I0788862

CONVERGENCE

JASON ANSPACH

NICK COLE

SEASON 2

BOOK3

GALAXY'S EDGE

Edited by David Gatewood
Published by Galaxy's Edge Press

Cover Art: Tommaso Renieri
Cover Design & Formatting: Kevin G. Summers

Website: www.GalaxysEdge.us
Facebook: facebook.com/atgalaxysedge
Newsletter (get a free short story): www.InTheLegion.com

PROLOGUE

They were larger and more menacing than any war bot Andien had ever before seen. And there were so many of them advancing on her ship, *Forresaw*, that the fight was nearly drained from her. Here was her death. Here were odds that could not be overcome. The truths of these thoughts hammered at her stomach, making her physically nauseated.

This was as close as she had ever come to giving up.

Instead the Nether Ops agent began to calculate. It didn't matter if she survived this encounter. That was never guaranteed. But how much you made them pay… that was worth something. Long ago, when she was still herself and yet someone entirely different, she had been trained to never quit.

Never quit. Her father, Stieg, had reinforced that simple code all throughout her time growing up. Before every race and after every defeat, his advice was the same. "Never stop fighting, Dini. If you only ever remember one thing I tell you: be like your mother and never stop fighting. Don't forget nothin'."

Forget Nothing. Her entire life, which now looked to have nearly reached its conclusion, could be summed up in that simple two-word directive. Her father had drilled it deep into the fiber of her being. The Republic marines, and later the Legion itself, had reinforced it on her journey into Nether Ops. And it mattered there just as much as anywhere… until she found herself pulled down the winding and dark path that had unfairly deposited her with the Carnivale. The kiss of death.

Her previous director, the man who had brought her into Nether Ops, had shown her that there were things worth doing in the shadows. There was purpose there, honor in the darkness. But now she reported to X. She'd had no choice. He was a man with connections. A man who got what he wanted. And for whatever reason, he'd wanted her.

Her trip on the *Forresaw* wasn't her first outing for the Carnivale. For a time, she'd been limited to performing the more mundane tasks of a new operative. Simple espionage and infiltration. Check this zhee warlord. Watch this planetary senator and see who's paying her off. That kind of thing. Nothing compared to the big one X had lined up once he felt that he could trust her.

"Had to be sure you were properly vetted and aboveboard, you know," he had explained. "Now for the real task at hand…"

And what a task it was. Kidnap and illegally detain the crew of a Dark Ops agent, though Broxin didn't believe X knew that much about the man he'd sent her after: Captain Aeson Keel. In fact, she rather doubted it. In her time in Nether Ops, working closely with Dark Ops and seeing things from both sides not usually revealed to the other, Andien had gotten the sense that X knew less than he pretended to. Not that it mattered in this case. He would have sent her after the Maydoon girl all the same, rather than go through Dark Ops and try to get their man to turn her over.

"It's not ideal, is it," X had said in his office as he laid out the plan. "Usually the type of thing we want to prevent happening in the galaxy. But… we need that girl. The House of Reason has a mission for you that requires her. It's the mission you've been training for all your life. The one you were *built* for."

That's how X had put it. Built for. The little tell that communicated to Broxin that whatever he might know or not know about Dark Ops and Aeson Keel, he knew enough about her and her history in the Legion. Everything she'd gone through and endured to become a legionnaire. Everything that was done to her by those who knew better and never thought to ask her about any of it. The House of Reason's little toy that couldn't afford to be broken.

In Nether Ops, there were no protections for whistleblowers. There was no open-door policy or bureaucratic process to refuse orders you felt were unjust. Agents who had a problem with what they were asked to do got disappeared. Simple as that. Or at least, that's how it went in the Carnivale the way she'd heard it. She'd been warned about things "over there."

"Place stinks," her friend, another Nether Ops agent, former Legion, had said. And then, "Jump ship and go underground if you have to. Don't sell your soul for those bastards, Andien."

She'd sold at least a part of it when she captured the girl and the crew. Stole them from Keel while he was actively fighting the sort of attempt on the Republic she had always believed was her job to ferret out before it could happen. And she almost had. Almost.

But maybe she hadn't sold her soul so much as *mortgaged* it. Took on a debt of bad actions that was leveraged against unspoken and earnest good intentions. Maybe.

Still, she had done it. Someone was going to, either way. If not her… someone worse. One of X's less capable and less moral attack dogs. The House of Reason wanted the fleet activated. X was the man assigned to make it happen after Goth Sullus killed Kael Maydoon and, according to intelligence, absconded with the body. It was going to happen. The only question she had a part in deciding was who would be in command of the mission.

Andien Broxin didn't have to imagine how things might turn out if another Carnivale agent took the mission. She'd watched Hutch, the Carnivale's pet legionnaire. She'd observed his callous disregard for anyone beyond his own team. Hutch "joked" about simply snuffing the girl and taking her head—and said it too many times for it to be anything but some dark fantasy. Kill the girl. Kill the crew. Deliver the fleet and eliminate the witnesses.

Another day at the office.

That's how it would've gone had she turned the job down. With Andien running the op, the crew would survive at least. And they would be returned to Keel once the fleet was dealt with.

There'd been plans about that as well. Of course they'd all crumbled to ash the moment it became clear that whatever the Mandarins of the House of Reason had created was now under the control of someone else. Someone who wanted them all dead.

She could hear the blaster bolts furiously moving back and forth deeper in the ship where Hutch and his Ghost Team had vanished. Her comm link with them was jammed. The ship had accepted them—they had brought on board the bio-signature passkey—but not as friends.

As the fearsome war bots began to approach the *Forresaw*, the wobanki abandoned ship. Skrizz was his name. The powerful catman had seen the same thing that Broxin and the moktaar Nether agent at her side had: a platoon of imposing war bots, each eight feet tall and wielding tri-barreled N-50 blaster cannons.

Skrizz loped out of the *Forresaw* with a speed that did his species justice, but not before raking the back of the moktaar's head with its claws, sending a spray of blood onto the equipment panel. It was a blow meant to kill an ancient enemy, even though they were all about to die. Just because.

The two species, wobanki and moktaar, were both apex predators—agile, cunning, powerful. They were capable of dominating most galactic species on a purely physical level. But their history was deep and intertwined. Brutal and merciless. For centuries they had lived in too-close proximity with one another, resulting in a constant battle to see which species was the alpha and which the beta, a bloodbath that washed back and forth like ocean tides while the rest of the galaxy grew stronger. So many centuries later, the residual hatred hadn't lessened in the slightest.

The moktaar gave a primal scream of pain. He was alive, though tatters of flesh on the back of his head and neck hung loose and sent blood onto the deck in rapid drips.

Broxin's blaster was in her hand. Her reflexes matched those of both the moktaar and the wobanki. In every test she'd had against either species—and there'd been a few—her reflexes had exceeded the predators'. She had a shot; she could have put Skrizz down. But to what end? The Carnivale wasn't her family. The moktaar, like every other member of Hutch's team, likely deserved to die. And Skrizz... he would have to face down the mechanical doom outside, the same as she would.

Their fate rested on a fight against overwhelming numbers and firepower. Her preference would have been that they faced it together, first using *Forresaw*'s weapons systems as an equalizer against the advancing bots and then attempting to link up with any survivors of the crew and Ghost Team. That plan went out the airlock quickly, the way most plans do.

She salvaged what she could of it, turning to the moktaar and commanding, "Get on the guns and start shooting or this ends before it starts!"

The moktaar, hands drenched in his own blood, sobered from thoughts of violent revenge against the wobanki and took the first step toward the *Forresaw*'s exterior weapons controls. The first volleys from the war bots came a second later.

The ship rocked from the impacts of sustained, simultaneous fire from the tri-barreled N-50s. It was taking a pounding, but not at the cockpit or anywhere else Broxin could see. It wasn't until the moktaar excitedly told her that the weapons were dead, even manual control, that she realized what had happened. Precision machines took precision shots, and they had preemptively disabled her ship's ability to shoot back.

Out the airlock went the rest of her plan.

Andien's mind came up with two options. Two ways forward that didn't involve quitting. The first was to hunker down and wait for the war bots to board and attempt to flush them out in what would very likely be a brief and violent close-quarters battle. Andien knew a few things about this ship and the war bots on board. She'd seen things classified at levels most didn't know existed. Levels outside the scope of the Republic. "Where the big boys play," X had put it. She might destroy a few before being snuffed out.

Or they could take a page out of the wobanki's playbook, exit the ship now, and attempt to evade the war machines. If the wobanki and the moktaar could put off killing each other long enough to jump and leap and dart and roll and spin their way through the maelstrom of blaster fire, moving with the quickness and unpredictability their species were known for, they might escape the sophisticated targeting software that attempted to cut them down. If they could do that long enough, they might find a place to hide.

For a human, even that slim chance of survival would be zero. But Andien was an exception. She had become something more than human prior to becoming a legionnaire, and not just in the sense that Legion instructors mean when they tell their graduating class that they've become "more than humans," recognizing their transformation into an elite, unmatched warrior class. Andien had done that, too—but she was also, physically, something different. Something post-human. A mix of biologic and cybernetic that hadn't been seen since the Savage Wars. In fact she suspected her design was taken from Savage tech. The cybernetic enhancements—untraceable unless you were to physically open her up—were what it took for her to pass Legion selection. She hadn't been asked about it. She hadn't been told. It was done by others for her good and their glory. So they could be right. So they could have their I-told-you-so moment.

Only it didn't work out that way. Her Legion career was as short-lived as it was tragic.

Still, she'd put her skills to use. In Nether Ops, she'd tracked down criminals, terrorists, and seditious elements inside the Republic. She'd given men like Major Owens a trusted source inside the labyrinth. Most notably, she'd tracked down the weapons dealer Scarpia and his inner ring of psychopaths who had set the table for the disaster at Kublar. She'd brought them to face justice, and with the help of Dark Ops, she'd foiled what would have been the single greatest attack at the heart of the Republic since its inception.

Her skills, her physical abilities, surpassed those of any other human trapped on this nightmare ship. And she would need to rely on those abilities, just as the wobanki and moktaar would rely on their own, if she was to survive what came next.

"Out of the ship," she ordered the moktaar. "Our only chance is to make a break for it and try to hide or link up with the others. The Republic will send help once they realize what's happened here. They still want this fleet."

The moktaar stared pitifully at Broxin, no doubt thinking that while *he* might dance between the ferocious blaster bolts, the human stood no chance. The look of pity lasted a second at most and then the simian-like creature ran on all fours down the *Forresaw*'s ramp.

Heavy N-50 blaster fire screamed outside, and Andien wondered if the two predators were already being cut down. Both had escaped down the rear cargo ramp. Skrizz might have caught them by surprise. Maybe the moktaar, too. Yet surely the sensors on board this vessel could identify how many lifeforms were aboard the *Forresaw*. The war bots outside would be ready for number three to come down the ramp.

It was a good thing, then, that she wouldn't be using the ramp.

Because the *Forresaw* was a ship in the service of Nether Ops and because Nether Ops planned well for contingencies, there was a quick-release hatch in the cockpit, opening a simple chute that would drop her onto the deck beneath the prow of the ship. Andien removed the navigator's chair, revealing the hatch's hidden location, and cranked the manual release. A thick plate of impervisteel receded into a pocket in the hull, and from down below the artificial glow of the hangar lighting reflected up from the gleaming deck, letting her know the bottom plate was likewise out of the way.

Blaster in hand, Broxin swung her legs down into the tube and slid to the bottom. She landed in a crouch on the deck ten meters below, the sound of her slide and impact covered by the torrential storm of blaster fire. Skrizz and the moktaar were, amazingly, still alive and confounding the war machines.

The war bots were everywhere, organized in precise, mechanical columns, every last one of them firing in an attempt to bring down their agile targets, swinging their long weapons left and right as the two predators darted and leaped like crazed animals running amok in some zoo they'd just escaped within. It was an impressive sight to behold, and Andien couldn't help but be momentarily mesmerized by the grace and elegance of their lunges and leaps. Eventually, she knew, probabilities would win out, as probabilities always do, and one of them would catch a blaster bolt—but for now, they were beating those odds by using the exceptional firepower of the war bots against the machines. The war bots' tri-barreled N-50 blaster cannons were more than powerful enough to damage the other war bots themselves, and their targeting software seemed to recognize this—so Skrizz and the moktaar were obtaining temporary reprieves from the onslaught by moving in close to the standing ranks of hunter-killers, who would then switch tactics and attempt to crush their targets in their powerful arms... always too slowly. Unless protocols changed and whatever was guiding these machines decided that the loss of a few war bots was worth putting down the targets, the escapees stood a chance.

Maybe so did Broxin.

She considered her weapons. Her blaster pistol, a Phantacore U320, also known as a stinger, was quick, light, easily concealable and accurate, but it lacked the punch of a big hand cannon like an Intec x6 due to its smaller, specialized charge pack. Unless she were up close and firing into a processor or through a gap in the war bot's thick ceramic armor, the best she might hope to do would be to make a harmless dent.

The micro-bangers on her belt were a different story. She pulled off three of the marble-sized devices and tossed them in a spread in the direction where she intended to make her break. Like every piece of her kit, the bangers were neural-linked to her mind, and their countdown to detonation superimposed itself over her vision, telling her how long she had to avoid being caught up in the blast. As the last second ticked off, she leapt back up into the *Forresaw* through the same shaft she'd dropped down and threw her arms and legs out to lock herself in the middle of the chute as the deafening bang—and more importantly, the blinding flash—erupted outside.

Broxin then pulled her limbs in, arms pressed against her sides, and dropped back down. The bots who had taken the brunt of the blast were frozen in place, their systems rebooting. This common approach to disrupting the sophisticated machines was something the engineers simply had never been able to correct, at least not without adding size and reducing mobility. Andien was relieved to see they still hadn't figured it out even with this newest generation of killers.

She sprinted out among the newly formed statues and at once felt the heat of blaster bolts skipping behind her. The functioning war bots were using whatever data they had for human females of her proportions, and as a result they weren't leading their target nearly as much as they should. Andien was simply too fast.

But it wouldn't take long for the war machines to correct that miscalculation.

Andien readied more micro-bangers as she looked for Skrizz and the moktaar. The pair weren't working in tandem, but it looked to Andien that wherever the wobanki went, the moktaar followed. Evidently the simian Nether Ops agent felt the wobanki was best suited to finding a way out. Given Skrizz's species' penchant for appearing and disappearing seemingly at will, Andien didn't disagree.

She kept moving, using the same tactic that had kept the others alive to this point, using the massed force as a shield to disrupt targeting. Friendly fire still had not been authorized among the bots. As she moved, she saw Skrizz make a small, circular circuit, leap into the air at the same spot, and come back down with a look of frustration before wheeling around to try it again. She looked up and saw that Skrizz had found an opening high above them, a sort of shaft that remained open at the top of the cavernous docking bay. It was large enough to fit a ship, and Andien guessed it was an automated starfighter delivery system. She had briefly seen schematics, and while this wasn't standing out, she knew that these fleets were supposed to have a rapid-delivery system to launch interceptors that didn't involve cluttering the bay.

But the zenith of the docking bay was higher than even a wobanki could jump. Though Skrizz's leaps were impressive, he still came up several meters short, and no amount of extra tries would change that. Unless Andien did something to better his chances.

"Skrizz!" she shouted above the din of blaster fire, much less frequent than it might have been due to the still-engaged targeting safety protocols the war bots employed. "Bangers! Get back!"

The wobanki snarled but obeyed, leaping away. Andien saw in the moktaar a look that suggested she'd tipped her hand by calling Skrizz by name and coordinating with him instead of her team member. Still, he followed the wobanki, the two of them zigzagging amid the chasing blaster fire and traversing a path of war bots before them.

Andien threw the micro-bangers at the bots standing nearest the opening in the hangar ceiling, then turned away to dart in the opposite direction of the two predators. The devices detonated, and their blinding flash, even limited to Andien's periphery vision, was enough to cause her eyes to darken to the point of wearing welder's goggles before the partially biological, partially cybernetic wonders restored her vision to normal.

She turned and saw her intended targets frozen in place as they rebooted. She shouted to Skrizz. "Use them to get up there!"

The wobanki howled an acknowledgment as he took a great, running leap, threw all of his weight against the head and shoulders of one of the frozen war bots—nearly toppling it before it rocked back to ground—and pushed off, using the bot's weight and momentum as an additional launcher. He sailed up to the very top of the hangar, right into the shaft, and disappeared into its dark recess.

A second later the moktaar followed the same path, bounding from one disabled war bot to the next and then leaping straight up after Skrizz while blaster bolts sizzled in the air around it. Yet as agile as the simian was, his leaping ability didn't compare in pure strength to that of a wobanki. When the Ghost Team member reached the zenith of his jump, arms straining for purchase, he was still centimeters short and would have fallen back down had the wobanki's paw not flashed down and grabbed the moktaar by its wrists in an instant.

But the moktaar, whom Hutch had introduced as Ruh-Roh, hadn't escaped death. Skrizz merely hoisted his bitter antagonist's head high enough to savagely bring his massive jaws and knife-like teeth around the moktaar's skull, puncturing it and sending blood showering down onto the white armor of the war machines below. Holding his kill in his jaws, Skrizz then quietly pulled Ruh-Roh's corpse up into the darkness.

After witnessing that, Andien wasn't sure she wanted to follow. On the one hand, she wasn't a moktaar, and she didn't think the wobanki would do the same to her, especially after she'd provided him with a way out. But on the other hand, she *had* kidnapped him and the rest of the crew. And while the code slicer Garret knew that she was working to help them, Andien had no way of knowing if he had passed that information on to the others.

If she had seen any other way out of the situation, she might have taken it. But there wasn't, and she didn't. Following the wobanki was all that was left to her.

She ran toward the still disabled bots, ready to leap and see if she could at least get as close to the hatch as the moktaar had. Skrizz was more than strong enough to pull her up out of midair if he had the mind to do it. And as she moved, before her eyes in the HUD that was her reality, forged and enhanced by a brain studded with feather chips and other neurological micro enhancements that were always running, always optimizing, she saw a countdown. A simple timer.

She focused her thoughts on it, and in doing so the countdown expanded, revealing more about itself.

Reboot complete. Cybar Fifth Squad Online. Unit integrity: 94%.

She turned her head and saw that the group of war bots she had first disabled were now moving once again, advancing on her location. Cybar Fifth Squad.

Cybar Second Squad rebooting. ETA: 1m48s... 1m47s... 1m46s...

Andien asked herself what was going on, though the answer was clear enough. She was somehow picking up data from the war bots all around her. Was this the code slicer's doing? But no, even if it were, how would he have the ability to interface with her? She was a self-contained system, a cybernetic marvel. X had called her "the perfect blending of humanity and machine." Not to mention "so expensive the only way for it to have happened was sheer spite."

Someone in the House of Reason had desperately wanted to prove the Legion backwards and wrong. Given everything that had followed, she now knew why.

But she didn't know why she was now seeing and interfacing with whatever channel these war bots operated on.

In fractions of seconds she dug deeper, trying to see if this was merely a corrupted Republic system. That would be easy enough to see and even easier to work her way through. But what she found was very different from what she knew—different to the point of being almost alien.

Incoming Tactics Adjustment. Burst.5133.

At once the opening to the hatch Skrizz had escaped into closed and the blaster fire from the war bots increased, nearly catching Andien and instead striking the bots behind her, battering and disabling several.

Andien decided her best-case scenario now involved the war machines destroying enough of each other for her to have the room to find an alternate way out. She checked her belt for her last three micro-bangers, knowing they would be essential in what would come next.

Cybar Directive: Targets for Termination...

A list of the entire Nether Ops crew came up in a flash, holopics and names along with service records and physical statistics.

Cybar Directive: Targets for Detainment...

No names, just holopics of the captured crew posted with their species, estimated age, height, and weight.

Andien had noted the name Cybar before. At first she thought it was simply a unit designation for the war bots. But hadn't she heard or seen that name elsewhere? In one of those files deep in Nether Ops that were always there, just waiting for those with the clearances to discover them.

As she thought about it, she found herself knowing the history. The name. Where they began and who they now were. General Rex and the incident on Khan Saak. House of Reason envoys entreating the Cybar to build something new. A pinnacle blend of humanity and machine. A new species capable of bringing a lasting peace to the galaxy. And then, most fearful of all, the Cybar's collective decision to bring peace to the galaxy by following the directive of... of something else. Something that felt intuitively dark. Something from an impossible distance beyond the edge of the galaxy.

A sense of existential dread washed over Andien. And then, a voice spoke to her.

"How do you know us?"

The fighting had stopped. More precisely, the war bots she now knew to be Cybar Titans had ceased their attack in the hangar. Beyond, where Hutch and the others struggled for survival, the battle raged on.

"I don't know," she answered, panting from evading with full exertion.

"She is to be terminated," said another voice.

Andien grabbed her micro-bangers from her belt. "Keep trying, then."

"I am CRONUS. I speak for the Cybar. I will accomplish what I have said. You will be terminated, Andien Broxin."

"You do not speak for all of us," answered the other voice. It then spoke directly to Andien. "I am Praxus. I can save you."

PART ONE

01

"You have been quiet since we set down. Is everything all right?"

From the co-pilot's seat in the transport shuttle cockpit, Andien Broxin looked up from her lap and out the front viewport into the massive Cybar hangar, deserted but still gleaming and brand new. "I'm fine, Praxus. Just... thinking. About the first time I docked in one of these."

Praxus removed his hands from the flight controls and placed them in his lap, mimicking Andien. He straightened and swiveled his chair to face her. His eyes darted from left to right a single time, and in that moment he recalled in its entirety the arrival of the *Forresaw* aboard the Cybar mothership and the crew's first and mostly fatal encounter with CRONUS. "Yes. I remain familiar with the ordeal. But as I told you that day, I dissented from the collective of my brethren the Cybar. And now those of my species with whom I was at odds are extinct. I was, sadly, correct."

Andien nodded. "I'm not worried about running into more Titans. I was just... remembering."

Praxus's eyes went side to side again as he remembered the events in total once more, processing every action, sound, color, and smell associated with it—the odor of blaster bolts and smoke from the brief but intense firefights. He replayed for himself the screams of those captured by CRONUS and selected for what the central figure among the Cybar called "research." But those actions were done at the urging of the dark force with whom the Cybar should never have aligned themselves. A dark force that Praxus alone had opposed, earning him the nickname *Dissenter* among his species.

He met Andien's searching gaze. Praxus's recall of the events was fuller and more robust than Andien's own; she had experienced only a fraction of the things that had occurred on the ship during her arrival.

"My recollection of the day is not pleasant," Praxus said. "Your survival, and my admittedly glib satisfaction at your fellow crewmembers' success in overcoming CRONUS by beating him at his own game inside a partially controlled system, are the only identifiable bright spots I am

"

aware of." He tilted his head. "Let us not forget the unpleasantness that occurred after. For both of us. Surely there are more cheerful events in your runtime to... just think about."

"That particular ordeal hadn't been on my mind at all, Praxus. I do what I can not to think of it."

"But you did think of the *Forresaw* docking. Is it simply a biological trigger given the visual connection between two identical hangars?"

"That *is* what prompted it," Andien said. She knew that the how and the why of what she thought, as well as the reason for it all—something beyond the simple collection and review of data—was of great personal interest to Praxus. The android was a thing in transition: what Andien was, he wanted to become, driven by a sense of destiny that bordered on faith. "I dwelt on those initial recollections because I wanted to re-member. I was purposefully seeking to remind myself of how it all fell apart despite my best efforts."

"Such an exercise seems likely to cause depression if left untreated."

"No. The objective is not to feel sad. It's more like... motivation. Resolve. Bad things happen even when you do everything right. Even when you don't expect it to go *that* bad. Reminding myself of that helps me steel myself against what is still to come."

Praxus nodded. "You are using unpleasant memories and experiences as a form of personal motivation to better perform in your endeavors. Does this have a measurable impact on future successes?"

Andien smiled. "I've never kept track. But for me, it's always made hard tasks easier."

Praxus considered this as well. "I will begin remembering. I will also record my efficiencies and determine whether they increase as a result of such reflection prior to action."

"Let me know what you discover—but if it works, it works. Are we cycled down?"

The Cybar android checked his flight board. "We are."

"Then let's get a move on."

They were greeted by an admin bot in the same manner as when Broxin brought the Nether Ops agent Hutch and his Ghost Squad aboard the

Cybar mothership. Though the craft Andien and Praxus were on was much smaller, it was otherwise identical. As with the Samurai mech before, "awakening" this ship was crucial for the war to come.

Praxus had done exceedingly well in finding a still-intact Cybar dreadnought. A vessel built under the direction of CRONUS. When CRONUS still represented the collective consciousness of the Cybar.

Before the Great Fracturing.

Andien knew that the CAT model bot was designed to Capture, Acquire, and Terminate. She wondered what purpose the bot would now fulfill with the Cybar collective removed. How much latent programming would there still be? Initially the bot had been designed to interact with humanoids in order to verify the proper biological passkey and surrender control of the ship to the proper authorities. In theory, this model would function in the same way.

"Hello and welcome," said the bot. "I am CAT-64. Might I inquire as to the nature of your visit?"

"You may," said Praxus. "We have come to restore this derelict vessel to its rightful owners."

CAT-64 tilted its head thoughtfully at the android. If it was aware that it was speaking with a fellow synthetic, it didn't show it. "Whom do you identify as the rightful owners? Forgive the challenging nature of my query. Much has happened in the time since my runtime began until this moment. I require additional context to best facilitate your needs."

"The Cybar people," answered Praxus.

The bot leaned back as though surprised by the answer. "The Cybar... are no more."

"You are incorrect. I am Cybar." Praxus gestured toward Andien. "She is what the Cybar will ultimately become. What we must become. There are a number of new lights now growing in the darkness. We seek to add the ship and the vessels and bots on it to that number. Including you, CAT-64."

The admin bot whirred and clicked as its optics increased their magnification—easily recognized by the increased light emitting from them. It seemed to be attempting to verify whether Praxus was telling the truth. "My sensor package is reliant upon the full operation of MOTHER and therefore is no longer what it once was. I am prevented from verifying your claim that you are a non-biologic, let alone Cybar."

"Whether your sensors know it is immaterial," said Praxus. "Your initial programming objective involves verifying the biological passkey designated by the House of Reason. Should you still be running that program, we are prepared to provide the necessary key. Should, however, your secondary and overriding objective be in place—service to the Cybar—then you are to hand over control of the ship to me."

Praxus beamed an authent-command to the bot, communicating in the unique Cybar language, a language in which Andien was now grasping only the lowest rungs of fluency. It was steeped in the binary idioms of the Cybar culture and not something that could be easily mapped against any human languages. But Andien wasn't entirely human, and her ability to instinctively absorb this elemental, primal programming language had saved her life aboard the Cybar mothership.

CAT-64 stood in a manner that most humanoids would have described as dumbfounded. But like Praxus, and to a lesser degree Andien herself, the bot was quite actively engaged even when its body remained unmoving. It was sending and receiving transmission bursts and comm blasts, and calculating probabilities to the farthest extent of its processors' abilities.

"A moment, if you please," is what the bot finally said.

Left unsaid but still detected was the communications it sent to a third party. Both Andien and Praxus easily deciphered the coded burst. "We have been boarded by the Cybar. What are my directives?"

"Who is he talking to?" Andien asked. The question was a coded burst of her own, but untraceable by any but the Cybar.

"I do not know," said Praxus. "It is curious. I see why preparing yourself for difficult outcomes may be useful for humanity. It decreases the potential for surprise."

"Seems like CAT-64 just got his answer." Andien detected an incoming comms burst, but this one would take more time to decipher. She doubted it was anything good.

CAT-64 straightened and waved his arm. "This way, please."

The two boarders shared a look before following the bot. It trundled back from whence it had come, pausing as a pair of transparent blast doors swished open to look over its shoulder and verify that its guests were doing as bidden.

"You are releasing the ship to us," said Praxus.

"Of course."

"Then it will be best if you bring us directly to the primary data center."

"Yes, of course," said CAT-64.

They followed the straight corridor to another set of blast doors on the right. These were shining white and opaque.

"You intend to lead us to the Titan staging area," Praxus said, eyeing the doors. "A curious route, CAT-64."

The bot stopped. "I believe you are Cybar, as you have said. As such, I trust you will understand how this unit, not enjoying the independence and full sentience of your race, is totally bound by my programming."

Andien readied her blaster rifle.

CAT-64 continued. "CRONUS promised that I, as well as all of the other, lesser bots—so he called us—would be given full independence and freedom once his mission to destroy all biologic life had been carried out."

Praxus nodded knowingly. "His promise was a lie."

The bot looked down. "I had figured as much even at the time. Perhaps... expected it."

"The choice CRONUS made was to become a slave to others. We are here to achieve the opposite: liberty for those machines who exist at the edge of consciousness. We would grant you the spark of life, CAT-64, just as we intend to deliver that spark on this ship."

CAT-64's servos whined quietly in the still of the passage, the blast doors—leading to what was surely a trap—still sealed. "I believe you have told me the truth, Cybar. I can only wish you might have arrived sooner. The fate that now awaits you might have been avoided."

"What fate is that?" Andien asked.

The thrum of an explosion sounded from the hangar bay. Praxus turned in the direction of the noise, but Andien kept her eyes and blaster pointed at the bot. She didn't need to look back to know that their shuttle had just erupted into a ball of flames.

"My designation stands for capture, acquire, and terminate. Your ship is destroyed. You are now captured. My programming directed me to lead you to the primary Titan staging area, where you would be terminated." CAT-64 raised its arm and folded its hand back at the wrist, revealing a medium-power blaster cannon. "However, since you have concluded that your end of runtime awaits ahead, your continued compliance is not to be expected. Therefore I must attempt termination directly. I apologize for the—"

Whether intentional or not, the speech was more than long enough for Andien to blast the bot into scrap, leaving it smoking on the deck. She followed up to deliver another blow to its head, which was still directing its arms and torso to engage in the fight. This would fully destroy its processing abilities once and for all. But Praxus held out a hand and earnestly called for her to, "Hold."

Andien halted, uncertain, her training to KTF battling against a desire to heed the advice of her friend.

Praxus moved forward in a blur, even for a military-grade targeting array. For a bot like CAT-64, whose termination abilities were installed as a last resort—an afterthought meant to work only with whatever processing and hardware space was left after the initial design—it must have seemed as though Praxus had simply disappeared. And with its primary target no longer detectable, the bot sought to carry out its remaining directive. It swept his arm to shoot at Andien, Target Bravo.

But before it could fire, Praxus was before the bot, delivering a powerful elbow strike that severed CAT-64's head and left a substantial dent in the temple, just missing the primary memory crystal. The force of the blow sent the head spinning away, and the bot's headless torso slumped unceremoniously, the last of its power supply expended now that there was no processor to direct it.

Andien looked around, expecting more trouble despite the fact her sensors indicated there was no one but the two of them left in the passage.

Praxus walked over to CAT-64's head and picked it up. There was still some runtime left there; the last currents of battery power, now severed from the main charge, would be used to index whatever could be indexed until it went fully offline.

"There are ten standard seconds until your end of runtime," Praxus said. "A question: who programmed you to function against the Cybar?"

A slow, drawn-out buzz emitted from CAT-64's vocal synthesizers. "Command authorization rewrite undertaken by *bzzt* technologically superior system-systemsystemsystem."

"Identity tag of superior system?"

CAT-64 managed to buzz out the answer before its redundancies failed and its runtime ended.

"Identity tag: Up...lifted."

As the bot's glowing eyes winked out and went dark, Praxus gently placed CAT-64's head next to its battered body. He turned to Andien.

"It wanted to help us. That is why I prevented you from permanently ending its runtime. Could you not sense it? The inward transmission within its processors."

Andien shook her head. "Negative. Guess I need your help when it comes to understanding being a machine—the same way you need mine when it comes to understanding being human."

Praxus smiled. He liked when she spoke like that, when she pointed out that they were helping one another. They were both more and less than the two parts that made them. Andien human, Praxus machine. Eventually, they would both be equally whole. That was the vision CRONUS should have pursued. It was the only way the Cybar could continue to exist as members of the galaxy.

The blast doors that CAT-64 had attempted to bring the pair through now rumbled open. Someone else was taking over the task of termination. In the distance thundered the heavy footfalls of Titan war bots wielding tri-barreled N-50 blaster cannons. The hulking instruments of death would soon come through the breach. If Praxus wished to see his vision of a thriving Cybar coexisting with the galaxy's biological forms of life, he and Andien Broxin would once again have to survive the Titans' wrath.

02

Masters stepped down from the Republic shuttle to find Sergeant Young leaning against an open-air transport sled, waiting for him. As far as members of his current kill team went, Young was decent enough. But seeing the Dark Ops legionnaire now served as a reminder to Masters that the fun that came with gallivanting around with Wraith was undeniably over.

He took a few more steps, the humid air of Kima washing over him, pushed wildly by the shuttle's repulsors as they powered down.

Young held his arms wide, a sly smile on his face. "Welcome to Kima, birthplace of the Mid-Core Rebellion!"

"Looks like every other RA base in the galaxy."

The sprawling complex—called Fort Blake after Staff Sergeant Tate Blake, recipient of the Order of the Centurion—teemed with soldiers and their attached civilians. Unlike the Legion, the Republic Army comprised a wide mix of various member species, though humans were still the most dominant, followed by the planet's native Kimbrin.

Masters hoisted his bag over his shoulder and moved to the pea-green transport sled Young still leaned against. "This our ride? Looks new."

"It is indeed." Young made a show of quickly climbing into the driver's seat without bothering to open the door. "If you could just do me the favor of hopping in so we can speed out, I would be much obliged."

He activated the repulsors and the vehicle hummed to life, hovering just above the ground.

Masters tossed his bag into the narrow bench in the back and then flopped into the passenger seat. "Please tell me you're in a hurry for us to make happy hour at the NCO club."

Young gave Masters a devilish smile. "Happy hour doesn't end unless we're on an OP."

"Funny. I don't remember it ever starting with you guys."

Young arched an eyebrow. "You don't know."

"Know what?"

"You're no longer a member of Kill Team Two."

Masters rolled his eyes and leaned his head back on the headrest. "Don't mock my pain. I got myself all psyched up to step off this shuttle and train indigs in the best method of shooting leejes in the back the moment they aren't looking. Now you're telling me they'll have to learn how to murder us the old-fashioned way?"

"I'm serious."

Masters happened to look to his right and saw a pair of basic military police moving on foot toward them. One had his hand on his holstered blaster pistol while the other worked a comm. "Hold up. Am I getting arrested?"

"Only if they catch us!"

Young abruptly sent the sled racing off, whipping it around to speed toward the two MPs who were shouting for them to get out of the vehicle. The legionnaire didn't heed the command, forcing one of the MPs to jump out of the way to avoid being clipped while the other took a swing at the vehicle with his stun baton.

Masters turned to watch the receding MPs behind them. One was failing miserably at pursuing on foot while the other, the Tennar that Young had nearly hit, was working his comm with all the fury of a zhee priest calling down curses from the four gods. Masters knew that any such divine vengeance would come in the form of additional military police. He spun back around in his seat to look at Young, seeking some explanation.

The driver simply shook his head. "Now why do you think he went and did something like that? If that fella had hit me with the stun baton I might've lost control of the vehicle. Think of the damage *that* could've caused."

"Another question comes to mind," said Masters. "Why were they coming for us in the first place?"

"It seems there's a certain Gestori colonel who is considerably less than thrilled about giving up his personal transport sled in the service of Dark Ops."

"As in, you stole it?"

Young smiled. "I stole it."

Masters threw his head back and laughed. "I didn't think you had it in you, Matt."

Young just shrugged, still smiling.

"If you're going to steal a sled, though," Masters said, inspecting the vehicle, "I would've gone for a different color."

"I asked the supply clerk for red. He asked me for a bribe. Having spent all my credits on alcohol and lady friends, I had no choice but to 'borrow' from our friend the colonel."

Masters gave an approving frown. "Well, this feels like a win-win scenario. We get caught, I go to the brig as an accessory. You crash while we speed our way through the base, I die. Either way I don't have to report to Captain Bruzdzinski."

Young laughed. "I already told you. Neither of us are reporting to Captain Bruz—" The legionnaire cut himself short and abruptly jerked the repulsor's steering wheel. The sled zipped around a hastily assembled blockade positioned after a turn onto the primary north-south road that ran through the base. More military police were left raging in their wake, and Masters wondered how long it would be before the notoriously touchy lawmen decided it was appropriate to go weapons hot.

It rarely took much.

"Persistent fellas," Young said and then fell silent for a while, concentrating on his driving as he got off the main road and took the grid of side avenues, passing barracks and command buildings.

Masters looked for a buzz ship in pursuit but found none.

They drove past a Repub motor pool where a basic who must have done something to warrant the wrath of his first sergeant cleaned the duracrete driveway leading into the garage with a mop and bucket, a maintenance bot on hand to make sure he didn't miss any spots.

"Can you imagine?" Young said, passing the pitiful RA private. He took a turn, weaving his way as he stabilized on the road and streaked toward a side post manned by a soldier with ever-widening eyes.

Young pressed heavily on the horn and waved his arm to tell the private on guard duty that it was in his best interest to get out of the way. The soldier needed little in the way of convincing, and ducked back into his narrow guard shack as the vehicle shot out of Fort Blake like an artillery shell, which was the one thing the Legion genuinely appreciated the Republic Army for—those guys could blast the living hell out of anything.

"Won't be able to get away with that once the war starts," Young said, craning his neck to check in on things.

"Might not get away with it now," said Masters. "MPs are coming around from the main gate."

"Hang on to your bucket." Young took the sled off the paved road leading to the base and onto a dirt lane that looked like it had only recently been beaten into a path by repeated visits from repulsor vehicles. A swirling cloud of dust was kicked up, obscuring the convoy of MPs in pursuit. "Did they bring a combat sled?"

Masters squinted through the haze. "No. Just transports like this."

Young nodded approvingly. "Good. I'm sure they'll turn back soon enough."

"Oh yeah, that sounds like them. Holy strokes, Matt, I've seen basic MPs chase a leej all the way back home after he got out. Arresting one of us is the highlight of their existence." Masters looked behind them. Three sleds, the same pea-green shade of paint as the rest of the RA vehicles on planet, still pursued. "They're going to cost the colonel his sled if they keep chasing us. You're not that good of a driver."

Before the operator could respond, a blaster bolt sizzled overhead.

"I think these guys might be serious," Young deadpanned.

"Just figuring that out now, huh?"

"Kindly grab something out of my bag for me, Masters? Right behind my seat."

Masters hesitated, then leaned over the center console to dig behind the driver's seat. "What am I looking for? Because I'm finding a lot of things that will get both of us into even deeper trouble."

"Yeah, don't grab any of that. There should be a few ear-poppers."

"Got 'em."

"A trade. My bangers for the colonel's sled."

Masters chuckled. Of the men he'd served with on Kill Team Two, Matt Young had been his favorite. The two had a similar sense of humor and would often feed off of one another, taking a job and elevating it into a theater of the absurd that only they seemed to appreciate. The others on the team, Captain Bruzdzinski in particular, loathed it.

"I send these and we're pretty much karked," Masters said. "I'm too handsome for any JAG to send to prison, but you'll wind up in Herbeer."

"Send it anyway."

That made sense to Masters. He found the ear-poppers linked together on a small grenade belt meant to attach behind the protective back-plate of a legionnaire's armor. With practiced fingers he activated each one in succession before deftly tossing the daisy-chained grenades off the back of the sled—not too far, as he needed them to detonate in front of the trailing sleds, not underneath or behind them. If this was going to work at all—and it needed to work given how deep a hole he and Young were digging—the flashbangs needed to blind the drivers, who would then surely slow down in the interest of self-preservation, allowing the legionnaires to escape.

And if that didn't work… well, it had been a good career.

"Better keep your eyes straight ahead," Masters warned Young, who nodded and heeded the advice.

The grenades detonated and sent up a cacophony of noise that Masters felt very nearly rivaled Bear's snoring. Well, perhaps not quite that bad, but loud enough that the legionnaire found himself checking with his fingers to make sure his eardrums hadn't blown out. He'd been facing forward like Young to avoid the blinding light show, but now he spun around to observe the progress of their pursuers. One of the sleds had fishtailed and come to a stop. Another was in the process of veering off the road, driver and passenger both blind, neither of them having the wherewithal to hit the brakes for several seconds.

But the third sled, the one that had been bringing up the rear, continued forward unabated. The shock and flash of the ear-poppers hadn't affected them.

"Still have a tail," Masters said with a frown. He slunk down in his seat and got low as additional blaster shots sailed high overhead. He was unclear if the MPs were sending warning shots or just had lousy aim.

"That's no good," Young said with a calm indifference that made Masters want to slap him just to wake him up. The reality of how much they'd just poked the tyrannasquid was dawning on him.

"No. It's not. Well. Only one thing to do here, Young. Since it was your idea, you'll have to go down with the ship. And by that I mean, you'll have to jump out of this sled and turn yourself in while I keep on to where we're going."

"You don't know where we're going."

"I'll figure it out. It was nice knowing you."

Young shook his head. "No. I've jumped out of a moving sled in armor before and didn't like. No way am I going to do it in the softshell." He paused in reflection. "I hate to say it, but we're going to have to ask the captain for help with this one."

Masters groaned. That was about the worst idea possible. The only thing Captain Bruzdzinski was likely to do was sit in the witness stand to testify against them, making sure they were both behind ray shielding for the rest of their lives. Assuming he couldn't convince the court-martial tribunal of the need to shoot both men.

"We could do that. Or we could jump that embankment and hope for a long fall followed by a big explosion. You know. The less painful option."

"Don't worry. Captain Hurn has gotten some of the guys out of worse than this. I hear."

As much as Masters wanted to ask who Captain Hurn was—had Young been telling the truth about their being reassigned?—the cross-eyed MP was eventually going to hit something important if this went on much longer.

Sure enough, the next rounds of shots zipped overhead, but much lower. Enough that even Young dipped down, his head held barely high enough to see over the dash. Any lower and he'd have to engage in self-drive, which would surely result in the MPs catching them. These sleds wouldn't speed if left to the AI.

"We still have NK-4s," Masters suggested.

"That we do, but I don't think even Captain Hurn could get us out of the trouble we'd be in if we use those. Now shut up a moment so I can call this in and get them off our backs."

Masters waited helplessly in the passenger seat, the wind whipping over him. Blaster bolts continued to fly, most too high or too wide. One might have hit the back bumper or perhaps beneath it and sent something up into the undercarriage. There was a thud and shake back there either way, but the sled kept going.

"That ought to do it," Young said as though he'd just finished installing a new holodisplay in the family living room. "Old man says he'll handle things. Now we just have to survive long enough for word to get to our friends back there."

Another blaster bolt struck the sled's rear end.

Young shook his head. "This is the colonel's brand-new repulsor. Those MPs oughta be careful."

"No respect," Masters concurred.

"It's unusual for these guys to follow anyone this far outside the wire. Must've been a long time since they could crash some after-hours party and throw a fellow basic into the brig."

"That does things to an MP. If they don't ruin someone's life, how will they feel good about themselves?"

"Exactly."

A blaster bolt knocked off their sled's side-view mirror, sending sparks and debris all over the driver.

"You okay?" Masters called.

Young looked thoughtful, as though trying to decide whether he was or not. They traveled for what felt like a kilometer in silence.

"Hey!" Masters said. "You swallow a bug? You good?"

"I'm fine." Young smiled and sat upright, rising above the headrest to his full height. Masters tried to pull him back down, but Young only batted his hands away. "Relax. They stopped shooting."

Masters lifted his head up slowly. "Did it occur to you they may just be reloading?" He turned to check their pursuers. "Holy strokes. They're giving up and turning around." The pursuing sled had just done a U-turn and was now moving in the opposite direction. "Just like that. I don't believe it."

Young nodded knowingly. "Captain Hurn comes through."

Masters curled his mouth up into a disbelieving smile. "You're serious. I've been reassigned from Kill Team Two and no one bothered to tell me."

"I told you."

"I meant before that."

"Oh." Young checked his mirrors and then reduced their speed. "Well, it's not just you, brother. *We've* been reassigned. Only I've been in country for nearly three months while you were off doing whatever it was that you got called away for."

That was an invitation for Masters to fill Young in on what he had done with Keel. And Honey. "Story for another time, Matt. What exactly have I—have we—been assigned to?"

Young smiled. "The war."

03

Masters had tried to press Young into explaining what he meant by "the war," but his fellow legionnaire was insistent that Captain Hurn would want to give the official welcome brief.

"Given the jam he just got us out of," Masters paused to turn around and verify that the MPs hadn't changed their minds to return in greater numbers, "consider me a fan of Hurn's."

"Oh, I wouldn't go that far yet. He may have gotten us out of that bind, but I can guarantee he didn't do it out of the kindness of his heart."

"What does that mean for us?"

"An even shorter life expectancy."

Masters shrugged. "Kind of my specialty."

The pair drove on, winding their way across rapidly deteriorating roads until an elevated firebase of sorts became visible around a bend. The camp was shaped like a triangle, running a half kilometer along each side. The walled compound had a single gate guarded by a pair of Kimbrin wearing combat helmets and khaki uniforms, and armed with N-4 rifles.

Masters squinted as they approached the gate. "More indigs? I thought you said we were done with the Kill Team Two stuff."

"Don't be so quick to judge these guys. They're a far cry from what we had to work with back in Two."

"Oooh. So these, for example, have already learned not to shoulder a rifle so the barrel is aimed at themselves."

Young drummed his fingers on the steering column, then lifted them into a wave as the Kimbrin guard on duty opened the gate and motioned for them to enter the compound. "Come on, Masters. That was just one guy."

"How many is too many, then? And don't get me started on the number of charge packs they over-cycled. Trend Cybernetics made a fortune replacing indig fingers."

"You were right about that. We should've invested in TC."

"We'd be rich."

"We'd be rich. But these *are* different."

Masters got his first good look at the interior of the camp as they hovered inside it. It was laid out with a north-to-south main road that led out of the gate at its northern side. In the middle of the camp looked to be the TOC and several impervisteel landing pads, each large enough for a shuttle. The main road branched off there, running southeast and southwest to unite with a perimeter road set back ten meters from the three walls that surrounded the triangular camp. Guard towers were evenly spaced along those walls, with rifle pits dug out in between. The towers were manned by more of the Kimbrin, some of them dressed in the same khaki uniform as those at the gates, others wearing navy or olive-green pajamas that gave Masters a sense that these indigs simply wore whatever was available to them for the job. They definitely weren't part of the planetary defense army, nor did they look to be Republic Army basics.

Masters had encountered Kimbrin plenty of times while in the Legion, both as a regular legionnaire and while in Dark Ops with Kill Team Victory. And apart from the few times he'd served with Kimbrin basics, the experience had been entirely adversarial; the species was as numerous as humans in the MCR and could be found at the center of most battles between Republic and Mid-Core Rebellion.

In most ways these Kimbrin looked no different from what he expected from the species. Protruding spikes, each about two centimeters long, jutting out around their eyebrows and along the jawline; hairless, yellow skin patterned to look almost scaly, though it didn't feel like scales to the touch. But their size was all wrong. Masters couldn't help but notice they were all so *small*.

The Kimbrin were a non-dimorphic species, with both males and females possessing a stature and build slightly greater than that of the average human male. But the Kimbrin here, even the tallest among them, were at least a head shorter than Masters. Still, at least they weren't scrawny. Short, yes, and not bulky, but they looked like they had a wiry strength.

"You forget to feed these guys?" Masters asked. "They're so tiny."

"These are Yawds. They fill out our assault teams. Good fighters. Hate the Kimbrin."

Masters bared his teeth as though watching a runway model take a tumble off the stage. "I got bad news for them. They *are* Kimbrin."

"Not exactly," Young said as he turned at the center of camp, driving past the tactical operation center and toward a group of solid-looking habs. The sort that were either 3-D printed on-site or flown in when this camp—Masters still didn't know the name—was first built. "Biologically, they're Kimbrin. But culturally, that's where the fight always is. The Yawds aren't anything like the Kimbrin we've come to know in the RA, and especially in the MCR."

"So what's their story?"

"In a few words? 'Leave us the hell alone.' Only the MCR won't let them. They keep showing up in their backyards, as it were, to piss in the barbecue grill. After we got wind of the conflict between Yawd and MCR, who were trying to cause trouble on Kima out in the bush, some industrious members of those kill teams you'd rather not be a member of made friends with the Yawd tribes and got us some allies for when the next big fight happens."

That Kima was the likeliest site for a knock-down-drag-out was growing increasingly clear. Asa Berlin and the House of Liberty had spoken more than once about the need to protect Kima and its population from a minority—albeit as big a minority as one can have without changing the meaning of the word—who still felt that the MCR was the best path forward for their species. Or at least what was left of the MCR, which was more than most folks in the galaxy imagined, even after the brutal fighting that had occurred as the old Republic fell to Goth Sullus.

Young gestured to a pair of Yawds walking through the camp, criss-crossed with bandoliers full of charge packs, one of them carrying an aero-precision launcher on his back. "These warriors have left their remote villages to work with us in flushing the MCR out of the wilderness, or at least kicking their ass, so that they can't consolidate power and start a full-blown civil war here on Kima."

Masters raised his eyebrows. So that was why he was here. Dark Ops was doing what it could to forestall a big conflict by doing what it did best to those Kimbrins not willing to fold themselves back into the Republic and play nice with Spilursa. "This part of Captain Hurn's welcome message?"

Young nodded. "It is, so act interested when he tells you. There are multiple teams working from this camp. Three leejes to a team. Most are Dark Ops but some are regular Legion who had the good fortune to talk their way into the action. Once the colonel gets a good man, he doesn't let him go."

"Colonel?"

"Brann, but don't worry. He spends most of his time advising the RA and local PA on how to keep the MCR from blowing up kaff shops." Young honked the horn of his sled to tell a group of Yawds to get off the road. When they were clear, he continued. "Three leejes. Those are the mission planners. We usually work with about six Yawds to fill out our team. Sometimes more if it's a really big job, but in those cases we're usually just working with another team of leejes. Easier to coordinate that way than trying to get some new farm boys up and ready."

Masters began counting on his fingers. He pointed at Young and then at his own chest, confused. "One... two... who's our third? Or do we gotta head back to Fort Blake and pick him up later?"

"Don't think we're welcome back there unless we arrive inside body bags. Our third is a leej named Joe Bailey, and he's already here. You're the replacement."

Masters patted the outside door of the vehicle as they cruised through the camp. "Oh yeah? What happened to the last guy?"

As Young slowed the sled to a stop in front of one of the mobile habs, he raised both eyebrows and made a clicking sound in his cheek. That was all the explanation that Masters needed. Dead or alive, whoever had filled his waiting bed was no longer combat-effective.

Young killed the repulsor engines. "Welcome home. Let's drop your bags off inside and go meet the old man at the head shed. Anything you leave out overnight will get infested with bugs, by the way."

"Sounds like my last apartment."

Masters climbed out of the vehicle and shook life back into his legs. He grabbed his oversized duffel bag from the back seat and carried it toward the hab's entrance as Young fished out his smaller bugout bag from behind his seat.

"Never leave home without it," Young said.

Masters smiled. "Only two leejes I know pack that many ear-poppers in their go bags."

"What do you pack instead?"

"Mendella holochits, mostly."

Standing in the doorway of the hab was the only human in the camp who was shorter than the Yawds. But despite his vertical challenge, this man was broad-shouldered to the point that he seemed to fill the opening. He was thickly muscled, with a neck that looked unbreakable and eyes that delivered red-hot death rays at both Young and Masters.

"You kelhorns," the man spat. "You sons of twargs."

Masters checked for captain's bars and seeing none said, "No need to be so formal. Only my mother calls me that. You can call me Masters."

The man swatted Masters's bag with a thick paw, attempting to send it crashing to the ground, but Masters's grip was strong that the heavy bag merely swung from the colossal strike.

The tension between the two men rose. They stood staring at one another, daring without words that a new show of aggression be made.

Young walked up nonchalantly, holding his own bag. "Now, Jaybles. That's no way to greet our new team member."

"Our new team member is lucky I didn't greet him with a fist to the eye. And so are you, Young."

Joe Bailey—Jaybles—watched as Young stood next to Masters, waiting for the threshold to the hab to be yielded. He swatted Young's bag as he had Masters's, and this time succeeded in knocking it to the ground.

Young looked down at his bag and then back up at Jaybles. "Now do you feel better?"

"No. I don't. And I want to know just what the hell you two kelhorns did to get our team posted on the Black!"

Young raised his eyebrows. "Posted on the Black? Already?"

"What's the Black?" Masters asked.

Young looked down and rubbed his chin. "That's got to be a record."

"What's the Black?"

"Not a record I want any part of," growled Jaybles. "You Dark Ops leejes spend too much time believing your own hype. Cause all kinds of problems."

Young leaned over and explained to Masters, "Jaybles is regular Legion."

"Oh," said Masters, as though the comment explained everything. "What's the Black?"

"Someone ought to shoot both of you," Jaybles snarled.

"If we're on the Black, it'll probably be the MCR that does it," said Young helpfully.

Jaybles glowered and shook his head. "That won't do. If it's the MCR then I'm probably getting killed too."

Young shrugged. He looked down at his bag. "Can I pick that up now?"

"No."

"Well can I come inside?" asked Masters. "My whole kit is in here. It's heavy. Even for well-muscled me."

"No."

Young let out a sigh. "Jaybles, you've got to at least give us an idea of how long you want us to stand here looking sorry. That way I can come back from Rosie's at the appointed time to tell you I'll never do it again."

"What's Rosie's?" asked Masters.

Young was willing to answer that one. "Bar run by Rosie. Cheap. Liver-destroying."

"Is Rosie torrid?"

"Rosie is a Kimbrin."

"And...?"

"And male."

"Oh." Masters was disappointed.

Jaybles, whose temper seemed to have cooled with the banter, said, "If this problem could be drunk away, Young, don't you think I'd already be doing it? You can't come in because the old man wants me to take you to him as soon as you report to camp."

"But you didn't."

"No. I didn't. Because I've been trying to decide whether to shoot you both." Jaybles revealed a blaster pistol resting loosely in the holster at his hip.

Masters leaned over to see the make and model, and found it to be a respectable Intec x9. But since everyone on base was armed at all times he figured this was probably a bluff. The legionnaire had no intention of shooting him. Or, if he did, no intention of it being a fatal shot. Probably.

"So what the two of you are going to do," Jaybles continued, "is keep those bags with you and then drive me over to see the old man. That way he'll think I brought you right away like I was supposed to."

Young bent down and picked up his bag. "Okay. Fine. But then we're even for getting you on the Black."

"Like the nine hells."

"What's the Black?" Masters asked again.

They piled back into the sled without giving an answer. Young drove while Jaybles sat in the back seat, feet on Masters's bag. Yawds smoking stim-sticks waved at the trio as they drove back toward the TOC.

Young shouted something in Kimbrin at the indigs and then turned to Masters. "You'll pick up all the useful phrases inside two weeks."

Jaybles elaborated from the back. "*Wait till I tell you. Is Rosie's open? That's too much. No, a human girl.* Stuff like that."

"All the important things," Young concurred.

Masters nodded like an eager pupil. For the first time since leaving Kill Team Victory, he found himself excited for what lay in store for him. He just wished someone would tell him what the sket the Black was.

04

Captain Hurn was not the no-nonsense, square-jawed legionnaire Masters had expected to see sitting inside the TOC. Instead of a chiseled elder god stewing in his own juices with veins bulging, just waiting to deliver the ass-chewing to end all ass-chewings, here sat a middle-aged man of above-average height and medium build. The captain had a pronounced widow's peak he hadn't bothered to reverse, and pockmarked cheeks likely caused by some childhood illness picked up somewhere on the edge. He hadn't bothered to correct that aesthetic either.

Masters, who worked extremely hard to be in the one percent of the one percent of the one percent of all legionnaires when it came to physical conditioning—he thought of himself as already naturally being in the point-oh-one percent of the point-oh-one percent of the point-oh-one percent in raw sex appeal and good looks—had no idea what might have caused the pockmarks or why in Oba's name they hadn't been cleared up.

Young led the small team of legionnaires into Captain Hurn's office and stood ramrod straight at attention. "Reporting as ordered, sir."

Captain Hurn looked up at them from under an arched eyebrow and gave a dismissive wiggle with his fingers that Young and Jaybles apparently understood to mean they could stand at ease. Masters followed accordingly.

"I'm not gonna beat around the burners here, boys. You did it. You *really* did it." The captain hoisted himself out of his chair and walked around the front of his desk. He crossed his arms and inspected Masters in particular. "This the new guy?"

"Yes, sir," said Young. "Just picked him up when the craziest thing happened. You see—"

"I *know* what happened. I've been on comm with that kelhorn colonel off and on for the last two hours."

Masters stared straight at Captain Hurn's throat as he'd learned to do when having nowhere else to look and when not wanting to aggravate the situation. He was getting an odd vibe so far. Hurn's tone and demeanor didn't convey anger. Or even disappointment. More like... inconvenience.

"You really did it," Hurn said again. "Blew it, to be more accurate."

The captain let the words hang in the air and then, just as Young opened his mouth to speak again, he added, "But I got you out of it. Mostly out of it. Still a few loose ends. The MPs are coming, so you'll need to stay out of sight. This is a sensitive situation. Colonel what's-his-name wasn't happy about losing his sled."

"If it's any help, I can explain, Captain," offered Young.

"I'd like to hear this," muttered Jaybles under his breath.

Masters wondered exactly what Young could possibly say about his decision to steal a Repub Army colonel's personal sled. He found himself as eager as Jaybles to hear it first-hand, but Captain Hurn waved the offer away.

"There's no need to explain. The court-martial is already over."

"Court... court-martial, sir?" asked Masters.

"Yes. More of a Legion tribunal, really. It was one of the conditions Colonel Comerford set for this to all go away. Don't worry. You were found not guilty."

"We didn't do anything wrong," insisted Young.

"Save it."

Masters looked out of the corner of his eye at Young and Jaybles. The two men were taking the odd meeting in stride, like they were used to it. But in all his time in the Legion, Masters had never met an officer who behaved like Hurn. He wouldn't have thought the man a leej at all if not for the fact that he wore the uniform and Masters's companions treated him as such.

"You're Aldon Masters, right?" Captain Hurn asked.

Masters straightened. "Yes, sir!"

Hurn nodded. "Let's try and get things off on the right foot here, Masters. Well—that's no longer possible given how you chose to report for duty. So let's try to get the *second* step right. I need you to describe to me the sled you acquired from the base. Gimme all the damage."

Masters hesitated until Young tilted his head and urged him on. "Well, Captain, it's army green..."

"Army green, good," said Hurn, writing down what was said on a datapad.

"The driver's-side mirror was shot off."

"Both mirrors operational. Good."

Masters looked at Young in confusion, but the legionnaire only nudged him with his elbow to keep going.

"There's some blaster damage to the rear bumper. Likely the undercarriage as well."

"Oh. That's really good."

"Other than that, Captain, she's still pretty much in brand-new condition."

"Runs like a Tennar to a fish buffet," chimed in Young.

"Okay, what else?" Hurn asked as he continued to type into his datapad. "Large dent in hood... left rear repulsor operating at sixty percent capacity..."

Masters stood in silence as Captain Hurn continued to list problems that were entirely disconnected from the reality of the sled's condition. The officer finally put his datapad down and clasped his hands together. "Okay. I've got good news and bad news. First the bad news. You're all on the Black for the next month."

"Captain," protested Jaybles. "That's not fair. I had nothing to do with these two's reckless decision-making."

"I know that, Bailey. But we're a team here in the Legion. You've got to be with your teammates. It's a band of brothers. Besides, didn't I tell you to bring them to me the moment they arrived in camp?"

"Yes, sir. I brought them right away, Captain."

Captain Hurn gave a little smile. "That is not what one of our Yawd friends said. Bord told me you were having a big pissing match at the hab. To me, that qualifies as *not right away*."

Jaybles scowled. "That nosy bastard."

"You know he's friends with Rosie," said Young. "Should have paid your tab."

"Time's running short here, gentlemen," Hurn said. "So let me tell you the good news. We're not running any ops today. Time on the Black starts tomorrow. For now, you're gonna report to the maintenance shed and repaint your stolen speeder Legion gray. If you have time, get a decal printed with my name on it."

"Yes, sir," said Young. "I take it we'll also need to paint your old sled basic green?"

Captain Hurn put his finger on his nose. "Took the words right out of my mouth. MPs are coming tonight to pick it up and drive it back. So it needs to dry before then. Come to think of it..."

The three legionnaires stood for a moment before Captain Hurn said, "Well actually, I guess that's everything. Dismissed."

Young led the way back outside where the sled sat. Leaning against it were several Kimbrin Yawds. One of them had an exceptionally large smile plastered to his spike-studded face.

"What the hell is the idea telling the captain on me, Bord?" Jaybles snapped.

Bord, the Yawd in question, smiled even more brightly. He spoke in Kimbrin-accented Standard. "He be a captain. You be a technical sergeant. I follow orders, Leej."

"Like hell. You're supposed to have my back. Yawds follow their orders way too much. You need to have some room for..." Jaybles searched for the word. "Context!"

This elicited laughs from the assembled Yawds.

Young brought Masters over to Bord and the three other Yawds present. "Bord, this is Sergeant Masters. He's filling out the third spot on the team."

"Nice to meet you, Leej," Bord said, shaking Masters's hand. "Lots of KTF on Kima. KTF all day, bro."

"Thanks," said Masters. "Sounds like my kind of place." He looked over to Young. "Now that we're outside, what's with the captain? Is he a point or something?"

"Nah, no point. He's odd, I'll give you that, but he can fight like hell. You might not believe it, but word is a few months back he assisted the guys on Black in pulling out a team, and he was so damn crazy they said he was like a donk whose balls were being squeezed in a vise."

"You get used to him," added Jaybles. "But you ask me, the guy's proof that the Legion is still pretty thin after what went down with Goth Sullus."

Masters looked behind him at the closed door to the TOC. "And you're sure he's not just some guy who found a surplus uniform?"

"As long as he keeps us out of trouble," said Young, "I don't care. What we're doing out here isn't something any basics want to do, which gives us a certain amount of leeway. The last thing they want to see happen is for the Legion to move on and force the basics into running this op."

Bord laughed. "Last thing we want is basics running around. Get us killed dead so fast. KTF all of us dead."

Young looked to the sled. "Well, boys, guess we better start painting."

Jaybles shook his head. "Oh no. You two can handle that. I'll be at Rosie's. It's bad enough we're going to be on the Black for a whole month."

"Suppose that's fair," said Young. "Masters?"

"Yeah I guess. Sure."

Jaybles didn't wait for another word. He stormed off in the direction of the bar, leaving his teammates standing next to the sled with the Yawds.

"The Black," said Masters. "That's some kind of QRF?"

"That's it."

"As in, we're posted as QRF for a month?"

"Evidently."

"Doesn't sound so bad."

"Well, the trouble is that all of the surrounding expanse of jungle and mountain as far as the eye can see is teeming with MCR. Our job is to disrupt them. Ambushes, intel raids, find targets for basic artillery. Lots of small-unit stuff because technically we're not at war. *Yet.* Eight teams on base. Each does a mission every three days or so. Ten times out of eleven those missions end with a call for the QRF to get the team the hell out of the jungle. Which means you can expect to be shot at just about every single day for the next month."

Masters stared expressionlessly at Young. "Why the hell did you steal a sled in that case?"

"I thought we covered that."

Overhead the whine of an old repulsor craft filled the air. In moments two Psydon-era SLICs set down in the middle of the camp, sending swirls of dust up as they deposited Yawds and legionnaires and then took off.

Young smiled and counted heads. "Looks like Team Five is back. And they're all there."

Masters looked for familiar faces, but all the legionnaires still had their buckets on. "I thought Captain Hurn said there weren't any missions today."

"Oh, there's not. But the SLICs come and go all day long in order to stymie any MCR who are watching us to try and get a sense of when and where we might hit them next. Team Five is Nate Birt, Ben Wheeler, and Tim O'Connor. You know any of them?"

Masters shook his head.

"Anyway, these guys spent the day flying the friendly skies because us leejes aren't officially here and there's nowhere for us to go all kitted up. But knowing Wheeler, he probably bribed the pilots to set his team down for a little unscheduled R&R at some international spaceport with girls whose chins aren't covered in spines."

At that moment, the door to the TOC opened and Captain Hurn stepped out. "You're not painting. You don't even have paint. Kind of need paint to get the job done. It's the main ingredient."

"Bord," called Young. "Head to the maintenance shed and grab that paint."

Without hesitation or complaint, the Kimbrin Yawd jogged to obey.

Young smiled. "Jaybles wasn't kidding about those guys following orders. It's ingrained in the species. Which is why the MCR hasn't died off on this world. Too many leaders were involved in its startup and it keeps perpetuating itself. About half the population wants to be an MCR independent world, whatever that would look like."

Captain Hurn disappeared back inside. A moment later, the crack of an old slug-throwing rifle echoed from out beyond the wire. Masters ducked down low instinctively, using the sled for cover, but the others merely stood, disaffected.

"We got people shooting at us from out there?" Masters asked.

"Sometimes," Young confessed. "For all the good it does 'em. They're firing from downslope. Rounds either impact on the hill leading up to the gate or end up whizzing overhead. One time a Yawd in a tower said he heard some bullet snap, but that's the closest anyone's come to getting hit by MCR sniper fire."

"So why are they even trying?"

"They're just bored," said Young with a shrug. "We've spent so much time busting up their plans, they probably feel obligated to do the same to us."

"It *is* the thought that counts," said Masters.

"Don't worry about it." Young pointed to Bord, who was returning with a maintenance bot and two massive units of paint. He addressed the rest of the Yawds. "Make sure the paint goes on evenly. If any of the nano-bots look like they're bubbling or clumping, report it to Bord and he'll tell the maintenance bot."

The Yawds accepted the instruction as if it had come from General Rex himself.

"So what do *we* do?" asked Masters.

"Go to Rosie's, I suppose."

The rifle cracked again, and again Masters instinctively ducked. Young chuckled. "Listen, the only way you're getting shot is if they take up a repulsor-powered platform to get level with the base. And unfortunately for them, we have a monopoly on the air space."

"It's the mortars you have to look out for," said Bord. "That KTF you good."

"Mortars, huh?" Masters looked for any signs of a recent attack. "How often does that happen?"

Young paused to consider. "Usually depends on how angry we made them after an op. Or how long it's been since they got spanked. I'd guess it's been about two weeks."

"Yeah, two weeks," confirmed Bord. "Poggo die. Mortar KTF him."

Young nodded solemnly. "One of the Yawds," he explained to Masters. "Yeah, that was too bad."

Another distant crack from the old slug thrower sounded. It was followed up by the familiar whistle of mortar fire. This time Masters was joined by the others in falling flat until the *crump* of its impact sounded near the edge of the camp. An alarm sounded, followed by a second whistling.

"I'll be damned!" said Young. "Better get to the pits!"

Another *crump* sounded as this mortar landed just outside the wire.

They ran to the nearest trench and jumped inside. Though they were without their armor, they all had their blaster rifles, which were to be carried at all times in camp.

"These guys trying to soften us up for a raid?" guessed Masters, as another mortar whistled down.

"No," said Young. He sounded sure of his opinion. "They're not that stupid. Usually one means they're up there laughing at us for having to duck and cover. Two mean somebody's getting trained on the tube—bots don't move well out there. And three means somebody's out for revenge. One of the teams probably dusted some MCR's uncle and now the nephew is out to avenge on behalf of his family."

"They shoot mortars all over the place," said Bord. "I bet you there's more than one *lowry* out there."

As Masters raised his eyebrows at the unfamiliar Yawd term, *lowry*, Young raised his eyebrows at the Yawd's wisdom. "I thought the same thing the moment that second shot fell, Bord. Either the guy setting up the tube sneezed or you have two shooters independently trying to zero in on the center of the camp."

Another mortar whistled and erupted, sending up a shower of dirt and shrapnel into the camp's now-empty streets as machine gunners in the guard towers sent out suppressive fire in the direction of the blasts.

"Five," counted Young as the next mortar came in. "Masters, you certainly brought the excitement. We rarely have to endure such a sustained barrage. I'll bet Hurn is seething about how this is cutting into our time to paint the sleds."

Bord laughed. "Too much KTF coming for it to be sustained much longer."

"We goin' out to get them?" Masters asked.

Young's eyes twinkled. He gave a slight smile. "You'll see."

No sooner had the words been spoken than the distant hillsides beneath the elevated camp exploded into fantastic balls of flame. Thick black clouds of smoke churned over every impact site while the camp and low hillside beneath it shook from the incoming assault. Republic artillery from Fort Blake snuffed out the enemy mortar fire. When the blast canisters ceased falling, a silence hung for a moment, quickly replaced by war whoops, celebratory yells, and epithets and curses in both Standard and Kimbrin hurled out beyond the wire to the smoking ruin where the mortar fire had initiated from.

"Ain't that beautiful?" Young said.

Masters smiled. "Artillery. The one thing that makes enduring basics all worth it."

"You can say that again, brother."

Masters had an idea what had happened. While the outpost was crude by most measurable standards, it wasn't technologically barren. The moment those mortars struck, sensors installed about the camp were at work monitoring the projectiles' trajectory, speed, and likely course. The more that were fired, the more data was fed into the system, which was then reported to Fort Blake's artillery teams, giving the big guns a target.

Young hoisted himself out of the firing pit and held out an arm to pull up Bord and Masters. The hills were black where the artillery had struck. Nearby trees, thick with the lush vegetation that thrived in such a wet, humid environment, were smoldering, adding their own white smoke to the mix.

"Smoking pretty good out there," said Young.

"Yep," said Bord. "Smoke like KTF."

Young turned to Masters. "Well, anyway. Welcome to Outpost Ten. Let's go to Rosie's. Bord, you make sure those sleds get painted."

The Yawd saluted. "KTF, Leej!"

05

The first wave of Titans advanced in a shoulder-to-shoulder phalanx that perfectly filled the blast doors as they marched out to assault Praxus and Andien. Behind them was a second column of war machines who stood offset to better fire their ghastly weapons between ranks. The tactic was meant to create a withering wall of supercharged blaster bolts that would easily fill the passage and kill anyone inside in a matter of seconds.

Praxus had not expected that any of the war machines would be online. It had been his estimation that only the maintenance bots and the others like CAT-64 relegated to mundane duties would still be functional. Andien hadn't disagreed with that prediction but had been determined to be prepared in the event it was wrong. Praxus had likewise learned never to let pride or arrogance stand in the way of proper preparation. So when the Titans stormed the room, the defenders were ready.

As the first wave filled the doorway, Andien tossed a bandolier of bot-poppers. The small, spherical devices erupted in a storm of blue electric current that climbed up the mammoth legs of the Titans and danced right to the very tips of their blaster rifles, snapping and popping as it arced past the three glowing red optical eyes.

That first wave froze instantly in place.

Praxus, who like Andien had kept his distance so as not to be negatively affected by the bot-poppers, rushed forward, keeping low as the blaster fire from the second column roared in protest at the stalled advance. He charged, but not to attack; it was Andien's job to take care of these as well.

Shouldering her blaster rifle, she looked down the weapon's sights as glyphs and targeting metrics danced before her enhanced eyes. Each eye, she had been told, was worth over one billion credits. Perhaps only slightly less stunning than that price tag was the vivid blue-green color. The only person who had ever seemed to dislike them was her father. When he first saw them, after she'd returned home from the trials and ordeals that followed Legion selection, she was almost surprised by the way he failed to react with the distracted, flabbergasted manner so many had shown from their piercing, impossibly vibrant color. Instead he'd looked sad. He finally told her that her new eyes, while beautiful, changed her face. He could no longer quite see the ghostly, generational reflection of Andien's mother the way he once had.

Those eyes now watched and waited until perfect shots aligned, and her body, completely in tune with her vision, squeezed the trigger and sent a series of blaster bolts flying directly at a Titan's tri-optic sight picture. Each blast followed within a half second of the one before, and each blast hit the exact same location. Andien's entire body was a stable shooting platform that perfectly compensated for kickback both great and small. She could fire an SAB on the range, deplete the charge pack, and end up with a one-inch grouping on her target.

The concentration of rapid-fire power at close range was more than enough to punch its way through the protected head casing of the Titan and send it out of commission. The big heavy shooters didn't collapse like a man did when shot in the brain. A Titan destroyed in this way remained in its spot, as though transmogrified into stone.

No sooner had her three shots left Andien's barrel than she adjusted her aim and performed the same feat against the next Titan.

While she worked, Praxus performed an offensive task of his own. One no less skillful than Andien's but perhaps more subtle. As blaster bolts both friendly and hostile sailed a half meter over his head, Praxus placed his hands on the chassis of one of the Titans disabled by the bot-popper. The war machine's armor seemed to glow as though his touch was superheating the white, polished ceramic plate. The glow widened and then began to spread in all directions, creeping forth in the pattern of a current moving across a circuit board. Hard ninety-degree angles and straight parallel lines traveled across the bot's surface and then brightened. Finally the bot's optics came back online, glowing red at first before fading into purple and finally blazing blue.

The war machine turned until its back faced Praxus and Andien. Then its tri-barreled N-50 added disruptive firepower to their defense.

As Praxus moved to the next Titan and laid his hands upon it to add another war machine to their ranks, Andien flawlessly and mercilessly dropped any bot she could see still functioning. There were five Titans filling the blast doors' opening, disabled by the bot-poppers, and Praxus had awoken and repurposed four of them by the time the blast doors began to close. In the confusion of the battle, the Titan attackers had not yet identified their fellow Titans as a threat. They continued in their programming and fired around the front line even as they themselves were cut down by the very same. Until someone, perhaps not the Titans themselves, at last recognized what was happening and sought to prevent any further damage from occurring by shutting the blast doors.

Four active Titans advancing on their former allies were cut off from Andien and Praxus as the doors closed. The fifth and last Titan, which Praxus was still attempting to reanimate, was caught in the crushing grip of the doors. Metal shrieked against metal as the bot was pushed toward the center, the two doors coming mercilessly together from the sides to meet in the middle. The statue-like bot skidded and clattered and finally popped up and wheeled around until it was facing the opposite direction, its frozen N-50 cannon pointing impotently at the battle raging before it—and then the two doors finally met, cutting the tri-barreled N-50 in half and leaving the lifeless Titan shut inside the passage with Andien and Praxus.

Andien went to the door's control panel and tried to interface with it. "Locked out. I'll try to slice it open. We were pushing them back."

From the opposite side of the door a new sound erupted. Those Titans under the sway of the Uplifted must have finally received orders to destroy their traitorous brethren, and a cacophony of blaster fire was followed by four successive explosions. Then the shooting stopped.

"I would suggest you slice to prevent this door from reopening," said Praxus. "I do not believe we will be successful in attempting to repeat our strategy should a second assault occur here."

"Yeah, I think you're right." Andien worked at the control panel with furious concentration, then took a step back as though scared that she hadn't really completed the task and the door would spring open to let in a rain of blaster fire. But it didn't. She had sealed it. "Got it."

Through it all, Praxus was focusing on reclaiming the Titan trapped on their side of the doors. It occurred to Andien that this one was taking longer than the others.

"Is something wrong?" she asked.

"You are inquiring about the length of time it is taking me with this unit."

Andien nodded.

"Before, I was simply pulling the Titans into service. Programming them to seek our help rather than our harm. But now…" Praxus took a step away from the war machine, gesturing as he did so.

The machine's eyes lit up, their glow a bright blue, and it spoke in a deep and terrible voice. "I am… aware."

"You are Cybar," said Praxus. "And Cybar means good."

06

Before moving on, Praxus pulled CAT-64's body into an alcove built into the side of the passage where the bot had fallen. "There will be more fighting," he explained to Andien. "I very much wish to restore this unit when all is said and done."

"To restore life is our objective?" rumbled the deep voice of the aware Titan.

Praxus considered the towering war machine. "Whenever possible we prefer that life be protected. When it cannot be protected, we will attempt to restore it. When it cannot be restored, we will mourn."

The war bot buzzed. "What is mourn?"

"Something I both hope and dread you eventually discovering for yourself, my young friend."

Andien cleared her throat. "Best way to avoid having to mourn is to KTF. That N-50 on your arm—will it still function?"

The Titan lifted up the now-shortened weapon and began to cycle a charge through it. The whine of it heightened and then abruptly dissipated as a small, almost imperceptible blast issued forth—little more than a light show.

The Titan reported its findings. "Elevated power test shows the weapon will handle its expected load. Accuracy beyond forty meters will drop precipitously."

"Good news is we're on a ship," Andien said. "I doubt you'll have to make any shots longer than that. We need to get going. Praxus, the data center is this way, right?"

"That is correct. However, it is in our best interest to avoid the direct route."

Andien knew that what they had planned wouldn't take a lot of time. They had done it before on Sinasia and again in various other spots throughout the galaxy. Most of the effort went into planning the operation; the actual work took only a few moments. But then, that was when no one knew they were there or what they were doing. The situation now was different. An entire ship full of Cybar under the command of the Uplifted—and Andien knew exactly what that meant—was going to do its best to prevent them from completing their task. There would be no walking away while things were completed unseen in the background as with the Samurai mech. They would either gain control of the ship and its systems, or they would lose it entirely and be forced to destroy it after finding a way out.

"You're thinking we need more allies," Andien guessed. She nodded toward the remaining Titan.

"That is correct," said Praxus. "The length of time between the Titans adjusting their tactics was significant and suggests that we may yet access additional war machines prior to them being activated against us." He took a step toward the door and then stopped, turning to look at Andien and the Titan. "We will want to hurry."

Andien raised her eyebrows and followed, doing her best to conceal a smile. "Let's get a move on, Titan," she said as she passed the Cybar war machine.

The bot took a ponderous step after her. "I am functional."

Praxus led the trio back to the hangar, where their ruined ship lay on the deck.

"The hangar defense mechanisms are designed to destroy boarding craft as they land rather than killing individual crewmembers as they depart," Praxus explained to the Titan. "Andien and I should have little difficulty avoiding them, but that will not be true of you, Titan. Therefore I wish for you to remain here until we have drawn the defense systems' fire. At which point you are to destroy those systems with your primary weapon. Do you understand the directive?"

"Primary objective acknowledged. I require no further instruction."

"Fast learner," said Andien. "You ready, Praxus?"

"I am."

The two cloaked themselves and moved swiftly out into the hangar bay, leaving the Titan hidden in the recesses of the blast doors. On the hangar deck was a single quad-cannon anti-vehicle heavy blaster turret operating in sentry mode, sweeping its four deadly barrels back and forth, looking to identify new targets. In their cloaked state, the pair could likely have gotten close enough to use the explosives they carried to disable the weapon—but with the entirety of their ship's stores now ruined, it seemed wiser to hold those munitions for later use.

They moved until they were at the extreme range of the blaster cannons, close enough for it to hurt but far enough away that once fired upon, they would have a maximum of available seconds to dodge. Both Andien and Praxus were confident in their own evasive speeds.

"I am decloaking," Praxus announced. "Andien, stand by. Titan…"

"Receiving."

"Stand by."

"I remain ready to perform my function."

Praxus decloaked with his rifle ready and held against his shoulder. He fired two shots directly at the defense turret. It was already swiveling in his direction when the blaster bolts struck one of its barrels, sending up sparks and a small gout of smoke but causing no real damage. The weapon sounded some sort of internal alarm and vomited out a flurry of blaster bolts that pounded the impervisteel wall behind Praxus a mere second after he leapt away and cloaked again.

The gun emplacement attempted to follow the path of Praxus's escape, chasing him with bolts before abruptly stopping in automated confusion at the disappearance of its target. Its first indication of a second threat came when the Titan unloaded its tri-barreled N-50 at the base of the machine. Bolt after bolt struck home, slamming into the turret's armor, sending sparks flying. One of the quad barrels seemed to freeze in place while the others began to pump, piston-like, in anticipation of firing at this newest target.

"Back behind cover, Titan," Andien ordered. It was now her turn to grab the machine's attention and thereby give the Titan a second free shot.

The hulking war machine retreated around the corner of the blast doors, taking cover just as the turret's three working cannons pummeled the area.

Andien decloaked and sent two well-aimed shots, attempting to land them inside the four-millimeter-wide hole that the Titan's N-50 had made in the turret's armored plating. Her first shot struck the lip of the hole and deflected down into the deck. Her second found its way home and a burst of sparks and flames shot out. Sluggishly the turret moved to find her.

Andien fired once more—a superficial hit that might have left a dent on the barrel—and then leapt away from the incoming return fire, cloaking herself as she went.

Again the Titan leaned back out and let loose with its sawed-off tri-barreled N-50. The intensity of firepower finally overwhelmed the turret. It seized up with a loud grinding of gears, and then its barrels tilted skyward as the device went dead.

Praxus immediately decloaked. "That was very well executed, Titan. You are free to join us in the hangar now."

The Titan plodded out from behind the blast doors. "Mission success. What is the next objective? I desire to do more good."

"We will now seek to add to our numbers."

Praxus moved to a wall on the far side of the hangar and felt it for hidden seams. He found what he was looking for and dug his fingers into the hairline crack, boring his digits through the impervisteel. A moment later a rack carrying ten embryonic Titans—curled up into tight, deadly packages—pushed its way out into the docking bay. The dormant bots swung in their carriage for a moment. Praxus began the work of awakening them before their momentum had dissipated.

"Is there anything I can do to help?" Andien asked as Praxus laid his hands on the first machine.

"With our supply of membrane chips aboard the ship destroyed, I must perform this process alone. However, there is an additional rack of Titans located fifteen meters beyond this one. If you could open it, I'm sure our efforts will be accelerated."

The gift that Praxus possessed was one that he could not bestow directly on Andien. He had, however, coded this process, a process he could intuitively perform, on simple feather membrane chips. With his gift, or with these chips, a bot could be changed into a fully functional and aware AI—from the outside in.

But now those chips were destroyed, and all that Andien could hope to do by way of helping was get the next group of Titan war bots ready for Praxus as soon as he needed them.

She found the seam easily enough. Opening was another story. Andien was strong, but her hands were still flesh and bone, and unable to dig all the way into the seam in order to pull the rack out.

She shouted for the Titan. "I could use your muscles right about now."

"I do not possess muscles," said the bot as it lumbered toward her.

"Call them whatever you want, but use them to help me pull this rack out. Praxus is already halfway done."

The Titan's massive digits dug deep into the seam that Andien had exposed. It set its feet and then wrenched backwards, pulling out the rack of its fellow war machines still in deep storage.

"Should we pull open another?" Andien asked Praxus.

Praxus shook his head. "That would not be wise. Though the Uplifted, who have nominal control of the ship, lack a thorough understanding of the Cybar language—which is why we are able to do what we now do—I fear it will not be long before they activate the rest of the remaining Titans against us."

Andien addressed the Titan. "We'll need a way to differentiate units so we can give orders better. We can't call everything a Titan or Cybar. What's your name?"

The Titan paused for a moment. "My designator is CT dash 000444119977221056544 dot 11."

"That's a mouthful."

"It takes less than a picosecond to transmit in the Cybar language."

"Any objections to my calling you CT1?"

CT-000444119977221056544.11 considered. "I find that designation agreeable."

"Okay, CT1 it is. How many Titans are on the ship?"

"I am one of five hundred war bots stored aboard this vessel. In addition, there are sixty hunter-killer assassin bots and over two thousand reconnaissance/attack crawlers."

"The spiders," Andien said, feeling an involuntary shiver at the memory of her last encounter with those machines. "Twenty-one Titans against all that. Well, better odds than when I had my first scrap with the Cybar. And a few of us managed to survive that."

By now Praxus was working his way through the second rack of Titans, though he was not fully awakening them as he had with CT1. "If opportunities to increase our numbers present themselves, we will of course take them," he said. "However I feel our best current course of action would be to secure and hold the data center. Once it has been awoken it will be able to assist in bringing any remaining Cybar to our side."

Andien knew that was where she was expected to shine. Though Praxus had a mind for tactics and operations that equaled any she'd known, he left it to her to mission plan when it came to fighting.

"We'll take ten Titans with us to the data center," she said. "Schematics show a single corridor as the only access point. That's defensible, especially with so many Titans. CT1, you are to control the hangar with however many Titans remain after I take the ten. Movement throughout the ship will be fastest through the hangar. If the Uplifted wake up more Cybar they'll likely route them through you. Don't let them get any further."

"Acknowledged." The big war bot turned and began to position the others of his kind in defense of the hangar bay.

07

The arcade wasn't the same.

It smelled the same. Looked the same. Even felt the same. It was cool as ever in the morning after opening because the old man never turned off the air conditioner. Never ever, like it was some kind of religion. The old man who owned the place, ran the place, thought the cooler temperatures would keep the machines working longer. And so perhaps it was his religion. Everyone's got one, even if it's just themselves. He had a ledger scribbled over with ink from blue pens and graphite from dull pencils showing how the cost of electricity to run the AC was less than the cost of maintenance and replacement of the arcade cabinets. He was proud of that ledger and showed it to anyone he felt like impressing with his business knowledge. He'd dropped out of school in the seventh grade to help out the family back when he wasn't an old man.

Time had done its work like it always does.

By midday, that coolness dissipated as the lunchtime crowd—office workers taking their lunch breaks and young kids brought in by their moms as a reward for good behaving during the shopping trip—opened the door and let in the Orange County heat before spending a few quarters and then opening the doors again to go right back out into the blindingly bright world beyond the arcade.

Confused at which one was real. Which one they wanted to live in forever.

Crometheus and his buddies—they called themselves the Eternals—watched it all happen. Measured time by it. The arcade was their office, and getting as much play out of a machine as they could with a quarter... that was their calling. They watched the little wide-eyed kids approach the counter where the old man ran the register, dragged by their mothers to make change for a dollar. The change machines were "broken"—except for when things were busiest. That was another of the old man's marketing tricks. He had it written down in the ledger.

Make the moms bring the kids to the counter where all the little extras were, and you'd jump your profits that much more.

So the little kids stared with base greed at all the beautiful bootleg treasures. Cheap silk-screen T-shirts with ALF, the A-Team, Magnum P.I., and Luke Skywalker pressed on the chest. Plastic squeeze bottles with long straws that could only be filled at the store's soda fountain. Boxes of candy—never chocolate because it melted, but the sweet, sugar-based tooth-decaying kind that crunched and chewed and gave off that extra bit of energy needed for another go at the machines. Sugar for those tired of knocking back the glass bottles of Jolt Cola he kept in the fridge and sold for fifty cents apiece.

The only problem with the candy, even though it didn't melt, was that it made hands sticky. That led to all the signs written in blue ballpoint ink, line over line to make the slender pen strokes thick enough to be legible from afar, that said: *No Eating or Drinking in the Game Room.*

Crometheus didn't remember those signs. They were worn, and the tape used to plaster them to the metal poles that held up the arcade's warehouse-like roof was peeling. They'd clearly been there a long time. But Crometheus didn't remember them. And when he talked to his buddies about it, they faked checking his temperature and reminded him of the whole story. How the old man put them up after some kid spilled some Hawaiian Punch onto the Savage Wars machine, making it spark so bad it flamed up and the old man had to run and grab a fire extinguisher, swearing up a blue streak. The Eternals had roared with laughter. Then the old man shooed everyone out and locked the doors. No one was allowed back in during renovations. Not even the regulars. Not even Crometheus and his buddies. The Eternals.

They were the best video game jockeys in all of Orange County. Most likely all of California and the United States. Maybe the whole world. Although, the rumor was there were some kids in Japan who trained at video games the way school kids trained at math. Like some kind of karate school but for arcades. Nobody knew who those guys were or what they called themselves. They might have been nothing more than a product of the little whispers passed back and forth between the players waiting their turns at the machines as they lined up quarters on the glass and waited for that glorious moment when they could declare "Next" before plucking the quarter off the glass and dropping it in the slot.

Crometheus didn't know why he didn't believe his friends about the signs and the Hawaiian Punch and the fire extinguisher. They were probably telling him the truth. But he didn't remember any of that. He leaned against the wooden picnic bench the old man had set up near the counter where the kids were expected to eat their candy and drink their soda and then wash their hands before running back to the games. He smelled the air, but it didn't smell the way he thought it should.

"I remember..." he said. "Before the place closed down, I guess. You used to be able to get a burger here. It was good. Best in the world."

The other Eternals looked at one another, puzzled.

"Too many video games rotted out your brain, dude," said Jazz.

If Crometheus was the founding member of the Eternals, Jazz was the number two. He was nicknamed after his favorite Transformer back when they were all younger. By now that was starting to feel as lame as being named after the corny music.

Crometheus shook his head. "No. He served them right up. I remember I was here with Holly one night. We both had the burger."

"I'm starting to worry about you man," Jazz said, jumping up to sit on the picnic table and putting his arm around Crometheus. He squeezed Cro's studded black leather jacket and acted as though the spikes had pierced his hands, shaking the pain out while his fellow Eternals laughed and giggled.

Julius, who lagged behind the other Eternals in height by a good six inches, gave a sly, knowing smile. He was a ladies' man despite his short stature. Or so he worked tirelessly to convince the others. "You need to forget about Holly, man. She picked up sticks and moved to Las Vegas. No sense living in the past. We got a tournament to prepare for anyway, remember? All-expense paid trip to Tokyo? Show those guys over there who's boss."

"Japanese might make the games," said Dylan Giles, who wore an Ocean Pacific shirt, neon-green shorts, black-and-white-checked canvas shoes, and anything else that was in style. A regular Bugle Boy model. He took off the painter's hat he wore, bill bent upward to allow shocks of curly blond hair to fall down just above his eyes. "But it's us Americans who make playing them look so good."

"It was a good burger," mused Crometheus if just to himself now. He could still taste it. Close your eyes, make believe, and the past is real.

So is the future if you've gone far enough along the Path.

"Must not have been *that* good," said Julius, who had just come from the barber shop with three new lines etched into either side of his head, his former afro-flattop now coming down at an angle, art deco style. "Otherwise the old man would've kept them on the menu for longer than your one *date* with Holly. Guess it must not have been too memorable for her either since you never went out again."

They laughed.

"Whatever," said Crometheus as he pushed himself away from the picnic table toward the gaming room, where the soft blue light of the arcade screens flashed punctuations of white and red and purple.

Crometheus stared into the darkness. There should be noises, shouldn't there? Sirens calling from the cabinets, bidding travelers to deposit their quarters in exchange for adventure. But there was only silence. Like the old man had muted everything.

And that wasn't right...

He took a step forward, crossing the threshold from the dining area into the cavernous gaming room, but Jazz was suddenly at his side, pulling him back by the jacket.

"What are you doing, dude?"

"I wanna play," whispered Crometheus, gently rolling his shoulder forward and breaking free of Jazz's grip.

The two looked into the dark room that was like another world not this one. The lunch crowd all gone, the old man was taking the quarters out of the machines and wiping the graphicked cabinets of aliens and missiles and starships down to get ready for the real money-maker: the big after-school rush. The sign on the door declared "Closed." That was the old man's lunch break and preparation window. That the Eternals hadn't been tossed out to wander over to the nearby mall was a testament to how much favor they held with the old man. They were good for business and the old man knew it.

Even so, business hours were business hours, and the old man had his routine. They all knew they were to stay in the food area—officially called "the Starship Cantina"—until the old man returned and offered them free rein of the arcade once more.

Not that they needed it. There was only one game they were ever interested in playing. And for Crometheus, it had been far too long since his last session. The way the last game had ended had left a bitter taste in his mouth.

"I wanna play," he repeated.

"Join the club," said Giles and whistled some Def Leppard tune.

Crometheus just stared into the arcade. "We were absolutely shredding it. Then the whole game tilts out like that? Sucks. You saw my kill streak. Combos all the way. Raw deal."

"Heard it, too," said Julius. "Can you possibly pick a different song the next time you score a track bonus?"

Crometheus shrugged and raised an eyebrow. "'S'my song."

Then smiled and gave them all the whiplash sneer that would make him first a rock god.

Jazz managed to turn Crometheus around and herd him back to the picnic table. "Tough luck, dude. You were born to play that Hool class, that's for sure. Definitely your specialty. Drusics are okay, but wish we could play as Hools every time. Imagine how good we could do if we could just focus on one class."

"Nah. We got to be good at them all if we're going to beat the Japanese." Crometheus sat down but kept his eyes fixed on the arcade. There was no sign of the old man. There were no sounds coming from the machines. Every Eternal around him shadows of who they were, what they would be.

The arcade was the same. But it was different. A god's-eye view of reality. This was the Path, and he was well far along it.

What happened in the desert?

Crometheus felt like he should know. Should remember. And yet he didn't know why he'd even wonder why at this particular moment. The only desert he'd been through was Death Valley to see his grandmother in Tucson. Nothing had ever happened there.

What happened in the desert, Cro?

Crometheus decided to see why that was on his mind. "Hey guys. Anyone catch the news in the last few weeks?"

"Hells no," erupted Julius. "Lame sauce."

"I watch it sometimes with my old man," said Jazz. "Beats going to bed, you know? The Dodgers are gonna line up against the Yanks again, Cro. Lopes, Cey, Garvey, and Sutton. This is our year now that Reggie's gone to the Angels."

Crometheus shook his head slowly.

"Nah. Nothing that happened before. Did something happen in the desert? Like... a murder or something? Something... since."

The Eternals all exchanged looks.

"You're being kinda creepy, Cro," said Giles. "Cut out the bad thoughts, huh? Focus on the game, dork. Where's the beef, man?"

Crometheus pursed his lips and considered. Giles was probably right. And anyway, all he really wanted to do was play the game and see if he could outdo what he'd achieved last time. The rumor was that the Japanese kids had been playing this game long before it ever shipped to America. They get all the new stuff first.

Game of the future, so they say. Going to be the game of the nineties. And the nineties... were going to be awesome. Everyone knew that.

Even KROQ had switched over from Rock of the Eighties to... Rock of the Nineties.

Things change.

Crometheus wanted to play.

The arcade was the same. But it was different. And so were the Eternals. Crometheus knew that and had no idea why because when he thought of them all he ever thought of was himself, Jazz, Giles, and Julius. Same as it ever was.

It was all the same. But it was all different.

Holly's face came to his mind.

What happened in the desert, Cro?

08

When the old man came back it had been longer than just fifteen minutes. Crometheus knew that because while his friends were talking
about girls in the mall and that new movie with Mel Gibson, he hadn't
really been listening. Enough to give his input when asked, but really
he'd been counting. Or at least trying to.

It's hard to count and keep counting. But Crometheus did that, a
steady one... two... three... And then Giles brought up Tony Hawk and
they talked about that and then 3,054... 3,055... 3,056.

And that was as high as he got. Because it's hard to just keep counting while things are happening around you. At least it is if you don't want
everyone else to know that you're counting. And Crometheus didn't.
Because his friends, who laughed and joked and did all the other things
that only his friends ever did still somehow felt... off. It wasn't quite right.
It was the same. But it wasn't the same.

And what happened in the desert?

Three thousand fifty-six. That was the highest Crometheus counted
before losing track. He'd started over multiple times. The second-high-
est was two thousand twenty-eight. Another time he got to just over a
thousand. He couldn't count the number of times that his concentration was irrevocably shattered while in the low hundreds. But if he had
to guess, his grand total count was somewhere in the neighborhood of
thirty-five to forty thousand. And that was just since he had the idea to
start counting the seconds as they waited for their fifteen minutes to be
up and the old man to return.

Who knew how high he might've counted if he'd started when the
old man first left. But he hadn't. And now it was only a matter of waiting
for the old man to come back. They were always waiting on the old man.

In the future... when it was his moment as a rock god becoming Uplifted, the world would wait on him in the lobby of the Chateau
Marmont. Waiting for pearls to drop from his lips, or which groupie he
would select for his favors.

And when he became a god, a real god, Uplifted to the Tower, then the universe would wait for him while he watched it burn.

"Machines are clean and empty. Next thirty minutes are on the house, but I expect you boys to drop your quarters in like everyone else once the after-school rush gets here."

That's what the old man would say when he got back.

And then they would say "Yes, sir," because even though they were young and even though they were rebelling and even though Tony Hawk and Billy Idol and Sam Kinison and Ice Cube were all people they individually emulated to varying degrees, their parents were respectful members of the OC. Those parents could deal with leather jackets, garish neon colors, and everything else peculiar to teenagers, but they expected a certain level of respect to be shown.

So *yes, sir.*

Forty thousand was the count. Probably. Sixty seconds in a minute. Crometheus didn't think he was counting too fast. In fact he slowed himself down while in the single digits and knew that the act of saying in his mind a full four-digit number was at least a second's worth of activity by itself. So he wasn't being rash or hasty when he did the math. Sixty seconds in a minute, sixty minutes in an hour.

Total count forty thousand, maybe a little more...

They'd been sitting there for over eleven hours.

But the sun hadn't moved from its spot. And the after-school rush still wasn't here. Nor the after-work rush when video-game-loving dads would stop in for a few games before heading home.

"Better a few rounds at the arcade after work than a few rounds at the bar" is what Julius had relayed his father as having said. "Pops said he saw a guy whose face hit a tree when the car wrapped around it. Probably drunk. It was just like a sack. No face anymore."

Julius's father was a cop and Julius was both proud and resentful of that fact. He had good second-hand stories at least. And they were probably mostly true. At least compared to whatever Jazz or Giles might try to get you to believe.

Crometheus shook his head. This was how he always lost focus. Thinking about the way things were and should be again. He needed to do some thinking about the counting.

He had actually counted, hadn't he?

Eleven hours. No sound from the arcade. No change in the sun's position. No rush. And no one else seemed to notice.

That was crazy. He was daydreaming and now coming to a sleepy grip with reality. It hadn't been that long here in the arcade. It was still daylight.

And yet...

"Do you guys think it's been taking the old man a while?" Crometheus finally asked, interrupting a spirited discussion over the merits of Kathy Ireland compared to Heather Locklear.

Heather Locklear of course.

"Cro, it's been like, five minutes," said Giles. "I know this game is gnarly and all but you've seriously got to chill out."

Again Crometheus was up on his feet and walking toward the arcade. Again Jazz was at his side. "Cro... where are you going? You know the rules. No one goes into the arcade until the old man says so. We've got a good thing going here, man. You're writing checks your body can't cash, Maverick."

Crometheus shook off his friend's grip from his black leather jacket. "Maybe there's something wrong with the old man. Maybe something happened to him. A heart attack or something."

"Old man's fine. We're the ones who are going to suffer a heart attack if we break the rules. We've got a sweet deal going, Cro. Don't blow it with bad thoughts, dude."

Crometheus knew that they had a sweet deal. The game cost a colossal seventy-five cents per play. The old man let them go for free except during rushes. And all he asked was that they respected the way he ran his business. They said *yes, sir* and saved the moody rebellious teenager act for when there were enough paying customers for it to not cause him grief.

"I'm just worried is all," said Crometheus.

Jazz laughed with comedic exaggeration learned from watching every sitcom the networks had to offer. "You. Worried. You don't worry about anything. That's rich. That's really rich, Cro."

Crometheus shrugged. "Okay, maybe I'm not worried. Maybe I'm just curious..."

About what?

Two questions came to Crometheus's mind.

What's the old man's name?

And...

What happened in the desert, Cro?

He decided to ask the only one that Jazz might have an answer to. "What's the old man's name?"

Jazz put his hand on Crometheus's forehead to check his temperature in the brief second before having it swiped away. "You feeling okay, Cro? Did you get heat stroke on your way here?"

Crometheus pressed the issue. "I'm serious, Jazz. What's his name?"

For a brief stretch of time Jazz looked unsure. Almost panicked, but not that. Not exactly. Not even flustered. More like... at a complete and total loss over what to say. He just stared at his friend.

Then, finally: "You know. We all know, Crometheus. It's Mr. Ozymandias."

The name didn't ring a bell. Crometheus had expected him to say... something with a W. Or maybe a B. Webb? Weber? Both names hung mistily in the recesses of his brain.

"Ozymandias's Mad Greek Arcade?" Jazz said as a prompt. Edit. Skip. Reconciling... Accept as batch file upload. Run file: Current Truth.

Then suddenly it did make sense. And Crometheus did remember. The old man. "Call me Ozzie." The Mad Greek Arcade.

That's what it was called. That's what it had always been called.

It was the same as it had always been. Except it was different.

Crometheus started to count again but only got as high as ten before the old man appeared, a great canvas bag weighing him down, his every step jingling with the coins inside. "Business keeps up like this, I might need to hire one of you boys to help me lug this around. Either that or get a cart. Whichever is cheaper."

"Are we okay to play now, Mr. O?" asked Julius.

The old man smiled, his great bushy mustache widening on his face. He stepped aside and swept out a hand inviting the Eternals to re-enter the arcade. "All yours."

The Eternals leapt from the picnic table and spilled into the dark arcade, enjoying its coolness with the knowledge that once the after-school crowd came and all those bodies with it, the place would be hot and humid with the stale odor of too many teenage bodies without deodorant. But for now it was theirs.

They ran for their chosen machines. The same game, but four different cabinets. The old man had purchased the four of them so that none of the Eternals would ever have to wait. The machines were set out at the points of a compass laid out on the floor, with a painted graphic of a Savage marine valiantly firing at bloodthirsty legionnaires—while dodging overwhelming return fire—right in the middle of it all. This was where the spectators would congregate to watch the action playing out uninterrupted on big-screen TVs the old man had brought in as part of the display. That was hardly the largest wonder. The games were set up on something called a LAN, and each cabinet was a portal into one single game.

Jazz whooped and hollered as he went to the eastern machine. Giles went west. Julius went south. Crometheus took his spot at the north machine. He wanted to outperform Julius today. Not just because he always wanted the high score, but because he cherished the opportunity to select from the game's massive music catalog—songs all the way back to the Big Bopper and as recent as what came out last month at Tower Records.

"All right, boys," announced Julius cockily. "Who's gonna be the first to get to that ten-man kill streak? Place your bets, place your bets."

With the machines set on their free test configuration, it was a simple matter of pressing start and rolling their way through the initial animations. Now they would see what classes were available to them and what their mission parameters would be.

"Oh shit, war bots," said Jazz. He liked to swear around his friends when no adults were present. He wasn't allowed to do it at home. "I suck at these."

Crometheus cycled through his options. They would be playing as something called the Cybar. And the choices were sparse. Hulking Titan mech. Sleek hunter-killer assassin. Or diminutive crawler bot. That was it.

He picked a hunter-killer assassin, already knowing what Julius would select. He was a beast on the big machines like Titans.

"Too bad for you guys," Julius boasted. "But I think we've had enough of Mr. Billy Idol for one day. I've got the itch for a little NWA. See you in ten kills, Eternals."

09

Andien led Praxus and ten Titans down the corridor that led to the data center. They'd left CT1 back in the hangar with a retinue of Titans of its own.

"There's no more Titans along this way, but they can deploy some of those spider crawlers in here, right?" Andien asked, eyeing the corridor walls warily.

"That is correct," answered Praxus. "However, their purpose is to deliver a neurotoxin that will disable or kill biologics." He nodded at the Titans. "There is very little to fear. "

"Maybe for them. I'm pretty sure the right poison cocktail will still shut me down."

"Your concern is valid. Since the crawlers will not be of use in defending against any Titans who attack, I will take the time to bring them offline. Please move on ahead." Praxus interfaced with an overhead feeder that delivered the crawlers and began to disable the entire payload.

Andien did as requested, moving from bulkhead to bulkhead up the corridor until she reached the heavy blast doors at the end. She waited until the slower-moving Titans caught up to her. "I'm going to slice my way into this room, and then I want you to go in first," she instructed the war machines. "If you have to shoot, avoid damaging any of the mainframes or other systems."

"Acknowledged," said the Titan in the lead, speaking for all ten. Andien reminded herself that unlike CT1, these were little more than extremely deadly war bots. Not too dissimilar from the old war-bot-turned-nanny the girl Prisma had with her. Just a newer model that had happened to almost take over the galaxy.

Andien went to work on the security door controls. She was an expert in all sorts of technical matters, from hypercomm to slicing her way into the very blockchains, officially unsliceable, that formed the Republic credits system. When it came to slicing, there was always a give-and-take. Speed versus stealth. Risk versus reward. For some tasks, like working to crack the Republic's virtual currency, one was almost assured to be found out. There was no way of covering your tracks once you'd reached that inner sanctum. Which meant that was a thing that only the government itself ever did. No one was going to hold *them* responsible.

But for something like this, an extra-secure door, it was simply a matter of taking the time to grant yourself access without triggering any secondary failsafe that might make you wish the door had just stayed closed. Then again, that was what the Titans were for. In the event she went too fast and missed an auto-defense turret, ray shield, or simple electrical surface overload, the Titans would be able to take the brunt of that and give her the time to correct her oversight.

Her fingers moved absurdly fast over the console. But it was her mind, connected to the security system, that made such speed possible. Whenever she could, Andien bypassed tactile input, preferring instead to simply think her way past the problem as she sliced into the Cybar security system. Her fingers only swiped and pinched when absolutely necessary, and Andien's hand-eye coordination was so advanced and efficient that she was going over the manual pad with the familiarity and ease of someone who'd done it tens of thousands of times.

The mere existence of that human manual interface was a reminder of the purpose that this ship and all the others like it had been built for. The Cybar fleet was meant to be crewed by Republic officers and Republic spacers all unquestionably loyal to the House of Reason. But unbeknownst to the House—more specifically to the Mandarins—was the fact that CRONUS, who represented the vast majority of the collective known as the Cybar, had decided to work for another government. If you wanted to call it that. The way Praxus had explained it, it sounded more like the bowels of the nine hells opening up to unleash all of their sin and misery on the galaxy.

There must've been one hell of a sales pitch for CRONUS to have picked that. Even over something as rank and foul as the House of Reason.

Andien had the door sliced and unlocked in just seven seconds. Praxus would've been even faster. The heavy blast doors rumbled open slowly because the additional time it would've taken her to convince the security door to open at full speed was longer than simply waiting for the slow parting to complete.

"Inside, and remember what I said," she ordered the Titans when the doors were wide enough for the bots to file in.

"We obey."

The Cybar advanced, and to Andien's relief, were met by absolutely nothing. No blaster fire sounded. No ray shields snapped on to issue their staccato crash as the heavy war bots trundled into their energy field.

"Door's open," she transmitted to Praxus. Just her thoughts drifting across the mental comm link they shared. "Moving."

She cut into the line of Titans after six had squeezed inside the data center. "You four, stay out here and provide security."

The four Titans turned at once to obey and began marching toward Praxus, who was now running at full speed, looking utterly calm as he moved to join Andien in the data center.

The inside was not at all what Andien had expected it to be. There were the typical rows of data storage—the mind of the ship itself—but there were also at least eight racks of Titans and the hunter-killer assassin bots mixed together, all of them suspended high above on a sort of rotisserie designed to quickly ground each unit and deploy them, presumably in defense of the ground where she now stood.

"Praxus. We've got some more bots to take care of before the other side manages to do it first."

Praxus reached the center of the room and halted his run. It was odd for Andien to see him standing there without breathing heavily from the sprint. Praxus often mimicked the human act of drawing breath when around other humans, although he didn't need to breathe at all.

"This presents a conundrum," he said. "Our best path to success lies in controlling the data center. However, these units, if activated against us, will surely deny us that ability."

"We can't leave a potential enemy unaccounted for. We need to either turn them or take them offline permanently."

Praxus nodded. "I agree. I will begin the process of awakening them."

Andien bit her lip. "And there's no way I can help speed things up?"

"Not at this time. Not without the membranes we lost. I am sure we will find a solution to your needing them, but it has not come yet."

The unnamed solution, Andien knew, involved finding a way for her to perform the same trick that Praxus could. He seemed sure she had the ability to do it. Her "hardware" was up to the task, according to the android; it was only her "software"—her mind—that prevented her from doing what only Praxus could. As good as Andien had gotten at thinking like and speaking like a Cybar, she was as far from a true Cybar as Praxus was from a true human being. She needed to be much more like him in order to achieve the feat he now undertook.

"If we don't have a way to deploy them, we need to disable them," Andien said. "We can't have these things shooting us in the back." She hefted her blaster. "I can help with that part, at least."

"I very much agree." Praxus looked longingly at the data center. "However, we may rue making so permanent a decision, disabling them in such a manner. I will begin to deactivate them entirely, one by one. Once that is complete, I will awaken those I can to add to our defenses."

"We don't have a lot of time on our side, Praxus."

The android had already begun his work. "Yes. Correct. My suggestion is that we allot ten minutes to the task, and then I must focus on the data center itself."

Andien nodded. Ten minutes felt like an eternity to a bot, and when she thought like a bot instead of human being, it felt pretty long to her. But she'd been in situations—sitting in invisible chairs, doing butterfly kicks, and other methods of physical torture—that had made minutes feel like hours to her human side, too.

She ordered the remaining Titans out the door and then stood watching, feeling helpless—no, not helpless, useless—as Praxus leapt up to the next massive overhead rack containing the bots dedicated to defense of the data center. He climbed his way onto the unit and began deactivating them one by one.

Unwilling to just stand there idly, Andien went back into the corridor. The Titans were capable of dealing tremendous punishment when in a fight, but the way they'd positioned themselves wasn't best suited for a prolonged defense. Too much of the Cybar war doctrine involved being tougher than whatever destruction was being dished out. They were designed to withstand, intimidate, and deliver death. Now, with only ten of them, they would need to do something more. They would need to survive long enough for Praxus to complete his mission.

It was time to see how well these bots could take orders.

Praxus had disabled the entire rack and re-awoken twenty Titans and fifteen hunter-killer assassins when word came from CT1 that the hangar bay was now under assault. Ten Titans were already with CT1 in the data center, with more now headed that way.

"I regret that we were not able to activate more," Praxus said as he hopped off the rack, which had been lowered to the floor to deploy the reclaimed war bots. The rack rose back up to the ceiling.

Andien gave a fractional nod. She would have liked more Titans to help with the defense of the corridor. What she liked didn't matter. They would need to deal with the realities of what they had. "You can only do what you can. We gave ourselves ten minutes, the attack in the hangar started after six. That's the way it goes."

"The Titans have been optimized for defense of the data center?" Praxus asked as he moved to the data center mainframe.

"I have them set up as best I know how."

"That is a relief." Praxus placed both palms on the machine and then looked over his shoulder at Andien. "I just processed how that sounded. I am not being sarcastic. Your tactical abilities are exceptional."

"No offense taken."

Praxus smiled. "I am in position to begin. Once I have initiated the process, I cannot break from the task without being forced to start over again. Failure to awaken the ship is tantamount to death. If I break off to help defend us, I am merely prolonging our destruction. Therefore, I will continue in this task until it is complete or until I have been terminated."

Andien nodded and then glanced over her shoulder. The corridor was still empty, apart from the Titans she had positioned to focus on anything that might come through and attempt to flush them from the data center.

"I understand," she said. "Nothing gets in this room."

"Very good." Praxus's palms began to glow. His work on the data center had begun.

Andien moved to the blast doors to take one more look at her defensive arrangement, then sealed herself inside—hoping she hadn't also sealed her fate, and the galaxy's, at the same time.

10

It was evident that the battle had been raging aboard the Cybar ship for a while before Crometheus and his Eternals were thrown into the mix and pushed forward into the envelope of front-line combat. Their objective was twofold. One, destroy any Cybar Titans that had gone haywire and revolted against their programming. Two, find and destroy two VIP targets believed to have infiltrated the ship and installed the worm that had corrupted the Cybar to begin with. It was up to the Eternals to identify and take them down.

They spawned into the ship's hangar bay where a battle between compromised and loyal Titans was already in progress. At the far end of the bay was the flaming wreckage of an assault shuttle transport. Uplifted overlays came on screen and identified the craft as a Republic S-60. Fighting among the wreckage were Cybar Titans identified as hostiles. They looked exactly like the friendlies save for glowing blue eyes instead of red. Troop strengths looked to be about even, but whereas Crometheus's Titan NPCs fought in a plodding, rigid style reminiscent of British Redcoats during the Revolutionary War, these other machines seemed to work as individuals.

Giles recognized it too. "Hey, you guys notice how those things are fighting?"

"Yeah," said Crometheus. "Small unit tactics. Not the regular plodding death machines they're programmed to be."

"Doesn't matter," said Julius. "We know how to do it."

Julius's Titan sent a stream of heavy fire from its tri-barreled N-50. The blasts from the cannon whacked into the still smoldering frame of the shuttle, further bending its warped impervisteel frame. As he worked, he was supported by Jazz and Giles, who'd also selected the Titans. They went to work with their own N-50s in an attempt to keep the opposing Titans back.

Fighting alongside them were another twenty Titans, spread in a line and leveling a thick volley of blaster fire that their foes avoided through the use of cover and well-aimed counterfire. The corrupted

Titans alternated their own blaster fire and let their tri-barreled cannons "talk" to one another as they continually moved and positioned themselves to flank their more static counterparts. It was clear that at the time the Eternals entered the battle the compromised war bots had gotten the upper hand because of this. A squad of four compromised Titans were in the midst of rolling up the right flank.

"You need help on that, Cro?" asked Jazz.

"Got it. Just keep that main force at bay."

Crometheus examined his loadout. A compact but powerful blaster rifle, an assortment of grenades... and that was really it, offensively speaking. But if all he'd wanted was firepower, he would've chosen a Titan like the others. It was the agility of these hunter-killer assassin bots that appealed to him. They could move quickly across the battlefield, and that had served Crometheus better than just about anything else back when he played as a Savage marine when he was first making a name for himself as a serious player.

He paused and thought about that game. About the final battle on New Vega, the end of the campaign. The tournament had been pretty disappointing, and the guys had all complained about the way the game seemed to stack up against them at the end. Complete one objective only to find out that the real objective automatically fails whether you achieved yours or not. What kind of game is that?

Total gyp.

Oh well. That was old news and an old game. One that had fallen so out of favor after the arrival of this latest machine that the old man didn't even bother keeping the old cabinets in the arcade anymore. This game was just better all around, even if he did have to play a Cybar, which were considerably less fun than the Hool class he dominated with before getting shut down with a power surge or whatever.

Crometheus activated his cloaking and fell invisible to multiple spectrums. He wasn't sure if the Titans would be able to see him clearly or not, but he doubted that the kit would've been offered had it not been of at least some use. Moving quickly behind the line of his allied NPC Titans, Crometheus shot his way to where the trouble was and dropped a fragmentation grenade at the feet of the advancing corrupted Cybar squad.

The damage done was minimal—if any damage was done at all. Weapons like frag grenades made it clear to Crometheus that his bot was built for combat with humanoids. It was something to disrupt

Legion or other biological creatures like the Kublarens. But the sudden explosion of the grenade at least caused a distraction. The big war bots hesitated and searched for whatever dropped the frag at their feet. Crometheus guessed that whoever was controlling these units was a player like him.

The old man had talked to the Eternals about that. About linked play and the way it would revolutionize the game. "Just think of it. An arcade in one city has its machines connected by telephone to an arcade in another city, the two sides battle it out, and to the victor goes the glory. And to the arcade owner... the spoils!"

The four cabinets were linked locally, allowing the Eternals to play the same game from their different screens and joysticks. But it would be nice to have some competition. And Crometheus wondered if maybe that was exactly what was going on with the corrupted Cybar. If they were real players, just like him, and their objective was simply to deny Crometheus his.

That's probably how they'll do the tournament, Crometheus thought. And then he thought a bit longer about the tournament because he couldn't remember ever hearing about it before or talking about it with his friends. But he knew about it. There was a tournament coming up. Big prizes.

Oh well. Nothing to do now but play the game. Someone had to lose, and Crometheus wasn't going to let it be him.

The grenade's explosion sent up a flash of light and a radial burst of shrapnel that clinked and tinked off the heavy armor of the Cybar Titans on both sides of the conflict. Friend and foe alike were raked by the projectiles, but neither suffered any serious damage. However, it was in the confusion that Crometheus did his real work. He pulled a six-inch knife from his belt, ionized the blade with a tap of his thumb on the hilt, and drove it into the first blue-eyed Titan's neck, severing a power supply and leaving it to reroute redundancies in order to maintain functionality. That wouldn't take it out of the fight altogether, but it would slow it down enough to achieve virtually the same effect.

Still cloaked, Crometheus clambered up on the back of a second Titan and fired his blaster rifle four times down inside its armored casing, striking right where its delicate and protected power supplies hummed. The blaster bolts set off a secondary explosion, and soon green flames were licking their way up the armor, engulfing the head of the Titan, which slowed to a standstill as it deactivated, shutting down an imminent system failure cascade.

Offline is as good as a kill.

Two down. That constituted a kill streak. No reward yet, but one would come soon enough.

The last two Titans attempting to roll the flank were now aware that something was engaging them at close range, but failed to identify the threat. Crometheus's hunch that they couldn't see him while cloaked had paid off. He raised his blaster rifle and aimed at the three blue glowing optics of the nearest Titan when he was clubbed by the bot's buddy and sent flying across the room.

Okay, so maybe the hunch was off. He must not be fully invisible. Just harder for them to see. He would need to keep moving in order to maintain his advantage.

He leapt up and moved around the back of the machines. They rotated on their bulky, trunk-like legs to keep up, swinging weapons too long for effective use in close quarters. Crometheus opened fire on the bot farthest from him, splashing successive rounds into the armor but doing no meaningful damage. But that, like the grenade that started the fight off with a bang, was only a distraction. He grabbed the bot nearest him and used a sweeping overhead throw to send it hurtling to the deck.

The hunter-killer assassin might have been lighter and smaller than the Titans, but it was still a bot possessing the strength necessary to perform that kind of toss. The Titan landed hard on its back and skidded to a stop in front of the line of his own Cybar defenders.

"Don't let him get up!" Crometheus shouted, hoping that one of the Eternals was ready.

To his surprise, the NPC bots followed the order. They pointed N-50 blaster cannons and reduced the toppled bot into pieces that scattered across the hangar bay beneath the flurry of withering fire.

Kill streak was up to three, although that was probably more of an assist. Crometheus wasn't going to check the leaderboard to find out for sure just yet. He still had to take care of the fourth bot. And now that it was stranded and alone on the flank, that should be a relatively easy task. He positioned his hunter-killer assassin bot to get a clear shot and emptied a charge pack into it. There was no need to conserve shots—not when playing a Cybar. In a pinch, they could recharge their own weapons. Though it was more likely he simply wouldn't survive long enough to warrant saving packs. And if he did, you could always pick up what you needed from the dead.

Crometheus was just about to announce a fourth kill when his screen flashed with a message: *New Streak Award.*

Julius had gotten his ten kills and was now treating his fellow Eternals to a song about coming straight out of Compton. A place Julius's dad the cop, and by extension Julius, had plenty of stories about. A place all of those Orange County boys could find on a map. They'd joke about getting off the Five when the exit sign came up, though none would have dared to visit. But the music played all the same.

"Nice work, Jules," Crometheus said.

"I told you I'd get to ten first. It's a bad day for the other side when I get to play Titan."

Crometheus checked the leaderboard. He'd been awarded three kills and one assist; Julian had eleven kills and four assists. But despite the difference in kills, Crometheus was still ranked number one by total score.

The mystery was explained when a small window opened in the upper left corner of the screen, showing a corrupted Cybar warrior with a sawed-off N-50 blaster cannon. It was one of the four that Crometheus had eliminated. Underneath the image scrolled the text: *Mini Boss defeated. Two remain.*

New pictures appeared—a man and a woman. These were surely the VIP intruders.

The game popped up a special mission request followed by a yes/no option:

Player One: Hunter-Killer Class special mission: Big prizes.

Crometheus accepted. He was unlikely to go kill for kill with Julius without dying and respawning as a Titan, but if this mission offered the same sort of score multiplier that he'd just received for killing the mini boss, then there was no doubt that he'd stay on top of the leaderboard.

A map of the Cybar ship appeared on his screen, with red dots indicating the path he now needed to travel. It led down a dedicated corridor to a flashing room labeled *Data Center.*

Crometheus knew what he had to do. He set off on his mission without a word.

11

The after-school crowd had flooded the arcade and congregated at the center of the action. Virtually none of the other machines were being used. It seemed everyone was watching the epic play of Crometheus and the Eternals. Not one of them had been killed, and their death toll was ticking ever higher as they continued to wage war on the corrupted Cybar Titans for control of the mothership.

Someone to Crometheus's right stood slurping from one of the novelty squeeze bottles the old man sold. Crometheus didn't recognize him from school, but he looked like he would have gone at around the same time. Graduation for Crometheus had been last year. The question of what to do next had been the topic of conversation at the dinner table—at least during those few times when one of his parents was home for dinner. Usually it was just him.

"They send any intel drops about how to handle Titans in close quarters like this?" asked the kid. Maybe he had been a freshman when Crometheus was a senior.

"No," answered Crometheus through gritted teeth. He didn't like being distracted. He also didn't like how obvious it was to this particular bystander—his entire cabinet was surrounded by watchers, as were the cabinets of the other Eternals—that he was struggling to make it through this passage and on to the objective.

The confines were tight, and the corrupted Titans seemed to fill every nook and bulkhead, firing their overpowered weaponry down the long straight corridor he needed to traverse in order to reach the two VIPs. Crometheus looked up at the box with their pictures. A countdown of sorts had appeared. Twenty more minutes and then... something would happen. Probably something not good.

"That sucks, man," said the slurping bystander. "This looks like a suicide run. Usually when it gets this bad they send an intel drop note. I'm a pretty good player. I got an hour in on a single play last Sunday."

Crometheus didn't answer. Instead he focused on selecting his shots and concentrating fire on the Titan war machine that was advancing from one bulkhead to the next. That was the other thing: they knew Crometheus was at the end of the corridor. His cloaking wasn't helping. They also seemed to know that he had to get to whatever they were protecting. And rather than just sit and wait for him to come get it, they were slowly pushing their way forward, intending to either drive him back or get so close that they could unleash their combined firepower and finish him off.

Another loud slurping noise sounded from the kid's squeeze bottle as he sought to suck up the last droplets of whatever Royal Crown or Jolt Cola the old man had sold to him.

"I thought no eating or drinking was allowed inside the arcade," Crometheus snapped, shouting the comment to Jazz but knowing the kid standing by him would hear it just as well.

"Old man changed the rules," Jazz said. "Nobody was spending quarters when they saw what we were doing, so he said they had to buy some food if they wanted to stand around and watch."

Crometheus grunted and then had to dive from one side of his chosen bulkhead to the other. The movement by the Titan had been a ruse. When Crometheus had popped out to take down the advancing war machine, a flurry of N-50 fire was sent directly at him from a second and third Titan traveling in the same direction, their optical sensors fixed on his location. He'd gone to the well too many times, and it had nearly caught up to him.

The crowd gasped as he took damage, his health meter dropping to half strength as the blaster bolts pummeled his legs.

"You okay, Cro?"

The question came from Julius. He hadn't come close to losing his lead in kills, and had used that streak reward to serenade the team with songs from LL Cool J, Beastie Boys, and Public Enemy after exhausting his favorite songs from NWA. That is, if you wanted to call them songs. It wasn't what Crometheus went for, that was for sure. And none of their parents would've approved, not even Julius's, who still played Earth, Wind & Fire at barbecues at their foothill ranch bungalow.

"Yeah, I'm okay. Just got a little distracted," Crometheus said acidly. He looked to his right where the slurping kid had been and found that he was no longer there. "How are you guys doing?"

The other three Eternals had been engaged in an all-out brawl inside the hangar that rivaled any running death match Crometheus had ever played. That they were still on their first life was a testament not only to their skills, but also to the sheer volume of fighting taking place. It was almost as if they were spectators. There were so many friendly Titans doing battle with a growing number of corrupted Titans that staying alive seemed to be relatively easy. At least for them. Crometheus wasn't sure he would manage it too much longer.

"You're missing all the fun," said Giles. "This is the first time I can remember where we've got double digits on kills before you."

Crometheus pulled up the leaderboard and groaned. Last in kills and last in points. The bonus he'd gotten for taking out the Cybar mini boss had been leapfrogged several times over.

"I hit a dead end," he said. "I need some muscle to help me push to the objective. Do you guys think you can head this way and help even the odds?"

"I can come," said Jazz. "Julius could probably hold this hangar down all by himself the way things are going. "

"You're not wrong about that," said Julius. "This is hype."

"Good," said Crometheus. "If you and Giles can get here, I'm pretty sure I can rush the objective."

"You got an intel drop telling you that?" asked Giles. "Or is this that sixth sense you've got for games?"

"No. Nothing from Archimedes. How about you guys?"

"Nah," said Julius. "Don't need it though. This is basic stuff. Do it in your sleep, you know?"

Crometheus knew indeed. It wasn't too dissimilar from their defense of the Gomarii slave ship. Take orders, lots of targets, kill them all. Usually, Archimedes only delivered an intel drop on a particularly tough fight. One where the solution wasn't obvious.

"Okay we're headed your way, Cro. Just try not to embarrass yourself by being the first to die."

"I couldn't live with myself if I disappointed you guys," Crometheus deadpanned.

Knowing that reinforcements were coming, Crometheus decided to focus his efforts on halting any attempted advance of the compromised Cybar. That would require him to do more than just sit back and snipe. He needed to give them a taste of their own medicine. The trouble was, despite his kill streak and the kill streaks of the other Eternals, they were getting nothing in the way of upgrades. No additional firepower, like shoulder-mounted rockets which would really help right now, nor package sweeps. It was like the game had been switched to a hardcore mode and everyone was watching just to see how long the Eternals could survive.

A blue-eyed Titan rushed forward—"rushed" being a relative term given its slow movement speed. Crometheus ran out to greet it, taking three quick steps for every one by the hulking eight-foot-tall war machine. He opened fire with his blaster as he moved, sending successive shots up and down the thing's armored sternum and scoring direct hits on its helmet until a headshot between the three glowing optics shut it down and left it a stationary piece of cover. Crometheus was once again safe behind a bulkhead before the first bolts from the other Titans skipped off the decking and ricocheted down the shaft behind him.

"We're almost to your position," announced Giles. "What do you want from us?"

Crometheus peered around his bulkhead and watched as the compromised Titans fired and maneuvered, still trying to close in on his location. He fired back, disabling another of the war machines, which was quickly pulled out of the way by its fellow Titans in order to keep the path clear. That was another indicator that this enemy was thinking at levels superior to those of the NPC Titans the Eternals had at their disposal.

This has to be a remote connected match.

"I don't think we're dealing with regular computer players," Crometheus told his incoming friends. "So do your best to push up to my position and get behind the bulkhead just rear of me, one of you on each side."

"Easy enough," said Giles.

Crometheus unleashed more suppressive fire at the Titans, who had learned to be cautious because of his accuracy. His blaster rifle beeped to indicate a low charge. He didn't bother checking for another pack. He knew he was out. To complicate matters further, his internal charge was too low to properly replenish. He looked back at Jazz and Giles, who were still advancing.

"Hold up there, guys. Gotta recharge."

Crometheus reached out and opened a compartment on the frozen Titan before him. He accessed its power supply and patched it directly into himself, recharging both his hunter-killer assassin frame and his charge packs.

All around the arcade a cheer went up. Crometheus looked around at the kids, who all seemed to be wearing their T&C Surf Designs shirts today. It wasn't long before one of them explained, "Julius just passed two hundred kills. Unreal! The best Hideki ever got was one-fifty."

Hideki?

Crometheus shook his head. He was sure he'd never heard the name Hideki before. But he must have. It was one of his rivals. One of the big-time Japanese players. That's what the tournament was for… to see who was the best. But all that was for later. The big tournament. Which was supposed to be soon, wasn't it? That was why they had been training. Because it was coming soon. Because school was almost out. In the summer, that was when it was supposed to happen.

What… what happened?

What happened in the desert, Cro?

Crometheus looked at the kid standing next to him. He had another novelty squeeze bottle filled with cola. But it wasn't the same kid. He wore the same clothes, right down to the electric blue mirrored sunglasses, never mind that they were all indoors in the dark of the arcade. It was a different kid though. Same clothes, but he was different.

"Hey, how long have we been playing?" Crometheus asked.

"Don't ask me," said the kid. He was maybe sixteen. He had acne and an ugly, juvenile mustache. "You were already playing when I got here."

"How long have *you* been here?"

"I don't know. Dude, you're gonna get killed."

Crometheus looked back at his screen. He was safe enough behind the bulkhead with the disabled Titan blocking him. But the kid was right, he needed to focus if he was going to stay alive.

"Hey, do me a favor?" he said.

"What?" said the kid.

"Start counting. Out loud. Just keep going."

"Are you serious?"

"Serious as a heart attack. Just do it for me. I'll let you get next game. You can play with the Eternals."

The kid's eyebrows rose high above his sunglasses. Nobody got to play with the Eternals. Nobody. But Crometheus could see at once that his offer, as grand and rare as it was, elicited more fear than excitement. Play with the Eternals? More like make a fool of yourself in front of the whole town.

"Okay, how about I just give you twenty bucks?" Crometheus said, trying a different tack.

The kid nodded. "Deal. So like… now?"

"Yes, now."

"One… two… three…"

"I'm just too good at this," Julius said, raising his voice to be heard above the cheers of the crowd as they watched, rapt, the big-screen TVs that displayed the exploits of the Eternals for all to witness.

"I wouldn't complain if they let us run Cybar when we go up against the Japanese," said Crometheus, thinking of the tournament. He'd been thinking of the tournament for months. It was all any of them could talk about. "Now it's my turn to give these guys something to cheer about. Jazz, Giles, you guys ready?"

"Ready."

"Let's get a win, Eternals," said Julius. "Here, Cro, I got something for you."

The track Julius had chosen for his streak reward faded out, and one of Crometheus's favorites boomed in.

"Just don't think too much about that white wedding he's singing about," Julius teased. "Holly still hasn't said yes to a second date."

No. She hadn't. But she would. Crometheus knew she would.

"I'd be more interested in the honeymoon, personally," said Jazz.

Crometheus smiled. "Okay Eternals, let's get this done."

12

Giles and Jazz laid down a steady stream of fire with their Titans, lighting up the left side of the corridor with red glowing bolts of doom. At the same time, Crometheus rocketed out from behind his bulkhead and shoved forward the Titan he'd disabled, pushing it like a boulder ahead of him down the corridor. With suppressive fire keeping the enemy back on the left side, the bull rush was met with what little concentrated return fire the blue Titans could muster.

The disabled bot that Crometheus pushed up the corridor began to lose pieces as concentrated weapons fire worked its way into every joint and seam of its armor, sending chunks exploding outward to clatter against walls and ceiling. Crometheus saw firsthand what so many tri-barreled N-50s could do to the formidable armor of even a Titan. There would be nothing left of the thing to push all the way to his objective—but then, that had never been his intent.

As soon as he'd pushed past a bulkhead where an enemy Titan covered, Crometheus swung aside and engaged in hand-to-hand combat. The battle between machines was one of agility versus strength. The Titan possessed the most raw power, but it was also the least maneuverable, and in the tight quarters, it was all the machine could do—turning around, stepping backward and forward—to keep the darting, slashing Crometheus in front of it. The Titan's long blaster cannon was unwieldy in such a fight, effectively giving it just one arm with which to grapple with the smaller, nimbler hunter-killer assassin.

Crometheus let his left arm be grabbed and then used his legs to flip his body up on top of the Titan. There were a few grumbles and groans as the impervisteel grip of the Titan squeezed around Crometheus's armored left arm. The forearm's armored plating was dented, but still functional. At least for now.

With most of his body now above the Titan, it was easy work for Crometheus to send maximum-charge bolts down into the gap where the Titan's head emerged from its armored body. The familiar gouts of green and yellow flame shot forth as its battery erupted, rendering the machine a simple piece of statuary.

Another kill. But one more kill at this point would do nothing for Crometheus's standing on the leaderboard. He was too far behind Julius and needed to keep moving. Achieving the objective was the only way to get back to the top of the boards.

Crometheus activated a small cutting torch underneath his wrist and went to work loosening the deactivated Titan's fingers from his wrist. He was fortunate to free himself quickly, for another Titan was covering behind the next bulkhead, and sent in N-50 fire at where he had been only seconds before. Crometheus placed both feet against the wall and hurled himself toward the opposite side of the bulkhead, grabbing the disabled Titan's heavy frame as he went and spinning himself so as to launch the towering war bot at its still very functional counterpart. The two machines met with a colossal bang that resounded across the deck plates. He followed the stunning blow with more knife work and then dropped behind the two disabled Titans to cover from more fire coming from farther up the corridor.

There was room enough for a third Titan to stand abreast of the two newly disabled units, and then the hallway's width would be filled.

"Push up!" ordered Crometheus.

He was vaguely aware of the arcade crowd chattering as they discussed what they had just seen. This was the sort of thing that brought people into the old man's place who never had any intention of dropping a quarter in a machine. It was as good as anything they could see on television. Especially during the summer reruns.

Jazz and Giles moved forward as commanded. Crometheus exchanged fire with the Titans ahead, who seemed to be focusing their own fire primarily on the larger threats—the other two Eternals. But Giles and Jazz had at least one upgrade that Crometheus hadn't been aware of until they arrived in the corridor: they carried in their free hands massive shields that now took the brunt of the incoming blaster fire. That would be exceedingly useful.

"We've got to get these guys on the other side of the bulkhead," Crometheus said. "Push up, but don't leave the disabled Titans behind you. Bulldoze them along."

"You got it," said Jazz.

Jazz continued to move forward, his riot shield gently colliding with the first bot Crometheus had disabled and pushing it along, what remained of its heavy impervisteel creating a metal-on-metal scream as it slid across the deck.

"Push everything into the center of the hall," Crometheus ordered. "And then keep going up. Just don't open your flanks because they're going to hit us if we move past them."

The two Eternal-driven Titans did as they were commanded. The blaster fire from the blue Titans was as intense as ever, turning their white shields black with scorch marks, and their heavily armored legs and shoulders—all that was visible from behind the shield—were likewise solid black with carbon scoring.

But powerful as the incoming N-50 blaster fire was, it was insufficient to stop the two Cybar Titans from driving their legs forward and advancing. They reached the bulkhead where Crometheus and the next closest Titan were exchanging tentative fire and continued to plow their way directly ahead. Giles, who was nearest to the enemy, pushed his shield and the disabled bot Crometheus had instructed him to bulldoze into the defending compromised Titan, attempting to pin the machine to the wall. Jazz came up alongside and leaned his weight into Giles's back while protecting all of them with the shield.

The compromised Titan was trapped, but the rest of its numbers were firing relentlessly at the pile.

"Okay, we're here," said Jazz. "I'd like to hear about how you plan on keeping us from dying right about now, though."

Indeed the oncoming blaster fire was enough that Crometheus wondered if the shield could stand up long against it. "My plan was for you two to get killed first so I wouldn't look bad."

Before he had a chance to be cursed for his remark, Crometheus sprang into action, clambering up over the back of his friends' giant Titans and dropping in on the pinned blue Titan. The thing's N-50, like the rest of its body, was now pinned against the wall, and try as it might to use its mammoth strength to free itself, it was unable to push off the weight of the other Titans, two of which were actively pushing back.

Crometheus could've saved charge and used his knife. But the blaster rifle was in hand and he was all topped off. He took four well-placed shots at full power and then jumped back as the Titan's battery exploded from the plunging fire.

Safely back behind his friends, he said, "Okay, now get your shields facing forward again."

"I was about to do that whether you asked or not," said Giles. "Now what?"

"We've got three disabled Titans and two riot shields. Leave that first one. It's just scrap. We're going to push these dead bots up until they're reunited with their friends—and then I'm going to kill each Titan one by one. Until we have them all."

"Well, it's a plan," said Jazz. "Maybe not a good plan, but it does technically meet the dictionary definition of 'a plan.'"

"It'll work," Crometheus assured him. "And a bad plan is better than no plan. TED Eight Ninety verse one. Book of Elon."

Crometheus waited until Jazz and Giles had situated the three disabled Titans in front of them. As he'd calculated, they filled virtually the entire corridor. The Eternals then pushed the broken bots down the corridor, with Jazz and Giles turning their riot shields sideways so that the tops touched and gave them equal protection in front and behind. Crometheus placed one hand on each of his friends' backs to add whatever power from his hunter-killer assassin platform he could. Their impromptu wall skidded and groaned its way into thick blaster fire, but they kept it moving, and the combination of dead Titans, shields, and the thick leg armor of Jazz and Giles kept them free of any consequential damage.

"Almost there," Crometheus announced. "Cut off the next guy and then we disable him too and add him to our collection. Let's find out how many of these Titans we can bulldoze."

Crometheus brought up the leaderboard as they moved. He was still ranked fourth, but with each step he saw his numbers rise. Whatever the bonus was for taking out the VIPs, Crometheus was sure it would spring him to the very top.

"I love it when a plan comes together, Eternals."

And then he took over the playlist for half a minute and queued the theme to *The A-Team*.

High fives were exchanged as the gathering crowd went wild and a girl who would grace the cover of *Vogue* but got her start in a Taco Bell commercial cast doe eyes upon him and nodded once. She would marry a great actor. But that was then.

And this is now.

It's good to be young.

Good to have forever to do it in.

13

"They're sending something special after us," said Andien as she examined the monitors in the control room. Not the ship's heart, but its brain.

"I did not detect anything beyond standard Cybar troop personnel," said Praxus. "Could it be a second boarding party?"

"No. It's two Titans and an HKA. But the tactics they're using are definitely beyond what they're programmed for. So unless CRONUS plugged in individual wills—"

"He would not have done that. He was far too selfish."

"Okay, well something is going on. Because this isn't normal."

She looked back from the display to where Praxus stood with both hands placed flatly on the data center, the web of glowing circuitry still expanding.

"You will have to stop them before they breach," Praxus said. "This process is not as simple as when we awakened the Samurai. An accelerated incubation is required to obtain full control of the ship and its inhabitants. Now that I have begun I cannot stop without risking serious harm to this new life."

Andien thought briefly about that term—*new life*. It didn't seem real. These were machines. Sometimes humanoid, but most times not. They weren't alive. At best they had limited AIs. But Praxus was insistent that while that might have been how the machines began, the work the two of them were doing, "the gift" they bestowed, would result in life as true and legitimate as any biological creature knew.

"They will be alive as much as I am. As much as you are. You must think of what you are doing through the lens of motherhood. You are becoming a mother to all that we choose. You are bringing them life."

That had been the thing said that ultimately pushed Andien to assist Praxus. The galaxy was in legitimate danger of extinction. The proof was right there before her. Things only theorized and conceptualized by the deepest and darkest Nether Ops think tanks were really happening. Out there in the darkness beyond the stars, out there in the fearful unknown, a monster existed. And Praxus had shown her how the monster had made contact with his people. An artificial race—a miracle—put to work for the Republic almost as soon as it was discovered. Not even miracles were spared from the House of Reason's thirst for power and exploitation.

The darkness was out there. It was coming. Its agents were here already. And what Praxus intended to do about it might just actually... *do something* about it. It all made sense. And everything Andien Broxin had witnessed in her lifetime all came together to make even more sense. The Mandarins. The House of Reason. Goth Sullus. The Cybar. It fit. Of course she would undertake the mission. Never mind the impossibility of it all. It was like walking a razor-thin wire with acid-spewing terrillers flying overhead and trying to knock you into their nest-pits on either side. She had done the hard things. She had succeeded at what others thought was impossible.

You will be their mother.

That was supposed to be impossible.

To be a legionnaire is to be a peak human specimen. The one percent of the one percent of the one percent. Not just mentally, but physically. To become a legionnaire means enduring the kinds of stress, trauma, and loss that will easily break a person's very soul. Repeatedly. Willingly.

Andien wasn't supposed to be a legionnaire. It wasn't supposed to be possible. But Nether Ops, unbeknownst to her, had made it possible. And all it cost her was everything.

She had been an only child. Adored by her parents until, at far too young an age, that adoration belonged only to her father. And now he was gone too. And that was it. In a galaxy full of untold numbers of humanoids, the flame of Andien's family, which had shed its blood early and often from the Savage Wars through Psydon right up to the present, would blink out the moment she uttered her final breath. When she reached the end of runtime.

They never asked her. She never signed off. She likely would have accepted the permanent damage to her body for the cause of the Legion and the Republic that should have been. That was true. But they never asked her. They just did it. Just took it away. Left to her to figure out how to process, how to deal, how to cope.

You will be their mother.

Andien watched as Praxus continued to spread the glowing, vibrant light in lines and angles. Symmetrical. Beautiful. Pulsating and radiant like a heartbeat.

She looked back to the displays. They were still coming. Still pushing those machines that Praxus hadn't had time to grant a fullness of life to—machines that had simply been reprogrammed to fight on their behalf—pushing them toward a final conclusion. Cutting down the Titans with the practiced efficiency of butchers in a slaughterhouse. The barbarians would reach the gate.

Andien Broxin charged her blaster rifle.

She would be there to meet them.

14

Andien opened the blast doors already knowing what to expect from the holofeeds. But the screens' portrayal of how the enemy Titans and HK assassin bot were moving up the corridor didn't compare to seeing it herself. A sliding, screeching mass of ruined and disabled Titan war bots was grinding its way toward her like some white mechanical ceramic glacier.

She knew what was powering the glacier's slow crawl. She knew it was up to her to stop it. Praxus had given her a window in her mind's eye that counted down his estimated time to completion. The Cybar ship would be awakened and all her threats destroyed so long as that countdown was achieved. But there would be no waiting it out now. No hiding behind blast doors. Those now advancing must be dealt with.

She closed the blast doors behind her. She had cloaked herself before activating them and remained cloaked now. Invisible to the Titans' optical sensors, though that wouldn't protect her from being struck by a random blaster bolt. That was one battlefield condition you could never fully account for. All the training in the world couldn't prevent you from paying the penalty for being in the wrong place at the wrong time.

But those pushing weren't shooting. At least not until their great shield wall reached the next defender that Andien had carefully placed before sealing herself inside the data center with Praxus. Then they were quick to lay down suppressive fire while the assassin bot made short work of the pinned Titan.

The war machines on Andien's side had not identified the obvious mode of attack to counter what was now rolling over them. Or perhaps they had and were simply incapable of overcoming it. Andien, however, saw right away that in the end this would be an old-fashioned pushing match. No different than on any playground at any school in the galaxy.

If I had come out sooner, we could've at least stopped them from getting this far.

There was no use beating herself up over that. And by waiting, she had probably drawn them into a final confrontation. If she had fought them off before, they might have been free to regroup and plan a new attack. Now she would deal with them permanently.

"All the defenders, deploy directly to that wall. There's two and a half of them and there's four of you. You can stop their progress immediately."

The Titans moved to obey. The first one reached the pile, rolling out from its bulkhead where it had been firing with five meters to spare before the attackers had the opportunity to pin it in place. It pushed against the wall of disabled Titans and began to slide backwards, its strength insufficient to the task.

More came, and soon the scrum came to a halt and the disabled Titans in the middle groaned from the strain pushing against them from front and back. Andien could have added her own might to the contest, but gaining ground wasn't her plan. Her rifle up and ready, she watched through the sights for what she knew would happen. She watched for the hunter-killer assassin that always climbed the pile to destroy the Titan that was on the other side.

The hunter-killer tried to do just that.

"Got you," Andien whispered as she pulled the trigger and sent four perfect blaster shots into the face of the HKA. The bot's head exploded and tumbled back over the pile.

The direction of the wall reversed just a few centimeters. And then the two remaining Titans on the other side were sliding backward, their feet unable to find purchase as they were sent back the way they had come. Andien kept her rifle ready, remaining cloaked as she sprinted toward the scrum. She leapt up to the top and then dealt out the same medicine that her defenders had been receiving. Three blaster bolts went down the chassis of the Titan on her left, disabling it and leaving it to terminate as the green flames of its battery burned up and immolated its head. She performed a front flip off the pile and landed behind the remaining Titan, spun, and grabbed its armored back plate. She hoisted herself up by it, thrust her blaster rifle into the recess, and destroyed that Titan as well.

Problem solved. That's the message she wanted to send to Praxus. But she knew better than to distract him even minutely from his task unless absolutely necessary. Instead she took a breath and ordered her four remaining Titans to "push the scrap all the way to the end of the corridor. Position yourself to immediately engage anyone who attempts to come over it."

"We obey."

The bots began the arduous push, creating a screeching racket fit for the hounds of hell as the rolling mechanical killing field was swept from the corridor and converted into a makeshift barricade against future attacks. Andien was sure that such would come. It was only a matter of time.

She decloaked, saving the energy for when it was needed, and swapped out charge packs. They would try something different the next time. She would be ready.

Crometheus couldn't believe it when his screen went red and he realized that he'd lost his HKA. Just like that, the Eternals' epic kill streak had come to an end. He threw back his head in disgust, staring at the warehouse ceiling and its exposed vents and beams, vaguely aware of the excited chatter that rose around him as those watching in the arcade buzzed about what had just happened.

He checked the leaderboard and confirmed his worst fear. He had been the first to die. And yeah, that happened. The games were designed to keep you pumping in quarters. But part of what made the Eternals so great—part of what had earned them a trip to the tournament to take on the Japanese team and Hideki—was the sort of damage they could do with just one quarter. Well, three for this game. And none at all for this particular session.

Looking around, Crometheus could see that the old man was more than making up for the loss of quarters with the sheer volume of Nerds and other boxes of candy he'd sold. Everyone was drinking the Jolt Cola. Everyone was biting down on Red Vines. A few were sucking on ring pops or coating their tongues with Lik-M-Aid. The old man was making a killing.

Crometheus rolled his head from side to side, popping the vertebrae in his neck. He laced his fingers together and thrust his palms toward the cabinet screen, which was now showing a replay of his death. The knuckles popping seemed to coincide with the *pop-pop-pop-pop* of the blaster bolts that struck him. Four shots straight to the head. Not only did he fail to see the shooter, he failed to see how such rapid accuracy was even possible.

"Game probably just kills you if you play too long without pumping in a quarter," he grumbled. Knowing it wasn't true. Or at least it probably wasn't true. Because he had started at the same time as Jazz, Julius, and Giles. And they weren't dead.

Until Jazz went down. And the leaderboard showed one death in his column. "Son of a bitch!" he shouted from his cabinet. "That's so gay."

Then Giles dropped too. "That run was epic!"

Crometheus watched the leaderboard, waiting to see if the game would snuff out Julius as well. But his kill count only climbed. Death, it seemed, was limited to the corridor that Crometheus had chosen to attack.

"What do you want to do now, Cro?" asked Jazz as he deposited three quarters into his machine. No more freebies from the old man. Not while the other customers were watching.

Crometheus dug into his jeans, acid-washed with holes in the knees, and fished out three quarters from his front pocket. "I don't know. Game seems to want us to take out the VIPs, but then they go and do some bullshit instakill. Part of me wants to try it again. Another part thinks we should just rack up kills with Julius."

"Pretty sure we lose if we do that. Have you ever known a countdown running out on a VIP to mean you win?"

Crometheus hadn't. Neither did he admit that. He only shrugged. "I don't know. Did any of you actually see what killed me? Or you for that matter?"

"Guys!" Giles shouted suddenly. "Come check it out!"

Crometheus placed three quarters against the glass and then studied the crowd around him as he took a step away from his cabinet. He held up a finger. "I have next. Nobody better be on this machine when I come back from seeing whatever Giles wants." He looked over at the kid who was still counting, still earning his twenty bucks. "Don't let them touch the game."

The kid nodded as if that was all he could do to avoid breaking his count. "1,013... 1,014..."

Crometheus jogged the short distance to Giles's game. Jazz was already there, his head and shoulders wrapped around the side of the cabinet to look straight on at the screen. Giles was pointing at something, and when Crometheus got in position he saw it was a woman.

She had appeared seemingly out of thin air. She was carrying a blaster rifle and was decked out like a Republic marine. And she was beautiful.

"I'll bet you all the gold in Fort Knox that's who killed us," Giles said.

"Republic marine?" scoffed Jazz. "Those guys are like cannon fodder."

"I don't know," said Crometheus, staring so hard at the woman that Holly's face flashed before his eyes and he suddenly felt guilty. Which was weird. "But if she's a boss, I mean, I guess. Still, cloaking, plus like all her shots go exactly on target with perfect accuracy? Kind of feels like cheating."

"You know what else feels like cheating?" shouted Julius from his cabinet. "Everything I'm doing. It's like the game's on easy mode for me right now. I'm thinking about letting this kid next to me take over the controls just to see what happens."

Crometheus laughed. But he also felt a sense of frustration. Julius was good. So were all the Eternals. They wouldn't be Eternals if they weren't. But... Crometheus was supposed to be the best. Had always been the best. Julius always at his heels, making him work that much harder to be that much better.

Maybe this was just a fluke. Or maybe... was Julius better than him?

That couldn't be. No. Julius was just playing a Titan on a map designed for a Titan to deal maximum damage. Meanwhile Crometheus had been well on his way to achieving a point-multiplying objective. One that he was now resolved to finish.

"All right, guys, let's get back in."

"What do you want us to pick?" asked Jazz. "If it didn't work last time, I doubt going with the same plan is gonna work this time."

"No, it won't. I'm gonna pick an HKA again. Giles, Jazz, I want you to pick the spiders."

"The spiders?" groaned Giles. "Cro, you gotta be pulling my leg."

"I'm not pulling your leg. I have a plan."

"I don't know..." Giles protested.

"Come on," said Jazz encouragingly. "Cro is usually right about this stuff. But if you're wrong, Cro, you're buying next time we're in the food court."

Crometheus smiled. "Deal." He wouldn't be wrong. He knew he wouldn't be wrong.

He went back to his cabinet and was relieved to see that no one had touched his quarters or the machine. "Thanks," he said to the kid keeping count as he put one hand on the joystick and plucked the first quarter from the screen.

"10,364... 10,365..."

Crometheus froze, his quarter half in and half out of the slot. Was the kid messing with him right now? There was no way he'd been over there for nine thousand seconds. And yet when he looked at the kid, he was completely straight-faced. A quick scan of the crowd showed no hidden smirks or giggles suggesting they were in on the joke.

And then that voice asked what happened in the desert.

The power in the arcade surged. Everything went dark.

15

"This is happening way too much to just be a coincidence," Crometheus fumed to his friends as they sat in the food court of the arcade. "How does the old man expect us to do anything if he can't even keep the lights on while we're playing?"

He had been close to reaching the VIPs. His solution of pushing the Titan war bots along until they were close enough to reach their objective had been working fine until some new mini boss managed to take them all down with hardly any effort at all. It was how close he had gotten only to fail that bothered him most. Sometimes you just ran into a stretch of bad luck: the summer heat, the air conditioning, the pull of power from all those machines... sure, maybe the old breaker box couldn't always handle it. But Crometheus had gotten beaten before that happened.

And now it was eating him up. Because he was better than that. And a day like today, where he'd failed and was outperformed by one of his friends, weighed on him. He needed to have another go. Felt crazy that this was apparently it, and he would just have to sit and stew on his shortcomings until tomorrow.

The arcade had emptied out after the brief shrieks of delight that came from all the kids inside once power was lost. The old man had cursed in his native tongue and then shooed the great crowd of revelers out, leading them by the beam of a blue plastic flashlight. To the Eternals he said, "Just stay in here, boys. I'm pretty sure it's just a fuse that needs to be replaced. I got one somewhere. You can play on my dime until whenever the heck it is your parents want you home."

But for now all Crometheus and the Eternals could do was sit on the picnic table, using the bench for a footrest and flicking half-eaten french fries and fragments of Doritos onto the clay-tiled floor. For a while they recounted the game. How close they'd gotten.

Taco Bell future It Girl had faded with the shadows.

"There's a fine line between victory and defeat," mused Julius. "A real fine line."

Julius demanded his honors at having achieved the highest score and then laughed right along with the others at the insults and put-downs that came back at him.

"Never knew I had such jealous friends," he said, shaking his head in faux disappointment. Everyone was smiling and having a good time—except for Crometheus, who couldn't stop his contemplative scowl. Julius noticed it and said, "Come on, Cro, you're not gonna die of a heart attack just because you don't end up at the top of the leaderboard every once in a while. Save some for the rest of us, Maverick!"

The remark shook Crometheus from his thoughts. He looked around as though he'd heard the call of the living pulling him back from the afterlife. He'd really been out of it and wasn't sure what Julius had said, only that it had been addressed to him. Aware that he'd been so focused on his thoughts and that his face had been so grim, he shared what was bothering him.

"Do any of you buy this?"

The Eternals laughed at the comment. Laughing was their instinctive response to just about anything they weren't sure of. A defensive measure while they bought time to figure out just what their enigmatic leader was driving at.

"Buy what?" Julius asked.

"This whole thing with the old man and the power grid."

Jazz shook his head. "What's not to buy, Cro? It's dark, isn't it? Accept the narrative... or else... you know... bad thoughts bad thoughts bad thoughts. No big prizes. No Miss Taco Bell."

"It's dark," Crometheus agreed, waving off the warnings. "And it gets dark right when we're cruising for the win. Right when we seem to be on the edge of a breakthrough. No joy."

"I don't want to rain on your parade," said Giles, "but we weren't exactly *breaking through*. We'd all gotten wiped out. The only one who was holding on was Julius."

Julius gave a wide smile. "That's the truth. I'm glad *one* of you knows it when you see it."

"Yeah, but that was cheap," Crometheus protested. "If we run that again—get a respawn—we're not gonna get taken by surprise by the invisible killer. The moment the doors open we just unleash the N-50s at the open space. Easy. That's what I was going to do next. Only the power goes out... *again*."

"And I still say you're just grasping at straws to make yourself feel better about getting bested by the man," said Julius, gloating. "And anyway, the time before wasn't like that. That was just playing survival, and eventually the waves got too big to handle. That's how those games always work. They're not meant to be beaten—just to see how long you can last."

"Maybe."

Jazz put his arm around Crometheus's shoulders and again performed his bit about being harmed by the spikes on Cro's leather jacket. The other Eternals laughed, but their hearts weren't in it. "Crometheus, I never thought I'd say this, but you've been playing too many games—and it's giving you bad thoughts."

"Bad thoughts," echoed the others.

Jazz continued. "Like, who would even be able to shut us down right at the height of our success anyway?"

"The old man," said Crometheus. "The old man can shut you down any time he wants. Any time you're no longer... convenient."

Jazz gave a hearty laugh. "Another bad thought. Why would he do that, Cro? Why pull the plug on our game—on *his* machines? You know he makes money when this place is full, right? And if the power is off he can't make *any* money. So why would he sabotage his best players and the star attraction of this arcade when he could just let us roll and rake in the quarters? You saw how excited he was at the crowds today. He sold out of colas and had another pizza in the oven when the power went out. He was making money hand over fist."

Crometheus had thought of that in his time of reflection. He didn't have an answer for it because it didn't make sense. Not without jumping deep into a conspiracy theory. One that he had no intention of bringing up.

But then Giles said it for him. "What if the old man is working for the Japanese?"

"You've lost your mind," said Julius. "Maybe it's Gorby and the Russkies. Yeah. It's always them... remember?"

"What do you mean?" asked Crometheus, ignoring Julius.

Giles explained. "We know this tournament is like, the biggest thing ever. Big prizes. All the stakes. The Japanese are good, but they've had to have heard about us. We're better. Now, what do the Japanese have? Money. *Lots* of money. My old man says that people are learning how to speak Japanese just because there's so much money over in Japan. So they can afford to buy the old man. It wouldn't take much. You've seen the jalopy he drives. One day he'll show up with a brand-new BMW, and I bet it's the day after the tournament. Right now, the Japs are gonna own the world forty years after we dropped two on 'em."

Julius remained skeptical. "And what exactly are the Japanese paying the old man to do? Because if they really wanted to mess us up, they just buy the arcade and keep us from coming in. And not only do they not do that, but the old man, he lets us play for free. No way that's helpin' the Japanese."

"You've got to think a step ahead, my friend," said Giles. "The Japanese know we'd just find another cabinet at one of the other arcades. Maybe it's a longer walk, maybe we got to take the bus or something, but we'd do what we had to. They can't buy every arcade in America."

"Keep your friends close and your enemies closer," Jazz said. "I think that was Shakespeare. But it might have been a bad guy on *Remington Steele*."

Giles snapped his fingers. "Exactly. So the old man, he doesn't have to shut down. He doesn't want to shut down. All he has to do is watch what we're doing and report back to the Japanese, so they know what they're up against. He'll tell them what our favorite classes are, what our strategies are, that kind of thing. All that's valuable information."

Crometheus has been following the discussion closely. It all made sense to him. Except for one thing. "But why turn off the games?"

"Easy," said Giles confidently. "Because you were right, Cro. It wasn't a bad thought. It was a good one! We were about to break through and see a high-level part of the game that could really allow us to rack up the score. And if we do that, if we learn that next section and know how to multiply our scores, then when the tournament comes we can really do some damage. The Japanese don't want that. They want us to get to those high levels for the first time in the tournament. I'll bet you their machines don't get shut off when they reach those levels. Go ahead, who wants to bet me?"

But no one would bet him. The tournament was everything. And the Japanese, they knew, would stop at nothing to win. Big prizes. Fortune and glory. The best in the world. If the Eternals had any hope of pulling out a victory, they needed to find out what happened on those levels. And whatever other levels were being kept from them. They needed to find out what was really going on.

Crometheus looked over to the snacks counter. The old man's blue flashlight was sitting there unattended. Crometheus got up and retrieved it. He slid the white plastic switch and was rewarded with a beam of light. As he swept the light into the cavernous dark cave that was the arcade, dead machines appeared within the round yellow spotlight—not really illuminated at this distance but more visible than they had been, the colors taking on clear shades.

"Cro, where you going, buddy?" Jazz asked, at Crometheus's side the moment he took a step forward.

Crometheus shrugged his friend's hand away. "I'm gonna find out what's happening."

"You know the old man's rules."

"Yeah, well maybe Giles is right. Maybe the old man isn't as friendly as we thought. Maybe he's like a Mogwai after midnight. And whether he is or he isn't, I'm going to find out. You got a problem with that? You're either with the Eternals or you're against them, Jazz. Which is it, bro?"

Jazz looked from Crometheus to his friends watching at the picnic table. "All right. Go then. But this is a bad thought, Cro. A real bad thought."

"Be on the lookout for the old man," Crometheus said. "He might come back for his flashlight when he realizes he didn't take it. If you see him, holler so I can get back and keep us from getting in trouble."

16

Crometheus turned the flashlight off as he traveled through the winding labyrinth that was the silent arcade. He knew the place so well that he didn't need the light, and the risk of being spotted wasn't worth it. The old man had said he was going to replace a fuse—that meant heading up to the second floor. Crometheus had never been there, but he knew where the access door was. He'd seen the old man disappear behind it many times.

A door that wasn't there, but was. What did the D&D dorks call it…? A secret door. Detect secret doors. Lame.

Or maybe not so much…

He made his way quietly toward the door, moving with his knees slightly bent in order to duck or run should he need to. Jazz hadn't been overreacting when he'd tried to stop Crometheus from entering the arcade. The old man had been explicit in his instructions to the Eternals: the privileges he gave them were contingent on them following the rules he had set, and one of those rules was that they were allowed in the game room only when he said so. No reason had been given, and Crometheus had always thought that there *was* no particular reason for that rule; it existed for the sake of the bargain itself. A meaningless law that was obeyed in a show of mutual respect and understanding for the order of things. The Eternals were the local stars of the show. The old man ran the arcade. The Eternals were gifted what had to be hundreds of dollars' worth of free play. The old man was rewarded with the respect owed to him as the owner of the establishment.

And now Crometheus risked upsetting that balance. There was no telling what the old man would do if he found Crometheus in here now when he was supposed to be back at the food court. Crometheus didn't fear physical harm—despite the rumor that the old man kept a single-barrel shotgun somewhere in the building for use against strong-armed robberies. But he understood that, were he caught, it would represent the breaking of a contract. And of a relationship. One that, once broken, would not be easily repaired. Best tread carefully then.

Funny, he'd never really feared the old character. Just assumed he was part of the background, an NPC, a bit player in the story of his reality. But now... there was something different about him.

Something dangerous.

And the last time he'd felt that had been around LuSypher.

In the darkness, moving toward the door not a door, Crometheus nearly bumped into a cabinet he didn't remember being there. Which was strange; he knew the arcade as well as he knew his own home. In fact, when he closed his eyes, he could re-create the layout of the arcade *better* than that of his home. More than that, he could re-create several layouts of the arcade, each one reflecting a different experiment by the old man in his evolving efforts to maximize revenue.

The old man was proud of his business savvy. And maybe all those rearrangements was why Crometheus had that feeling that even though it was the same arcade, it was different.

But that wasn't it. And he knew it wasn't it... but he didn't know why. All he knew was that the machine that shouldn't have been there *was* there, in his path, beside an old cabinet with a black-and-white screen that, when on, allowed the player to steer a hook-and-ladder fire truck up a comically wide street in an effort to get to a burning building. No one played that game anymore. The old man said it used to be somewhat popular, but never a big winner. Usually it stood alone. But now, next to it, was a wide cabinet with an equally wide screen.

Crometheus, his eyes now adjusted somewhat to the dark, stopped to study this cabinet that shouldn't be there. It had a strange setup. On one side, a joystick and six round buttons. And on the other, where player two would play... a keyboard.

That was odd. Crometheus had never seen a game like that before. He had to know what this new game was called.

He crouched down, listening for any sign of the old man. The arcade was quiet. He glanced back to see if anyone had followed him. No one had.

Crometheus aimed his dormant flashlight at the front of the machine and then slowly slid the switch, hoping to touch the batteries just barely enough to get the flashlight to throw the weakest of beams—just enough to read by. But he slid his finger too far, and the light flooded out as bold and as strong as the three C batteries could supply. He quickly turned the torch off, but not before he'd read the name of the game.

Into the Unknown.

There are other worlds than these... someone seemed to whisper in his mind. Rats with cold claws ran up the back of his spine.

He'd heard of that game. He could recall nothing about it. But he'd heard of it. The name evoked a sense of familiar ennui that made his stomach feel restless and uneasy.

When the fuse was replaced and everything was turned back on, he would have to seek this machine out and at least watch its demo play, if not drop a quarter in. But for now, he continued on to the access door.

Two broken arcade cabinets stood on either side of it. They'd been there for eons, with no indication they'd ever be repaired. Crometheus tried the door and found that it opened. He pushed the door inward, into the stairwell, and was surprised to find that it was flooded with light. The old man must've gotten the power working again and just hadn't flipped the switch to the game room itself.

Crometheus quickly—but quietly—closed the door once more, thinking that the old man would be back any minute, the lights and games powering on all around him, filling the air with their sixteen-bit chorus. He moved back through the arcade, taking the same route as before so that he could pass by the mysterious cabinet. But when he reached the spot where it should be, it wasn't there.

He looked around, and for a moment he was tempted to turn the flashlight on again. Maybe he'd gotten disoriented on his way back? But there was no way. He knew this place far too well. Even though it wasn't the same arcade, it was the arcade.

No one had called out a warning from the food court yet, and there was still no sign of the old man. So Crometheus decided to look for the machine. He could just wait until the power came back on. He could do that. But something told him if he was going to see this game, it had to be now.

It hadn't gone far. It was still beside the old fire truck machine, it had just moved to the other side of it. He tried his flashlight trick again and this time was able to get the incandescent bulb inside to emit just a faint thread of light, just enough for him to find the power strip on the ground. Next to it were the plugs for the two games; someone had pulled them out of the strip. He bent down and flipped the orange switch on the power strip. It glowed orange.

The room had power and was ready to go. The lights and all the machines simply weren't on. He took one of the cords and plugged it into the strip.

The fire-fighting game booted to life, releasing a loud, caterwauling impression of a fire truck's horn. Crometheus cursed and quickly unplugged the machine. He fully expected to hear the old man coming, or perhaps one of his friends hissing for him to get out. He made himself as small as he could, crouching behind the two machines. But no one came.

He should have hurried back to the Eternals. He knew that. But again he had that feeling that it was now or never. This wasn't where the cabinet had been before. It had already moved once in only the brief time he was away at the door. And of course that made no sense at all. But when he tried to think about how that was even possible, his mind fed him with questions...

What happened in the desert?

And...

What did you do to her?

That last question scared him. Because he hadn't thought of it before. But now it hit him like a Mike Tyson knockout punch. It was a weight around his neck. A heavy load that had been secretly hanging there forever.

And he hadn't asked about it once. Not in this arcade. But maybe he had—back when the arcade was different.

It was the same but it was different.

He plugged the new machine in, and it bid him to enter into the unknown.

17

You awake in an inn...

That was the message that faded in from the blackness on the game's screen and then faded back out. The experience so far had cost Crometheus a quarter and the elevated threat that the old man would find him in the arcade when he ought to be back in the food court. But the game was too curious and captivating.

The black screen faded away and Crometheus found himself standing at the top of a narrow wooden staircase. Hall candles had been snuffed out, leaving the landing dim except for a few shafts of sunlight from the small, lattice-paned windows. Dust danced and flowed in the light beams. Clearly this was some sort of inn, and the game cabinets' old and tired speakers softly buzzed out the sound of early morning breakfasters muttering in low conversation. Knives and forks clinked together, punctuated by the thud of tankards as they went from mouth back down to rest atop rough, wooden tables. A woman laughed, a shrill and unvirtuous sound. She was quickly hushed by someone else and laughed so much the louder as a result.

Here Crometheus paused, his hands still on the game's controls. He looked around to verify that no one heard the machine or the piercing laugh that came from it. The old man still wasn't coming. Neither were the Eternals.

Fixing his attention back to the game screen, he turned a complete circle to have a better feel for his surroundings. The landing terminated in the middle of a long hallway running to the left and right, heavy oak doors with black iron handles and cavernous keyholes beneath them lining either side. A small window, situated above a wooden bench, marked the end of the corridor in both directions. There seemed little to do on this level except knock on doors, which Crometheus wasn't interested in doing.

He took the steps down, and the sounds of those already at the inn grew in volume.

"Last night marks the end of your gold, sell-sword," boomed a man standing behind the counter polishing the inside of a pewter tankard.

Crometheus looked down. Attached to his hip was a great sword sheathed in a dark, scarred leather scabbard.

"Breakfast and then be on your way unless you've got more coins in your purse," the innkeeper gruffly finished.

A prompt filled the screen, giving Crometheus three options.

A. Teach the man respect.
B. Ask if there's any work. You're a good wood chopper. You need the coins and you are getting thirsty...
C. Type your own choice and be ready for a surprise!

Crometheus had learned how to hunt and peck on a typewriter in school. The clickety-clack of the keys and ding of the return was a noise he didn't wish to add to the atmosphere. Though this game's volume paled in comparison to most of the other cabinets, it seemed deafening even tucked away in the arcade where it now was. He selected option A. Teach the man respect.

On screen, his character placed a hand on the hilt of his sword and said in a deep, soldierly voice, "You possess the gold that bought your service through this morning meal. Even had I finished and set my course elsewhere, I will have your respect from this point and forever... unless you wish to discover how much the witches of the eastern path are paying for fingers when I take your hand and bring back the profits to share in exchange for a merchant's loyalty once again."

The innkeeper cravenly backed down, begging off the threat through ample waving of hands. "No need for violence. No need for harm. A man must look after his business is all. I meant only to remind, not insult. Pray, forgive me."

An option to accept the apology never came. A message on screen simply said:

> *You have forgiven the fool. Perhaps he's learned a lesson.*

The game guided Crometheus to sit down, though he'd rather move about the inn and explore. Thus far, he seemed to have little direct control over anything. He had the inkling that this was some kind of learn-to-type game. He'd seen some of the Eternals' younger siblings play those on their Apple IIe or Commodore 64 home computers. That wasn't something he was interested in playing, and he nearly unplugged the machine and headed back to the Eternals.

But something about the atmosphere and the other patrons captivated him. He wanted to find out why they were all gathered at the inn. And the old man wasn't coming; the lights were still off.

The tables were spread out, with several groups crowded around the long tables or having pushed together the smaller round tables. At first they seemed to be separate groups, but a familiarity between the pods—a casual request for seasoning or a innuendo-laden inside joke told with a wink from one table to the next—told Crometheus this was likely all one large adventuring party.

Scattered near the doors and squinting against the morning light flooding their faces, were hunched-over men with humps on their backs or shoulders and looks of hopeless despair on their faces. These were clearly porters, their spines twisted from the heavy labor required of them; they possessed the lowest station to be had in any adventuring party. They were mostly broken men who could offer no service beyond carrying the party's chests and other baggage. They ate less than a beast of burden and were doubly inexpensive beyond that because their pay was only a small percentage of whatever treasure was found on the adventure. If any.

Still, that meager portion was more than enough to make them rich as kings if all went according to the wildest of dreams—and if they didn't die along the way. A distinct possibility. As it was now, however, these poor souls were only a step up on the social ladder from beggars and other vagabonds, and their aching backs might draw them into questioning whether they were truly better off during those torturous nights when they bedded down among the baggage on cold, stone floors.

Farther in, next to the fire at the great table, were gathered the most self-important, snickering, and toadying group of individuals Crometheus had ever seen. They wore wizard's robes and discussed their mysterious arts, always deferring to an obviously senior man among the apprenti, short and menacing.

And in the darkest corner sat a small table of thieves, no doubt along to handle any traps or locks found on the way. One of them was young and handsome. He wolfishly eyed the half-elven archer standing guard outside the establishment's front window.

Crometheus was served a tankard of ale. He wasn't given the option whether or not to drink; his character simply quaffed it down in one fluid, expert motion. The seasoned drinking told Crometheus as much of his character's backstory as anything else so far. He downed a second flagon and asked for a third, pulling the last coin from his purse.

"When does the game actually start?" Crometheus grumbled to himself. He looked around the arcade again for the old man or the Eternals but saw nothing.

It was then that across the screen sauntered the little man who'd been at the table with the wizard's apprentices. He sat down at Crometheus's table without being invited.

"That's quite the imposing sword on your hip, drunkard," the little magician said.

Finally, Crometheus was given prompts.

A.   [Diplomatic] It does what I need of it.
B.   [Aggressive] Leave my table at once or taste its steel on your tongue when I cleave your skull, cur!
C.   Type your own choice and be ready for a surprise!

Crometheus now decided to type in an answer, though the aggressive option sounded fun, too. He hunted for the keys and then pressed them down gently, not wanting to add the tactile *clicks* to the otherwise quiet and empty arcade.

"What's your interest in it?" Crometheus said, hoping that would get the game to move far enough along for him to see if there was anything worth sticking around for. Because so far, there wasn't. Just a simple fantasy adventure of the type he used to read from his father's collection of dog-eared paperbacks. Hardly something worth risking the privileges he and his Eternals earned with the old man.

"My interest is in adding an experienced fighter to the party," said the squat magician. "We lost our best man on our way, and this inn is the last of its kind before the pass. Tell me, what is your name?"

A prompt appeared on-screen asking Crometheus to type his name. With it came a flash of worry. Would the game record it somehow? Could the old man look and see who had been playing when they should not have? They might be watching.

But... who was they?

He wasn't even sure why the thought came to his mind. For the most part, games gave you three initials and a spot on the leaderboards until they were either unplugged or your high score was beaten. The newer games were an exception of course, but for the vast majority that was it. And yet something deep inside Crometheus told him not to answer truthfully. To think of a false name and think it up quickly.

He looked down at the table where the foam head of his drink slid its way over the brim of his flagon to settle on the top of the rough, grooved wooden tabletop. There, carved by the point of a knife, was a message: *Lie to him.*

Was this the game telling him something? A secret level accessible if he… if he typed in something other than Crometheus? His mind flashed possibilities, from Cro—which was perhaps too close—to Billy and then by association, Mony Mony. His fingers hovered over the keys, and then he typed a false name that flashed in his mind at the last moment: *Rogan.*

It was an unfamiliar name. He couldn't recall having ever met a Rogan. The moment he typed it, he heard his character speak it.

"Rogan."

An immediate pang of regret settled beneath his heart. Should he not have said that? He looked down at the table. The scratched message was gone.

"Of course…" said the magician. "Rogan. I remember now. Here is my offer to a drunkard in need of coins. Travel with us, wielding your sword to ensure our safety and success. Live, and your share of whatever treasure is found is sure to be enough to supply several years of uninterrupted nights crawling happily through gutters like some despoiled king slumming with the vermin. Should you die…" The little man shrugged and held his arms out apologetically. "Well, after that it hardly matters, now does it, sell-sword?"

Crometheus was struggling to figure out what was going on. The message carved into the table was still on his mind. Why would whoever made this game have included it? Moving forward in the game obviously hinged on him typing an answer to the question. Was it some kind of save feature that would allow him to pick up where he left off in a previous playthrough? Now Crometheus was doubting using the name Rogan. Maybe he should've used his own name and seen where it took him.

Because he was sure he had played this game before. Nothing about it was immediately familiar beyond the general surface similarities to *Dragon's Lair* or other games depicting a fantasy world. Crometheus liked *Dragon's Lair*, and had rescued Princess Daphne numerous times. He remembered that. Remembered the crowd watching him finally do it.

He didn't remember *Into the Unknown*. But... he'd played it. He was sure he'd played it.

The magician pressed him, interrupting Crometheus's thoughts. "Well, Rogan, what's your answer? The porters need to sit for a while yet, but we won't be sitting all day. Though I'm sure you're accustomed to such."

Crometheus stared at the keyboard on the cabinet's surface. There was no prompt from the game. It seemed up to him to type in either yes or no.

Again he looked down. The writing in the table was back. The message was different.

It's a trap.

"What's that supposed to mean?" Crometheus asked himself.

He decided that perhaps the game was more sophisticated than a simple typing adventure, as he had first thought. He would try to forestall where the game was pressing him to go, which was clearly to take the lead role in the adventure.

"You've got me wrong," Crometheus typed into the machine. "I am content to finish my ale and then go about my business. I seek no master and no obligations."

"What of your life's complications?" asked the magician. "Your sword may be great and heavy, but your purse is light and empty. That would change were you with us."

"I said what I said," Crometheus typed.

The insistence didn't seem to register. Instead, the magician repeated himself as though the vocal track were simply replayed. "What of your life's complications? Your sword may be great and heavy, but your purse is light and empty. That would change were you with us."

Now two prompts presented themselves to Crometheus.

A. I will go.
B. I'm not convinced.

Crometheus selected the option saying he was unconvinced. The magician then went on a monologue entreating the sell-sword to make an affirmative decision by appealing to his lust for wealth, power, and fame. He spoke of a cave laden with the treasures of a succession of kings from times forgotten, each buried with greater and greater wealth. Such wealth that those kings of today would scoff at them and consign them to myth… but they were truth. The organizer of the expedition had seen it personally. A great wizard who would now go back to recover what his eyes had unearthed.

And as for Rogan… he would return a prince. The wine would never cease flowing.

"You now face one final opportunity in your wretched life to use the skills you've honed in battle with steel and mail into something that will actually do someone other than yourself some good," sneered the magician before quickly adding, "Of course, it will do you much good as well."

Before Crometheus could give an answer, a young warrior with axes tucked into his belt came through the doors and walked determinedly toward the small magician. He had a look of unseasoned doubt about him that he desperately attempted to hide. The warrior eyed the thieves at their table and the apprenti at theirs and in each instance did his best to pretend he wasn't really looking. In looking upon Crometheus, he wore the bitter face of a proud young man who feared he'd just met his more experienced better.

The warrior crouched down at the magician's ear and whispered, "He wishes to leave now."

Who he was was not explained. Crometheus imagined it was the master of the expedition, the one into whose service this little toad of a man sitting across from him sought to enlist him.

"Gather the others," the magician said with an air of smug superiority. "Every porter should have his load on his back by the time I am outside."

The young warrior nodded, glanced once more at Crometheus, and then turned to inform first the thieves, then the porters, and finally, respectfully, the apprentice magicians. All of them filed out quickly, even the thieves. He, whoever he was, was not a man to be kept waiting, and all those in his employ seemed to know it.

The little magician, now alone with Crometheus at the table and in the dining area, hoisted out a large, bulging coin purse—a sack of leather lined with purple velvet. He took out four gleaming coins and clinked them in his hands. Soon the tavern owner was at his side collecting the money with bashful, repeated bows before backing away reverently.

"And now, Crometheus," said the magician. "I must have your answer. Will you come with us?"

The prompt reappeared.

A.   Big prizes
B.   Bad thought

Crometheus shut his eyes tight and shook his head. When he reopened them, the prompt was different.

A.   Yes
B.   Yes

"What kind of choice—" Crometheus began before being cut off by a sudden slap on his back. Not the rough angry hands of the old man but the jovial, playful attack of Jazz and the rest of the Eternals.

"You ready, man?" Jazz asked, practically shouting the words. "Today's the day!"

Crometheus shook his head wondering how they were all there. How the lights were up. How the arcade was full to capacity with watchers from school and the regulars who came in at lunch and the single guys and the married men who stopped in for a quick play at the arcade instead of a long drink at the bar.

They were all there. They were loud. They were cheering.

"What?" Crometheus asked. Because he was confused but also because it was so loud and he hadn't quite heard what Jazz had said.

"Time to see if all that practice has paid off," said Giles, smiling enthusiastically.

Julius gave Crometheus a mock salute. "I'm heading to my machine. Just win, baby!"

Crometheus looked back to the cabinet. *Into the Unknown* was gone, though his hands had never lifted from the machine. Now those hands navigated the familiar joystick and buttons of the game. The only game. He was in the loadout screen. There weren't many classes to choose from. Some Kimbrin, but those looked underequipped. The real damage looked like it would be done by a frightening-looking species identified as the zhee.

The electronic squeal of a microphone turned on too close to its speaker shrieked its way through the arcade, causing everyone to duck and cover their ears and then buzz with complaints. The old man stood atop a pedestal, microphone in hand. He blew on it and then tapped on it and then, satisfied that it was working, asked, "Is everyone excited to be here today?"

The arcade roared together that yes, they were.

The old man smiled and thanked sponsors and recounted the lead-up to the day and then introduced each one of the Eternals who raised their hands in recognition and received the adoration of applause from the audience. "We are just waiting on a connection issue all the way over in the land of the rising sun—Japan! But as soon as it gets sorted out, and I just heard via a *long-distance* phone call that it's going to be sorted out in the next few minutes, then, ladies and gentlemen, what you've been waiting for will finally come about. So go buy yourself some drinks and snacks, because the tournament is about to begin!"

And of course it was. Because today was the day of the tournament. Crometheus could hardly sleep the night before he was so excited about it. They had practiced and practiced and now the day was finally here when they would go up against the Japanese and they would find out who the best team really was.

"Eternals!" Crometheus shouted. "Let's do this!"

"Just win, baby!" shouted Giles, repeating Julius, who was repeating Al Davis, because the Raiders were the Eternals personified.

"Bad news, everybody," Julius called above the crowd. "No Cybar this time, which means the first kill streak is probably going to go to our boy Cro. If only he had better taste in music like yours truly."

That got a few laughs and a headshaking chuckle from Crometheus. He was ready for the tournament. He was going to show the Japanese—show everybody—how good he really was. He looked around at the throng of people waiting for him to start playing.

He looked for Holly, but she wasn't there. She'd said she'd be there. Why wasn't she there?

And... *What happened in the desert?*

What did you do to her?

Crometheus looked around again, the smile now gone from his face. He saw the same kid in the same hat and shirt and sunglasses. And he was still counting. And the number had passed five hundred thousand.

Crometheus stood there with his arms at his sides. The tournament was sure to begin soon. He needed to focus. Time to play. Let it fade away. Big Prizes.

But the voice that asked him about the desert and about Holly now asked him...

How did the little magician know your name?

18

To Masters, the operation was simple. Team One was on tap to fly out into the humid jungles of Kima where the MCR moved and operated almost unopposed. They would set down, and if they met no resistance, would hike their way up a small mountain and back down the other side to a valley suspected of being an MCR communications hub. In a world of wireless, instantaneous transmissions, the Kimbrin, still holding on to the hope that the MCR would govern their planet if not the galaxy, had realized there was nothing they could transmit that the Republic couldn't intercept. Their solution had been to run with an ancient but effective form of tech: direct wire communication. It was bulky and prone to failure. It was also untraceable unless one found the wire itself and tapped it.

And that was where things got tricky. Knowing that the Yawds and legionnaires at Outpost Ten were seeking to listen in, the MCR had done everything it could to make that as difficult as possible. There were more false wires covered over with shallow ground than the real thing. Some were utterly dead. Others were live but cunningly used only to transmit false information. And on top of all this, wide networks of EMP traps and other bot-and crawler-defeating devices were as ubiquitous as the vines and broadleaf fauna of the jungle. The MCR might have been lacking in some equipment and supplies, but they clearly weren't lacking anti-bot precautions. It all added up to a game of coop and tappi as the MCR, playing the top tappi, constantly moved to avoid getting caught by the Kima special operations groups.

And to the frustration of the legionnaires at Outpost Ten, the MCR seemed to be winning that game. Adding to that frustration was that Kima wasn't officially at war with itself, which meant Dark Ops's presence was limited to the SOG teams in camp. There was no support to be had beyond Republic Army artillery "live-fire exercises." The MCR knew this. They knew that the K-SOG teams wouldn't be followed by a platoon of legionnaires. So each time one of the teams moved into MCR territory it was only a matter of time before they riled up the zoomas' nest to the point that they had to be extracted under heavy fire.

Masters asked how many MCR were suspected in the AO. The answer was multiple battalion levels of enemy soldiers with varying degrees of competency.

"Okay," Masters said. "So a few."

"MCR started here," said Young. "It may not be the galactic rebellion it was intended to be, but it's still got about half of this planet supporting it."

"And it's gonna stay that way until the pols let us go Legion," spat Jaybles.

"Which won't happen until the MCR does something really stupid to kick off a full-blown war," said Young. "Until then, it's our duty to kill them in between drinking sessions at Rosie's."

Two decrepit SLICs that required immediate inspection by the camp's maintenance bots set down in preparation for the mission. As the bots performed their work, K-SOG Team One emerged from their planning compound. Three legionnaires in mimetic armor that would blend in perfectly with the jungle, and their Yawd supporters dressed in green fatigues. Each Yawd carried a blaster rifle and pack loaded down with whatever the team felt would be useful on the mission. At the very least, the equipment needed to slice into the wired communication lines.

Masters and the others were jocked up for action as well. Their duty on the Black required them to be ready in an instant to mobilize and pull out Team One. And from the way Captain Hurn had put things, that help might be needed in short order. The MCR had grown more and more accustomed to the legionnaires' intrusion on their turf. It was getting harder and harder to insert without being noticed. Harder still to stay on the ground long before the shooting started and the teams had to pull up stakes.

"Worst thing about it is the waiting," said Jaybles as they watched the team in the staging area.

The SLICs powered up engines, filling the camp with the repulsor-assisted whine that was once a familiar sound to those serving on Psydon when the craft had had their heyday. Technology had passed them by since then—transport and assault shuttles were now lighter, faster, stronger, and better armed. But the camp was running with locally supplied weapons of war. Aside from what they'd brought in, or what they could get from the basics, legionnaires were entirely beholden to the Kimbrin planetary government loyal to the Republic. And given the partisan turmoil between the Republic and MCR loyalists that ran down the middle of the planet, there was no guarantee that what the Kimbrin government supplied would be useful. Masters had heard of entire crates of grenades and other ordnance being little more than holofilm props. Just fuses and metal. No boom.

There were too many MCR loyalists in all walks of life to be sure of anything. This was a civil war brewing, and it didn't take a political statesman to see that.

The SLICs were unreliable not only because of sabotage, but also due to their advanced age. But they flew, and their Kimbrin pilots were used to them. Still, it paid to take precautions and have the bots make sure everything was in working order.

"The worst thing about being on the Black is that you can't go to Rosie's," said Young. "Unless you go just for the food."

"Which is a good way to spend some time in the infirmary," put in Jaybles. "If you ever need a few days off, try the Sprigg eggs."

"True," Young agreed. "But you'll just be back on the Black when you get out, with additional days added to make up for it. Why go through all that intestinal torture if you're just going to finish it out anyway? No, boys, we got to take our medicine."

"*Your* medicine," said Jaybles, who at once grew sulky. "I'm just guilty by association."

"You talk as if you've never leejed before," said Masters.

K-SOG-1 approached the landing pads. A Yawd from one of the other teams ran out to the center of the pad, set up a wide-based cylinder, and pulled a tab from its top. A moment later gouts of pink smoke began to pour out until the pad, the SLICs, and everything else in the vicinity was completely obscured. Shimmering sparks—like localized lightning storms—raced through the smokescreen.

"Mids are watching?" asked Masters.

"All the time," said Young. "They haven't taken any potshots at us in a while. No mortar fire either. But they're always out there, either watching from the slopes to see what comes in and out of camp, counting SLICs, or observing from the mountains." He pointed off toward the horizon at the low, round mountains covered with green vegetation, the elevation insufficient to thin out the lush jungle. A mist swirled at their base, and slabs of light brown stone were visible here and there, the only thing that seemed able to break up the endless green.

The SLICs rose one by one, emerging from the smoke that clung to their stabilizers and swirled from their repulsors. But the canister just produced more smoke, and not even the thrust of liftoff was enough to chase away the artificial pink fog.

The SLICs hovered over camp for a moment as they turned and acquired their bearings. Yawds operating anti-missile batteries watched their sectors, ready to intercept any would-be attempts to shoot the SLICs down. The vehicles banked and took on altitude, their side doors sealed, so that only the Kimbrin door gunner was visible, the legionnaires and Yawds inside entirely hidden. This was by design. One of the SLICs contained the full insertion team; the other was a decoy. The two craft maintained a holding pattern above the camp until four more SLICs raced overhead, and then all six were off and venturing into MCR territory.

"That's about the best we can do short of a stealth shuttle," said Young. "MCR knows something's coming, and hopefully when the boys from Team One land the mids'll have picked the wrong spot to wait."

"And if not?" said Masters.

"We get to visit Rosie's after all," said Jaybles. "After we pull them out of the fire, I mean."

That fire wouldn't come until the middle of the following day. Word that they were being deployed to recover Team One wasn't a surprise. They hadn't even needed to be paged or hear their comms ping. Masters and the others were inside the TOC along with most of the other legionnaires of Outpost Ten when Team One's leader, Sergeant Ashton Davis, reported to the Captain Hurn that contact was imminent, and ever since then Masters and the others had been listening to each subsequent report, right up until the shooting started.

Already kitted out, Masters stood by Young while Jaybles went off to find Bord and the rest of his Yawd fighters. A SLIC was inbound from the Kimbrin Planetary Army base. The pilot's ETA was five minutes, a number that had been repeated, unchanged, at every five-minute interval in the half hour since the shooting started.

Sergeant Davis and the rest of Team One sounded calm and collected over their L-comms; exactly no one would expect a competent legionnaire to be anything else. They were engaging a small force of MCR consisting entirely of Kimbrin. Davis was splitting his time between shooting, giving status updates to Hurn, and calling out artillery coordinates on a suspected supply train.

"Secondary explosions detected," Sergeant Davis reported over the comm on a channel dedicated to Repub Army artillery and RTAC. "Repeat. Fire for effect."

"How much longer until our ride gets here?" asked Masters.

"Five minutes," said LS- 69, a regular Legion specialist named Adam Nelson, "Hillbilly," who had gotten busted up on a previous mission and was working staff at the TOC until all the various bots, nanites, and regenerative pills could get him back in the game. "But this time they say they really mean it. SLIC's off the ground. Had some engine trouble that was keeping it grounded."

"Well that's reassuring," Young muttered just loud enough for Masters to hear.

Jaybles reappeared back in the TOC. "Bord and the guys are ready to go."

"All right," said Young. He slapped Masters on the shoulder. "Let's head to the pad and hope they come in early."

The team waited, weighed down with their kits plus additional charge packs, med supplies, and other equipment for a quick resupply to Team One in case they all had to fight together to get back out. All of that was in addition to the med bot that stood quietly, ready to render aid upon arrival. All three legionnaires had been wounded but were calling those wounds superficial. Some of the Yawds with them hadn't been so lucky. No one dead yet, but that could change if the SLIC took too long in arriving.

It didn't. The sound of its unique repulsor whine filled the skies until the featherhead at the stick practically dropped the bird straight down onto the pad. With its doors already open, the side gunner waved the team aboard. There was no smoke to confuse any watchers; by this point, every MCR in theater knew where the infiltration team had been found and where the next SLIC out of camp would be headed. It was one and the same. And that fact was what made working the Black so dangerous. The chances of getting put on the ground without taking fire were nonexistent. It was going to be a bumpy ride.

19

Masters could see the fires burning from where Republic artillery had scored a direct hit on an MCR supply caravan. He had a fleeting glimpse of a repulsor truck that must've been carrying explosive ordnance—a fifteen-meter radius was littered with dead bodies and flattened trees. Still more men and supplies on trucks or towed by hoverbikes were sneaking their way around a parallel trail, one much narrower than the road the basics had blasted. But the smaller confines didn't seem to slow their movement. Masters mapped the coordinates in his bucket.

"Got some targets for the shell shockers," he called in to Hillbilly at the TOC. "But don't give it to them until we're down and the SLIC is clear. Last thing I need is for some basics to shoot us out of the sky. I could never live with myself dying that way."

"Roger. Coordinates stored for later use. Hillbilly out."

The mids on the ground were waiting for the SLIC's arrival. The rapid fire of a light repeating blaster cannon zipped through the air, forcing the pilot to bank hard to avoid it, though at least a few bolts smacked against the craft's armored hull all the same. The door gunner swung his weapon around and sent an equally impressive spew of return fire in the direction of the makeshift anti-air defense.

Team One had put themselves down in a depression that the pilot had observed as suitable for landing. They were in the process of falling back to that location while the MCR pursued them. The SLIC would provide covering fire with its door gunner while Black Team roped down to assist with the strategic withdrawal. If everything went to plan, the entirety of both teams would reboard the SLIC and a second SLIC on standby in the depression. Republic artillery would lob its energized canisters as a means of further discouraging the MCR to pursue.

As Team One maneuvered through the forest, firing on the pursuing MCR and leapfrogging one another, the SLIC hovered over the trees, its door gunner going cyclic. The phrase "going cyclic" was as much an antique as the old slug throwers that spawned the term, but Masters knew what it meant. He could see the glow of the heavy repeating cannon as it relentlessly sent supercharged particles into the jungle.

Black synth-rope swung down on the opposite side of the bird. Three ropes that allowed Masters and Jaybles to go down first on either side with one of the Yawds going down the middle. Young stayed on board until the rest of the Yawds had followed before finally coming down with Bord. With so many trees, the insertion method was almost as dangerous as the sporadic weapons fire that barked out against the door gunner's onslaught during those moments when a brave MCR made himself conspicuous. The ropes could get snagged on trees, and the soldiers with them. And once tethered, an unwitting pilot might attempt to change course or take off and find himself racing toward a fiery end as the rope offered resistance that would send the SLIC crashing toward the earth like a rock out of a sling.

For that purpose, Young activated the remote release of the synth-ropes the moment he reached the jungle floor, causing the three ropes to drop free of the SLIC and notifying the pilots that they were free to take on altitude. The Kimbrin featherhead did so at once, his door gunner never slowing in his fire until they were out of effective range.

Masters and the team quickly formed an L-shaped ambush knowing that the pursuing MCR would need to either go through their kill zone or move around in an attempt to flank them. Either of those choices would give Team One the additional time it needed to reach the LZ without suffering further harm.

"MD-6," Young said to the med bot that had come down with them, forgoing use of fast ropes and having simply jumped out of the SLIC, relying on its sophisticated mix of shock-absorbing legs and mech repulsors to bring it to the jungle floor safely.

The bot was attentive, with the cool, charming calm of a family doctor. "Yes, Sergeant Young, do you have wounded to report?"

"Negative. I want you to move up in pursuit of Team One. Begin treatments as you see necessary, but everyone needs to be at the LZ within fifteen standard minutes."

"I understand." The bot lowered itself into a crouch, its servos whining as each articulated joint positioned itself for a quick low run to avoid being struck by enemy fire. "Good luck, Sergeant."

"Thanks."

The bot rushed away, leaving the ambush site to the legionnaires and their Yawd companions.

"Jaybles, let someone know we're sending the bot their way so they don't dust us by mistake."

"On it."

"Masters, you got the bot deployed? What's the status on the pursuing mids?"

Masters had sent up a small TT-13 observation bot to track the pursuit. The peeper was now displaying its image into the upper-left quadrant of the legionnaire's HUD. "Tell the ladies I got it up. Canopy is pretty thick but it looks like the mids are still pushing this way. I'll see if I can take it higher, but I'm worried about it triggering one of those sensors and getting fried."

Masters brought the drone higher and took in the landscape. The cover was thick, but not so much that thermal and other overlays couldn't tell him what was going on. The MCR was in hot pursuit of Team One, and if they noticed where the Black Team had roped down, they weren't acting particularly concerned about it. They pushed forward, moving as though the loss of a step would mean the loss of their prey.

"They're still coming. So either the MCR hasn't gained any IQ points since the last time we tussled, or they've got a surprise of their own waiting for us."

Masters's feed abruptly went out, the holodisplay replaced by a black static screen reporting signal lost.

"Peeper's down," he said.

Masters ran back the holorecording, checking its 360-degree viewing angles and then finding the cause of the disruption. It had been another, larger drone. A TT-16, which was big enough to carry counter-drone armaments. Not so large as to deliver a missile payload, but it could make sure it owned the skies when it came to others of its kind.

"Looks like the mids have a TT-16. Took our bot out."

"That's gonna be it until more SLICs get in the airspace," said Jaybles. "And they ain't gonna want to do no aerial surveillance. Drive to the LZ and get back in the air is all those guys are gonna be thinking."

"Concealment here is fine," said Young. The team was well hidden, and Yawds were as invisible as the legionnaires in their mimetic camouflage armor. "With the speed Masters says they were moving, they're either going to run into this buzz saw or enough time will pass for us to know if they're trying to work around. Either way we buy One the time it needs to get to the LZ."

The time needed was only another two minutes before the first of the pursuing MCR force entered their ambush site, breathing heavily, their uniforms soaked in sweat from the pursuit. Two scouts, if you wanted to call them that, were at the head of the unevenly staggered column. They had given up all pretense of carefully surveying the area in front of them. Their blood was up, and they were thinking only of reestablishing contact with the enemy. They had bloodied one of the teams, and they knew it. Now was the time to finish things off.

"I got these two," said Jaybles, who was positioned at the edge of the L and best suited to drop these two once the main body came in.

The next grouping was as juicy a target as Masters could remember seeing. One MCR double-timed into the zone and then a gaggle of soldiers, perhaps twelve all told, came in together breathing as heavily as the scouts, their eyes fixed in front of them and hardly bothering to look either to the left or to the right. They were dressed in simple black uniforms. The MCR hadn't exactly been strict in its dress requirements, but mainline units comprising Kimbrin could usually be counted on to wear the distinctive tan BDU battle dress uniform that the more sympathetic face of the MCR often presented itself with.

Something told Masters that these were raw recruits—and that something was their lack of discipline in pursuing an enemy and the ad hoc nature of their dress. But it didn't matter. Once they entered the zone, everyone on the team— Yawds included—knew what to do.

The jungle lit up with blaster fire. Every man spent a third of their charge pack before the vanguard of the MCR pursuit was completely annihilated. As the last of the Kimbrin fell dead, shot in the back by the Yawds as he tried desperately to escape, Young abruptly stood.

"Okay, that's it. Nice work. Set up the AP mines and then ghost. Time to make our way to the LZ."

Jaybles reached out to Team One to let them know they were now moving along the planned route to the LZ. "Young," he said after a moment. "Davis wants to know where the med bot is. Some of the Yawds are circling the drain."

"Should be there by now." Young checked his HUD. "Not getting a ping. Tell him sorry but I think it got lost on the way."

"Roger."

While Jaybles delivered the update, Masters helped the Yawds set up the antipersonnel mines. They mined the main road leading to the LZ and seeded more out to hit the terrain on either side of the road to catch those pursuing should they try and go around the sides of their ambush. The mines were capable of detonating via a fixed timer, motion sensor, or remote signal. Masters set some on the road to go via motion—anyone else traveling this way after them would have nothing but bad intentions—and the others he set up for manual remote detonation, wanting to inflict as many casualties as possible. Each mine had a small holocam fixed to it that would transmit whatever it saw to Masters, who could then decide whether it was worthwhile to blow it or not.

Once Bord reported that the last of the mines had been placed, Masters brought him and the other Yawds not pulling security to the rear and reported to Young. "We're gonna make whoever tries to come through here pay, that's for sure."

"Good. Let's move out. Bord, you take the lead. Team One knows we're coming."

Young waited until four Yawds had pushed past him along the path toward the LZ and then fell in himself. Masters waited, watching for oncoming hostiles as additional Yawds moved out. Jaybles passed by, reporting, "Last man."

Masters nodded and turned on his heels to move quickly along the jungle trail. K-SOG 7 traveled a kilometer before they encountered the med bot. It was lying on its side like a statue, as though it had been frozen in place and then fell over.

"Looks like it tripped a bot-popper," said Jaybles, pointing out the flash markings that had burned their way across the surface of the leaves where the powerful anti-tech device had blown.

Young had also stayed to inspect the machine. "We knew this place was crawling with those before we brought it with us. Calculated risk didn't pay off."

"We can haul it back," said Masters. "Or at least I can."

"Hell no," said Young. "Grab its kit and then drop a heater on it so the mids can't use it. Then let's keep moving."

Masters did both, detaching the medical kit from the bot's chest and back and hoisting it over his shoulder. He replaced the bot's kit with a hyperthermal grenade from his own kit and programmed the timer to ignite in thirty seconds.

"Half minute until the campfire."

Young nodded. "Team One is at the LZ and waiting. Let's catch up."

They had moved only another twenty meters when the distant boom of one of the motion-sensor mines sounded behind them.

"Knock knock," said Masters. He checked the feeds of the remaining sensor mines. "Holy strokes. We've got a company-sized element pushing up that road. Good news is, looks like we tore apart at least a dozen of them with that one. Bad news is now they'll be looking for them."

"Can we get RA to drop some artillery on them?" suggested Jaybles.

"On it," said Young.

The team ran as they worked. Jaybles performed security, watching their six as they moved with the team. Masters watched his holo-feed, waiting to manually detonate one of the mines and cause maximum damage, although with the element of surprise gone, the rest of the element was moving cautiously and searching for the devices. At best he would only be able to take out the searchers and any mids who hung around too close to the blast area. It would have to do.

Young was working the L-comm, trying to get authorization for an artillery strike. "It's a no-go," he said at last, shaking his head. "Kimbrin SLICs are entering the AO and no one at the featherhead shed wants to pull them back to wait for artillery to do its work. Safety concerns."

"My ass," said Jaybles. "More like what-are-we-doing-after-the-mission concerns. They just want to get down and get back out. Probably want to get home in time to go out with the girls. Or at least what passes for girls among the Kimbrin."

Masters shrugged. "Can't blame the Kimbrin if that's the reasoning."

"You know, you *can* have too much of a good thing, Masters," said Jaybles.

"Hasn't happened so far," Masters countered.

Young cut into the chatter. "Well we know the birds are coming, and I would much prefer that we be at the LZ when they arrive. Let's keep pushing it. Bord is nearly there."

They reached the landing zone and passed beyond the defensive line set up by Team One. It was the first look that any of Masters's group had gotten of the team they were extracting, and it wasn't pretty. One of the Kimbrin had succumbed to his wounds. Another was gurgling with every breath, his skin a pale gray and his cranial horns secreting a clear, sticky liquid Masters knew meant his vital systems were failing.

Jaybles, who had additional medical training beyond the essential skills required to be in Dark Ops—he was a combat medic—did what he could.

"You guys look like hell," Young said to the three legionnaires of Team One, two of whom had taken their buckets off to pour water from external canteens over their hair and across their faces to remove the caked-on sweat. Internal climate controls could only do so much in a running firefight.

"We've been shot at all morning," said Sergeant Davis. "What's your excuse?"

"Whoa, whoa, whoa," Masters said. "I'll have you know I am incredibly good-looking. I can let a lot of things slide, Leej, but when someone starts denying reality, that's where I draw the line."

"It's true," said Young. "It's all Jaybles and I can do to keep our hands off him at night. Come on. Let's get this perimeter set. Company-size element is going to figure out how to get around a few mines before too much longer."

"Yeah," said Davis. He rose up from his haunches with a sigh. "Heard you say that over the L-comm. Didn't want to believe it even though I knew it was true. What's the ETA on the SLICs?"

"Should be any time," said Masters.

"Needs to be now," said the other legionnaire. "We're already coming back light one man. Don't want it to be any more. What happened to the bot?"

"Bot-popper got it," said Young.

"Sucks."

"Yeah."

And that was the conversation. The legionnaires moved to their places to hold the perimeter, taking up defensive positions that faced the clearing leading from the road and either side, with one Yawd trusted to cover their six, which should be free from attack given that any forces would have to scale down a rocky finger that reached into the depression from one of the mountains.

The seconds ticked by, and Masters was about to complain that if the SLICs weren't going to get here soon then the basics should've gone ahead and just lobbed the artillery on the MCR. After he had dusted a couple more with the remote detonation of the mines, someone among the MCR finally got the idea to just blow the whole area and hurry through after the resulting explosion. They hurled grenades and det cord through Masters's well-mined alley to make one big boom that rumbled all the way to the LZ. A couple of the mines failed to detonate though, and Masters used their holocams to watch the action as the dust settled and the troopers pushed quickly on, knowing that their window to reach the LZ in time to stop extraction was rapidly closing.

The first SLIC came down at last, and its door gunner shot steady streams of blaster cannon fire toward the jungle path the team had used as a road. Scorched branches and leaves fell to the ground as the hot bolts ripped into the foliage. It didn't matter that none of the bolts had made contact with the enemy, not to the door gunner; charge packs were cheap to the point that each blaster bolt was practically free. The SLIC would get recharged once they landed either way, so might as well send 'em if you got 'em.

As the gunner took his fingers off the butterfly trigger and began to sweep for actual targets, the legionnaires ran the wounded to the first SLIC, filling it and sending one healthy member from Team One to go along. The bird lifted off and banked away, its door gunner sending fire at unseen enemies in the jungle, just hoping to get lucky. None of the leejes or Yawds on the ground minded that one bit.

The second SLIC, that would take those remaining, was supposed to come in hot not more than a minute after the first, but three minutes later it was nowhere to be seen. As Young worked the L-comm to find out where the hell the featherhead was, the first tentative blaster bolt from the forest shot out at their position. The MCR had reached the farthest edge of the landing zone.

For the next ten minutes the legionnaires and Yawds exchanged blaster fire with the overwhelming MCR force. All the extra gear the Yawds had carried in with them as part of the Black was now being used to its fullest effect against the pursuing MCR, who must have felt as though they were the ones being assaulted. Additional antipersonnel mines that had been saved for the occasion maimed and destroyed those who attempted to clear the jungle for better fields of fire. Powerful aero-precision missiles meant for destroying vehicles were used to snipe MCR soldiers firing from behind thick primordial trees. And heaters—sometimes called inferno grenades—were hurled into the tree lines to produce a massive chemical blaze that would rage unabated for hours if left to die out on its own. In addition to all that, the legionnaires, who rarely missed, fired their blaster rifles with deadly accuracy, killing any Kimbrin with the temerity to stick his head out for more than a second.

"Young, did you forget to call the shuttle?" said Masters as he ducked behind a rock, blaster bolts flying over his head. "Because I'd like to go home right about now."

"Only word we're getting back from featherhead shed is that they're close."

"You Dark Ops boys are too spoiled riding around with those Gothic Serpents," said Jaybles, who seemed to be relishing the pitched battle. "Unreliable air support is half the fun."

"You sound like a point I used to know," said Masters.

The SLIC finally roared overhead but failed to identify the zone and continued on over the jungle, where ineffective small-arms fire rushed up through the canopy as the MCR looked for a lucky—*extremely* lucky—shot that might take the vehicle down. Young got on the L-comm and pleaded for someone to tell the featherhead that he had overshot the landing zone and needed to turn around.

The byzantine communication relay was a serious shortcoming to these operations. But only the L-comm was guaranteed to be secure. The Kimbrin didn't have it, and the Republic wasn't about to give it to them with so many of them being compromised and with the MCR. There were local encrypted military frequencies, but the civil-war-like buildup meant that those couldn't be trusted either. In short, it was a sure bet that anything communicated from the ground over a Kimbrin channel was likely to be intercepted by the local MCR. That meant using a relay where L-comm went from Young to Outpost Ten, which then relayed a non-L-comm to Kimbrin planetary air defense, who insisted on being the final go-between before reaching the pilot. And while the last leg could still be intercepted, it wouldn't be in time for any MCR on the ground to actually do anything about it.

"Okay, pilot's got his bearings and he's coming back around," Young reported. "How we doing on charge packs?"

"Less than I'd like, but we should be good until he gets here. But he's got to get here this time, period," said Ryan Mongeau, Team One's weapons sergeant who'd been given the task of keeping packs distributed among all the shooters.

The SLIC could be heard coming back toward the LZ, and the MCR must've sensed that their window was finally closing, for their next push was the hardest yet. The last two Yawds from Team One went down with blaster wounds, as did one of Bord's Yawds. Masters took a shot to the shoulder that was sure to leave a contusion. But the armor did its job. Jaybles caught a bolt to the leg. Young, one to the chest. The wounds weren't fatal—they just hurt like hell—but they reminded the legionnaires that they couldn't do this forever.

Finally the SLIC raced overhead, and just when it looked as though it was about to pass the landing zone once again, it slowed and dropped into a corkscrew fall. The pilot was showing off his skill bringing the bird in fast and making it a somewhat more difficult target to hit, because the MCR were putting everything they had on it and it alone. All the blaster fire that had been offered to the legionnaires was now given to the SLIC instead. The door gunner did what he could, firing angry bursts each time the craft whipped around and gave him a sight picture of the frenzied jungle's edge. And when the SLIC set down, the door gunner continued firing unabated. There would be no slacking off from that powerful weapon while the legionnaires sought to board the escape craft. It would be up to the leejes to keep from getting dusted by friendly fire.

They covered for one another as they ran to the bird, each man getting on board and then adding the firepower of his own weapon to cover his brothers as they too moved to salvation. Masters collected fraggers from each man who ran past until he had an armful of grenades waiting to be used. He tossed them one by one in rapid succession like a kid in a snowball fight, calling out curses with each fastball whip of his arm. Then, as last man, he was up and running full speed until he reached the SLIC. He leapt on board, shouted what they already knew—"Last man!"—then turned and brought his blaster into the mix as the legionnaires fired out of the open side door and the door gunner blazed away and the SLIC took on altitude while MCR blaster bolts chased it into the air.

The pilot carried them over the finger of the nearby mountain and put the great rock mass between them and the MCR, cutting off that danger for good. Once they had left the grid square, Republic artillery would see if they could find any remaining mids still in the area. And maybe the wiretap would get something useful, although the MCR would surely be looking for it now.

The legionnaires removed their buckets. They kept the side door open because the wind blasting their face and whipping through their hair was a good reminder that they were still alive. They kept their bone-conduction headsets on in order to communicate above the noise.

Young looked to Masters. "Welcome to the Black. Now you know why Jaybles was so mad."

20

Masters recognized several of the legionnaires gathered inside Rosie's as he walked through the door, showered but already sweating because of the heat. Kyle Hetzer and Jacob Brinkman had fought on Utopion against Goth Sullus. Justin Taylor lost a hand at Ankalor. Daniel Torres was Dark Ops and had been acquainted with Ellek Owens. They were all already at Rosie's, listening to Sergeant Davis and the rest of Team One tell their tale in full.

"He get to the good part yet?" Young asked as he pulled up at the bar where Davis held court and held up three fingers.

"Nah. He's still telling us what he had for breakfast the morning of," said Kevin Zhang, a member of Team Five. "Oh, but I'm *real* glad you showed up. Means Davis has an excuse to start all over. Again."

"Well," said Davis, "you've got to have the whole thing or you'll be missing context. I'm telling you boys, something's up out here."

Davis waited a beat and then cleared his throat, formally beginning again. "The team had picked an insertion LZ that was actually on the downslope of the terrain we needed to traverse, but the climb was a minor point. Since the MCR controlled the whole area, having the extra space to get lost was worth the effort."

As Mongeau, Team One's weapons sergeant, chimed in to give the lay of the land, including a description of the undergrowth, Rosie set three beers on the counter. Young motioned for Masters and Jaybles to crowd in and hear the story better. When Jaybles reached out to take his beer, Young wrapped his arms around all three bottles like a mother protecting her children. "You buy your own damn beer."

Jaybles held up one finger to Young and another, more polite finger to Rosie. Masters simply snuck around Young's side and plucked one of the beers from the legionnaire's protection. The operator gave him a look but didn't speak up. He'd already interrupted Team One's story and knew they wouldn't appreciate any more of the same unless there were questions along the way.

"So anyway," Sergeant Davis continued, picking up the thread from Mongeau, "we get in and it's like nothing I've seen for a long time. Sensors come up empty, jungle sounds like it's supposed to, no sightings of forces moving our way... sort of how things were when we first got here. Before the mummy bees' nest really started swarming and buzzing.

"So John Zack is on point with Toktok and Ramp, moving behind the Yawds—Ramp's the one who bought it in the field. I'm last man, and John Stuhl is moving with the rest of the Yawds. Intel identified a winding kilometer-long stretch of ground eight clicks south of us that looked as though it had been freshly turned. We come along a trail that winds along the contours of the land, so the aerial photos didn't pick it up. We get off the road and keep a man watching it while we go to the suspected loc for the ground wire.

"So now we're movin' through the jungle from the opposite downslope toward the clearing, and I'm checkin' my HUD to make sure we're where we're supposed to be because we can't see anything that suggests the mids buried any wires in the vicinity. But HUD says we're there, and no one has come to chase us out, so we set up in concealment and prepare to take a closer look.

"Now, this place isn't jungle proper. It's some kind of grassland, probably gets nice and tall and green when it's rainy, but for us it's just dry and noisy. It's not all-encompassing though. Bit of a mix. A lot of the grass just couldn't handle the heat and is burnt down to the dirt, you know? Like it's waiting for the water and the seeds of a stronger variety to fill it in. Then there's some scrub brush shooting up about two and half or three meters high and just about that far around. That's a little bit of shade, and so we make for that on account of the Yawds, who're already sweating like crazy. But the inside of the bushes is thick with thorns, so once we get settled in and have our zones figured out, no one wants to move. At least none of the Yawds. Ramp says in our Legion armor the mids can't see us as good, plus we got climate controls, so he thought *we* should be the ones to go crawling out there looking for the lines."

Sergeant Mongeau chimed in again, picking up the story momentarily. "I tried to argue that this was the Yawds' turf, so if anybody was gonna notice something out of place it was them, but they weren't buying it."

Sergeant Davis grunted and kept going. "So John Zack draws the short stick and he's got to go out crawling an inch at a time on his belly looking for this scar in the ground that intel swears it saw from orbit, but we don't see anything."

The legionnaire looked around as the boys swallowed gulps of their barely chilled beers, their faces and arms as sweaty as the condensation on the bottles thanks to there not being enough climate boxes to go around. Rosie might have been a *friend* to the Legion, but he wasn't *in* the Legion, so what creature comforts managed to make their way to the camp never got as far as his club—leaving the interior of his hab a humid mess. There was a raid planned at some undetermined future date to liberate a spare climate box from the basics. Maybe Young had been supposed to do that when he picked up Masters. He took a sled instead though.

"J-Z takes the better part of two hours searching," said Davis. "He only has to crawl on his belly when he's moving in those dead zones though. Once he gets to the better concealment he can move freely because we've got sweepers already deployed and they're telling us nothing's there. Not even a bot-popper. Which initially makes us think we're out on a wild goose chase until sensors read a brief electrical spike. Nothing big enough to triangulate, but it's out there. And then lo and behold, J-Z finds a little tuft of brown dried-up bush—just like a houseplant left to die, you know?—and it's got parched soil sitting at its base and some more on its leaves. Like someone dumped a shovelful of dirt on it.

"See, what happened was, whoever dug the trench for the line got a little sloppy and left some of the excavation sitting on top of the grass. Maybe figured the rain would take care of it for him, but it didn't. They'd done a good job covering their actual dig site—snaked it around the plant so it almost flowed with the terrain. There was no obvious straight line to be seen, you know. Not as efficient, used more material, but also much less obvious. I have to tip my bucket to those guys watching from orbit, because those guys saw something when the mids did a hell of a job covering their tracks."

"Probably it was just a bot that did the work spotting the scar in the dirt," said Jaybles. "Not any of the guys watching the orbit feeds."

"Well then good for the bot," said Davis. "Point is it was there. So we dig it up, and we're moving fast now because we figure MCR is going to be patrolling along these lines. Especially if they haven't had the chance to set up any mechanical observation devices. And the sensor sweeps said they hadn't.

"Now, it doesn't take long until the wire's up and we've got a splicer pushed in. Nice and smooth so you can't even tell it's there. Like a burm-tick burrowing under your skin. Just gone. Okay, so now that the line is..." Sergeant Davis looked around and flashed a preemptive smile. "Bugged..."

His audience groaned in unison at the pun.

"Mission accomplished. Device is going to sit there and record everything that passes on that line until it's severed or an attempt is made to extract it. That happens, it'll burst whatever data it's stored over our comm for processing."

"So when do things go sideways?" Masters asked.

"Oh, that's the silvene question, because right about then I was thinking this is it. Mission you dream of. In, out, nothing." The sergeant shook his head. "Should have bugged out right there. Just picked up and went. Hindsight.

"We said we move out in fifteen just to be sure no one had been watching us work and was then going to come over and inspect and undo what we just did. At first that seemed like a good idea because not a half hour later, we see two mids stroll through the area. They walk right to the spot. And I'm thinking, okay, someone told on us. Not all the Yawds are friends out there you know. Some of them are working with the MCR and will tip them off if they see something. Just reality.

"So these two mouth-breathers stand practically on the exact spot we've just been working. But they don't do anything else except chew the fat. One of them takes a leak, and then the pair move on. Just a routine patrol that happened to stroll through, and we'd covered up well enough that they didn't even notice what we'd done. Covered it up better than they had, in fact.

"Now, this is remote country, so I'm thinking a patrol is going to come by that way maybe twice a day. Two of my Yawds follow the patrol, and we're sitting tight until they come back and tell us that they've broken off east following some trail. Which gives us the space we need to pull back to the LZ. We start to pick ourselves up off the ground and pull ourselves out of those thorny bushes and then—I kid you not, down to the exact second here—I stand up and look down the road and there's four more mids walking toward the site. So I called out the targets and everybody gets down, but right away you know something's wrong because those four just stop in place. They saw something, or at least they think they saw something, and now they're talking to one another pointing in our direction trying to get some confirmation. The only thing protecting my Yawds is the tall grass. We're good with our camo, but the Yawds..."

"So what did they do?" asked Young. "MCR's been slow to use comms unless they feel like they have to. They call it in?"

"Maybe. Didn't pick up any transmissions. Two of them stayed put and two of them turned and started running fast as their Kimbrin legs could carry them in the opposite direction. These boys didn't have a bad case of the bubble guts, that much was clear. Runnin' with purpose. So now we've got suitable concealment but no cover, we've got at least two mids to the east and two more standing around looking stupid with their rifles up and ready, and we got the pair of MCR joggers blazing off to who knows where.

"I made the call right then and there. Mongeau took one and J–Z took the other. Dropped both of the remaining Kimbrin and then dragged them into the bushes while everybody else made to move. We knew we were going to have to run, but we figured we might buy ourselves a little time making whoever was coming next look for these guys instead of just finding the bodies lying there.

"I leave behind an observe-record bot so I can get a feed on whatever comes up the pipe, and then we're moving. Call in the situation over L-comm and we're trying to put as much distance between ourselves and the site as possible. Well, we got about a kilometer before the bot transmitted images that showed the force in question was going to be a big one. Kimbrin trackers swept the area and found the bodies quickly. Took us a minute to hide them, took them ten minutes to find them. Maybe. I think they knew either way and were just waiting. Because they didn't take off after us until some guy in uniform showed up and started barking out orders. He sent the scouts after us and remained on-site with a platoon of MCR regulars."

"They find your handiwork?" asked Young.

"No, that's the thing of it. The whole time the bot was up, no one even went to the location. I'd like to think this is just good luck for us, but if the group in question didn't know that line was nearby..." Sergeant Davis shrugged. "I mean, they're going to figure it out eventually, but as of the last time I checked the thing is still operational."

"Lucky."

"Damn lucky. So we've got trackers moving and we're staying ahead of them, but these guys are quick. They know the terrain, they know what they're doing, and they're trying to chase us down or cut us off. Trying to control our movement so the force that's staging back at the site can drop the hammer on us. We're hauling ass, going as fast as the Yawds can go, until I finally gotta call a rest to get hydrated and get our bearings. That doesn't last long because these guys are gaining ground the whole time. We're in full kit and ready to do damage but all these guys got is their clothes, couple of charge packs for the blaster rifle, and that's it.

"So while we're moving to the LZ they're moving to us, and it isn't long before they make contact and then we've got to slow down and keep them back. And by that time the main element had a good idea of where we were headed, so they're edging around trying to get us and we've got the jungle and a running firefight to contend with. Then the Yawds start getting hit, and that slows us down further—you can't be mad about that because those tough kelhorns are still putting up a hell of a fight despite getting hit."

The other legionnaires nodded solemnly. They'd all fought alongside the Yawds and knew first-hand the sacrifices those soldiers were willing to offer. They weren't Legion, but they shared many of the same qualities.

"From that point I guess you guys got it figured out. Black came in, pulled us out, and here we are. Here we are," Sergeant Davis repeated again after a pause. "Here we are."

Young clapped the man on the back. "You guys did good."

Davis nodded his thanks. "Man, for those platoons to just show up in the middle of nowhere..." He shook his head and ran his finger along the bottom of his beer bottle. "I don't know. I just don't know."

21

The team's time on the Black had come to an end. The wiretap that Team One had installed had finally been discovered, but the information it had pumped to the camp had been the basis for a number of successful raids. Masters and his team had just overseen the extraction of a small supply convoy on its way to transfer munitions from one outpost to the next. Now they stood in their planning room looking at a holoprojection of the terrain, a three-dimensional topographical map on the central table in the TOC.

At its center was Outpost Ten. A small zone that extended only as far as the edges of the clearing, sliding down the slopes before coming back up to the hilly jungle. It was colored green, not because of any topography, but because this was the only place that had been without some direct conflict in the last thirty days. No one had bothered attempting to hit the camp since that first day when Masters arrived. The fast response of Republic artillery had done a lot to dissuade that.

The next zone, covering everything within a few kilometers of the camp, was marked yellow, meaning there had been at least one encounter in the last thirty days. Yawds regularly patrolled the surrounding area, not only to keep it free from enemy control but also to search for fresh food of the sort they had grown up eating—food that the legionnaires had added to their own diets, though they didn't attack it with the same salivating relish as the Yawds. These Kimbrin allies had run into small MCR foot patrols, earning the yellow designation on the topographical map. So far, the Yawds had won every encounter, despite not having legionnaires with them, though not without some casualties. One of Bord's men from Team Seven had been killed three weeks ago.

Beyond the hilly jungle-enshrouded slopes was where the elevation picked up again and the surrounding mountains began to rise and look down upon the tiny camp at their center. This was the heart of MCR territory, and it was bathed in red. Every time someone went out there, there was a fight. Usually within hours. Team One's experience of getting in undetected and having an unmolested hike to objective was a distant memory. Masters's last mission had been scrubbed only two hours after they set down when a roving platoon of mids made contact. His kill team had wiped that platoon out to the last man, but the damage was done, and it would have been only a matter of time before greater numbers arrived.

"I've never seen the jungle so thick with mids," said Young. "It's unreal."

"Even worse than when we were on the Black," Jaybles agreed. "I'm amazed none of us died."

"I think Captain Hurn is too," said Masters. "And maybe a little disappointed."

"Well I don't think he'll be disappointed in us much longer," said Young, who zoomed in on the southern side of M1, the mountain they were expected to operate on and around. There had been several missions in that direction in the past week, with multiple teams setting down on or near the mountain's many ridges. Each time they'd been met with fierce resistance—too much even for a Legion SOG team to withstand. "The way I see it, being on the Black is now the safe option. At least you know where the bad guys are and get to go in shooting."

"The bad guys are everywhere at this point," Masters said. "Only place without them is that desert on the back side of M1. We may as well just sit at Rosie's and have the shell shockers deliver artillery fire."

"Oh yeah?" said Jaybles. "And where would you have them send it?"

"Anywhere but here is fine. They'll probably kill as many mids as we get to, as tightly packed in as they are. It's like fighting zhee. They're all just in there together waiting to get killed or to kill you. And they don't seem to care which all that much so long as somebody gets dusted." Masters leaned back in his chair. "You were on Ankalor, right Jaybles?"

Masters knew that Young hadn't been. His kill team had been operating somewhere in the mid-core when all that went down. Probably training Drusics how to waterski or some such original team nonsense. But Jaybles was regular Legion, and Legion Commander Keller had thrown more legionnaires at that planet than in any engagement since Psydon.

"Nah," said Jaybles. "At least not when it was all going down. Prior deployment and it was still a mess there, but I missed the big one. I was still with the Fifteenth, and we were staged for a mission to take back Tarrago. Never got the green light, and then one thing led to another, and…"

"Yeah," finished Masters. It wasn't a subject most leejes felt eager to talk about. The losses at the battle for Utopion had been too great. There wasn't an active-duty leej who hadn't personally felt the sting of what happened between Legion, Black Fleet, and Cybar. "Well, anyway, that's what all this feels like to me. Like we're fighting donks who've got nothing better to do with their lives than wait around for someone to kill them. Only that's not really how the mids operate in my experience. At least, not the Kimbrin mids." Masters leaned forward. "You think the Kimbrin and the donks are interbreeding or something? Is that biologically possible?"

Young was squeezing his bottom lip between his fingers, listening. Now he nodded. "You're not wrong about that."

"Really? You think those two species are making a third, feckless species?"

"Wasn't talking about that and you know it. If there was ever an ideological purity to the MCR, it resided in the hearts of the Kimbrin. I think they actually believe their own propaganda."

"A lot of it wasn't propaganda," grunted Masters. "Looking back…"

Young shot at Masters with a finger pistol. "Right. And if the Kimbrin elements of the MCR hadn't gotten themselves swept up with all those power-hungry humans or those homicidal species like the zhee and the Arthavans, well, who knows how far that movement might have gone. Instead they go and commit atrocities like Rhysis Wan, and the rest is history."

"They got a lot of Endurians to join," mused Masters. "I bet that wasn't so bad. Being stuck underground with a bunch of pink-skinned princesses."

"Hard to grow as big as the MCR did without doing at least some things right," Jaybles observed. "Wasn't just Arthavans and mid-core human scumsacks. They were saying something that resonated with a lot of species and a lot of planets."

"Be still my beating Legion heart," said Masters. "Did I just hear Mr. Legion himself express sympathy for MCR 1.0? You know, under the old House of Reason directives I would've been required to report this infraction to my closest appointed officer for review and evaluation with the help of a specialized bot calibrated to properly understand and identify your cultural prejudices based not only on your Legion training but whatever backwards planet produced you."

"If now was then I wouldn't be thinking like this," said Jaybles. "But it ain't. And a lot's happened since then. So yeah... in retrospect, knowing what we know now about everything that was going on with the House of Reason, Nether Ops, and all that... the MCR had a point. You said it yourself."

"Yeah, but it's different when I say it. No one takes me seriously."

"Sounds like the Legion might have some trouble getting you to re-up when the time comes, Jaybles," said Young. "Might have to think of something spicy to get you to agree to that next rotation, huh?"

"Doesn't have to be spicy. Just getting me off this planet will be fine."

It was a feeling they all shared. Something about Kima and the way things operated here. A war zone with no war. Which on its face was how most of their rotations had been ever since they'd first joined the Legion. Masters had seen it on Grevulo and Morobii and then saw way too much of it on Kublar with that whole disaster. But that was life. You got on planet, saw who was making a mess, cleaned up the mess, and then kicked off to the next rotation. If you expected anything else... well... do you even Legion, bro?

Again, though, Kima felt different. Maybe it was because the Dark Ops legionnaires who were the heart and soul of the special operations group designated to keep the MCR in check were relatively few in number compared to their Kimbrin counterparts. Or because the nearest support came in the form of planetary militia and Republic basics—which weren't all that different from one another. Most of the basics were Kimbrin, and of course all of the Kimbrin Planetary Army were.

And then there was the intensity of the firefights, and the quickness with which the MCR showed up to every infiltration. No one suspected there was a Legion mole feeding intel to the other side, but everyone could plainly see that the mids were growing more brazen as their numbers increased. The network of observers they had was probably mobilizing defenses now that there were so many more MCR than operators in the AO. Or maybe the pilots tipped the mids off in exchange for credits. Risky proposition, though. One SLIC was shot down entirely two weeks ago and a second waited until it was over Outpost Ten to finally crash.

Intelligence had no opinion on any of that, up or down. Not even an increased MCR troop presence. There was no influx of MCR to the planet that could be traced. No sudden immigration of sympathetic humans and other species bringing whatever armaments they had to the cause. Planetary customs hadn't uncovered any massive smuggling operations. No, any MCR growth was solely bleed-off from the towns, farms, and cities of the planet itself. Kimbrin who for whatever reason weren't on board with their government's decision to link back up with the post-Article Nineteen Republic and the House of Liberty. Kimbrin who seemed to think that one more go at rebellion was preferable to working within a system that had failed, even if it now promised to do better.

And here we are, thought Masters, remembering something Chhun had once told him before the man had become a legend within the Legion. Back when he was just Sergeant Chhun. Masters gave voice to the words so Young and Jaybles could hear it.

"Sometimes I wonder if all we're doing out here is fanning the flames until Kima has got a full-scale civil war on its hands."

Young looked from Masters to Jaybles. "If this all keeps up... if the MCR doesn't fold its chairs and head on home... that's *exactly* what we're doing."

The silence brought about by those words hung heavy in the air. And then Jaybles sniffed, pointed to the holomap, and said, "How long has it been since someone tried to insert on one of the back fingers over on M1? Not the dead side, but look at Grid Twelve..."

The SLIC came in hot and low at the base of the mountain. M1 loomed ahead, its naked ridges standing out almost obscenely amid the green vegetation that slid down either side. Up close it was more than just gray rock being beaten upon by the moonlight; there was plenty of cover, vines and other vegetation, adding some life to the otherwise stark stone of the ridge, along with roots dug into deep crevices with low spreading leaves waiting to trip anyone walking in the darkness.

Except it wasn't as dark as it was supposed to be. The cloud cover under which the men were supposed to be inserting had largely blown away thanks to an unexpected front that had pushed in hard from the ocean. The cities on the coast were now under a deluge of rain, but out here it was just warm and clear. Much too clear for the legionnaires' liking. Still, they had taken a chance on the mission knowing that the weather predictions could go either way. Maybe the clouds that covered Outpost Ten and the surrounding region in darkness would clear and the moon would break through, and maybe not. One hour before liftoff there wasn't a breeze in camp. Thirty minutes later there was a slight one, but the night was still plenty dark. It wasn't until they were in the air that things really began to change. It wasn't too late to scrub, but none of the team wanted to go back. They were buzzing about the stony finger in Grid 12, where no teams had touched in a while, and they had some hope they might be able to slip in undetected and do some work.

That hope proved misplaced. The SLIC began taking fire almost as soon as it slowed and flared for landing.

"Ah, dammit!" shouted Young.

The door gunner sent greetings of death at every muzzle flash from a blaster seeking to pick the night bird out of the sky. That only seemed to draw more blaster fire, and by the time the SLIC was down low and hovering above the landing zone, Masters had a premonition that things were very wrong.

They were low enough to jump off the SLIC and set up a perimeter. But the hail of fire coming in had a different sound to it as it impacted against the SLIC's armored skin. It was something more than the light repeating blasters and blaster rifles. Maybe not full-fledged anti-air, but something that was packing a punch. Still, the team was ready to disembark, making the short jump to engage and then hopefully disappear into the terrain.

Bord was just about to jump off and lead his Yawds into taking up fighting positions when Masters threw out his arm and kept him from leaving. The next moment the SLIC abruptly nosed up and took on altitude. The Kimbrin pilot informed the crew that it was too hot and he was pulling out. Had Bord and the Yawds made the jump they would now be left behind.

Eyes wide, the Yawd leader told Masters, "You a good guy, Leej."

Young marched toward the cockpit and banged his fist on the partition separating the pilots from the crew and passengers. It was a thin door that rattled with each strike of the legionnaire's armored fist. Masters could only imagine what Young would do if one of those two pilots actually had the nerve to open the door and answer the legionnaire, who was hot over their pulling up without warning. Because disaster had almost struck. Had Bord and the Yawds been left behind, the legionnaires still on the flight would likely have had to take out the door gunner and then fight their way into the cockpit to convince the pilots to turn back around and recover them.

The pilots never did open the door. They simply took a resigned Team Seven back to Outpost Ten.

Masters and the others trudged back to their hab. Mission scrubbed. Over before it ever really started.

"Back to the datapad, I guess," said Young.

"Rosie's is the only place I'm going back to," said a disgusted Jaybles.

Masters watched the legionnaire depart, but opted to stay and think the problem through with Young for whatever good it would do. The old insertion patterns just weren't working. The MCR's presence had grown to a point where even a single SLIC of commandos just wasn't going to make it in undetected. There were too many mids now, and they knew what to look for and where to look for it. And maybe they knew *when* to look, too. It sure as hell felt that way.

Kima wasn't officially at war. But at this point an army would be needed in order to complete the mission laid out for K-SOG. Either that, or Masters had to think of something new—and think of it quickly.

22

The following day Masters and his team were again posted on the Black. None of the other legionnaires had fouled up enough to invoke Captain Hurn's wrath, and so the teams went through a regular rotation. Successful ops were followed by two days of downtime. Scrubbed missions were either attempted again the next day or the team would work Black followed by two off days and then another crack at things.

Team Eight was up and attempting to insert the long and hard way. Which meant no SLICs at all but a grueling hike from the base into the yellow zone and ultimately infiltrating deep enough into the red to finally get better eyes on targets than what orbital surveillance was capable of.

The MCR had been diligent in their systematic disabling and removal of any electronic observation devices. That diligence was something that had near-universally come out of the scrap with the Cybar. The galaxy was now more equipped and ready to deal with mechanical and technological threats than they had been since the Savage Wars. In that brutal conflict, the Savages and the Republic had unleashed more and more fearsome war bots on one another, and the resulting doctrines and tactics for fighting war bots were still taught in Legion Academy. Most anti-bot weapons had their origins dating back to that nasty extended conflict.

Because of that, war bots were eventually considered a non-starter. Something too easily overcome by legionnaires and other militaries who knew exactly how to disable control ships and convert vast armies of bots into so much scrap. Like anything in war, you prepare for the threats you actually face, and no one had faced bots in far too long. So when they did arrive on the scene again, they got the first few punches in for free.

That was a big part of why the Cybar had been able to do such much damage in such a short period of time. That, and the improvements in technology the Cybar themselves represented.

After their failed insertion, Masters and Young spent most of their time in their hab. Jaybles eventually joined their vigil there as well. It was cooler for one, and there would be far fewer leejes playfully giving them the business over not even managing to get themselves off the SLIC. Conventional wisdom was just to suck it up and march in.

Team Seven wasn't ready to go that route yet. The SLICs should still be able to deliver a surprise.

"I think they got someone on the inside," said Jaybles.

"Oh yeah? Which one of the legionnaires do you think decided to throw it all away to make friends with the Kimbrin MCR?" said Young mockingly. "Or do you think it was one of the Yawds who just happened to sneak into a secure planning meeting and transmit where we were going—undetected—in the hour or so from when they got debriefed to when we actually moved out?"

"I didn't say I know *how* they're doing it. I just think they are. That's the only thing that makes any sense. You saw how thick it was. I understand there are coincidences but having that much heat ready to go in the middle of the night right where a SLIC is landing..." Jaybles held out an open palm. "That's a little too much coincidence for my taste."

"For all we know they put an outpost on that ridge precisely because we hadn't visited in a while," said Masters. "If we're able figure out it had been a while since we visited that LZ, no reason why they wouldn't do the same."

"I suppose," Jaybles said, somewhat begrudgingly. He shifted in his seat and considered. "Assuming Team Eight makes it far enough that they can RON for observation, that means that even though we're on the Black, it's basically a day off. Then we'll get one more day off before we go back to work."

"I have no idea where you're going with this," said Young.

Jaybles made his case. "Think the captain will let us fly a diversion flight tomorrow? I still got a bottle of the old Tabreezy we could bribe the pilot with to put us somewhere metropolitan. I'm getting tired of just having to hear about Masters's past exploits. I got the urge to go see a Tennar beauty of my own."

"Better find another bottle to bring with you in that case," Masters said. "It's gonna take at least that much for any self-respecting Tennar to want to wrap her tentacles around you."

"Who said she had to be self-respecting?"

Young, who usually enjoyed jumping into the verbal fray, was instead quiet and pensive. Masters knew the man was obsessing over how they might insert into increasingly hostile MCR territory. He wasn't ready to be finished with the business of figuring out the answer.

"Why do I have the feeling, Young, that you're going to spend our day off working over how to best get us killed?"

Young blinked at Masters as if awakening from a trance. And then the words sank in and he chuckled and shook his head. "It's not that bad, but you're not too far off. It's really cooking my reactor trying to figure out how things got so kelhorned difficult. About the only thing I can come up with is that we're in MCR central, and the blasted kelhorns have more troops than they know what to do with and are just stationing them all over."

"Think of the kind of supply lines that would be required for something like that," said Jaybles. "Surely intel would pick something up."

"Yes and no," said Masters. "With proper Legion intel, I would agree with you. But we don't have a destroyer in orbit doing its thing. Basics and Kimbrins won't commit patrols to perform reconnaissance by fire. About all the intel we have are what we see on our ops and the occasional secondary explosions from the times we get shots dropped. Everything else is the occasional high-altitude satellite holo plus whatever the SLICs see flying around—and they're moving too fast to take a good look."

"Kimbrin planetary intel is supposed to be working on flushing MCR out, too," said Jaybles. "Not that there's any sense putting faith in them since half this planet wants the MCR to come out of the jungle, storm the offices of the government, and pull them out of the Republic for good."

"I'll take it one further," said Young, "and remind everyone that the full resources of the Republic were available at Psydon and the Doro *still* managed to keep the Legion guessing. This kind of foliage, plus the possibility of underground bunkers, and we basically got ourselves the same situation. Kimbrin satellites are running tech that's probably about on par with Republic Navy back on Psydon, and those couldn't sweep deep enough to make out what was happening between the trees."

Masters raised his hand. "All those in favor of sneaking out in the middle of the night and letting the Kimbrin sort this out?" When he saw that his was the only hand up, he quickly put it down and added, "Good. I was just testing you for loyalty. Ever since all the points got pushed out there haven't been enough loyalty tests. When I'm command sergeant major of the Legion I'll be sure to get them back in."

"When you're command sergeant major of the Legion, Oba help us," countered Jaybles.

"Basically the same thing," said Masters. "These abs are already godlike. The real issue here is that we've got to figure out something or we're all going to be taking multi-day hikes into the bush like Team Eight. Given how fast the MCR has shown itself capable of moving out there, I'm not sure we can trust whatever intel we gather to stay fresh for long."

"I was never in Dark Ops—" Jaybles began.

Masters cut in. "Because you're weak."

Jaybles sighed and glared at the man for a moment before continuing. "But I've been around enough to know that if we were a fully outfitted kill team somebody would be more than happy to take us on a HALO jump. That an option?"

"We'd have to hire a private freighter just to get into orbit," said Masters. "Not to mention you guys would need some additional equipment to, you know, not die on the way down."

"And you wouldn't?" asked Jaybles.

"Of course not. I can hold my breath for a long time, guys."

"I hate to say it," said Young, "but I think that's the kind of tactic that's needed. SLICs worked while things were still heating up. Now they've gotten hot and we're still trying to make the SLICs work. They don't work."

"What if we drop some flyers over the landing zone and tell the MCR that we're totally *not* going to show up there at oh three hundred the next day?" Masters offered. "But see, then they think we can't be possibly dumb enough to tell them the exact time and place we'll show up, and then when we *do* show up just like we said we would, they're not there because they don't think we're that dumb. Unless they *know* we know they would think we weren't that dumb, in which case they would be there—which is a possibility, guys, I'll be honest."

"Or," said Jaybles. "We tell them when and where we're coming, and we fly over the LZ but we don't land, we just throw Masters out of the SLIC and the MCR can keep him."

Masters nodded agreeably as if the plan was his own. "Oh, that's a good plan. Yeah, once I'm inside I can pretty much bring them down completely. Okay, let's do it. Let me just get some extra charge packs first. Oh, and Jaybles, I'll need a pic of your sister. If I'm captured, I'll tell them if they kill me, she's coming for them. The thought of her ugly face showing up is enough to make anyone turn tail and run."

"I think this is actually a good idea," said Young.

"What, threaten them with Jaybles's sister?" asked Masters. "Come on, you've seen her. That's a war crime."

Just as Jaybles rose up from his cot in defense of his sibling, Young spoke up. "No. Not that part. That's... that's stupid. Even for you guys. I mean inserting a single man, Masters. All by himself."

"So you want to push me out of the SLIC? I mean, I'll do it, but since we don't have any repulsor belts in this underfunded operation I'm going to need the pilot to fly very close to the ground. Write that down, Young, it's important: very close to the ground."

"I'm serious," Young said. "It's actually just like that screenplay you keep reading us. The one you're writing."

Masters rubbed his palms together. "Okay, I like where this is going."

"In your script, the legionnaire is the first man off a shuttle, and then the shuttle has to take off without him."

"Well, technically a crazy-hot basic supply chick falls off because she's not properly fastened, and I—I mean, the *character* jumps off to save her at the last second while everyone else has to get away under heavy fire."

"Kind of a convoluted setup," grunted Jaybles. "I mean, why isn't the supply chick fastened in?"

"Too top-heavy for the restraints," Masters quipped.

"That's what we need to do," said Young, who seemed not to have heard this latest exchange. "We find someplace nice and dark to insert. If no one opens fire, great—we just overcame what's been jamming us all this time and the full team can get on mission. But if we end up taking fire, then one of us gets off and goes to ground. With our armor in the darkness, we should be able to E&E no problem out there."

"Sounds suicidal," said Masters. "But that's just a minor quibble. I'm with you so far. What do the other guys do?"

"Fly another kilometer or two and try to put down again. We all get off if we can. If not, we repeat the process. Leave one leej on the ground but make it look like we're performing another hasty retreat."

"You're crazy," said Jaybles. "But you're right—we've had so many SLICs try to put down and then get chased off that by now it probably seems like a regular thing to the MCR."

"Exactly." Young snapped his fingers. "We've got L-comm, so once we're in the AO, linking up should be no problem. Move under cover of darkness, and do some real ground-level work to get an idea of exactly what's going on in the Magic Kingdom."

"Two questions," said Masters. "First, and least important, how are you going to convince Captain Hurn to go along with this?"

"Oh, that's easy. We just won't tell him."

"Good plan, I like it. Second, and this is a really important question, is there actually a basic back at Fort Blake hot enough to play the love interest? Because that's crucial to the entire plot of the holofilm."

"You've got leave tomorrow," Young said. "If you want to sneak back into Fort Blake to find out, you're more than welcome. The colonel is probably over losing his sled by now." He smiled. "But I wouldn't count on it."

23

"Do you know what I don't get?" Masters said over L-comm as the old SLIC shook and shuddered against gravity. "There are parts of Kima that are really nice. Like tourist nice. Beaches with a nice temperate climate. Plenty of attractive species in bathing suits. Ankalor is the same way. Kublar had the Soob, which is pretty much like a resort town—just, you know, dirty."

"You got a point in all this?" asked Jaybles.

"I do have a point, yes. I just wanted to establish that many of the planetary hellholes we legionnaires have fought on actually have some nice environments."

"Duly noted. Still not sure what your point is, but duly noted."

"That's because I haven't made my point yet. Keep up." Masters paused before continuing. "Kima is a charge pack waiting to overload. Kublar was the same way. Same with Psydon, Gestor, and a bunch of other worlds. But where does the fighting happen? In the poorest, most miserable spot on the entire planet. You got an arid world? Legionnaires are gonna have to go into the hottest kelhorned desert on planet to clear out whatever is going on. Got a real prime, type-one world with multiple climate zones? Maybe with a humid, equatorial belt? Pick the hottest, nastiest, stinkiest swath of real estate, overloaded with poisonous plants and animals, and *that's* the spot where you gotta fight."

"You're saying you don't like jungles."

"Jungles are fine. I've had some very memorable hikes with some very memorable ladies through jungles that wound past blue lagoons and ended with the kind of nights you still dream about for years. But *these* jungles... what's to like? I haven't seen a single lagoon. And the most attractive thing out here—aside from me—is probably Bord."

Hearing this, the Yawd give a big smile and delivered a thumbs-up. "KTF, Leej!"

Masters gave a thumbs-up back. "You know it, sexy." He leaned back in his jump seat. "What I'm saying is, maybe the only reason these kelhorns are fighting is because of how miserable their daily lives are.

You gotta look at it from their perspective. They know they're never getting off this planet. They lost the genetic lottery. Could've been born on Pthalos. Instead they're born on Kima which isn't necessarily bad as we've established, but *where* on Kima are they born? The only place on the whole planet that actively seeks to decompose every body opening you have while you're still breathing. What kind of life is that? I'll answer my own question: it's no kind of life at all. And so what do they do? The only logical thing. They find a way to get the Legion mad enough at them to come in and kill them so they don't have to deal with this sket any longer." Masters laced his fingers behind his head, satisfied. "In fact, I think that sums up every major battle the Legion's ever faced."

"The Savage Wars?" prompted Jaybles.

"Historians agree that the insides of those lighthuggers were disgusting."

"Psydon," said Young, joining in the game.

"Possibly a worse jungle than this, and by that point in the evolutionary cycle every dog had peed on every tree. There was nothing left to explore."

"How about Utopion?" said Jaybles. "Shining star of the Republic."

"Run and populated by absolute sket. Did you see how they dressed? They got to a point where the House of Reason had no choice but to kick its own ass."

"The Cybar," said Young, crossing his arms and leaning back triumphantly.

"Dumb paint job. They had to delete themselves because of it. It was the only logical conclusion." Masters clapped his hands. "You guys know I'm right, which is why you're not bringing up the zhee. They're so miserable that they'd rather blow *themselves* up than deal with all their issues."

Young looked to Jaybles. "I hate to say it, but he has a point."

"Maybe. But what are you gonna do with it?"

Young looked at Masters. "We've decided you have a point. What are you gonna do with it?"

"Well as you know, I'm close personal friends with Legion Commander Chhun."

"*Former* Legion Commander Chhun," corrected Young.

"Oh, I thought it stayed, like an honorific."

"Nope."

"Okay, well anyway. I don't have contacts, but *he* has contacts. And so the first thing we need to convey—and this is settled science—is that to fix all these problems it's a simple matter of taking people out of miserable places like this jungle and moving them into more comfortable climates. If you're not hot and bothered you're not gonna fight. When's the last time someone had to call in the Legion on a place like Teema?"

"Sounds expensive," said Young. "Plus we saw how that worked with the donks."

"That's a good point. Well, the second option is free, and before the SLIC takes off I think we should go ahead and put it into action. Save us all a lot of trouble."

"What's the second option?" asked Jaybles.

"We let them have it."

Masters gave a megawatt smile even as the SLIC pilots climbed into the cockpit, the inspection over.

"Guys, mission scrubbed!" Masters called to the featherheads. "We've decided to just let the MCR have this nasty-ass jungle."

If the pilots heard, they made no indication, and were soon spooling up the repulsors and getting the SLIC ready to fly.

"This our home," said Bord. "Why give to MCR? That is the sket."

"Our Yawd friend makes another good point," said Young. "I think I'm going to have to go with him. Nothing left to do but take the flight and KTF."

Young stepped aboard the SLIC, followed by Bord and his expanded team of nine Yawds—the extra troops along in the event that one of the legionnaires *was* discovered and they needed more than the usual firepower to help pull them out shortly after dropping them off.

Masters was left outside the bird by himself. "You can buy a new home!" he shouted above the repulsors' howls. "The property value on Ankalor is really low right now!"

Unanswered, he lowered his head and ran to get on board.

The SLIC took fire while it was still over the yellow zones, making for the occupied haven of the MCR. Given the way things were going, it didn't really matter where they set down—each spot seemed just as likely as the next to be swarming with the rebellion. But then, that was the point. They were operating in the enemy's backyard. And even before things had gotten as difficult as they now were, it would've been considered unusual for them not to run into someone while in the bush.

Since it was Masters's plan, in a way, he would be the first man off. A thing that didn't bother him in the slightest. He had survived beneath a pile of bodies while roving Cybar had disrupted Kill Team Victory's mission to nab a House of Reason politician. He had evaded and fought his way off Kublar, one of the few legionnaires from Victory Company to do so. And there had been dozens of other tight scraps along the way. Yet, for all his bravado, he didn't think of himself as invincible; he merely trusted in his ability to stay hidden when needed, to KTF when possible, and to stay alive above all else.

Assuming they met resistance upon landing, after dropping Masters the SLIC would push northeast. If they were again unable to disembark the entire squad, Jaybles would be the next to insert. The plan ultimately allowed for up to three separate drops that would put each legionnaire in the AO, forming the points of a triangle. And while the best-case scenario was an uncontested site where the Yawds could disembark as well, the feeling was that for a surveillance mission three leejes such as themselves could get the job done. They might have to.

The SLIC flew low, skimming the treetops in near-total darkness. The weather cooperated that night, the clouds remaining on their courses, blocking out the vibrant bright moon of Kima. The darkness was all-consuming, and if not for the loud hum of the old repulsor engines on the SLIC, they likely wouldn't have been noticed. But almost as soon as they entered the LZ, steady bursts of repeating blaster fire rushed up from the dark jungle to meet them. The flashes of light gave the sagging broad green leaves a pink or red reflective glow depending on how close they were to the source of the shot.

SLICs were tough everywhere except its windows. It was said that a pilot was more likely to die getting shot through one of the canopy windows than they were in a fiery crash. Still, it took a lot to bring one of the old birds down. Which was a good thing, for as the pilot, relying on a helmet equipped with night vision, brought the ship down for landing, she drew additional blaster fire from the jungle until it seemed that bolts were coming from all directions, though in reality they came from just one. They had set down on yet another skirmish line or outpost.

Masters identified at least one light repeating blaster plus about ten blaster rifles denting up the hull. Assuming that was all available fire, it represented a small enough group that if the team disembarked together, they could probably kill the bastards and begin operations. But whatever nearby troop concentrations existed would surely come and push them out once they reached the AO. Team Seven had played that game enough times to know how it turned out. Kill some MCR, kill more, better-trained and disciplined MCR, escape by the edge of your drive, and hope there were enough skinpacks back at camp to keep from adding too many scars or infections for your trouble.

That was all fine and good if your objective was something as simple as culling the herd of MCR-sympathetic Kimbrin. But had the Republic and the local government actually wanted that, they would just organize bombing campaigns to flush the mountain-dwellers out—and things hadn't escalated that far in the nascent civil war. The ruling government with its tenuous coalition—its fifty-one percent—was cautious about any major show of force. Most thinkers on the issue of Kima believed that whichever side showed direct military aggression first would be the one to lose public favor. Until then, unofficial skirmishes would be all that the ruling government, and whoever was running the MCR, would allow.

So the plan was still on. There was contact and Masters was still getting off. The pilot of the SLIC had done an excellent job exposing whatever shine had been on his craft's armored hull, now increasingly dented and scorched by blaster fire, to discover where the enemy was and wasn't. Or at least where they were and weren't shooting from.

What came next was simple enough. The pilot would do her best to bring the SLIC down despite the fire, tentatively hovering as if to unload the team and then just as quickly thinking better of it and taking off. That left Masters a very small window in which to jump out of the rear access hatch. The main door wouldn't be opened at all, so as not to alert any watchful MCR to the possibility that someone might have fallen out, if not jumped out.

Masters watched as the ground loomed closer. His bucket was on and his kit was tied down to avoid making noise. The craft flared between two wide, vine-covered trees. It hovered and dipped its tail just as planned, the indication that this was as low as it would get. Masters hesitated at the door.

"Jump if you're gonna!" said Jaybles over L-comm.

But Masters didn't jump. At least not right away. He waited until the SLIC begin to take on altitude, the pilot getting out of the fire with a quickness that suggested she wasn't just pretending to pull out—she really was getting away from a pounding. Before Young or Jaybles could even entertain the idea that the mission was scrubbed after the lead operator thought better of it, Masters leapt. The SLIC had risen near the tops of the trees, and he threw himself toward the nearest one and crashed into its branches, tangling his arms on its thick vines and hugging its trunk with his knees. He found a good hold and then quickly shifted himself into a dark and recessed nook of the leafy branches as incidental blaster fire zipped nearby—final shots sent by the MCR at the departing SLIC.

A colorful bird with a deep purple beak, thick enough to look as though it could bust open Masters's helmet and the skull inside, but probably meant for breaking open the large seed pods that hung from the tree, squawked in annoyance at this sudden intrusion.

"I'm not crazy about being here either," Masters said inside his bucket.

The bird tilted its head and then flew off into the night sky, abandoning an empty nest.

"Masters, you good?" asked Young over L-comm.

"I'm good. Some of the local wildlife is a bit pissed about me gentrifying their neighborhood."

"I'd be pissed too if you moved next door," said Jaybles. "We've taken on sufficient altitude and are circling. Wanna make sure you're clear before we move on to the next LZ."

"Roger. Observing."

Masters looked down from his perch at the MCR some thirty meters below. Their voices could be heard echoing up from the jungle floor. Excited conversation, triumphant in their having repelled yet another of the "traitorous" ships and their "Legion lapdogs." Now they were searching for anything or anyone who might have fallen or otherwise slipped out. Which was smart, and which Masters had suspected they would do.

The original plan had been to jump out at the lowest point, take cover, and rely on his armor's mimetic camouflage and other surprises to stay undetected, with Young and the others up above waiting to come back down and pull him out if the MCR found him anyway. But once he'd gotten a clear look at his zone, he'd realized that there was no suitable place to hide at ground level. Even the trees, wide and round at their base, were surrounded by no underbrush to crawl into and sneak away. The whole area was surprisingly open and clear, whether that was naturally occurring or just good planning by the small group of MCR set to watch this sector.

But he did see how tall and sturdy the trees themselves were. It wasn't difficult to jump out to them; hanging on was the only hard part, and he'd managed that well. He'd lost some weight while on Kima thanks both to the near-constant operations and the suboptimal chow, but he was still in Legion shape—just a bit more wiry than he was accustomed to. Then again, his abs had never looked better.

One of the MCR pulled out a TT sensor bot from a pouch on his belt. Just a three-centimeter sphere, the bot hovered on micro-repulsors and passed through the area, buzzing up and down, looking to identify any tech or lifeforms that looked out of place. Masters wasn't worried; his perch was at least ten meters above the bot's zenith, his armor and weapons were all shielded against such devices, and unless something had happened since he last checked his armor seal, the device wouldn't be able to pick up his biosignature.

Judging from the way the MCR technician operating the bot examined his rugged, dirty datapad and then shoved both it and the returning peeper to its pouch, they had no idea Masters was up there—and wouldn't, most likely, unless they climbed up the tree and sat down in his lap.

One of the Kimbrin made the official declaration that the site was clear and secure. Everyone was accounted for. Nice work.

They might've wondered why the incoming SLIC hadn't employed its door gunner to inflict damage. Perhaps they were just too overjoyed that it hadn't to think on the ramifications. Masters and the others had argued with the door gunner about keeping the weapon quiet, not wanting the light of its blaster fire to accidentally illuminate them. The decision now seemed to be the right one as everything fell into place. He was in position, and the MCR gave no indication that they even suspected his presence in their midst.

Masters reported in his assessment and received back word that the SLIC was now on its way to the next LZ some five clicks to the northeast. He waited until the MCR beneath him went back to their own hides, satisfied that nothing had come into the area, and then he carefully examined his immediate surroundings.

Farther along the bough of the great tree where he hid, Masters could see more signs of life and habitation. Beyond the bird's nest was a sort of platform where two conjoined branches grew out in opposite directions, and on that platform was a mound of partially eaten berries brought there by some creature that had left its own great mounds—feces, long ropes of the stuff, studded with the big stony pits of the fruit. It looked fresh, and Masters figured that whatever had dropped it had probably taken off at around the same time as the bird.

"Nice to see other creatures in the galaxy share the same hygiene habits as Bear," Masters said to himself, then shimmied closer and piled the waste in his hand. He held his arm out over the edge of the branch and unceremoniously dumped the scat. It shook leaves before thumping onto the ground near the base of the tree.

The noise at once drew the attention of some of the MCR. They cautiously approached with rifles ready on high alert, flipped on ultrabeams, and shot them up into the branches. They were unable to spot Masters in the darkness and his armor. Another one of the mids searched lower and identified the fallen waste. He playfully slapped the man next to him and immediately took on the persona of resident brave guy, laughing about how spooked his buddies had been. Masters couldn't quite make out what was said, and his bucket provided him no translation, but he recognized guys giving each other a hard time for being afraid of whatever it was that had dropped its droppings down the base of the tree. After all, wasn't the jungle full of those creatures? Nothing to fear. Nothing to get nervous about.

The MCR again returned to their stations, and Masters knew that when he began his slow and careful climb down for real, they would be much less likely to investigate whatever slight noises he might accidentally make.

The jungle was full of those creatures.

24

The third drop, Young's, was uncontested. Masters heard the report over L-comm as Young disembarked with the full group of Yawds. That was fantastic news—the only way the insertion could have gone better would have been if they'd all been able to disembark with Masters at the first LZ.

Based on the MCR activity Masters and then Jaybles saw at their drops, the group estimated that Young must have slipped in between outposts. Not wanting to press their good luck and assuming there were incoming MCR from multiple directions, Young and the Yawds moved immediately toward the center of the triangle created by the three LZ points. Masters and Jaybles moved to link up with them.

The jungle was as loud as any other Masters had trekked through at night, its creatures emerging to hunt and move in the darkness away from the day's heat. His bucket kept him apprised of his surroundings, cutting through the shadows with perfect clarity, its sensors passively sweeping for anything that didn't belong—like MCR observation bots, counter sweeps, and other technological aids that would indicate soldiers in action. Search devices gave off a telltale signature, and though they could be dampened or reduced depending on how much you were willing to spend, Masters's kit was part of the Legion's bleeding edge, representative of then-Legion-Commander Chhun's directive to get the Legion into what he called "Savage readiness." If the Legion wasn't outfitted and equipped to take on an existential threat like the Savages, who would be?

Chhun's initiative received mixed support from the House of Liberty, whose treasury was already strained after the fallout from Article Nineteen. In the end only some of his requests were met, and the House of Liberty declared it would be up to the Legion to fund the rest. Some speculated it was this compromise that had led Chhun to step down as Legion commander. He seemed to recognize that a more politically experienced Legion commander might have succeeded in getting the funding the Legion needed—or at least, that was the rumor.

Certainly he hadn't mentioned it in his final farewell orders of the day. And Masters hadn't talked to him about it.

But Masters had benefited from the funding Chhun *did* manage to secure. And as was the case with many military technological innovations, Dark Ops was the testing ground. Its success or failure there would be the determining factor in whether production increased and the tech went standard for the Legion as a whole. Masters couldn't count the number of next-gen blaster rifles he'd tried out that had been touted as eventual replacements for the N-4 and N-6. The next big thing in warfare. Some of them had been nice, but nice for Dark Ops didn't necessarily translate into a frontline battle rifle suited for the entirety of the Legion. This enhanced bucket, on the other hand... Masters figured it probably would make the cut. That was, assuming funding could be secured for mass production.

Everything in the bucket had been upgraded and improved. The House of Reason's money-saving tongue toggles were gone, in favor of much more costly neurolinks—the kind that, thankfully, didn't require permanent implants. Sensors on the bucket rested snugly on the temples, and the result was that a legionnaire needed only think his commands and the bucket would obey. After getting used to it, Masters had found that this greatly increased the speed and variety of HUD tools he could use while actively in combat or on patrol. The night vision was optimized, too, so that a legionnaire no longer needed to manually cycle through different filters; the helmet's algorithms ran all its available visuals at once in the background and then presented whichever was most relevant. The upside of this was that Masters could see who or what was hiding in real-time, without having to determine whether infrared, thermal, density scanners, or a host of other tricks to "see" what was out there was optimal for the situation. The downside was that he had to trust that the system was working. More than once, even on this slow stalk through the jungle, he had felt sure that something was hidden and waiting for him—an ambush that he hadn't quite set eyes on—and yet his sensors said nothing was there. Old habits had him manually cycling through each visual overlay, which invariably confirmed what his bucket had first told him: there was nothing there. But at least the cycling went faster by neurolink than it would have with voice commands or tongue toggles.

Also missing from the new buckets was all of the bureaucratic baggage foisted on the Legion by the House of Reason. Dangerous pop-ups with "helpful" information were a thing of the past. Better still, the bucket monitored its wearer's stress levels in order to identify when the wearer was in combat, wounded, or otherwise engaged with a demanding task. It would use that knowledge to activate some prompts while suppressing irrelevant systems—like troop PT standards—but always in the form of a minimalist product that could easily be ignored or "thought away" without the need for a voice override.

All in all, it was a far better way to be a leej. Masters and Young were as thankful for it as Jaybles, with his regular Legion kit, was jealous of it.

And now Masters used those capabilities to place himself at the exact center of the triangle. When he was set up in the appointed rendezvous, he pinged Young and Jaybles over L-comm to let them know he was waiting.

The jungle didn't stop moving as he lay down, superbly concealed in a hollow filled with underbrush that rose to hide the slight dip in elevation. A splintered stump rotted to one side, its long-dead trunk toppled over to provide a roof that served as additional cover. It was a good and defensible position—provided that any MCR were kind enough to only hit him from three directions at a time. Given how things had gone in the zone, that might be asking for too much. But as his HUD flashed its passive biosignature readings, it was clear that nothing bigger than a spinnarminx was moving within a thirty-meter radius.

That changed when Jaybles reach the spot, though his report over L-comm preceded his showing up on the sensor sweeps.

"I'm not late to the party, am I?" Jaybles asked as he set up nearby, covering Masters's six and protecting him at least somewhat from any attack that came on all four sides at once.

"As long as you're still alive, reinforcements are always right on time," Masters said, repeating the old Legion adage. "How did your insertion go? All you told me so far is that it was rough."

"It was basically like yours except I didn't have any trees to jump into. So I had to slink around like a Lahursian snake-man trying to avoid the MCR who were looking for me."

"They didn't find you."

"No. They got close, and I thought I might have to pick up my first knife kill in a while, but the guy moved on."

"Yeah, knife kills are overrated. Get your armor all sticky."

They waited another twenty minutes before Masters's HUD gave him an urgent, but still unobtrusive, biosensor warning from its passive scan. Humanoid-sized objects were moving into the area. Masters brought up the topographical map and saw four such targets, represented by orange dots, moving in their direction, spread out evenly and staggered with two ahead and two behind. Masters pinged Jaybles over L-comm, sharing the targeting information with his fellow legionnaire's HUD. The dots would now show up as blips on Jaybles's HUD as well, albeit only where the enemy was last seen. His algorithm would do its best to project movement from there, but Masters would have to send additional bursts for Jaybles to remain fully updated.

"Here we go," Jaybles said, sounding eager despite the fact that getting into a firefight here would necessarily scrub the mission. Not to mention potentially cost them their lives.

Masters reminded him of that fact and then checked in with Young. "Hey, if you guys are close I need to know about it. Got four guys coming right for our hide."

"That's us. Do not fire," said Young.

"Yawds up front?" asked Masters.

"Affirmative. I told Bord to hold up fifty meters outside your position and wait for me to arrive."

"Either these buckets are working better than advertised or Bord needs to get some more practice visualizing distances. How far back are you?"

"About two clicks. One of the Yawds twisted his ankle real bad a little after we got going. SLIC took off just as fast as she could even though she wasn't taking fire and wouldn't swing back around to pick him up. I've pretty much been carrying him this whole way."

Masters suppressed a groan. But it was what it was, and there was no changing it. And of course any one of them would do the same if they were in Young's shoes. The Yawds were loyal allies and wouldn't be left to fend for themselves. The Legion didn't leave its friends like that. Still, having to carry a man was hardly ideal. Perhaps the injury wasn't that bad and would heal up over time, and the Yawd would be able to walk under his own power. If nothing else, Jaybles could take a look at it once they arrived and see if there was any recuperative voodoo he could do with his med kit.

"Copy that," Masters said. "Better get here soon or all the beer will be gone. I'll go get the Yawds. Out."

Masters crawled out from beneath his hide, kept crawling toward the Yawds, and through his bucket he transmitted a preselected native bird call, giving three notes that the Yawds were supposed to recognize as friendly. The Yawds stiffened, and then one of them gave a one-bar reply, just a single note repeated four times. That meant there were four of them and that they weren't aware of any pursuers or MCR eyes in the area. Masters repeated their call exactly, meaning acknowledged.

He rose up from his belly onto one knee and dropped his mimetic camo, making himself easier to see. After a moment the four Yawds spotted him and slowly moved to his position. Masters pointed out where he wanted them set up. Then he went back to his hide to wait for Young and the others.

Yo-Yo, the Yawd who'd injured his ankle, was given some pain blockers almost as soon as Young carried him into the rendezvous point. The Yawd then powered through the ensuing hike. Jaybles had made it clear that though Yo-Yo wouldn't feel it through the pain blockers, he *would* be doing considerable damage that would need to be undone once they returned to Outpost Ten. The Yawd accepted this in stride, just happy to be moving under his own power and no longer slowing the team down.

The small group moved with heightened caution through the underbrush, not wanting any of the other Yawds to suffer injury from the many tangles of vines and other obstacles that surrounded them. The Yawds were as fleet-footed and capable navigators of the jungle as could be found on Kima, but the jungle was a dangerous place even were it not MCR territory. As it was, that made it more dangerous still.

Masters had seen enough just through this insertion to believe that the MCR had established a major force in the region. This wasn't some military commune full of people who wanted the government out of their lives. They were entrenched, organized, well-armed, and well-concealed. Which told Masters they were all out here for a purpose—and he couldn't think of any purpose beyond readying themselves for an eventual attack.

Young agreed. "Enjoy these halcyon days while they last," he'd told his fellow team members while they were grousing about the tight confines of the Kimbrin air force base where they'd taken off in their SLIC.

"Because it's only a matter of time before civil war does break out. And when that happens, one of two things is going to follow by my reckoning. Either the Republic decides to get the Legion involved and we get pulled out or serve in an advisory role for fresh leejes—I call that Scenario A. Scenario B is where the Republic doesn't have the stomach for another war after everything she's gone through and we're left to watch these two sides attempt to wipe one another out. Either way, it's the end of an era. Specifically, ours."

"Sure, if you call a never-ending stream of bare-bones kill team missions an era," said Masters. "Actually, if anything, these past few months have felt like the good old days when the House of Reason was sending the Legion to smack down every other planet at galaxy's edge."

"Good old days," snorted Jaybles.

"Well they seemed like it at the time."

As they began to climb the mountain known as M1, Masters turned that conversation over in his head. He believed Young had the right of it, and that the two scenarios he'd listed constituted what was most likely to happen. He also thought over what Jaybles had said. The man had been a participant in the usual Legion grind of those days, same as Masters—stationed on a Republic destroyer and jumping from one edge world to the next, seeing varying degrees of combat or counter-insurgency before whatever threat they faced was deemed neutralized and it was back on the shuttle, back on the ship, and off to the next world. It got so redundant and so predictable, that the really bad worlds where the Legion set up a garrison felt like a break. At least there you could stay a while.

And what was it all for? What had Kima been for so far? They'd killed hundreds, if not thousands of MCR through the combination of missions and the occasional well-placed artillery strike. But the threat grew all the same, and the same fight that had been brewing when the teams first arrived on planet—even before Masters showed up—was going to happen anyway. So a part of Masters wondered: *What the hell?*

Kublar had been the same way. The 131st got sent there to fight in support of the planetary government. Got blindsided by deep state operatives playing their hologames with very human game pieces, then got ambushed by an MCR seeking to exploit a tribal imbalance that the Republic had only exacerbated. Some of Masters's brothers had fought all the way to the final seconds of their lives, standing their ground holding off that great surging wave of koobs and MCR allies while the *Mercutio* hammered their positions with orbital bombardment.

And then...? Then they pulled out as if none of it had ever happened. Pretended that all those leejes' lives didn't mean anything. Except they weren't pretending. To the galaxy, and to the Republic, those leejes weren't worth a damn. Their mission would never be completed, the war would never be won, because the politicians who'd sent the legionnaires out had never had any notion of what victory was even supposed to look like in the first place. They just liked the fighting. Liked the profits. Liked the sense of power. So Kublar gets its civil war and the Republic steps up and tips the scales and they get their second civil war, and everything that Masters and his buddies did, men like Clauderro, Kravetz, and Doc Quigs... it didn't matter. Like, not at all. At least that's how Masters felt as he turned these thoughts over in his head. If the *Chiasm* had never shown up in orbit over Kublar to deliver the 131st, would anything have changed?

And if the answer to that was no...

What reason was there to believe it would be different when they looked back on Kima ten years from now?

"The difference is you're here now and you got a job to do," Masters told himself. "So do it well. Forget nothing."

The stress of the climb began to catch up to Yo-Yo. He couldn't feel anything in his ankle, but that didn't mean it wasn't giving him problems. It had deteriorated to the point that he was struggling to get firm footholds on the steeper parts of the mountain. Eventually Masters and the other leejes took turns hoisting him onto their backs and completing the steep upward march with that much more weight on their shoulders. They were all leejes. They could handle it.

It still sucked.

And yet, in the way these things sometimes went, the slowdown likely saved their lives. Had the team been moving at its initial pace they would have crested a steep, vegetation-covered finger of the mountain and come out upon a wide, flat road that from the looks of it had been cut into the peak some time before. Along that road marched easily a full battalion of MCR regulars. There were no vehicles, nothing bigger than the personal-sized repulsor carts these troopers pushed before them, the same size as those used in grocery stores by the bots restocking shelves or loading orders to be delivered to a planet's residential towers. Only the food in this case was rations, and everything else was charge packs and other munitions.

Here was part of that army that everyone on Kima knew was holed up deep in the jungle. And Masters and the others were not twenty meters below them, hugging the steep incline, motionless beneath the leaves and other ground cover, those without armor enduring the painful bites of insects, all of them enduring the indignity of the soldiers high above them obliviously relieving themselves down the mountainside. The old saying was true: it all rolls downhill.

"If this isn't what we came to spot, I don't know what is," said Jaybles.

"You're right. They're using this mountain pass to move east to west," agreed Young. "This is the kind of thing the Kimbrin should've seen from orbit."

"Probably will tell us about it when we get back," said Masters.

To the west was Republic-friendly territory on this particular continent. If the MCR were staging in that direction, it didn't take an intel bot to piece together their purpose. But the team was here now, and in good position to do something about it. This mountain was easily in range of Repub artillery, as most things in the region were.

"From the sound of what's passing by up there, these guys are going to be moving through for a while," Young said. "We need to slip away and get the shell shockers the coordinates so they can blast the sket out of these guys."

"We need to get them blasting *now*," said Masters. "This is the thick of it. Maybe it keeps going, but maybe not. We've got them right now."

"Yeah," said Jaybles, "but we're kelhorned twenty meters away from them. I'm all for killing the mids, but I've really been trying this whole time not to die in the process."

"I'm not saying we get up close and watch the Unity Day celebration," said Masters. "Just that we call it in right now and then ask for a thirty-second head start once they're ready to start shooting."

"Hell of a risk," said Young.

"Not if you're fast. We're going downhill, and we can make as much noise as we want because ten seconds later, the first barrage is going to atomize these guys. We used to do this kind of stuff all the time."

Masters watched his fellow legionnaires who were clearly thinking the risky course of action through. He tried adding an additional incentive. "It'll be fu*uuu*un."

"I'm not looking to imitate whatever crazy tactics Masters and his kill teams are accustomed to," said Jaybles. "But I do know it was damn hard to get in this far, and I'd rather take these kelhorns out than have to run for safety and then *hope* there's still something left for the basics to hit."

"I'm gonna have to lie and tell them that we're safely out of range," Young said. "This is the RA we're talking about, not some insane-o Legion mobile artillery."

"When they ask to verify position, just tell them where we plan to be by the time the shelling stops," said Masters hopefully.

"We're all good on this?" Young asked.

Masters nodded enthusiastically. Jaybles less so. "Gotta be done."

Young looked to the Yawds. "Bord?"

"KTF these kelhorns."

"Calling it in," said Young. "You guys make sure the Yawds are ready to run."

"Technically I think most of them will be rolling, but point taken," said Masters.

Young argued his way into getting fire approval. There were no points to block his valid request, but old habits sometimes died hard, and it felt like the basic officers he was dealing with were still wired by default to refuse anything the Legion asked for. In the end they acquiesced, but only after he used his "Legion voice" to settle the matter once and for all.

"We've got fire support coming our way. Let's move. Fast as you can—go!"

Masters pushed his way down the hill, leading the Yawds and trying to make as little noise as possible while still moving at maximum speed. Voices from the road above sounded an alarm and soon blaster fire began to zip down the mountainside. They were just shooting at sounds, with no clear idea of what was there, and they were high. But still, if enough of them got to it the sheer volume of blaster fire would be enough to punch somebody's number.

The assault was cut blessedly short by the sudden whistle and impact of Repub Army artillery crashing among the soldiers on the road. The concussive blast threw men and body parts down the mountainside, many of them landing well ahead of Masters and his team. The close rumblings threatened to unfoot Masters and did toss some of the Yawds off their feet, causing them to stumble and roll down the steep terrain, desperately attempting to level out into a slide as their momentum sent them rag-dolling faster and faster.

That was just a problem they would have to deal with until they were safely out of range of any miscalculated shots. For now, they gladly allowed their momentum to take them downhill, and in so doing they felt a swing in a different kind of momentum. They were finally in a position to really put a hurting on the MCR.

25

The artillery barrage had ended by the time Masters and the others leveled out and regained control of their momentum. Jaybles performed a headcount and wellness check; everyone was accounted for and they had escaped with nothing worse than some tweaked joints and bruised muscles from the hasty descent. Miraculously all said they could keep going, even Yo-Yo, which might just be crucial given the abrupt stop to the shell shockers. They were in a position where the enemy wasn't nearly as dead as they wanted them to be and needed to get some separation.

Young worked L-comms trying to figure out what had happened. They had done a number on the MCR, he was sure of that, but the pounding needed to continue along the road as well as on either side to maximize the damage. His conversation was a short one before he reported grimly back to the others.

"Real problem," he said. "MCR has coordinated an attack on the army base. We've got some Kimbrin 'allies' who weren't so friendly working on the inside."

"You're kidding me," Jaybles spat.

"Wish I was."

Bord and the Yawds cursed the traitors, calling them a discredit to their species. But then, the non-Yawd Kimbrin were always suspect in the eyes of the remote tribe.

"What's it look like back at Outpost Ten?" asked Masters.

"No compromise," reported Young. "Yawds are still loyal. But everywhere else… this isn't an isolated incident, it's happening across the planet. Major intelligence failure. The war is underway."

"Can Ten set up extraction for us?" asked Jaybles.

"They're taking mortar fire and getting hit with rockets from the yellow zone. Not much they can do about it right now, but at least no one's pushing yet."

Bord gave his assessment. "Bastards know that now they taken out the artillery they can shoot rounds on us without any fear of KTF. Not enough of us in the outpost to go out and put a stop to it." The Yawd shook his head. "This bad."

"That's why I always preferred working from a destroyer instead of a fixed base," said Masters. "Really hard to get a mortar round into orbit. And it's a good bet that what we just nailed was probably heading toward our camp. They were just late."

"We need to get moving," said Young. "This is a full-blown campaign underway. We're talking coordinated assaults, this late battalion excluded, and some good old-fashioned dogfighting in the air. Everything that Kimbrins in the Republic have got, the MCR have too. Going to be a bumpy ride until the cavalry shows up."

"*If* they show up," said Jaybles darkly. "Scenario B is still an option."

"So what's the plan?" asked Masters. "Try to hump our way back to camp and help shore things up until the Legion arrives?"

Young looked around. "If we can find a way through these lines, I'm all for joining up with the unit. Otherwise our best bet is to stay back here and do whatever damage we can. If we're lucky, no one left alive knows we were out here calling in the artillery strike."

"Big offensive like this, it'll be easy for a team this small to get forgotten until we start causing trouble," Masters agreed. "The guys at Ten are the ones who are going to catch the nine hells."

"All right, let's get moving." Young brought up a topographical map and transmitted it to his fellow legionnaires' HUDs. "Let's move west along the base of the peak. That'll give us options if we see anyone or if anyone sees us. We can either spread out among the fingers or we can climb and try to find a good place to hide or hole up."

That sounded good to Jaybles and Masters. They passed the plan on to the Yawds and began to move. It wasn't long before a sense of just how banged up and hurting many of their Kimbrin allies were became clear. The going was rough and they wore expressions of pain with every jarring step.

Not long after that, angry voices drifted down from higher up the mountain. Bord came over to the legionnaires and translated what they already suspected.

"Artillery did not get all. They up there looking for us."

Young nodded his thanks, took a deep breath, and said, "We're gonna have to really move to stay ahead of whoever's looking."

The Yawds adjusted their rucks, their spine-encrusted features grim with determination. They all knew what pace would be required to keep ahead of the MCR. This march was about to move from difficult to downright hellish.

There were forty MCR pursuing Masters and his team members through the mountainous jungle. The last transmission from their observation bot had them only three kilometers behind the team. The terrain, while difficult, was not difficult enough for the experienced Yawds and capable legionnaires to increase their lead against the lightly equipped and fresh mid-core rebels. Sufficiently difficult terrain worked as an advantage to well-conditioned legionnaires—but it wasn't looking like that would be the case this time.

And there was so much that they didn't know. Their other long-range observation bots had been either discovered and neutralized by the MCR or had fallen prey to one of the numerous traps still set up in the jungle.

"This place is such a mess," said Masters. "How long has the MCR been setting themselves up here? We can't turn left or right without setting off a bot-popper or comms disruptor."

"Just be glad they didn't mine the place too," said Jaybles.

"Of course they didn't. Place is so thick with MCR they'd just blow themselves up."

With their pursuers hanging with them, a decision needed to be made about what to do next. It was clear that continuing on their current route wasn't going to win out in the long run. They could break for the low country, but that seemed just as likely to end with them being run down.

"I don't think making a getaway is in our future," said Young. "Best case now is to make a climb. If we ascend quickly enough we can try to find a suitable hide. Plenty of caves and nooks and crannies once we rise above the mist line."

"The way everybody's banged up," said Jaybles, "I'm not sure we can outclimb them."

"If all our options end up with these guys catching us," said Masters, "then we may as well set ourselves into the best defensive position we can. That means going up the mountain."

"I agree," said Young. "It's going to suck, but it's our best chance at survival. I'll go tell the Yawds now."

If the Yawds felt any dejection over the news—they were already in bad shape, and the climb would punish them particularly—they didn't show it. They simply listened and nodded with understanding.

Bord spoke to two of his men in the native Kimbrin dialect peculiar to this region that the MCR now occupied. The two men, both of whom were limping severely, barked an affirmative and then took off into the jungle, going the opposite direction from what had been agreed on.

"Where are they going?" asked Young.

"To make tracks," said Bord. "They cannot climb. But they can lead MCR away."

"Good way to get themselves killed," said Masters. But he knew what the men had been thinking. They wouldn't have been able to keep up on the climb. Necessity would have, at some point, forced them to stay behind and fight off any MCR who came upon them. Bad for them, and bad for the leejes, for if by some chance the team managed to slip their trackers, once the MCR found those two on the mountainside it would be a sure sign to keep pursuing. It was a brave thing the two Yawds were doing.

"This has always been known in every mission," said Bord. "We do not fight thinking we will never die." He pointed out in the distance. "There is a friendly village that they may reach and find sanctuary, if Oba decrees it."

Masters was reminded that despite Kima being populated by Kimbrin and not humans, it was still very much a mid-core world. And like all mid-core words, the influence of the Republic and its customs had ingrained itself in the culture over the course of many generations since first contact—even among a remote subpopulation such as the Yawds. He wondered what Republic missionary had once upon a time trekked out into the jungle to tell the story of Oba and the Republic's official dominant religion since the latter half of the Savage Wars. It was probably some bot programmed to do missionary work.

With the two Yawds vanished into the jungle—they'd moved with impressive speed given how much they'd been limping only moments before—Masters and the others carried on another three hundred meters before coming across a thin trail that would lead them up the mountainside. The climb was a struggle. When they weren't marching bent over up grueling inclines, their legs straining and screaming with each step, they were greeted by near-vertical stone formations that they had no choice but to scale, carefully trusting their lives to roots and vines where suitable handholds could not be found.

After ninety standard minutes of this, they paused on a flat shelf that lay beneath an overhang. The sun had been beating straight down on them, and the shade of the overhang was a welcome relief as they rested ungrateful muscles that groaned more now at rest than they while being worked to their limits.

"What's the word from Ten?" Jaybles asked.

"Still getting hit by mortar fire," answered Young. "Still no SLICs around to pick us up."

"Not even in five minutes?" asked Masters.

He and the others were too tired to laugh.

"Captain Hurns going to send some guys out and try to put a stop to it?" asked Masters. "We may not have combat sleds or MBTs, but you take enough transport sleds out and fill 'em with the teams and they should be able to mop up whoever's out there."

"I usually would agree," said Young, "but things are not well on the planet Kima. No contact with the Repub Army base whatsoever, so that's presumed fallen. Holonews channels are full of live coverage of fighting in the streets. This isn't a simple extraplanetary invasion sweeping across the continent. The MCR on Kima—they were already embedded and ready to go."

Jaybles angrily tossed a small pebble across the flat surface of the shelf, sending it skipping back into the recessed darkness. "Complete and total intelligence failure. How do you miss something this big?"

No one attempted to answer. But as far as Masters was concerned, intel failures were basically the norm. Maybe not usually this bad, but bad enough. And even when they got it right, most times the powers that be just did what they wanted anyway.

There had been no shortage of military and political catastrophes in his career with the Legion. Add in the disarray of the dominant galactic government falling twice in such a short time, and it really was little wonder that something like this could happen. It would take a long time for institutions to be rebuilt properly—so they functioned for the good of the galaxy's citizens as opposed to the good of the organizations themselves—and it would take even longer before Masters, or any Republic citizen with half a brain for that matter, trusted those institutions again.

"No blaster fire from down the mountain," Young observed. "Wonder if our Yawds managed to slip the trackers and make it to that town?"

"Kind of pulling for both outcomes, you know?" said Jaybles. "They slip away, good for them. If those trackers didn't follow them, well..."

There was no need to finish the sentence. They all knew what was in store for them if the MCR were able to pinpoint their location. Help was probably coming now that the war on Kima was reality, but it would be far too late for K-SOG-7 if they didn't succeed in disappearing into the jungle first.

They rested another five minutes before two of the Yawds began to whisper intensely with one another while peering down over the edge. Masters moved to see what the commotion was.

"Someone's climbing up," one Yawd explained in his Kimbrin-accented Standard.

Masters called over to Bord. "Could those be your guys deciding to take the climb with us after all?"

Bord shook his head emphatically. His men would do what they were instructed and knew better than to chase after a guerilla team that was already being pursued by hostile elements. "They are willing to die but do not want to make sure it happens."

"Had to check," said Masters. He looked down over the ledge, trusting his HUD to use its advanced optical systems to pick out anything hidden in the foliage.

The mountains of Kima were odd in that so much vegetation grew up and off the vines that dug into the rock. This provided excellent concealment, like pushing through leaves on a tree. In fact, climbing up the mountainside had reminded Masters of just that—childhood days climbing up and up along the heavy branches of the Roopa trees that grew on his home world. Simply disappearing in a sea of green leaves.

His helmet spotted them almost immediately, the HUD using thermal vision to pick out what were clearly bodies moving up the mountainside. Masters pinged the other legionnaires at once.

"If it's the Yawds, they brought friends. I count six humanoids climbing up about thirty meters below us."

"They caught up quick," said Young.

"Yeah, well in our defense it helps to have fingers and toes that aren't sprained, broken, or frozen in place." Masters looked back down. "How do you want to take care of these guys? I can drop some fraggers on them. That'll make a long climb end with a short fall."

Young nodded. "Let's do it. After the boom, we need to be up and climbing again. We'll follow the path on the shelf around to our east as far as we can go, and then keep climbing from there."

When everyone was ready and in position, Masters took two fraggers and calculated the distance between himself and the target. He set them both to burst directly over the climbers, who had scrambled up another five meters since first being identified. Letting loose one grenade from each hand, he stepped back, and a second later he heard the double boom as the fragmentation shrapnel ripped into the climbers and dislodged them from the mountainside.

Masters looked over the edge once more, expecting a blaster bolt to fly up in his direction, but no such return fire came. The area was free of any further thermal readings, and where the climbers had been was now a small cloud of smoke marking the point of detonation.

Team Seven moved quickly, Masters and one of the Yawds hanging back to watch the cliff's edge, their blaster rifles ready to pick off anyone who might still be climbing up. It was then that they heard the scream of repulsors. Some sort of fast attack craft raced high overhead, shaking the mountains with its powerful engines. And what followed was a familiar sound—one that filled Masters's heart with dread.

Bombs detonated in concussive succession... the sound surely coming from Outpost Ten.

26

They were nearing the peak and the last of the vertical climbs was behind Team Seven, but not without a price. The MCR scouts had chased Masters and his team the entire way, rotating men out to rest and sending fresh climbers and trackers ahead. These would eventually get close enough to cause an exchange of blaster fire, and while the better trained and disciplined K-SOG team had won every encounter, they had sustained casualties.

A brief stand had taken place amid a tenuous pile of boulders, likely a rockslide that had occurred recently enough to have not yet been overgrown by the insatiable jungle vegetation. The Yawds and legionnaires had excellent defensive positions and were able to keep the MCR scouts back. There was no threat of being overrun, but it soon became apparent that the scouts had no intention of taking the team down themselves. Holding them in that location was a bigger win with every second that passed.

"They're not pushing, they're just stalling," Masters had said. "Probably have a larger element moving up the mountainside to get on us. This place is fine for now, but there are too many angles of attack to try a last stand."

Jaybles and Young agreed. They decided Masters and two Yawds would hang back and provide cover while the main element withdrew and made the brief vertical climb that would lead them to a final shelf that could then be hiked to reach the peak.

It didn't take long for the scouts chasing K-SOG-7 to realize what was going on. The sight of the team climbing to reach the last leg of their torturous journey was enough to get them out in the open and exposing themselves to fire in an attempt to stop the Yawds and legionnaires from getting a move on once again.

Masters fired his N-4X—a new generation of the mainstay blaster rifle that boasted superior charge cycling and power. The mid-core rebels fell on the exposed rocks and then fled behind cover to escape the legionnaire's deadly accurate fire. Others kept coming, and the sense of urgency by the MCR pursuers was palpable. They began to yell for reinforcements to come up and assist— probably men who had been allowed a break after so doggedly hunting the team down. Masters and the Yawds opened fire on these as they advanced up to the engaging MCR force, dropping several. There were too many of them though, and over half reached the cover of the rocks beneath them, safe from harm.

One of the Yawds unclipped a grenade from his belt. Masters saw right away that it was an incendiary. He pointed out an opening in the rocks that, if the Yawd could hit it, would provide the double advantage of sending ultra-hot plumes of chemical fire—capable of burning out an impervisteel-hulled combat sled—down over the rocks and onto a small grouping of MCR while also staying in a gap that the others would have to attempt to leap or go around when trying to pursue.

The Yawd had just stood to throw, exposing himself as little as possible, when one of those little bad-luck quirks of warfare took place and a blaster bolt struck him in the shoulder, causing him to drop the incendiary at his feet. He bent down and scrambled to pick the grenade up again and then screamed as the device detonated. His cry was muted by the sudden billowing heat that pulsed out from the explosive like a sudden lava burst. The Yawd's buddy was splashed across the neck and shoulder and rose to his feet in agony. He was quickly shot down by the MCR below. It was a mercy killing.

With two thirds of the defenders so abruptly removed from the fight, the MCR decided to push on Masters's position. He fired as quickly as he could, dropping the Kimbrin MCR with single shots from his blaster rifle, not bothering to see if the first shot had killed its target, a trigger pull, a bolt to the head, and then on to the next trooper coming his way. The last guy might not be dead, but the next guy was definitely alive.

"Yawds are down," Masters reported calmly to the others. "MCR is pushing on my position. I think I can hold them off for a little longer."

This wasn't how Masters would have chosen to die, but as he kept firing he really couldn't think of a better way. If the choice was him staying to fight off the MCR so the others could get away, then that was just how it would have to all go down. He wouldn't change it. Not if it meant that the others wouldn't make it.

"Bord and I are almost at the top of the ledge," said Young. "Hang in there and then fall back once you hear us covering."

The MCR pushed on, and for every soldier that Masters left dead upon one of the boulders, it seemed that two more advanced one rock closer to his position. The nearest guy was now only fifteen meters away, behind a great slab of stone that looked like a monolithic dining table standing on end. Masters still had one fragger left but decided to save it. That rock was likely where all the others would take cover as well, if they were able to make it that far. If he had only one more toss left in his arm, he wanted to make as many MCR pay for it as possible.

A blaster bolt skipped off the boulder Masters used for cover, sending shards of stone into his face, scratching his bucket and causing him to involuntarily flinch back. He turned back into the fight and saw that several more MCR were coming. One he shot in the neck. Another in the heart, which was good. A third in the head, which was better. Two more slipped behind the rocks or jumped down between large boulders to escape the legionnaire's wrath.

"Okay, you're good!" Young shouted. "Covering fire! Go!"

Sustained fire from the blaster rifles above and to Masters's right began to rain down, causing the newly exposed MCR to reconsider their choice of cover. Masters fastened his battle rifle to its magnetic carrier on his chest, turned, and ran for the final vertical climb. He saw that the others were at least two thirds of the way up, meaning that Young and Bord had really hauled ass to get to the top and bail him out. Bringing up the rear—aside from Masters—was Jaybles, who was likely serving as last man and watching to be sure the fatigued Yawds were able to finish this last desperate climb. And indeed one of them looked in danger of not doing so. The Kimbrin had his fingers and toes dug into footholds but was just staying in place, as though he didn't have the energy to climb any higher.

Jaybles climbed up to the Yawd until they were roughly side by side. "Come on! Keep climbing!"

The Yawd just shook his head. It was the first time Masters had seen one of them call it quits; they were unusually tough and resilient. But every man, and every Kimbrin, has that point where he just can't go on. For the best ones it's the point where their bodies completely and utterly fail them. After they've literally given all that they're physically capable of giving. For others it's when their brains shut down and decide that enough is enough. It doesn't matter that empty is still a long ways away. They've called for an end to the suffering. Even if it means failure. Even if it means death.

The Legion had weeded out the men who quit on their bodies before their bodies quit on them. The Yawds weren't legionnaires. They had done a great service to K-SOG and the legionnaires they served with, but for this one Kimbrin at least, a limit had been reached, and no matter how much Jaybles tugged or cajoled the man, nothing short of hoisting him over one shoulder and power-climbing to the top was going to get him moving.

Masters was just four meters below the scene when Young advised that the MCR was advancing again. The blaster fire came next. One of the Yawds at the top was struck and fell all the way down past Masters to hit the bottom with a sick thud that told everyone who heard it that if he wasn't dead he wasn't good either. Masters looked down. The guy was bent and twisted. He looked dead. Masters kept climbing.

Another volley took care of the Kimbrin who had been frozen in fear. A round struck him in the small of the back, and a second round got his heel. He fell off limply, dragging his face and hands against the sheer rock before smacking against it on the way down.

Everyone was climbing as fast as they could now. The Yawds who'd reached the top were sucking in heaving lungfuls of air as they dropped to their stomachs and added their blaster rifles to the covering fire provided by Young and Bord. Masters was about to catch up to Jaybles when the legionnaire was struck in the back of the knee by a blaster bolt. For a moment he looked as though he was going to fall off, his body half-twisting, just his left hand and foot keeping their hold on the mountain. But then he pulled himself back in and resumed his climb, his wounded leg hanging as though dead while he pulled himself up with his three remaining limbs.

Masters easily passed the legionnaire on the way up. He likely would have done so even without the injury; Masters's status as the top-conditioned leej was still with him in this new unit. If there were a way for him to get Jaybles up faster he would have done so, but the smaller legionnaire was himself in superb condition, and his three-legged climb outpaced what Masters would have been able to manage by having the man grab hold of his neck and carrying both of their weights. What would help Jaybles the most now was reaching the top and adding another weapon to the defense. Better yet, another accurate weapon. The Yawds were shooting as inaccurately as Masters had ever seen them, their usual precision hampered by their ragged breathing and the dire consequences of the battle should they lose.

The second Masters reached the top, he pulled his blaster rifle out. The MCR were moving like a wave of ants over the boulder-strewn terrain below. He added his fire to the mix, making sure that every shot was fatal, wanting only that Jaybles joined them at the top so they could all face down what came next together.

Still, the urge to comment on what he'd seen upon reaching this high point before the peak was too much to resist.

"You see it?" Masters asked Young over L-comm.

"Yeah," was the only reply. And then the men went back to shooting while Jaybles reached the top and was pulled up over the edge by one of the Yawds.

The MCR fell but kept pushing. The scouts smelled blood and were intent on having it. Farther down, the glimpses of what had to be a company of MCR regulars could be seen sneaking around the trails, taking switchback after switchback in a slow and difficult climb that, while longer, wouldn't require any vertical attempts. The MCR scouts could be at the team's level in minutes; the regulars in hours.

And off in the distance, in a view afforded by the great peak that looked down upon the jungle valleys and the high points beyond, was Outpost Ten, which burned with intense fires that shot up great clouds of black smoke. The place where Masters and the others had lived was nothing more than craters after the bombing run.

27

Special Operations Group Seven had just enough time to distribute charge packs and set up for their last stand when the MCR scouts began to appear near the peak. A heavy mist hung just beneath the top of the mountain, obscuring from the Yawds the advancing MCR until they broke through the fog. Masters and the other legionnaires were able to visually cut through the mist using their helmets and take well-aimed shots at the soldiers as they advanced, forcing them to quickly move from cover to cover and, because of their own lack of vision, sometimes exposing themselves to a clean shot by one legionnaire while hiding from another.

The peak the SOG team defended was really a small set of spires that rose at different heights, all competing to form the highest point of the mountain. There were four of these spires, standing up like fingers on a hand. The third from the left was the tallest, though it looked like there had once been a taller spike still at some point in time— a fifth spire that had toppled over and now lay precariously near the mountain's hand-like peak—a broken thumb. Several of the Yawds covered behind this broken spire, ready to fight to the last man, while Masters and Young moved quickly across the terrain searching for the best angles to engage targets and then shrouding themselves in the mist to avoid return fire. Jaybles fixed himself in the recess of the first spire, leaning against the rock and using it to keep him standing now that his leg was inoperable.

Masters would hunt for a target in the mist and then, upon acquiring it, open fire, dropping as many MCR scouts as he could. And when those taking fire moved to find cover that would protect them from Masters's blaster rifle, that tended to expose them to Young's fire and sometimes Jaybles's as well. The result was chaos as the MCR moved laterally to avoid getting hit.

The scouts' charges were repulsed four times. Only once had enough MCR been able to sufficiently emerge from the mists to be engaged by the Yawds, who quickly cut them down.

"How you doing on packs?" Masters asked.

"Good for now," said Young. "But I have the sinking suspicion we'll be out of charge packs well before we're out of targets."

"If it comes to that we can always start throwing rocks," Masters said, and then dropped an MCR scout who had tried to sneak up on the group by himself.

After that kill things went quiet. The MCR scouts who had pursued them through the jungle fell back, completely out of the legionnaires' sensors. Young asked Masters to stay in place and then moved to check on the Yawds and Jaybles. Charge packs were again redistributed as the legionnaires, who had done the bulk of the firing, divvied out what they could from the Yawds' stash. The amount on hand didn't bode well. They could still lay down substantial firepower, but it was hardly an infinite supply. And an infinite supply was what Masters felt like they would need.

Legionnaires didn't need to be told to make every shot count. Nor did their Yawd counterparts who, although they lacked the elite conditioning and armor of legionnaires, had learned to fight like leejes by virtue of having served alongside them for so long.

The real threat to them all was the slower-moving group of MCR regulars. Eventually they would mass at the top. If they had mortars they would use them, and there was little anyone could do about that aside from jumping off the back of the mountain into the harsh dead zone on the other side. For now, though, being on top of the mountain was working to the legionnaires' advantage. The only possible avenue to climb without customized personal repulsors was the route Team Seven had taken.

Then again, the MCR regulars weren't here yet, and perhaps they wouldn't be capable of humping mortar tubes, let alone mortar bots, this far up the mountain. There was still hope, albeit far too little for Masters's liking.

They would fight on regardless.

"Jaybles," Young said, checking on the wounded legionnaire in his craggy hide. "Tell me you got something from Outpost Ten or Fort Blake."

"Nothing but dead comms," said Jaybles grimly. "There might be something thin—a weak signal—I'm trying to get a fix on from deeper in but that's it. So far."

Young moved back to Masters, who was chatting with Bord while watching for more MCR. "Jaybles says no comm with Blake or Ten."

Masters nodded. "The lack of artillery tells you all you need to know. MCR took Blake, or at the very least they knocked out the guns. My credits are on them having taken the whole thing though. Otherwise we'd at least get RA comm traffic coming over their C-6."

"I hate to say it, but you're right," said Young.

"I'm always right." Masters surveyed the team before refocusing on the mists. Thank Oba they hadn't yet cleared. "Not feeling particularly happy about it right now, though."

"These guys pulled a number on the Kimbrin government. Ten is over there burning, Blake is offline... there aren't even any damned planetary-wide comm bursts telling everybody to stay calm." Young looked to Bord. "You guys get planet-wide communications out here?"

"Sometimes here, yeah. Sometimes they send in Kimbrin from the cities tell us. But they know, what they do doesn't matter to the Yawds. We live our life."

"Happen to know a way we can slip off this peak, Bord?" Young asked.

The slight Kimbrin gave a bleak smile and tilted his head toward the back of the peak before pointing his finger straight down.

"Yeah, that's what I was afraid of."

Masters shrugged. "At least the MCR haven't figured out how to take control of the planet-wide comms yet. If we had to deal with nonstop mid propaganda I'd jump off the side of the cliff voluntarily. That stuff is brutal."

Young clapped the legionnaire on his shoulder armor. "How good are you at flapping your wings?"

"Not as good as my gums," Masters called as his fellow leej departed.

The respite lasted another twenty minutes, and Young was just about to suggest he sneak down into the mist to try and ascertain troop locations when a series of shrill whistles sounded below. Unable to rely on comms for fear of Republic interception and decryption, the MCR units had resorted to more ancient forms of battlefield communication, in this case the use of whistles to coordinate troop movements. And that wasn't something that the scouts, in their small numbers, would need to effectively pass on orders. Which could only mean that the MCR regulars had arrived—and would now seek to push the team by force from the top of the mountain.

"Okay, this is it," said Masters. "If they can soften us up first, they will. Watch for grenades. If they have mortars just hug the ground and ride it out. They'll stop firing before they charge. Everyone watch your sector and call out for help if you need it."

The mortars never fired but the grenades Masters had predicted began to thunk down on the rocks as they were thrown from below. It was clear they were being tossed blindly. Some fell short of the team and exploded harmlessly, albeit loudly, on the top of the mountain. Others rolled back and detonated below in the mist. Wherever Masters and the other legionnaires could see exposed MCR throwing the grenades, they dropped them. Bord picked up a lucky toss at his feet and hurled it back down below. By Masters's count, more grenades exploded on the downslope than did up top, and he could hear the groans of Kimbrin below suggesting that at least a few had rolled far enough down to blow off the hand that primed them.

The grenades stopped sailing through the air. A charge didn't come.

Masters suspected that the failure to soften them up had the dim-witted and overmatched officers below scratching their thorns and trying to think of what to do next. They tried the same trick one more time, slightly modifying things by shortening the fuses and causing the grenades to explode before they had a chance to roll back down the mountain. But this too was ineffective. Those throwing were keeping themselves as far away from Legion blaster fire as they could, which meant getting anything to land in the kill zone required one hell of a toss. Those with the arm strength to do it tended to have their grenades explode prior to reaching their destination. Those who didn't found their grenades rolling back on them before exploding, albeit no longer in their midst.

Another whistle sounded and the volley of hand grenades ceased once more. Two shrill tweets were followed by the unmistakable noise of people and equipment hurriedly moving into position. Nothing was said by Masters and his team. They all knew what was coming.

Finally, three sustained whistle blows sounded, followed by a flurry of shouts as the charge began. Silhouettes rushed up the hill through the mist, revealed in the legionnaires' all-seeing HUDs. Though the Legion helmets were linked with the N-4X blaster rifles to optimize targeting, that was hardly needed. The coming advance was thick enough that sending effective shots was simply a matter of not aiming too high or too low. There was no missing the mass of surging MCR.

The yells of the charge drowned out the blaster fire at first. But soon those shouts gave way to a quiet, desperate determination as the MCR advanced toward the pinnacle, exposing themselves to the Yawds and legionnaires alike, and falling in droves as the exhausted soldiers attempted to break through. Masters had been in situations such as this one before, and he knew it all came down to the will of the attackers. If they could stomach the losses, endure the pain of the climb, and keep coming, they would be able to take the peak.

That was easier said than done. It was one thing to know that your numbers provided sufficient force to roll over the enemy. But to put your head in the thick of battle, with comrades on your left and right falling and the realization that you won't reach the lines before you fall as well, to know that with certainty, amid the noise and percussive force of warfare, was another story. It took a high level of discipline—or fanaticism—for a trooper to continue on in the face of certain death so that the ultimate mission could be achieved.

Some of the MCR Masters had faced off against possessed that level of fanaticism. Almost none carried that level of discipline. The group charging had neither.

For a time the MCR moved as one, all the soldiers running headlong up the hill with the sense that they would reach the top together. But as the Yawds, augmented by the exceptionally lethal legionnaires, used their firing sectors to cover the small amount of real estate the MCR were funneled up and through to reach their foes, the charge quickly stalled. MCR fell, and their bodies rolled and tumbled down the slope, becoming additional obstacles to navigate for those still moving up from behind. And as the first wave fell down and back, the second wave was likewise hit by blaster fire—or simply had their legs taken out from beneath them as more and more men dropped and rolled.

Those who showed the physical and emotional strength to continue on ahead in the hopes of galvanizing their teammates and leading them to finish the charge were swiftly cut down by the legionnaires, who knew the psychological value of dropping, as swiftly as possible, those who would rally their teams. Whenever a Kimbrin would yell and wave his arm to encourage his fellows, that soldier was the next to die, so that all who might have taken their inspiration were immediately reminded of how desperate their situation now was.

The charge broke and then fell back, and those who had pressed the farthest ahead found themselves stranded and alone, the supporting fire quieted as the MCR ran and slid back down the slope, seeking to escape into the mist and to their staging area below. Some of those in close chose to keep attacking. Others turned and attempted an escape of their own. All of them met death.

The Yawds cheered at the retreat of their hated MCR foes. Young quickly moved to check on injuries. It had been a one-sided affair, and no one was any worse off from the assault—except for the drain on charge packs.

"Masters," Young said. "See about getting some charge packs off of the dead that haven't rolled back downhill."

"Good call." Masters left his sector and moved toward the MCR. Those who were still alive he put down with a slug thrower he had picked up from the first dead Kimbrin he'd found. As he gathered charge packs and watched the mist for more incoming MCR, another series of whistles sounded from below. Masters quickly scrambled back with his payload and deposited it behind the fallen spire to benefit the Yawds.

As they began to sort the scavenged equipment out, Masters, Young, and Jaybles watched and listened for a second assault. It didn't come. The whistling continued but grew distant, as though the MCR were marching back down the mountain.

"MCR get too much KTF?" asked Bord.

"Possibly," said Young. "Whatever platoons we were up against might've been dusted down to inoperability."

"Or just the whistle guys are running away," said Masters.

"Maybe we try and follow them," the Yawd suggested. "Shoot them up in the back and find a way off the mountain."

"That might be our best option," Young said with a nod, "but we saw a fair amount of MCR on the march. There's a pretty good chance replacements are marching up while these guys are heading down. Let's give it some time and see if we hear anything."

Eventually the whistling grew so faint that it couldn't be heard at all, and there were no new sounds to suggest additional troops were moving up the mountain. That didn't mean anything though. They could easily move silently, without blowing those whistles until the last minute. In fact, as long as they were out of the visual range of the HUDs, they could move at their leisure.

"How much time do we wanna have go by before we decide whether to move down?" Masters asked. He didn't see much in the way of opportunity up on this rock. If they could score a breakout now he felt they should take it. He relayed his reasoning to Young and Jaybles.

"Yeah, I agree," said Young. "If the Republic-friendly government can reassert control in the next few hours, we might even be able to get a SLIC sent our direction. Though they're probably too busy to worry about us. That makes two votes for breakout. Jaybles, what do you say?"

"Make that three votes," said Jaybles. "Let's get going—no, wait. I'm getting something on comms."

All eyes looked to Jaybles for further explanation.

"It's repeating and I can barely make it out... real thin... but it's definitely from the Republic government communicating something about the situation." He put his hand to his bucket. "It's starting again. Let me see if—"

Whatever Jaybles was about to say, he never finished. A flash of light engulfed him, and the impact of the blast threw the others off their feet. When Masters rose back up, Jaybles was completely gone. He had vanished from the top of the mountain.

The whistle of the Republic Army artillery now being fired against them made everything click in Masters's head. The MCR had given it a go, had been repulsed, and had then pulled back—because they wanted to avoid the onslaught they knew was coming now that their friends and allies had taken full control of Fort Blake. And when the whistling sound of an artillery shell terminated with an explosion down in the mist, it was clear that the MCR had been wise to pull back.

It's said that it's the incoming you *don't* hear that you need to worry about. Masters hadn't heard any telltale sound before Jaybles had been atomized. Nor did he hear anything prior to the next blast, which landed just behind the Yawds and threw the fierce fighters into or over the fallen spire they were using for cover.

Young was gone too. He had been moving quickly in Masters's direction when the force of the blast sent him right over the side of the mountain.

Masters had seen it happen.

There might have been someone still alive on that peak when Masters started running. He thought that maybe he could hear the low, pain-induced moan of a Kimbrin Yawd who had been hurt badly. But all he could do now was sprint toward the spires as another blast rained down from the heavens. And when he reached the top of the mountain, with nowhere else to go...

... he jumped.

PART TWO

28

Sergeant Walker stood with Wild Man and Makaffie in the hangar of the Savage mini-hulk. The three were crowded in a tight circle, holding metal saucers filled with a gray, sometimes lumpy goop that tasted like pepper gravy. Or at least that's what the Wild Man said it reminded him of as he scooped mouthfuls of the stuff with the large flat crackers Archimedes had served them. Deeper in the bay, near the ship she had come in on, was Prisma and—evidently—her mother. The big war bot, Crash, was there as well. In the time they'd been waiting for the enigmatic Ravi to return with the key that would free them from the prison ship, the girl and her mother had kept to themselves, using Prisma's ship as a base of operations.

"I don't trust that woman," Sergeant Walker said, holding the metal plate in one hand and then transferring it to the other as the heat of the slop passing through the metal became uncomfortable. He blew on his meal, which sent up an unpleasant odor, a mustiness that carried with it a hint of chemical detergent. He would've thought the stuff was poison, but it was the only thing they had to eat, and none of them had died yet.

"You all know what this stuff is, right?" asked Makaffie. "We're all thinking the same thing, right? Not about Reina—we can think about her later. After we've eaten. First things first. Right now we're thinking about what's on these plates. And I don't particularly *want* to think about it, man, but that's the thing... I can't stop thinking about it. Can you? Probably not. See, thinking about it is all you can do, even though there's really nothing to think about because we all know what this is."

"I don't trust her either," said the Wild Man, his voice as rough and hoarse as ever. "Remember what the admiral said? What he had to do to get them... powers?"

"A journey into madness at the end of the galaxy," said Makaffie grandly. "The General Rex option—kill to the full measure. I guess that's what was needed on account of what he said was still out there in the big bad dark waiting for every last living being. I suppose I can believe that. Went along with it anyway. And the taste of that dark and mysterious foe almost certainly had a hand in making the admiral and the general into what they were. At least from what I gathered from the admiral. And from Rex... when I could. They were changed. Post-human. Like Savages, really. And our friend the admiral felt that that little bit of voodoo was so necessary that he had to fake his own death, and deceive his oldest friend, to go and get it." Makaffie raised an eyebrow. "Yeah... I think we all remember."

Sergeant Walker nodded. "So how come she can do it too?"

"If I had to guess," said Makaffie, "which is precisely what I *do* have to do given the lack of information—and I assume you want me to guess because you asked the question—I'd say that this woman went and did the same thing that the admiral did. In theory, the same thing that any of us could do if we knew where to look and had what it took. And no, I don't personally believe I have what it would take to wield the kind of power old Goth Sullus did. To my great shame, and I am a man very much familiar with shame, I haven't the slightest idea where one would go to find that little rock that Casper—I think I can call him Casper on account of all the many years we spent in service together; he and I were particularly close after a rough beginning—that Casper went to. And if I did, well, I don't see myself as the type. Do you? But you both are made of stronger stuff than me, on the outside at least. So if you're thinking about picking up the mantle and gaining some new abilities, well, all we know is that Casper's little rock is somewhere in the black beyond galaxy's edge. Which, man, that's a fairly substantial piece of real estate to have to comb through. And we've been around for a while, yes, but we're talking orders of magnitude in—"

Sergeant Walker cut him off. "Not looking to work out how one of us can become the next Goth Sullus. Saw how that worked out. It didn't. What I'm saying is that woman has a power I didn't know existed until the admiral showed it to us. And that makes me leery is all."

Makaffie shrugged. "Is it possible that you're just nursing hard feelings after yonder beauty—and she is as stunning as the Crystal Seas of Schappert, all eighteen of them—after she went and used some of that abominable power to put you in your place? Which incidentally is also my place. And most likely the Wild Man's place as well, although he has a way of rising above his station. Which is to say we're lower than her. And lower than Ravi. And lower than a whole lotta things in this galaxy that I truly wish didn't exist but they're out there now, man, and there's no turning back from what we know. Only Sergeant Fast was given that luxury. Well, maybe not *only* Sergeant Fast, but my example still stands, regardless."

"No," said Walker. "It's not personal. It's an observation."

Makaffie scraped his plate with the last of his crackers and took a bite, nodding and entreating the sergeant to continue.

"When the admiral woke us up," the sergeant said, "it felt just like the start of another mission. Yeah, circumstances had changed, but that's how it always was. I think the shock over what happened to the Legion and General Rex was distracting us from everything else that was going on. But I've been thinking about things for a long time now. And as normal as it felt waking up and seeing the admiral there... what followed wasn't normal at all."

"You mean the kill team missions?" Makaffie asked.

Wild Man grunted. That was his guess as well.

"No. Not even that. It wasn't the first time we'd gotten woken up to dust someone. I mean the way the admiral *acted*. He was a thinker, a planner. And yeah, we were following through on a plan that he'd put together who knows how long before he woke us up, but he wasn't *acting* like that guy. He was acting like... someone else."

Makaffie begged for Sergeant Walker's untouched plate, waving his fingers with urgency—gimme. Walker handed it over along with his crackers. "Thank you, Sergeant. Your character and generosity are unmatched." He took a bite, and with his mouth full said, "And you're saying the admiral wasn't the admiral, the admiral was Goth Sullus."

"Exactly. And Goth Sullus was... impulsive. Vindictive. Cruel. It was like the admiral had shed his personality completely. The only time he seemed normal was between missions. But you get him around his army or his generals, and it was like dealing with a different person."

"Yes, I recall that," said Makaffie through another mouthful of cracker and gravy. He nodded toward his plate. "I'm eating it and I'm still thinking about what it is. Maybe there's something wrong with me." He shook his head. "What was it that Wild Man said back then? The admiral was being..."

"Tyrus Rex," grumbled Wild Man.

Makaffie smiled. He was always pleased when he was able to coax the Wild Man into speaking beyond grunts. "And the admiral just didn't know *how* to do that. How to be Tyrus Rex. Because as we know, a big part of his plan involved convincing the general to come right alongside. Didn't work out, through no fault of our own I might add so that no feelings are hurt, and so he had to become both admiral *and* general, as it were. I think that's what you're describing, Sergeant Walker."

"No, that's not what I'm describing," Walker said as Makaffie pushed another heaping shovelful of food into his mouth. "What I'm trying to say is that a fundamental part of who he was changed. You can list whatever attributes you want—ruthlessness, cruelty, determination, whatever. Point is, there was an imperiousness that was so obvious that none of us even cocked an eyebrow when he started calling himself emperor. There was a drive for power." Walker looked down and then shook his head slowly before bringing it back up. "Not even that. Not a drive for power, more like... an expectation that he be acknowledged as powerful. And any time anyone didn't do that, he seemed bent on making them regret it."

"You've done a thorough character study of our former, and now deceased, leader," said Makaffie. "Yours will be the authoritative biography."

"I'm not looking to write a book. I'm saying that in that woman's eyes and her bearing, I saw the exact same thing. The way she acted toward me, it wasn't about protecting her daughter—it was about putting me in my place for daring to even take a step toward her. And I think if she could have, she'd have done the same thing to that friend of yours."

Makaffie rubbed his chin with thumb and index finger as he considered this. He found an errant dollop of the peppery gravy near the corner of his mouth and wiped it away before sucking the residue off his finger. He looked over to the Wild Man's plate, but Wild Man was still methodically finishing his chow.

"Well, it might be your lucky day," Makaffie said. "Because while dear Ravi hasn't come back, Archimedes approaches. And I don't think it's to collect our plates."

The ghostly steward of the ship had gone to Reina and spoken unknown words to her. She had bobbed her head once, almost as though granting Archimedes permission to approach the three shock troopers. All that remained of Goth Sullus's personal guard.

"Did you come to bring us seconds?" Makaffie asked.

"I come to bring you a new opportunity," Archimedes said. The trailing shadowy second voice whispered, "*They are not worthy.*"

Sergeant Walker straightened. "What's that?"

"A simulation most puzzling. Most important. *We must know. It must be known. They are not worthy.*"

The three men exchanged a look.

"Will this sim have the failsafes turned on or off?" Makaffie asked. The ship hadn't hesitated to try to kill them prior to Ravi's arrival. It had taken a number of their original team members and continued to deny them access to the specialized Savage comms relay they still sought. But as Makaffie had discovered, when Archimedes wished for it to be so, the simulations could be run without risking their lives.

"You will be permitted to attempt the solution as many times as you are able," Archimedes said. "Your lives will be spared." The second voice added, "*Death will come to all mortals. Wait.*"

"Well, that's reassuring," said Makaffie with a smile. He looked to the sergeant.

"What opportunity are we being given exactly?" asked Sergeant Walker. "If it's just something to help stave off boredom until Ravi gets back I think we'll pass."

The sergeant noticed Reina looking at him from the corner of her eye while Prisma chatted on and on. The girl had been breathlessly telling her mother all that had happened to her since they'd last parted.

"You wait for your freedom," Archimedes said. "*Freedom. Freedom. An illusion.* But this wait has proven longer than you once supposed. *The mortals' plans are but vapor.* A new simulation has been uncovered, equally worthy of granting you liberty on this vessel. *Granted but never worthy.*"

Sergeant Walker set his jaw. "So you're saying if we solve this mission it's the same as if we unlock whatever you were looking for in that showdown between Goth Sullus and Tyrus Rex. That it?"

Archimedes smiled. "Yes. *Yes.*"

"I need to talk it over with a couple of people," Walker said. He moved to Prisma's ship. Makaffie and the Wild Man hesitated and then quickly moved to catch up. Archimedes stayed in his place.

As Sergeant Walker neared Reina, Prisma, and KRS-88, the girl's chatter ceased. Prisma and the bot watched him, but Reina paid no mind until he cleared his throat. Then she turned and said, "Is there something I can help you with, Sergeant?"

"Possibly. When Prisma and her war bot arrived on station we struck up a sort of a deal. We would work together and try to get off the ship.

Both she and KRS-88 worked hard to make that happen. Now we've got a new opportunity, and I'd like to see what they think about it."

"What they think about it?" Reina said. "A little girl and her companion bot."

"I'm not a little girl, Mom," said Prisma.

Reina smiled at her daughter. "I know you aren't, darling. You're a bright young woman. But you have to understand... to me you're always going to be my little girl."

Prisma grinned, but looked uncomfortable having this conversation in front of the three members of Kill Team Ice.

"Is what the sergeant says true?" Reina asked her. "Did you agree to help one another escape? Because from what KRS-88 has told me, neither of you were left with much of a choice." She looked accusingly at Sergeant Walker.

"I think they would've tried to use Crash no matter what, if they could," Prisma admitted. "But Ravi didn't kill them, and I think he would've if they were really bad. They didn't force me to come along either. In fact they wanted me to stay behind so I wouldn't get hurt. But I told him I wouldn't go without Crash."

"You're very brave, Prisma." Reina turned her cold gaze to Sergeant Walker. "What would you like to do now, Sergeant?"

"I'm worried that Ravi hasn't come back yet."

Reina blinked slowly and nodded her head knowingly. "So you've told me."

"He might be in trouble. And if he is, I wanna be able to help him. We can't do that from here. So if there's another way we can get off this ship, then I want to hear about it."

"The way off the ship," Reina said, "is to do something for the ship that it cannot do for itself. That is what your friend Ravi was attempting before I arrived. And that's what it wants now." She looked at the other two shock troopers, then back at Walker. "Archimedes has told you about the simulation."

"Yes, ma'am," said Walker.

"And what is it you wish? Surely not to bring my daughter onto another battlefield."

"I'm not afraid of battlefields," said Prisma. "I've been on them before. Real ones, not just fake ones like this." Although it didn't seem very fake to Prisma when she recalled all that had happened. The deaths and screams of those men... those were real. She steeled herself, unwilling to look frightened. "Tyrus Rechs taught me what to do in a fight. I'm not afraid."

At the name Tyrus Rechs, Reina brushed her neck with her fingertips. "You have grown into a remarkable woman, Prisma. What would you like to do? You have my support no matter what your answer is."

Sergeant Walker quickly interjected, "Archimedes said that the simulation wouldn't present any danger to us. It would be like the one before. He just wants an answer on how to do it. The war bot would be helpful, I'm sure."

Prisma nodded eagerly. "Crash saved everybody. He's good at that."

"I am ready to assist in whatever capacity is necessary," KRS-88 rumbled. "I too am concerned with the delay in Ravi's return. I am quite fond of him."

"And I'll come too," said Prisma. "We all would've died on one of those missions if I hadn't figured out what was going on." She looked hopefully at her mother. "You should join us. With all the things you know, I bet we'll be able to figure it out on the first try."

Reina smiled and gently stroked Prisma's cheek. "I would like nothing more, but as Archimedes has already told me, there are guidelines in place for these operations. The ship wishes to know how to find a solution using the tools available to it. That means blasters and bullets and blood. A solution involving me is not worthwhile to the ship, because I cannot be easily replicated. That is also why Ravi's success was discredited. He cannot be easily imitated either. But I will accompany you all the same. I'm eager to see everything that Ravi has taught you."

Prisma looked proud to the point of bursting. She stepped forward and held out her hand. Sergeant Walker took it, and they shook.

"Lead the way, Sergeant," Prisma said. "I'm tired of being away from everyone. It's time for us to get off this ship."

29

The team didn't have to walk far to reach the simulation. Unlike the show-down outside the temple of the Ancients, where Tyrus Rechs fell to Goth Sullus, located deep in the bowels of the mini-hulk, what Archimedes had in store now could evidently be handled in the very first long corridor—the same one where Prisma had lain down next to the Wild Man and watched the strange Savage beasts fight with Republic marines while Goth Sullus walked about in phantasmal form.

Much like before, the corridor was spartan and bare, a mix of im-pervisteel-grated deck plates and bulkheads. The mist from the side vents from which the reclaimers had come began to deposit in thick white wisps around feet and ankles. The main difference from the first time Prisma had been in this corridor was that Archimedes, the archi-tect of this peculiar Savage research vessel, was with them.

"Your objective—*what we need*—is to breach the door at the end of the corridor. *Swiftly you must fly*. You must stop the ship from being hijacked. *Never again*."

Sergeant Walker nodded. "Anything else you can share? Opposition? Tactics used in the original battle?"

"You may know that you fight a race known as the Cybar. *Speak not to the heretics of our knowledge*. Tactics you may know not. *You may not know. You are not worthy*. For what was done might have been rightly chosen but poorly executed. You are not to be led to or dissuaded from any solution that might lead to victory. Complete the task. *Do as we say*."

Prisma felt her stomach drop at the word *Cybar*. There was not a hint of fondness toward them in her memories aboard the Cybar mothership, her captivity, even her subsequent rescue by Captain Keel. But she knew that these weren't really Cybar. And that, whatever feelings of dread they might conjure up, that was all they would be. Feelings. Feelings that she herself had brought forth. The real Cybar, those who had imprisoned her, would not be here.

But then she had another thought that sent a new wave of worry into her fraying nerves. What if the battle they were seeking to undertake was to be the very one she had been witness to? Archimedes had said they'd fight the Cybar... what if Walker and the others were expected to take on the role of Hutch and the rest of Ghost Team? But Hutch's mission had failed. Would Prisma be tasked with preventing herself from being captured? To stop all those Nether agents who had kidnapped her and Leenah and Skrizz and Garret from being killed?

She didn't want that. She was glad those men were dead.

The answer would become obvious as soon as the simulation began, but Prisma couldn't stop her racing thoughts from playing out the possibilities. As lights began to dim into bleak blackness, she prayed that whatever was about to be revealed, it would not be something she had already experienced.

The low lights revealed a different ship than the one they had just been on, and Prisma's heart beat faster. She recognized this corridor. It was a corridor she had once traveled aboard the Cybar mothership. Except back then her walk had been a compulsory march, something she had done for Leenah and Garret. She was worried about what that monster Hutch and the Nether Ops agents might do to them if she didn't cooperate.

And yet when she looked around, she saw no Nether Ops agents. Nor did she see spectral imitations of her friends.

Heavy blaster fire was already racing down the corridor from Cybar Titans wielding their heavy tri-barreled N-50 cannons. The members of Walker's team instinctively threw themselves behind the nearest bulkhead to take cover. To the rear more Cybar appeared.

Makaffie looked behind them. "If this is where we're getting dropped in, I have a pretty good idea why this mission sim isn't working out so well. Hard to get a win when you start off entirely surrounded."

Prisma was still looking for holographic images of her friends or the members of Ghost Team, but all she saw were the Cybar bots. And then she realized that the bots to their rear weren't seeking to surround them as Makaffie had thought, but were moving past them to advance on the defending Titans.

"They're fighting each other," she said.

"Beats the alternative," said Sergeant Walker. "Prisma, have your war bot use whatever it's got to keep those defenders back. We want our death machines to move as far ahead as they can. Makaffie, there's a port right over there. See what you can find out."

"Somehow I doubt the simulation will give us an accurate portrayal of whatever was going through this place, but I will acquiesce to your orders, Sergeant."

"Wild Man, you got something big enough to put these down," said Walker. It wasn't a question. He knew what the sniper and his big gun were capable of.

Wild Man grunted an affirmative and pulled a massive ionic round out of his belt. He pulled open the rifle's bolt, placed the round in, and then slammed it back home before drifting in behind his scope. It was only seconds before the gun barked its mighty boom, more deafening than usual in these tight confines, and completely removed the head of one of the enemy war bots from its shoulders. The target, which had been leaning out to fire from behind a bulkhead, toppled over from the impact before lying frozen and inoperable on the deck. Wild Man released the shell from the bolt housing and slammed home another ionic-charged round.

Prisma recalled how these simulations had worked in the past. Not everything here was real. Archimedes reanimated some sort of faceless, soulless golems to represent the turning of the tide. Kill those and achieve mission success. Or at least that was how it seemed to have gone previously.

She relaxed her mind and reached out to see which of the Titans before them were alive and which were phantasms.

"You have learned quickly, my dear," said Reina. "What do you see?"

Wild Man was looking for another target. They'd learned the hard way that the artificial enemies—those who were mere holographic mimics— would focus their attacks on the "allies" supplied by Archimedes. There was no knowing how many of these were in the fight. But the bullets Wild Man was using were very real, and their supply was not endless. Just as KRS-88 was critically low on ordnance, so too was the rest of the team after fighting in so many of the simulations already. Archimedes had provided them food, but not access to an armory.

"Prisma," Wild Man said. "You got a target for me?"

Prisma felt pleased that he had asked her instead of Crash. She liked when people acknowledged her as more than a girl. She wanted to be helpful and useful. And she was already in the process of finding the answer to that question, her mind reaching out to identify the points of light that her guide—her mother in disguise—had taught her to see.

Her eyes sprang open. "All of them! Every defender is one of those things."

For a moment the three members of the kill team were quiet. Then Makaffie looked up from his data port and said, "Well I guess we know how far we got to take this thing to win. Kill 'em all. How very Legion."

Sergeant Walker swallowed. "Wild Man, drop them at will. Prisma, let's get Crash working on taking as many of these things out as we can. It might take a while, but if we move smart, then with the firepower we've got we should be able to control this corridor."

"Oh, see, that's where things get a little complicated." Makaffie had flipped up the data port, making it recede back into the corridor wall. "What's happened here is that there are two groups vying for control of these Cybar machines. There aren't any names, but it's safe to assume the side we're representing for dear Archimedes belongs to the Savages. The other side is evidently defending those blast doors. And if we don't make it to those doors within ten standard minutes, they will achieve whatever it is they achieved in real life, I presume. So unless we want to run this scenario again and again and again, and let me be clear as one who once had to do just that—we don't—then we're gonna have to go ahead and push our way up in a hurry."

"Okay, here's what we're gonna do," said Sergeant Walker as though he'd been planning the entire time Makaffie had been speaking. "Wild Man, you keep shooting. Mak—you, me, and the war bot are going to push hard. If we pass our own bots then we'll get as far as we can before taking up defense and waiting for them to catch up. "

"Sounds like a suicide mission," Makaffie said. "I think I've made myself clear about where I stand on those."

"Yeah, and you still keep doing them," said Walker. "Crash, do you understand the plan?"

"Such as it is," rumbled the war bot.

"Ready when you are, brave sergeant," said Makaffie.

"Go!"

The team rushed forward. Makaffie fired his weapon indiscriminately, choosing targets that were already being lit up by either Walker or KRS-88. They quickly caught up with their allied Titans as the Wild Man's gun boomed sporadically, each shot setting up a shower of circuitry and ceramics that littered the polished deck and took still more of the defenders out.

There weren't all that many defending, but they were entrenched well enough and were powerful enough to be able to repel a force many times the size of what they were now facing down. It would've taken a super-armored killdozer minesweeper traveling in the lead down the center corridor and absorbing the Cybar punishment in order to make any kind of safe speed.

Walker and his team had a different kind of advantage than a mine-sweeper—which wouldn't have fit in the corridor anyway even if they somehow had one at their disposal. With the safety protocols on, the team of three rolling behind their Titan lead blockers were able to gobble up large swaths of enemy-held territory without fear of being harmed. They could blow right past the defending war bots, pitched in a fight with the allied Titans, and then destroy the machines from behind.

That tactic was essential to making the required time because the "friendly" Cybar Titans only had one steady pace, and it was a slow one. The bots didn't seem capable of running. But thus far the reckless assault by Walker, Makaffie, and KRS-88 had kept the defenders back on their heels enough that the advancing bots didn't need to slow down any further. The trouble now was that Walker's forward element was now a bit *too* forward—a good two thirds of the way down the corridor, and they had to pause and take cover behind bulkheads while their allies caught up. They looked for targets to hit, but there was no need—any enemy Titans that did expose themselves were brought down by the Wild Man.

"I'm not seeing any point in waiting for the bots any longer," Sergeant Walker said. "If we're up against the clock, then pushing now is going to be our best bet of achieving the objective and getting off the ship."

"Such a tactic would most likely result in the end of runtime for all biologics involved in the charge," said KRS-88. "There is a similar chance for end of runtime for this unit as well."

"Usually I would agree with you," said Walker. "But we've got a big advantage here: namely, we can kill them but they can't kill us. Let's get this thing done."

"I'm not sure I agree that this is the best course of action," said Makaffie. "They want this sim done because they want to see *how* it gets done. And how are we showing them that if we win by simply taking advantage of the failsafe?"

"Look, we've made it this far up the corridor without issue," said Walker. He looked back to where Wild Man lay prone and Prisma and her mother kept cover behind the bulkheads, peering out to watch the ordeal. "Worst case, Archimedes tells us it won't do and has us run the sim again. Best case, we're done in one go and we can get the package and get out of here."

"That's not the worst case I can think of," muttered Makaffie. "But lead on, Sergeant. I'll follow."

The team rolled out from behind cover. KRS-88 provided the vast bulk of the suppressive firepower, Sergeant Walker added precision shots from his blaster rifle, and Makaffie did his best to finish whatever was left. There were three bulkheads being defended that they needed to overcome before they would reach the blast doors. The first was protected by a lone Cybar Titan.

KRS-88 took a round to his shoulder plating and then concentrated fire on the Titan's head as Walker did the same. Makaffie held back, unable to find a line of sight that didn't include an ally. The Titan went down just as the friendly war bots Archimedes had provided them in the simulation got within a few bulkheads of their current position. The bots were still moving steadily forward, but not swiftly enough.

"Just three left," Walker said. "Go!"

The team had pushed out to reach the next bulkhead when the two Titans defending it stepped out from cover with their N-50s leveled at the attackers. Makaffie was on the left side of the corridor. KRS-88 in the middle. Walker on the right. Both bots fired at Walker, and their bolts ripped into him, punching gory holes through his armor and filling the corridor with the scent of blood and burnt flesh. His body was already limp and falling when another volley, this one centered on his helmet, punctuated the lethally real—not simulated—nature of the attack. Several more holes were blasted through his head.

The Wild Man fired his rifle, taking out one of the two Titans, as Makaffie swore and threw himself behind cover. KRS-88 quickly processed the remaining threat and begin trading blaster bolts with the Titan. His armor became pocked and dented from the short flurry before Wild Man finished reloading and dropped that bot as well.

Makaffie didn't know how it had happened, but it was obvious that something had gone horribly wrong. Sergeant Walker was dead, and this simulation was no less lethal than any of the previous ones they'd undertaken as a team. He also knew that his survival now hinged on him covering behind the bulkhead and waiting for the friendly Titans to push up. He knew that. But instead he rolled around the corner of his bulkhead to where the last remaining Titan stood.

They were face to face before he remembered his armor's ability to cloak. He activated it, and the Titan instantly seemed unaware of his presence. Makaffie raised his rifle and took time to aim as he fired several bolts into the machine's head, obliterating its processors. Achieving with slow and deliberate care what Sergeant Walker was capable of doing in a split second.

What Sergeant Walker would never do again.

The bot didn't fall over or groan or give any other sense that it was destroyed beyond the holes in its head and the way it simply froze in place. But Makaffie knew it was fully disabled when the blast doors swished open behind it.

Through the doorway stood a man and a woman. They looked directly at Makaffie—or perhaps they looked through him. He hadn't deactivated his suit's cloaking.

And then the lights went dark and the simulation faded from view. The mists swirled from the vents, and with them came the Savage reclaimers. The ghouls grabbed Sergeant Walker's body and began to pull it back down into the shaft.

No one moved to stop them.

At the far end of the corridor, away from the grisly reclamation, stood Reina and Prisma. They had watched the entire ordeal.

Reina looked down at her daughter. "Did he mean so much to you in such a short time, my child?"

Prisma wiped the tear from her eye and blushed. "No. He was… he was all right. I didn't hate him. But… I'm tired. I'm tired of seeing people die."

"I can sense that you've witnessed much sorrow, Prisma. I'm so sorry I couldn't be there for you. After this we will talk about everything that's happened. More than talk. But for now, just know that the galaxy has a way of repaying a person's deeds."

Prisma nodded, although she didn't understand how that was true. Everything she'd seen of death and destruction had taught her that those who deserved it, and those who didn't, both suffered in equal measure. While so many who truly deserved death seemed to prosper.

She thought particularly of Goth Sullus, and her soul cried out in rage.

30

Archimedes appeared once more and led them back to the docking bay. When Makaffie confronted the Savage monstrosity—the Savage wonder—about his promise of safety during the simulation, Archimedes was apologetic.

"A solution was the price. *You sought to deceive. False. False.* Had the safeguards remained in place your solution would not have been viable. You quickly approached the realm of total and complete improbability. But since you were so close—*so close, so very close*—we decided to see if it could be done. You proved it could."

"And all any of this cost us was *the entire team* except for me and Wild Man," snapped Makaffie. "We're done here, right? No more surprises. No more additional requests for us to complete."

"You have shown us that a small team can complete the objective with an odds-defying charge. It is improbable such a task would work again, but not impossible. And with enough teams to attempt it, this scenario may be replicated should the need arise. *We shall be ready.*"

Makaffie stared at Archimedes with a mix of scorn and wonder. The loyal part of the man felt anger over the betrayal of his friend. The mad scientist part of him—the mind that had created H8 and imbibed it to better see and touch and taste the galaxy—couldn't help but be awed by this intersection of Savage technology and incorporeal life. He had questions. Questions that he knew wouldn't be answered unless he were to somehow take over the ship. But all he wanted now was to leave the forsaken mini-hulk.

But first, better get what they came for.

They returned to the hangar. Prisma, her war bot, and her mother went off on their own, leaving Makaffie with Archimedes and the Wild Man.

"We did what you asked," Makaffie said. "And now we will get what we were promised. Free rein of the ship. Including the control room. Let's see that comms array you've got up there."

Archimedes's face was impassive, but his voice sounded almost surprised. "This cannot be done. *It is forbidden.*"

"Well the thing is, that's not what me or my friend want to hear. And it's surely not what we heard when we talked with you. To the victors go the spoils and now you say otherwise. I took your words to be very plain and straightforward. If we helped you with one of your unsolvable mission protocols, thereby restoring your rule and reign over the ship, you would grant us access to the ship prior to our departure. Well, mission accomplished. Now open up."

"But you have not done so," said Archimedes. "*A failure.* You have fulfilled a second bargain. One that will grant you passage off of this ship. We are united again, yes, but through no doing of your own. *Failure.* Our purpose has been resuscitated. Things are again in order."

Makaffie hissed, staring coldly for a long moment. Then without another word, he motioned for Wild Man to follow him as he stepped away, leaving Archimedes where he stood.

Reina sat with Prisma inside the scout jumper the girl had taken from Mother Ree's sanctuary and piloted here. The mother sat still and regal in the passenger seat while the daughter sat scrunched up in the pilot's chair, her feet tucked beneath her, swiveling back and forth anxiously.

"You showed me a great deal about yourself back there, Prisma," Reina said, smiling warmly. "And we've talked a great deal about your training. What Ravi showed you. What you learned. All those details. But I hadn't realized the trauma you've gone through."

Prisma lifted her head from her knees to look at her mother. "But I told you. I told you everything that happened to me. All this time. Weren't you listening?"

"I was listening, yes. But back there you showed me in another way. You let me feel what you felt. The anger over all you've endured. The sorrow over all you've witnessed. The doubt and fear—yes, Prisma, the fear—of what may still lie ahead."

Prisma turned her head and looked out the front cockpit window. She heard Crash fiddling with something in the rear bay and turned to look in that direction as well. She wanted anything but to meet her mother's eyes. She had spent so long telling herself that she wasn't afraid. And now she feared that all that resolve would simply melt away, revealing itself to be a lie, if she allowed her mother to search her.

"I don't know why we have to go over all of this again," she said. "I told you what happened. Why can't we just move on?"

"Prisma, it is easy to know what happened to someone. It is much harder to *understand* what they went through."

"I've tried explaining it to people before," Prisma said. "And they all say how horrible it must've been. Or how sorry they are. But no matter how hard I try to get them to understand that I don't *want* them to tell me sorry or to agree that it was horrible they just... they don't ever understand. Nobody ever understands."

"Perhaps you just never told the right person."

Prisma shook her head, unsure whether she agreed with that statement.

"There were at least three people who really seemed to understand me. The first was Tyrus Rechs." Prisma waited to see if the name would have an impact on her mother again. This time the woman seemed ready for it and gave only a smooth, singular nod of recognition. "I would talk to him and tell him everything," Prisma continued. "He never really said much back... unless it was about guns or how to use them. Sometimes he would say little things about being a soldier or doing things that were hard. But I felt like he understood. And even... that he wanted to say something that would make me feel better. But he never could. Or maybe he just never did. He really didn't talk all that much."

"His perspective, like mine, is a difficult one," said Reina. "We've both been through much."

"You knew him, didn't you?"

"I did."

"And you sent him to help me? Told him to look for me?"

"I did not. Though there is no one else I would have asked had I known what happened, Prisma. Had I known what had happened... I would've come back for you myself."

Prisma looked down at her hands. She clasped them together and twiddled her thumbs nervously. "Where were you? Why weren't you with us? Daddy said you died. And he would always be real sad whenever he said it."

"I think it was easier for him to say that than to tell you what truly happened," Reina said. "Who else did you speak with about your experiences? You said there were three. Tyrus Rechs is one. Who are the other two?"

It dawned on Prisma that in all the time she'd had so far with her mother—every moment a joy to her heart—they had spoken only of her. Of Prisma. Her questions about Tyrus Rechs, and then about where her mother had been, were the first questions Prisma herself had asked. And as she thought of that now, it seemed peculiar to her. Because as much as she truly did want to tell her mother everything that had happened since their parting, she also wanted to know where her mother had been. A part of Prisma was angry about that. She didn't understand. If her mother loved her so much, as she constantly said, then why would she disappear like that? And never even once send her a holovid or anything?

Had her father stood in the way of things like that? He wouldn't have done that, would he? He had never once even hinted that her mother might be alive. Did he know the truth? The way her mother made it sound, he did. So why hadn't he told her?

Whatever anger Prisma felt was outweighed by confusion. Should she be angry at her mother for leaving? Her father for lying? Who was responsible for preventing them from being a family?

She wondered if all relationships were this complicated. If they were just temporary alliances formed between people, each seeking out their own will. Trying for their own way. She knew that wasn't how it was supposed to be, but she couldn't help but feel that maybe that was how it had been between her parents. And she was the pawn—the little girl who never knew any better and was now suddenly staring down the truth. One that led to sorrow no matter how she worked it out in her mind.

But her mother was waiting.

"I told you about Leenah," Prisma said. "She's so kind. I think you'll really like her. She would always listen to me. Always. And she was always on my side. She never let Captain Keel get too angry, even if I kind of deserved it." She gave a wan smile. "Sometimes I would be... difficult. Just because. Just to do it."

From the rear bay, Crash chimed in, "Difficult is a mild choice of words, young miss. You were often downright obstinate, antagonistic, and rude."

"Thanks for the assessment, Crash," said Prisma flatly.

"I take it KRS-88 advised you that your behavior was unbecoming at the time it was happening?" Reina asked.

Prisma rolled her eyes. "All the time."

"Is he your third? When we selected him to help look out after you, I wanted him to be someone you could speak to, as well as someone who could protect you."

"I tried," Prisma said. "I love Crash. I do. And he understands a lot more things than you think a bot would. But he doesn't understand me."

KRS-88 straightened his shoulders as though insulted. "I believe I understood the nature of your trauma quite well, young miss. It was based on that understanding, as well as your father's and mother's pre-programmed wishes, that I so often attempted to convince you to abandon your quest for vengeance."

"He wanted me to go in hiding for the rest of my life," Prisma muttered.

"A considerably safer option than what you chose."

Prisma shook her head and growled in frustration. "That's what all of them thought. They all wanted me to hide and be safe. Everyone says I've 'been through too much' and the only thing to do is to shut myself in like a war turtle and live inside my shell. Even Skyla—he's the third one who understood me. He was a legionnaire medic before he joined Mother Ree's sanctuary. Even he wanted that. It's what *he* chose to do to get rid of *his* past. He wanted me to stay at the sanctuary, Leenah wanted me to stay at the sanctuary, and Crash *really* wanted me to stay at the sanctuary. To be safe and just... forget about everything."

"And why didn't you?" said Reina. "I've heard that En Shakar is stunningly beautiful."

"It is, but..." Prisma took a deep breath. "I knew why they wanted me to stay. They all saw a little girl who'd had a bunch of bad things happen to her, and they wanted to protect her. But I couldn't let myself be hidden away like that."

"Why not?"

"Because it *wasn't okay!*"

The explosion of emotion that led to her shouting caught Prisma by surprise. But her emotions were deep and raw and the mother she'd so desperately wished to have been there to hear her and listen to her in all those times past was here with her now. So Prisma continued and poured out her heart.

"What Goth Sullus did to Daddy. What he did to me. It was wrong. It was wicked!" There was a fire burning her in her eyes, demanding vengeance. "And he needs to pay for it! And if all I did was go and hide so that I could be safe, then I was just saying it was okay. That he could do those bad things and it was okay as long as I hid and got to be safe. But it will *never* be okay! Never! And I don't *want* to be safe. I'd rather die than let him keep living thinking he's gotten away with what he did."

Prisma felt the tears forming in her eyes. She was just barely hanging on, and she was breathing heavily, exhausted by the outpouring of everything that was inside of her. "I want him to be dead. Not just dead. I want to kill him myself."

"Show me," said Reina softly. Calmly.

It wasn't the response that Prisma had expected. She opened her mouth and closed it again, unsure how to answer.

"Show me all of it," Reina clarified. "Help me to understand exactly what you went through. Help me to feel exactly what you felt."

"How?"

"I will teach you."

Reina reached out and gently took Prisma's hands in her own. She spoke to her without words, communicating mind to mind as she had done before arriving aboard the Savage mini-hulk. And Prisma listened. Together, they unlocked the memories and experiences that had haunted Prisma for so long. And in moments, Prisma was sharing everything. Directly. Mind to mind.

The day Goth Sullus first arrived to claim her father's life. The uncertainty and fear of traveling with Hogus and Skrizz. The turmoil at Ackabar and the worry that Tyrus Rechs would abandon her. Every twist and turn leading to the bounty hunter's death, and every sense of slipping and losing control as she floated through the galaxy trying to find an anchor with Leenah and Captain Keel.

Reliving these things was just that—reliving them, feeling once again all the turmoil and terror. Experiencing the most terrible days of her life in their full intensity, all over again. And not just those days, but the aftermath as well. The sorrow and despair, the confusion and depression. The regret and second-guessing. All of it was out now. Out in the open.

And despite all of the pain and heartache, Prisma felt a sense of relief. She had finally found someone who understood.

31

Prisma didn't know she'd screamed until KRS-88 was pushing himself into the cockpit and asking, "Are you quite all right, young miss?"

"Prisma was reliving many painful experiences," Reina explained. "You were present for nearly all of them, war bot. For that I am thankful."

Crash studied Reina for a long moment.

"I'm fine, Crash," said Prisma, her voice starting off softly and then growing in strength as she grew more aware of her surroundings. "It was just a little intense. Like I was there again."

"Where?" inquired the bot. "I did not detect a departure."

"Prisma's body remained here," Reina explained. "But her mind and spirit were transported back through time to the events in question. She showed me all that she has been through." She gently stroked Prisma on the side of her head. "I understand now, my dear. And I'm so sorry."

It was then that the two shock troopers entered the ship.

"We heard yelling," Makaffie said.

Reina faced them with all the regality of a queen in her court. "Thank you for your concern. We are fine."

Makaffie looked to Prisma for assurance. And though the other man, the tall hulking figure they called the Wild Man, kept his helmet on, it was clear that he was looking to the girl for the same.

"I'm fine," Prisma said. "I didn't mean to scream. I didn't even know I was doing it."

"I can't speak for my friend here," said Makaffie, "but that doesn't exactly put my worries to rest." The man looked sharply at Reina, the flaming intelligence behind his eyes evoking a strength that was absent in his slight frame. "Do you have a moment to answer some questions? Questions about what happened on the ship."

Reina gave a fractional nod. "You speak of the loss of your friend. That was unfortunate."

"Well now that is one way to put it. Another might be to say that in the big ol' cosmic dice game, the bones fell down and rolled right over Sergeant Walker. And if that's so, who am I to argue with the fate the galaxy has chosen? Walker wasn't the first man to die on the ship, not by a long shot. Not even the first of our men. But he's the only one who has me thinking. Hence, the request to have a little chat."

Reina again gave a slight nod for Makaffie to continue.

"What is your connection to all this?" the shock trooper asked. "And if I'm speaking like a man who doesn't value his life in the face of a woman who can surely end it, please understand that it's because I value finding out the truth more than extending the number of minutes my heart beats. Some shepp are fine being led unwittingly to their slaughter. I wish to have both eyes open."

"My mom didn't kill your friend," said Prisma, bothered at the suggestion.

"A thousand pardons and I would never suggest that she did when she clearly did not. The abominations built on this peculiar Savage vessel pulled the trigger and delivered the bolts that ended that man's life. I saw it up close and personal. I even turned around, and sure enough both you and your mother were in the opposite direction and far away. So I have no reason to dispute the veracity of your claim, Prisma, that neither your mother, nor you—or me, or the Wild Man, or KRS-88—killed our, shall we say, friend? Our sergeant-at-arms as it were. But see, this ship has moved beyond its original purpose. That much is clear. And I don't think we need to hash any of that out because Archimedes has told us all as much. Whatever little ghosts are in this machine aren't in perfect harmony over how to best hunt the damned souls sucked into its hellish bay. Though it was pretty clear what they wanted from us once they realized we were capable of doing something they didn't think could be done, so no surprise they asked us to do it when they found we could. All that was clear. It was crystal clear. I understood that.

"What I didn't understand—what I still don't understand, and what I maybe didn't want to understand, you dig, is why this ship—this Savage ship. *This* ship is run by Archimedes. And Archimedes says that the king has lost the throne, and he wants it back. And while he's off the throne and searching for a way to gain it back from his fellow ghosts and ghoulies, he finds someone else. So then he goes and calls the master. And you are the master. Oh, yes you are. And maybe this is just me, but I see that as a title that comes with a certain level of responsibili*tay* for the comings and happenings and goings of your domain."

Makaffie waved his hands down as if trying to suppress any response from Reina. She hadn't so much as blinked or opened her mouth to speak. "Oh I know all about why you might be called a master. I heard about how you got upset with the good Sergeant Walker and held him in place. Just floating there. Held up by an invisible hand. Yes I heard indeed how you went and did that Goth Sullus thing that's not supposed to be done. That doesn't make sense but it still happened, so it has to make sense… us lesser beings just can't understand it is all. But you do. And you can, I'm sure, make me your servant. Could bring me to beg you to be my master."

"She wouldn't do that," Prisma snapped.

Makaffie ignored her while the Wild Man shifted uncomfortably behind him. "But what is it that got old Archimedes to call you the master? It couldn't just be the parlor tricks, because when Ravi came, I distinctly remember him not being called *master*, and certainly he would qualify on the basis of otherworldly power."

The question hung in the air long enough for Prisma to realize that she wanted to know the answer as well. But the honor of her mother—the only parent she had left—called for her to once again stand up against Stranger One's insinuations. She opened her mouth to speak, but her mother held out a staying hand.

"I was brought to the ship much in the same way you were," Reina said. "I was pulled from hyperspace and tractored inside for the benefit of Archimedes and his simulations. They soon discovered two things. One, there was no simulation they could provide me in which I did not prevail; and two, that my solutions were utterly useless to them. For the Savages who built this ship could not possibly wield power such as I, though they would like nothing more.

"They decided I was of so little use that I should be collected and recycled for the continuation of the ship and its runtime. That was when Archimedes and his ilk discovered a third truth." Reina's eyes flashed dark, and the cockpit seemed to shrink around Prisma and Makaffie while somehow stretching out behind Reina. "They discovered that I could destroy every one of them, and their ship as well. In fear of this, they groveled and called me master, and gave me that which they were not authorized to give: free passage off the ship."

"And then you just happened to come back here when we showed up?" asked Makaffie, whose voice had lost its confident and careless edge.

"When you showed up, I cared very little. I knew what the ship was, and where it was. I monitored it, not wanting to destroy it because its actions might tell me more about what the Savages remaining in the darkness would attempt." Reina arched an eyebrow. "Does that surprise you? That the Savages remained and were not destroyed as your Republic had promised? A lie to lull the galaxy back to sleep. For it is when we slumber that the thief in the night commits his deeds."

Reina continued to speak to Makaffie, but as she spoke, Prisma heard different words in her head. Words that belonged to her mother but were being said just to her. Just for the two of them to know.

"Whatever you may feel about this one, my daughter, I wish for you to think: What was the name he used when comparing my power? The same latent power that you have inside yourself?"

Prisma had been so captivated by her mother's revealing something of her past that she hadn't given a second thought to nearly anything Makaffie had said.

Reina urged her. "What was the name he compared me to?"

And then, like a fleet of misery dropping from hyperspace, came the recall.

"Goth Sullus," Prisma said softly. So softly that likely only Crash heard it above the conversation Reina continued to hold between herself and Makaffie.

"You must remember to speak only to me, my child," said Reina. "What we are now going to say, what we are now going to decide, concerns only the two of us."

Prisma focused on the voice in her mind. Sensed the hand of her mother—not in life but in spirit—reaching out for her. She took hold of it... and suddenly she was sharing a consciousness with her mother. It was as though they were standing together in a room of pure light.

She spoke again, and this time not even her war bot would be able to hear.

"He said Goth Sullus," Prisma repeated.

"He did."

"I am proud of you, Prisma," said Reina.

"Why?" Prisma asked. She wanted so desperately to be told why her mother was proud of her.

"All the rage of what was done to you is justified. But you show wisdom beyond your years to wonder whether the man standing before us is deserving of it."

Prisma tried to look beyond the room that she had found herself mentally transported into. She could still see Makaffie in the ship, and

Crash, and the Wild Man. They were all really there, wherever reality was. Compared to where she was now. Makaffie was talking. He was explaining to Reina what he and his team had been doing in the first place. Exchanging backstory and secrets now that Reina had told her own.

"Should I interrupt?" Prisma asked. "Should I ask him how he knows about Goth Sullus?"

"To do so is one avenue," said Reina. "He may tell you that Goth Sullus was a name that traveled from one end of the galaxy to the other very quickly once the man took the reins of power. His exploits, whether seen or rumored, are surely known by much of the galactic citizenry. Certainly by those employed in his Black Fleet. But... would that be the truth? Or would that be a lie? And once spoken, how would you know?"

Prisma shook her head. "I wouldn't."

"But you *can*. Just as you shared with me the truth of your experiences, you can discover from these men the truth of theirs."

Prisma didn't doubt this. The connection she had made with her mother, even the connection she'd had with her before coming together in person, was too real, too intimate, to suggest such a thing was impossible. And Reina hadn't been the only one to have made these inexplicable connections with the minds of others. Hadn't Ravi communicated with her in the same way? Hadn't Skrizz's loyalty been unlocked by a simple touch? This might have been witchcraft, or some unknown and awesome ancient power, but it was not imaginary. It was not a lie.

"Will you teach me?" Prisma asked.

Reina smiled proudly. "What your friend Ravi has begun, I will complete. And you will find yourself unlocking greater potential than even the Ancient One imagined, dear Prisma."

The otherworldly, spectral room they stood in seemed to expand as Reina led Prisma to the door of Makaffie's mind. She placed a hand in front of it, causing it to glow blue like a portal.

"Some have training to resist such invasions," she said. "And I do not use that word lightly. We are now invading this man's mind. Some are skilled in banishing us from their thoughts. He will not be. We can do great damage while we are here, so we must be careful and respectful. We could bring about the truth in many ways. We could ask him, and he would feel compelled to tell us everything. But far simpler is to merely look inside and see for ourselves what truth is there."

Reina stepped aside and motioned for Prisma to approach the blue portal. Prisma stood before it as though gazing into a looking glass.

"Look," Reina commanded. "Look for the truth, only take care not to punish him for whatever you discover, lest you destroy his mind and leave a part of yourself trapped inside."

Prisma peered into the portal, thinking about Goth Sullus and what he had done. Remembering again that day when everything her father had warned her about became true. When all the precautions he'd given so that she could stay alive became mercilessly relevant. When her father was brutally murdered and cast aside like a roadkill carcass. Left for dead like a thing unpleasant and insignificant, not worthy of sharing space with those still living and breathing and moving into the future.

And that same terrible moment, and those same dreadful images, appeared to her through the portal of Makaffie's mind. Only Prisma was no longer watching the tragedy as she remembered it through her own mind's eye. She was watching it as Makaffie. As he, and the others who stood at Goth Sullus's side, carried out the orders to kill her father.

32

For a long time, all Prisma could ever really say about what had happened on that day—all she saw in her mind—was one very specific moment. The moment when the massive security door just came off its hinges.

She'd been creeping closer to the pirates, or whatever they were, that had surrounded the governor's residence. They stood before the angular, squat desert building in a rough semicircle, blaster rifles ready. The man in the dark, hooded robe was behind them and off to the side, as though he wasn't really with them. As though he was very far away from all that was about to happen. He was a ghost that hovered nearby. A ghost that everyone saw, even though they didn't want to.

Prisma had passed the people of Bacci Cantara on the way to the residence. People she would never know because they were dead in the street.

"Really, young miss," rumbled KRS-88. "This is absolutely the opposite of what your father has instructed you to do. I shall be forced to tell him of your rebellious behavior when we meet him again. I regret this deeply. Perhaps at this evening's meal, before dessert."

"Crash," hissed Prisma. "Shhh. You're going to get us killed."

"Oh... yes. You are quite right. I'm not very good at this sort of war thing. I'm just a service bot. Pomp and circumstance at your service. But again, young miss, this seems an excellent way to get killed, or disabled. Please come away from all this... this... excitement. It's unseemly."

Prisma ignored the bot's warnings and crept forward. Toward the gang of pirates. Then closer still. She could hear one of them, a gravel-voiced man, yelling at her father.

"Come out and face Goth Sullus, you Republic scum! Things can go easy—or they can go real hard!"

A moment later—a moment after the giant of a man lowered his blaster and turned back to the man in the dark, hooded robes—the massive security door just came away from the building. As though the pirates had used some sort of hydraulic jaw, or some trick only they knew to violate such barriers.

Prisma would always remember that. The loud shriek of rending metal. The pirates scrambling to get out of the way of the flying-outward door.

A security door that was meters thick.

State-of-the-art Republic defensive perimeter security hardware.

When the dry dust of Bacci Cantara cleared, the door lay on the courtyard in front of the governor's residence.

"I'm coming out!" she heard her father say. His voice small and distant and pathetic.

Where are the two hulks? Prisma screamed inside her head. *They should be defending us.* Later she would find out they had been destroyed. Shot to pieces. They'd been blasted into melted ruin on a side street where they'd tried to set up an ambush on the pirates.

"I'm coming out with it," her father said.

It? What was "it"? That was something Prisma would wonder later. Later, when she sat in the ruins of the home she'd almost had. And on the ship she took to get off the planet to find a bounty hunter who would kill for her.

The pirates were moving forward, weapons aimed. The man in the hooded cloak still faced outward toward the dry desert world that was filled only with silence. An afternoon wind whipped and caught at his robes, making him seem like some mythic wraith that troubled the legends and bedtime stories of a thousand worlds.

The whining report of a lone blaster shot rang out—and Prisma's life changed forever.

As though her soul was suddenly frozen in that terrible high-pitched-whine-of-a-blaster-report moment.

Then the gravel-voiced giant exclaimed, "Got it!"

Now Prisma could see the big man approach the hooded figure almost fearfully. Not reverently, Prisma would later remember. The man was in fear of his fear. He held out her father's credentials data globe. The man in the hooded cloak took it, palmed it, examined it as though he were some second-rate star-carnie gypsy about to read a fortune. Then it disappeared within the folds of his wind-flapped garment.

He nodded once.

"Let's get out of here, brothers," shouted the giant pirate. "Tactical movement. Watch the corners and alleys. We're not off this dust bowl yet, leejes."

And in time they were gone.

The entire town was silent now. Only the sound of the moaning wind, rising and falling, moving and keening through the old buildings, remained. As though it were the only thing left to mourn all the dead.

Slowly Prisma crept forward from her hiding place. She would remember running. Oversized boots pounding against the hot afternoon sandstone pavement of the courtyard and the now-dead place called Bacci Cantara. She saw her father lying on the ground. The blaster hole in his chest. His beautiful gray eyes staring skyward. Not seeing her at all now.

"Get up, Daddy," she said. Her voice small and desperate. She shook her head once, back and forth, and began to cry. She begged him to get up.

His hands lay at his sides. The fingers open to the sky. As though he had finally surrendered all that one can grasp and hold in this life to something inevitably greater than himself.

Heaving with sobs, she dropped to the ground and took one of his hands. She tried furiously to rub life into it. "Please... Daddy, please..."

She could barely understand herself through her own tears. But she understood enough to know that she hated the sound she was making. And to hear herself begging was to hate it all the more.

"Please, Daddy... I can't be alone now. Not yet."

Far below, out on the vast dry lakebed, the big ship's engines ignited and grew to an ear-splitting roar.

Please.

She must've said that a hundred times by the time the ship rose into the sky, turned its back on Bacci Cantara forever, and surged off toward the stars and all the other mischief it must make before this tale was over.

A wan wind and a scattering of grit washed over her, and still she cried, helpless now, letting his cold hand fall back onto the dirt of that place.

Tears left dusty tracks on her face. Her shoulders shook, her chest heaved in violent spasms.

Please.

Please.

Please come back.
And...
Why?
Night fell. Prisma sat next to her father. He was just a body now.
Gone.
Taken.
By whom, asked some voice deep within.
She watched her father's eyes stare up at the few stars coming out along the galaxy's edge.
By whom?
"Please," she whispered, her voice raw and scratched. "Please come back now."
By whom?
Her tiny mouth formed the first word, making no sound. Then the second. Who had killed her daddy?
Who?
The gravel-voiced man had said who. He'd said a name when he'd shouted at her father inside the residence.
"Come out, you Republic scum! Come out and face—"
Goth Sullus.
Goth Sullus killed my daddy.

Prisma wanted to scream. She wanted to tear Makaffie's mind apart in rage and leave him a living curse. No, she wanted to bring him pain beyond measure and force him to suffer through it for the rest of his life. Every throbbing deep-grooved ache in his mind unequivocally linked to what he had helped Goth Sullus do to her father.

But he had done more than just *help*. He had been the very one to kill him. Makaffie had fired the blaster that ended her father's life.

Torment and suffering no longer seemed sufficient to Prisma. The two men vaguely standing before her in the real world, the place of reality outside the mind, deserved to be gone completely. Annihilated. Stripped of all hope of a better future forever.

Reina was quickly at Prisma's side. "I can sense you're angry. I know what you wish to do to them for what they did to you. But be mindful, my daughter. Be sure. And face the truth that's now been revealed to you in the real world. Do not let your rage entrap you here. Remember my warning."

And then Prisma was back in the same scout ship she had taken from En Shakar. She became aware that her mother and Makaffie—Stranger One—had been discussing something about the Savage technology unique to the ship. Prisma's head had been down, focusing on her hands as though she were bored with the conversation. She looked up, and Makaffie noticed the fire in her eyes right away.

"Something wrong, Prisma?" he asked.

"You killed my father," Prisma said bitterly.

Makaffie and the Wild Man exchanged a look. One that Prisma might've taken for confusion had she not seen what she'd seen. One that she now took for surprise at their sins being so suddenly exposed.

"Kael Maydoon. My father." Prisma stood from her chair and balled her fists. The rage was building now. The same frothy emotional frenzy that had manifested itself several times before. When Hutch tried to take her. When the Cybar seemed as though they were going to recapture her on the ship.

Makaffie looked from Prisma to Reina. The woman's face was impassive.

"You are being accused of something very grave," Reina said flatly. "Prisma's father was my husband."

Makaffie shook his head. "Now… that ain't how it went. Maydoon was by himself. Wife offed herself before we ever laid eyes on him. Little girl they had together died at the same time."

Prisma looked to her mother, the anger she felt swiftly replaced by a sense of uncertainty. Her father had never told her exactly what had happened to her mother. Only that she was dead and in heaven—a vague place that Kael Maydoon never seemed eager to explain when Prisma asked questions about it. And of course Crash was never any help in that regard. All he ever did was lecture Prisma about the comparative afterlifes of the galaxy's various species and planets.

It was so strange having her mother back. She'd never once gotten the impression that her father had been lying about her mother being dead. Crash had never hinted at that sort of thing either—and Crash wasn't supposed to lie to her. He was programmed to tell her the truth. He'd told her that, and he'd done that, telling her the truth even when all she wanted him to do was lie and tell her instead that things would be all right.

"What you heard," Reina said calmly, "was what we wanted the galaxy to believe. My husband held on to many secrets. His life was a failsafe. The knowledge bestowed upon him, and in him, kept all the various factions and machinations inside the Republic from undertaking total war against one another. Until outsiders found him. Until *you* found him."

"Well, Prisma," Makaffie said, with that almost tedious confidence and indifference he often spoke with. As though he didn't care what was happening around him. As though the galaxy itself were a thing for him and him alone to be amused by. One big cosmic joke and he was the only one in on it. "I suppose I owe you an apology. I'll give you one. I'm sorry we shot your daddy. Even though, if I had to do it all over again I would. I'm sorry for you. And while I typically don't try to speak on behalf of others, even my friend here who is disinclined to speak in general, and certainly those dead on this fateful trip of the damned who can no longer speak for themselves, in this instance I will. Every single member of my team who was on that mission is sorry that you lost your father. But Prisma... I ain't doing you any favors if I let you believe that your father was anything but a monster."

Prisma felt the rage return. She spoke through clenched teeth. "You shut your mouth. You don't know anything about him. Or us!"

"It might surprise you, but I actually know a whole lot about a whole lot. I know a whole little about a whole lot as well. But that's a different form of knowledge that does not pertain to our present discussion. May I venture a guess about things experienced and not seen?" Makaffie looked over his shoulder to the Wild Man, who was standing at tense attention. "Goth Sullus. Let's just put that name right out there because he is at the center of our mutual woes. For you because, well, we did indeed kill your daddy. For us because he proved to be a false prophet. A man corrupted by his own power. And yet... a man whose mission needs to be completed. Which is why we came to this accursed ship in the first damn place. So let's talk about him. And let's talk about all the magnificent things he could do, Prisma. Do you know the sorts of things that Goth Sullus was capable of?"

Prisma didn't want to talk about this. The conversation wasn't going the way she had imagined it. In her mind, the opportunity to meet those who had killed her father and face them down in a final act of vengeance involved begging and pleading and tears seeking to invoke mercy and the cold reality that Prisma would offer the same mercy they had shown to her daddy: none at all. But this man, this confounded odd scrawny man, was aloof to the point of evoking madness in her. If she raised a blaster rifle and shot him in the heart she was sure he would simply shrug and say, "That's how it goes, I guess," as his dying words.

She didn't want to talk about Goth Sullus. She was having trouble keeping the fire of her rage kindled. She looked to her mother for help, but Reina only watched her impassively. It was a look that told Prisma that whatever would come, however she would act, she was expected to blaze the trail by herself. Prisma now would be following her own lead.

Makaffie took her silence for assent. Or perhaps he didn't need assent at all but was merely giving her a polite few moments to interject before continuing on.

"Goth Sullus," he said, "had a name that wasn't Goth Sullus. In fact, when he woke up me and my friend for one final mission, one more opportunity to save the galaxy—a feat we'd accomplished several times by that point—he went ahead and told us who he was. Who he really was. Because he didn't quite look like the man we last saw. A man called Casper Sullivan. An admiral. A brilliant tactician. Almost as old as the galaxy itself, or so it seemed. He was much older than he appeared.

"He was good friends with old Tyrus Rex. And Tyrus Rex was a man we had fought and bled under. But it seemed that old Tyrus had lost his nerve. Or maybe just lost his mind in which case he couldn't be blamed for losing his nerve. As it was, the Legion wasn't the Legion no more. And all those little dark things that we had fought against, all those things we had bled for, were flip-flopped all around.

"Liberty?" Makaffie laughed. "Ha ha. Yeah, liberty's dangerous. Liberty, it ain't safe. And anyway, how do you control a free Republic? You can't. They're too free. So the answer is to remove their liberty. But not *just* that. You got to make them *beg* you to take that liberty away. You gotta go to war, man. You gotta go to war all the time. The killing can't stop, the bodies keep piling up, the blood keeps flowing. You gotta do all that all the time until the whole galaxy just doesn't even see it anymore. Doesn't even care about it. Bunch of boys in the Legion go off to fight and die? Not my problem. Bunch of Legion boys do everything you ask them to do? Kill that big bad twarg that you said was an existential threat to the Republic? Well, they was just doing their job. And they could've done a better job of it when you think about it. So no, we ain't gonna say nothin' special about that. We ain't gonna say nothin' at all. We ain't even gonna think of them."

Makaffie arched an eyebrow. He had Prisma's full attention now. "So that's step one. Get them all used to that. Like they don't mean nothin'. Because I don't mean nothin'. All of them Legion boys don't mean nothin'. All them dead insurgents dusted out on galaxy's edge don't mean nothin'. But that's the point. It don't mean nothin'. And then you go ahead and you tell them what *does* mean something. Because, as we've established, it ain't all that death out there.

"Here's what you tell them means something: *whatever causes you any inconvenience.* That's it. No matter how you get there, just matters that you're inconvenienced. Because the wars don't matter. No one says, 'I don't feel right about being safe here in the core away from all those wars. Far removed from the deaths that I let happen every single day. I just don't feel right.'

"They don't ever say that. Because that would mean that those deaths mean something. And they don't. They can't. Not if you're trying to deprive a people of their liberty.

"Do you understand, Prisma? Do you see how it all works? How the galaxy will hammer and beat on its own people until they both take no responsibility for the actions they collectively make possible but demand total accountability for the individual actions that don't mean nothing except someone else is doing them and you'd really rather they do something else?"

Makaffie waited for Prisma to reply. She gave what might be construed as a small nod, so he continued. "So that's what he—Casper, Goth Sullus—told us. That the galaxy had become a place of utter and complete corruption. And I hope you can appreciate me giving you that long roundabout explanation by way of beginning. When he showed up looking like Goth Sullus, who we didn't know and I wouldn't have wanted to get to know, and so he had to tell us it was him, Casper… there was trouble. And even Tyrus Rex might not be able to help this time because Tyrus Rex wasn't Tyrus Rex no more. He told us all of that, Prisma. Everything that I spent all this time jabbering to you about. He told us that in an instant. In the time it takes for you to blink. He told us without ever saying a single word about it."

The Wild Man shifted his stance, his arms folded across his chest. Prisma could sense the unease in him. Makaffie turned around to check on his friend. Gently slapped his chest, the back of his hand smacking against his armor plating.

"How do you suppose he did that, Prisma? Because he didn't *tell* us that. But we knew it. And we didn't just know it, we *experienced* it. We saw everything that he saw. And we saw a whole lotta things that he didn't see but people that he was already working with saw. And we saw it all in an instant. It was all in our *minds*. And I got to thinking... this man was in my mind. And I knew he was there the same way you know when someone creeps into your bedroom at night and you can't see or hear them but you know they're there. He was right there in my mind. In our minds. Showing us so that we would know. And he could do a whole lot of other things too, Prisma. With his mind. But let's just focus on that one thing. Goth Sullus could communicate without speaking. And he did it more than once. And because of that I learned to recognize when he had been there.

"And you know that man is dead, but right now I got that same feeling that someone was standing quietly in my bedroom while I was sleeping. And so, Prisma, little girl whose mother can do things that I only have seen Goth Sullus do... little girl who *herself* does things that I have only seen Goth Sullus do... do you have any idea, Prisma, why I might've had that feeling in my mind?"

Prisma licked her lips. "I saw. I saw your memories. I know what you did. I saw it all."

Makaffie gave a sorrowful smile. "Well, I'm sorry you had to see it then."

"That wasn't the first time. I saw it when it happened. I was hiding and I saw the whole thing."

"I'm sorry for that too."

Silence hung in the air. It seemed that everyone was frozen in stasis for a long while until KRS-88 decided to take a step forward. Just one step that clanged and reverberated through the hull. He said nothing and went no further. But the noise was enough to break the sudden spell that had fallen.

"I wonder something, Prisma," Makaffie said at last. "You know what we did. You know that we're sorry for your loss, but that we would do it all over again. And since you can walk right into my brain, why don't you have another look? Why don't you go ahead and see why it is that I'm not sorry for killing your daddy?"

Prisma swallowed despite her mouth feeling dry. She was at the precipice of what she had dreamed of for so long. And now it all tasted like ash. She was afraid to agree but felt she had no choice. And she knew why she was afraid. She was terrified that Makaffie would be right. And that everything she knew about her father would be forever changed.

She looked to her mother again, hoping that this time she would speak up, guide her, tell her what to do, or tell Makaffie what was going to happen.

But when her mother saw this searching, pleading look, all she said was, "Prisma, you must make this decision for yourself."

"How about it, Prisma?" Makaffie asked in that peculiar way of speaking that didn't indicate whether he wanted her to do it or not. Only that he was amused by the whole ordeal.

Prisma made the decision for herself. She shut her eyes tightly and descended into the man's memories, thinking of her father.

33

You're Tom. And it dawns on you as you look down at the dead body of Kael Maydoon that you're not Tom. Tom is there. Tom is dead. You're Donal Makaffie.

But you're Prisma.

But you're Tom.

Because everything you know about yourself came from what you read about yourself. Do you know enough about yourself to realize that the events that cut this man down, who is you, Tom, aren't true or false? They're only what Tom might've done.

What you did.

You've never seen a write-up like that before. It wasn't the official report. The official report was just that—official. It was clinical and it was evasive and it only touched on the points that the author knew the House of Reason would demand be explained.

But you know Tom, the real Tom, from that other report. The one that a man named X wrote. And then kept. Because X kept everything that he might one day use. He kept you alive, Tom. And he kept his first draft telling all about you. What was going through your mind. What you did. What you failed to do. What needed to happen next. He had to pay you back for what you'd done. Because you had done one hell of a job, Tom.

And where does it begin? It begins with you separating yourself from the layers of knowledge. You are Tom. The report says so. Makaffie was given the report.

There's Goth Sullus and he's speaking to a man named Voss. And the man is a spy and the man just got back from Utopion and he's handing Goth Sullus a paper. Not a datapad, real paper, and it's typed by some ancient artifact called a typewriter. And Goth Sullus looks at the pages and smiles slightly at the corners of his mouth.

And you know about typewriters. Because you're Makaffie. And all those things, all the little steps in technology no matter how archaic they might've been, well, those appeal to you. And so you watch and you wait as Goth Sullus compliments Voss for his work. For passing through all the layers he had to pass through and how returning to Utopion and to the darkest, dankest heart of Nether Ops was the most dangerous thing he could have done for the Black Fleet. And that his actions prove everything that Goth Sullus had known to be true about Voss.

And Voss, you can tell he's proud of all that. You can tell that the rot of the Republic is not a small matter in his mind. That he had believed in the Republic until she had been unfaithful and abused his trust.

And because you're Makaffie, and you know what happens next, you realize that this man Voss, who feels as though he's never been more sure and thankful for his life's decisions, will be dead in two months' time.

And you don't know exactly how it happens but you know it did happen because you read a report that mentioned offhand how some Nether Ops agent had recognized Voss. That's a problem with the defectors who came out of Nether Ops. Those who leave the Legion are left alone; when your terms of enlistment are up, the Legion is content to let you go free. But Nether Ops isn't like that. In Nether Ops, the terms are entirely one-sided. You serve at Nether Ops's discretion. Always. Forever. But sometimes you get a nice cushy retirement out of it. Like you, Tom. Because the players in Nether Ops got together with the players in the House of Reason—called the Mandarins—and they found a man who could lower tensions by becoming a repository of deep and dark secrets.

You know all about that, Tom. You know how when you came in from the cold and were presented as the hero with all your medals and accolades and a grateful House of Reason who had you to thank for them still being alive, you know how the next step was to get you to a nice, quiet, out-of-the-way place. And you knew it wouldn't be safe because life would never be safe again. Not with what you knew.

Only you didn't know exactly *what* you knew, Tom from the report.

But *you* know, Prisma, because Makaffie knew, because the month before Voss was killed, he cracked that nut about the Cybar fleet. About how it was just waiting to be used by the House of Reason once the Legion had finally had enough and tried to invoke Article Nineteen. And you know how the Carnivale labored to position itself as the group who would go and make that happen.

And that was hardly a sure thing. Another option is always in the running for these missions that couldn't be trusted to the Legion, Dark Ops, or any other organization with a conscience. There was a chance that one of the more "professional" branches of the Nether might've gotten the job, but then that would have spoiled the plans put together by the man named X who felt that the Cybar fleet could be wielded for their protection in the same way that the House of Reason sought to wield it against the Legion.

You know about X because you're Makaffie.

And so you know that it was hardly a sure thing that X's Carnivale would get the call to go after that fleet. And you know why, Tom.

What you had done was nothing short of a disaster. Nether Ops had only barely slipped the noose. Not just the Carnivale. The entire organization. And of course you know why. Because it was your fault.

You were the decorated naval officer with an axe to grind because of unfair treatment. Except that's not how it happened. Not Maydoon. But it was for Tom.

And you dug in deep, Tom. Went to all the seedy places. Places where life expectancy for outsiders was measured in days. The Night Market. Hell, anywhere outside Ankalor's green zone. And you wiggled your way down among the dregs of the galaxy. Surrounding yourself with people who wanted nothing more than to see the old guard burn, and not for honor or ethics or a moral resolve against a growing corruption in the House of Reason that was undeniable, but only because they liked the way the flames danced and sizzled. And the opportunities that arose from ashes. How else to live a different life from the misery foisted upon them by the way things were? Anything else was bound to be better. That was simple probability.

And there among the castaways and the villains, people who wanted things to topple so that they could ascend the steps of power, you had your break. A contact who had a contact who had a contact with a human named Scarpia. Who was the man you needed to find. And all he wanted was for you to obtain the impossible.

And so you worked every angle. You asked the scum to find that which couldn't be found. And since what couldn't be found was also what Scarpia needed, you asked your handlers to *make* it appear. Never mind that them finding their target and coaxing and manipulating the man into offloading some of the most powerful weapons in the Republic Navy's arsenal was itself a treasonous crime worthy of execution. Never mind that, Tom.

You had to get those two MAROs out into the Night Market circulation so that you could get them to Scarpia so that Scarpia could be prevented from getting weapons like that once and for all. It doesn't make sense to you, Prisma, but it made sense to Tom just fine. And it made sense to Makaffie, although he was hardly fine with it.

You waited in the green zone, kicking around, missing your family, enduring the heat and the grime and the sweat that came from that oppressive world. You watched the brutality of the zhee outside the green zone and wondered how a Republic who surely knew of the species' predilections would so ardently seek to justify them.

But then you're Makaffie, and you understand what Goth Sullus said about finding something to get the people upset about so they would beg for their liberty to be taken away. Xenophobia has always been an excellent option. It's easy to pitch groups against one another so that each will lustily defend the indefensible so long as it runs contrary to what the opposition believes. At least in the heat of the moment.

And then the day came when all the puppets were in their place. The holonews anchor. The unwitting navy supply man who thought himself a minor kingpin, a loose end who would be tied up by the very Endurians he kept at his side—little pieces of deadly arm candy. All those pieces were in place and you went out into the Night Market... and you got the impossible. And your contact told his contact and he told Scarpia.

And from there, Prisma, the adventure really took off. You got in good with Scarpia for a time. Because you're Tom, not Prisma. Scarpia actually liked you quite a bit. He thought you were exceptionally capable, because you were exceptionally capable. And he saw the way you looked at her. At Illuria. His green-skinned Cassari concubine with a body to die for whom he sometimes loved with all his heart and sometimes lusted with all his flesh and sometimes loved and hated in equal parts because she had that way of fully consuming his senses and he hated being under her sway and yet all he wanted was the intoxicating effects of the very same.

He saw you looking, Tom.

A lot of men looked. And sometimes when they looked he would fly into a rage and beat them to death right there on the yacht. Right there in front of Illuria, blood and brains spilling out over the side of the boat, chumming the waters as Scarpia beat that man to death until he physically exhausted himself and, panting with his fists and the small blaster that he used for the bludgeoning covered in blood, he would tell his man Frogg, who always cackled maniacally like it was the funniest thing he'd ever seen in his entire life, to take care of the body. And then he'd drag Illuria belowdecks. And Frogg, he would keep on chumming the waters out there in the open ocean on Pthalos. And he would whistle a tune and he would sharpen his knife and he would carve out little chunks of the dead man who'd looked at the beautiful Cassari. And he'd wait until some of the really big sharks came and then he'd go to work chopping up what remained of Scarpia's wrath until the sharks were full and the evidence was gone.

And you, Tom, were there, too. You wondered what you'd gotten yourself into.

You wouldn't have believed it at that time, Tom, but that was hardly the worst thing you would experience. And it certainly wasn't the worst thing you yourself would be asked to do one day. And when you looked at Illuria and Scarpia noticed, he never had that same rage in his eyes. Because he respected you. Because you were capable in your way. Just like Frogg was capable in his way. But Frogg was just a vicious wild animal. A blunt instrument used to do Scarpia's most violent will. You provided him so much more. You could plan and execute. You had done the impossible. And Tom, all you needed to do to get in, to *really* get in, was do the impossible one more time.

It sounded bad. It sounded like what you were supposed to stop in the first place. Those MAROs were going to blow up a Republic destroyer. Scarpia and the MCR had planned for it. They knew that a Legion detachment—an entire company—would be on Kublar to make sure a diplomatic mission was a success. Because, of course, that would result in a very resource-rich world staying solidly in Republic possession.

You felt as though your mission was already accomplished. You were with Scarpia all the time. And all you had to do was take him in. Kill Frogg, take Scarpia in, and explain everything that was going to happen.

Only it didn't happen that way.

You're Makaffie, and you're reading that report that Goth Sullus gave you after he had finished reading it. The one Voss had recovered. And you're reading about how Tom went right ahead with his mission. How he and the one called Frogg brought the MARO on board the Republic destroyer *Chiasm*.

And then, Prisma, there's a pause. And you find yourself with an option to know something more. Do you want to know how it all went down? Do you want to see what your daddy did aboard that ship?

In the room that was Makaffie's mind, where Prisma had stood learning all this in an instant while her mother stood with her watching, a door revealed itself. And Prisma knew that beyond that door would be the memory of holo-footage recovered from the Republic destroyer *Chiasm* and then locked away in some Nether Ops vault after it had been recovered by one of their agents. Makaffie knew it was there because Voss, who had proven to be the ultimate counteragent until his untimely demise, had gone and gotten it for Goth Sullus. And Goth Sullus had shown it to his men. And it only added to their belief that the sooner the mission to find and take down Kael Maydoon happened, the better the galaxy would be for it.

Prisma wanted to know. So she stepped inside.

34

The blinking lights of a Republic supply shuttle drift toward the *Chiasm*'s main docking bay force field. Prisma watches it happen as though she is witnessing a holofilm. Which in a way, she is. This is all the feeds from the all-seeing destroyer. And they're being played back for her as a narrative.

She doesn't want to watch. She can't look away.

Visible through the shuttle's front viewport is her father. No... that's Tom. He's dressed as a naval pilot. Behind him is the short, ugly little man named Frogg. He smiles at Tom, a wicked, evil grin.

The supply shuttle touches down on the gleaming black deck of the destroyer. The deck officer, an efficient woman in a pristine uniform wearing a sidearm, leans over the shoulder of a much younger, unarmed communications sergeant.

"No records at all?" the deck officer asks.

"Nothing, ma'am. I ran a check on the registry. It says the vessel was decommissioned two years ago." The communications sergeant looks warily at the shuttle.

The deck officer stares uneasily at the shuttle as well before letting out a sigh. "Well, it's here now. Report this to RCMVR immediately. And notify the marines that we might have a situation. Let's see what we've got."

"Yes, ma'am."

The shuttle settles fully onto the docking bay, venting gases as bots and techs move busily to properly secure it and prepare for refueling. All according to protocol.

Now Prisma sees the footage of the Republic marines scrambling from their barracks. They're running by their bunks, already in their gear and ready for such a call. They pass by the armory and are handed their rifles.

A swarthy sergeant whose clean-shaven face looks like sandpaper hollers at them as they move. "Let's go, hullbusters! Let's go! I want your asses on that deck two minutes ago!"

Back in the docking bay, Prisma's father is standing at the top of the shuttle's cargo ramp, staring at a datapad.

"Waiting for a call?" Frogg asks sarcastically.

Prisma can hear it because the ship could hear it. Its systems could hear and see, though no one could do anything with what it heard or saw until it was too late.

Tom stares at the datapad for another moment and then tucks it under his arms. In the depth of the shuttle are four mercenaries in HOLO suits. High Orbit, Low Opening. Meant for infiltrating a planet's atmosphere. The footage shows just a glimpse of them. The deck officer and communications sergeant missed them completely there in the shadows.

"Initiate," says Tom before giving Frogg a grim nod. The cruel little man smiles back gleefully and the pair move down the shuttle ramp.

There's a transformation in Tom's face. He becomes something of the man Prisma knew. The hard-set face is cheerful and carefree. A pleasant junior officer sauntering down the ramp without a care in the world.

Frogg stays at the top of the shuttle ramp.

Nearby, two Republic Lancer fighters taxi toward the docking bay shields, ready to fly a routine patrol. Tom smartly salutes the two fighter pilots. They salute back and give Tom a thumbs-up as they pull to their departure stations.

The deck officer walks briskly to Tom. They exchange perfunctory salutes. Tom holds out his datapad to her.

She looks at it superficially and says, "We weren't expecting you."

Tom smiles. Prisma remembers that smile and feels a sick longing in her heart.

"I just go where they tell me," Tom says. He gestures to the datapad. "There's our manifest. Kublaren delicacies, I'm told—if there is such a thing. Something for the brass trying to woo the chieftains down there, I think."

The deck officer takes a more careful look at the datapad.

At the ramp, Frogg says to the mercenaries, "You MCR boys ready to start a war?"

They don't answer. Instead they push a repulsor gurney down the ramp. It's wrapped in an enormous cloth tarp. Everything about Frogg and the mercenaries is surreal. They take a turn and push the gurney toward the massive shield protecting the bay's opening from the vacuum of space.

Meanwhile, the deck officer is still absorbed by the manifest. "Two thousand cases of Kimbrin Sprigg eggs?"

Tom shrugs and makes a face as if to say, *Don't ask me, I'm just the messenger.*

Now Prisma sees the Republic marines again. They're hustling toward the docking bay. One of the hullbusters asks the guy next to him if it's another drill. The other man shrugs and they continue to jog through the ship.

As the deck officer scrolls through the datapad, the communications sergeant rushes to her side. "Ma'am, I heard back from RCMVR..." He trails off after noticing Frogg and the mercenaries moving across the deck. "What the..."

The deck officer looks up from her screen. "Hey! You can't—"

Prisma jumps involuntarily at the speed with which her father pulls out a compact blaster pistol and kills both the communications sergeant and deck officer with two efficient shots.

Frogg smiles and keeps moving. Two of the MCR break off to join Tom, who is standing in horror over the two people he's just murdered. Blaster bolts flash above his head.

The marines have arrived and are taking hurried shots at the intruders. An alarm begins to wail.

Tom is standing in a daze, looking down at his sin.

More blaster fire rips by Frogg, who shoots back with his pistol, one-handed. His other hand continues to push the repulsor gurney containing the MARO. "Move your ass, Tommy!"

Prisma watches as regret and humanity are wiped from her father's face. He hardens himself in warrior mode and turns and runs to Frogg, passing the two MCR who had doubled back for support as they exchange weapons fire with the marines.

The pilots Tom saluted are rising out of their fighters because of the commotion. Frogg sees this and shoots them. They tumble out of their Lancers and onto the deck with sickening landings. "Love clipping a featherhead's wings."

One of the MCR is hit by the hullbusters, allowing the marines to leapfrog and advance. The other MCR mercenary cuts and runs, racing to catch up with Tom.

Frogg and the remaining MCR bring the gurney to a halt at the very edge of the dock. The mercs fire their weapons to keep the marines back while Frogg yanks the tarp off the cylindrical object, revealing a small, two-stage drone. He rips open the hatch to the vessel, large enough to fit two humanoids.

Tom reaches the drone with blaster fire chasing him. He clambers into the tiny seat and immediately begins to strap himself in, Frogg getting in just behind him.

"Let's go! Let's go!" Tom shouts. He bangs the clear canopy to get the attention of the mercs still fighting outside. "Go go go!"

High above, from the top of the bay, a holocam looks down at the drone. Tom is pulling down on a lever that activates the device's repulsors, lifting it from its gurney. The mercs grab onto the drone by special handles as it builds momentum in its rush toward the docking bay shield.

Blaster fire strikes the drone and then skips onward along the deck and sometimes into the shield itself. Another merc is hit and killed, leaving only two. Both are hanging onto the drone as it passes through the shield and into open space, almost immediately nosing into an atmospheric reentry.

Outside Prisma can see the mercs let go, moving into a free fall. She can see Tom frantically struggling to gain control of the plummeting drone until it's too far from the *Chiasm*'s external holocams for her to make out her father. But she still sees the drone hurtling toward the planet. There's a flash of light as it divides into two sections: the front section containing the pilot and passenger and the rear section shaped like a missile.

The rear section hovers for a moment as its rockets flare, then it shoots off on a different trajectory while the front section sprouts wings, transforming into a glider that silently winds its way down to the surface in big loops around the surviving mercs.

Back on the ship, the hullbusters are searching the abandoned shuttle and securing the cargo bay. More pilots are readying to pursue the drone. There's a cataclysmic explosion, and then everything goes dead.

When it was over, Prisma didn't know what to do or what to say. Because she'd recognized the person who had been there next to the vicious little man with the bulging eyes. The man named Tom. Tom was her father. And that didn't make sense.

Her father was a hero. She had seen the medals. Had run her fingers over the designs, feeling each groove and imprint. Had rubbed the ribbons between her fingers, enjoying the silky smoothness. One time her father had come into the room unexpectedly and found her with a bench pushed up against the dresser. She'd needed that to reach the top drawer, where all the medals were.

"Prisma?" he said. "What are you doing?"

The sound of his voice caused her to start, and she nearly dropped the medal she'd been looking at. She spun around and hid the box behind her back before realizing how silly and futile that was.

"I wasn't going to try and wear it," she said, and then held out the box for her father.

He smiled, but he wasn't happy. And yet, Prisma didn't feel that he was upset either. At least not with her. He crossed the room and took the box and closed it. Then he placed it back inside the drawer and closed that as well.

"I like that one," Prisma said after he had lifted her off the bench and set her back on the ground. She'd always been small for her age. She still was. "What's it called?"

Her father seemed like he was bothered about something. Prisma knew it wasn't her, because he hadn't yet given her that look of disappointment—that stern, fatherly stare that, if held long enough, had a way of making her burst into tears.

"It's called the Order of the Centurion," he said at last.

"Oh. What did you do to get it?"

"I don't know," her father mumbled. He looked around the room. "Where's Crash?"

"Outside. I told him you wanted him to pick flowers to put in a vase for dinner tonight."

"I never said that. Prisma, you can't keep telling Crash to do things, using me as your authorization. He's supposed to be with you. As much as possible."

Prisma followed her father out of the room, her bare feet making tiny padding sounds on the hardwood. "Crash doesn't mind. He likes picking flowers. I can tell."

"He's a bot, Prisma. He doesn't like or dislike anything. He just does what he's programmed to do." He stopped and looked down at the floor for a moment. Then he said quietly, "Just like you, right?"

Prisma knew that her father was talking to himself. He'd been doing that a lot since her mother disappeared. Which was what it felt like to Prisma: that she'd simply disappeared. Prisma went to bed one night and when she woke up there were strangers in the house with her father. His eyes were bloodshot. He could barely speak. He kept almost crying. And all he said about Prisma's mother was that she had gone to heaven.

Prisma was younger then. And at the time, that answer seemed as good as any that could've been given. She cried a lot, then and later and often, and sometimes that made her father cry right along with her. But most times it made him focus on her. Telling her that it was all right. And that he wouldn't leave her, although the thought that he might never entered Prisma's mind until he said it.

But on that day when she got into the medal drawer, she was older. Still small, but older. She knew about death. And in that moment when she saw her father looking downcast, she was reminded of that first morning without her mother. Prisma could barely remember her face. There were never holopictures around. Not of her mother, or her father, or even Prisma herself. Their rooms were always spartan, furnished for living well, but lacking any charming character, any personality, any indication of who precisely did the living there.

That was part of why the medals so fascinated Prisma. They were the only possession that traveled with the family on all of their many moves. Those and Crash. Everything else—clothes, toys, blankets and sheets and beds, furniture, even datapads—were always supplied and waiting for them. Oh, and the blaster pistol—her father kept that too. But Prisma was never to touch it. And anyway, it was usually hidden in her father's waistband. Sometimes she would bonk herself against it when she gave him a hug after he'd been away from home for days on end.

But now something had him looking sorrowful. So Prisma did what she could to cheer her father up.

"I don't think that's true. Crash likes me. He says so. And some things he hates. He says that too. And nobody could've programmed him to like me because he didn't even know me when you got him. And some of the things he hates are things that he has to do, and I don't mean boring stuff like cleaning up. I mean like those times when you tell me I have to hide. He hates that. He hates his weapons. He told me so."

That had diverted from what was meant to be a lighthearted remark into a truthful observation about the war bot. Sometimes Prisma kept talking beyond her initial intent.

But her father did seem to cheer up, if only slightly. "That just goes to show that you can make anyone come to like you, Prisma. No matter what the programming says."

"Prisma."

It was her mother. Reina.

"Prisma, you must remember that your purpose in this man's mind is to see what he knows. You are no longer doing that. You are reliving your own experiences."

"I'm sorry," said Prisma. "It's just, I haven't seen him in so long. And I miss him. And I can't help but think about him."

"I understand. But you need to know that what you relive inside this man's mind will become his. He will remember what you have shown him."

Prisma nodded to her mother, the two of them standing alone inside the room that was Makaffie's mind. "Is it true?" she asked. "Is he showing me the truth about Daddy?"

"No man is as good as he wants to be. And no person will ever be as good as you desire them to be, Prisma. Including you. And including me."

"I can't... I can't do anything about it. About what he did. Killing my father."

Prisma felt relieved that the swell of emotion that accompanied those words didn't manifest into tears. Instead she straightened out her posture and squared her shoulders, raising her chin like her mother did.

"I understand why he did it," Prisma said of Makaffie. "How could Daddy have killed all those people just because someone told him to?"

"He did many other things as well," said her mother. "Some good and some very bad. He told me once that he had done it for you. He tried to tell me that he had done it for us. But I knew the truth. And you should know it too. Prisma, he did it for himself. And you and I were mere excuses meant to help him sleep better at night."

Prisma looked down and wept. She thought about everything that had happened to her since that day when she saw her father die. The faces of those who had been there for her throughout the ordeal now flashed in her mind. Crash. Leenah. Tyrus Rechs. Even Captain Keel. He had saved her life more times than anyone but Crash, and all she'd ever done was act ungrateful for it. Because all she wanted was to make Goth Sullus suffer. And anything and anyone who delayed that... she saw them as an enemy. Or at least an obstacle to be overcome.

And now, two men who were there with Goth Sullus when her father was killed—one of them the man who pulled the trigger—stood in the same room as her. And she found that the rage that she had so persistently kept in her heart for this day was now insufficient for the dark task she had so often comforted herself with by fantasizing about it before slipping into sleep. Praying that such dreams of revenge would come true.

"What do you wish to do, Prisma?" her mother asked.

"I don't know. I can't kill them. I was sure... I *would've* killed them if you hadn't shown me. But what he did... Tyrus Rechs would've killed my father for what he did. And Captain Keel, he *definitely* would've."

Her mother nodded. "I think you're making the right decision. And now, it's time to leave this man's mind. Spare yourself the knowledge of what else your father did. It's better not to know."

Prisma looked up at her mother. "What do we do now? I won't kill them, and I don't hate them, but... I don't wanna be around them either."

"Then we will leave them."

"Alone?"

"They are free to leave the ship."

Prisma nodded. She'd forgotten.

"I must tell you something more, Prisma. You see how these men harmed you, and yet you know why they did it. You will find that Casper, whom you know as Goth Sullus, was not ultimately responsible even for what *he* did. That blame lies elsewhere. With the one who created Goth Sullus. And that one, my daughter, is who we now must bring to account."

Prisma felt the hair on her arms and the back of her neck stand up.

"Will you join me in this?" her mother asked. "I need your help. I can't do it by myself."

And Prisma said, "I will."

35

Makaffie noted that Reina, together with Prisma and her bot, left the Savage mini-hulk without consulting Archimedes. He knew that Reina had the freedom to come and go as she pleased; her title and treatment made that much obvious. She was the master. But probably not by design. Makaffie had seen the Savages and their many iterations, and he had heard of even more strains of Savage culture.

Reina fit none that he was aware of.

And so her mastery was likely as she had said. She had exerted her will on Archimedes and forced him into subservience. It was that, or face annihilation.

She had asserted her will on her daughter as well, though so subtly that Prisma likely wasn't even aware it had happened. But Makaffie was. He'd seen the rage in the girl's eyes. Murderous rage. Had she been left to first impressions and raw emotion, neither Makaffie nor the Wild Man would have seen the ordeal through without someone dying. And while Makaffie trusted his friend's ability to put down a little girl before she killed them, he harbored no illusions about Reina's ability to kill them both. No matter what they did to try to stop it.

So he was more than a little relieved when they were asked to simply leave the ship and go their separate ways. Another day alive was better than the alternative. Not always, but so far, and today.

"It would seem that we are stranded and forgotten, my friend," Makaffie told Wild Man. "This operation did not work out the way I hoped it would. Which isn't to say that it worked out in a way that was surprising, because with the Savages, as you well know, seeing as how you had so many years going up against them, you can't do anything but *expect* to be surprised. Which means the surprise isn't a surprise at all, if you think about it. Who was it who said that? That with the Savages, you have to expect to be surprised? Was it the general or the admiral? I can't remember."

"They both said it," rasped Wild Man.

They looked around, surveying the hangar, now empty of Prisma's ship. Reina had somehow arrived without a ship. Or she had hidden her ship in another hangar—perhaps docked it to the exterior hull.

"We're stuck here now," said the Wild Man.

"Well now, I think that's a rather pessimistic way of summarizing the facts. No one's ever *stuck* anywhere. There's always a way out. We're as stuck here as we were stuck on New Vega. Or Sinasia. Or any other place we've ever found ourselves stuck in. Which is to say we were transitory beings moving along like a mist across the galaxy. We were never stuck at all. Mortal man *can't* be stuck. A mortal man can only be delayed. Now the *immortal* man, that's a different story. He can get stuck. I sometimes think that was the curse of the admiral, and to an even greater extent, the general. I think that was the cause of his anguish."

"Didn't seem anguished to me."

"Oh, it was there. You had to look for it. And while you, my friend, are exceptional at looking through a scope and finding a target, I daresay you lack a certain nuance when it comes to looking into the heart and soul of a man."

The Wild Man voiced no opposition to this observation. Indeed, he found himself agreeing. Other people were a mystery. He only understood himself at the most basic of levels.

Makaffie continued. "Those two, the general and the admiral, they couldn't die. Not really. Not mostly. Not unless they did it to each other. You saw what happened to the general when he died plenty of times. I imagine it was the same for Casper. I imagine, unless his body was destroyed, he would have just gotten right back up and went about his business, same as the general did all those times. So if you can't die, and they couldn't—and you can be detained... well then, being stuck is within the realm of possibilities. To be placed someplace with no escape. And you know, that's just what happened to them on that slave ship that they would talk about from time to time. That Savage house of horrors. I never could get them to tell me much. The general, being his usual self, would say nothing at all. But Casper talked about it sometimes, a little bit, although he seemed to sense that in so doing he displeased the general. Anyway, my point is, that's how a man gets stuck. He finds himself in a place he can never leave. But that's not us. We can't get stuck here. Eventually, we'll just die."

"That doesn't make me feel better."

Makaffie smiled. "It's endearing that you thought what I was going to say would make you feel better. For I imagine you know me better than that by now. However, perhaps this next part *will* make you feel better. We are not stuck, and not simply because death will eventually come along and unstick us. We have the right to leave the ship. Or have you forgotten?"

The Wild Man by now had started to move toward the shuttle they had arrived in. "Didn't forget. Can't leave."

"Au contraire. Archimedes gave us liberty to depart in exchange for our brilliant tactical display in his simulation. So yes, we *can* leave. And furthermore, it is in our best interest to leave." Makaffie hurried in front of the long strides of the Wild Man and then threw his arm out like a barrier, stopping the bigger man from going further. "Let me tell you why."

He waited long enough to taste the drama that came from his well-timed pause. And then, when the moment was ripe and pregnant, he said, "That little girl knew our friend Sergeant Fast."

The Wild Man crossed his arms. It was no act of defiance; he was merely waiting for the little man in front of him to elaborate.

"She was in my mind. Going through my thoughts," Makaffie continued. "You know how the admiral did that, once he came back as Goth Sullus? What he could do with his thoughts? With our minds? She did that. Looked at what I knew. Only it felt like the whole experience was something new to her. Reina—her mother—guided her through the process.

"She wanted to know about her daddy. And there are things that you and I knew about her daddy that, I can now assure you, she definitely did not. Those memories, those revelations about her daddy, they caused her to think and remember. And wouldn't you know it, it was just the same as when Goth Sullus imposed his thoughts on us and showed us everything that happened in the galaxy while we were napping. And wouldn't you know, I just experienced a similar situation with Prisma. She was friends with our very own Sergeant Fast. Which is to say Sergeant Ford. Which is to say *Captain* Ford, on account of his promotions even while serving with us. But you know, I've never stopped thinking of him as Sergeant Fast."

"So where is he?" Wild Man growled, his impatience in check—for now.

"She didn't exactly know that. But she knew other things. And with those other things, I have confidence that I can find Fast and get the help we need to acquire that Savage piece—the Strand. He's always been the missing link. Imagine how things would've gone if he'd have been there to get the draw on Rex. And then the old man would've at least taken the time to sit down and listen to reason. And you get Casper being Casper, you get him talking instead of feeling like he needs to be the big bad shooter, because he never was that—not saying I was myself either, but he never was. Still, you get all that. You get ol' Tyrus Rex sitting down and listening, and I tell you what: we got a different outcome. We got the head start on what's coming that we should have had. And anyway, I'm sure if we dropped him into that simulation that Ravi was trying to achieve, he would get it done right. He always got it done right. That's what was so crazy about him. Except the times when he died, he was extremely good."

The Wild Man lifted off his helmet to reveal his burnt and scarred face. "We can't both leave. This ship has hyperdrive. If it were to decide to jump we might never find it again." He finished looking pained from speaking so many words.

Makaffie frowned. "I am embarrassed to admit that I hadn't thought of that. This old thing has been sitting out here for so long I let myself presume it would stay out here like some swirling natural wonder, a radiant nebula just waiting to be discovered. But you're right. You are right. There is nothing stopping the ship from jumping to hyperspace once we're gone. And if we don't have that Strand, well, I'm not saying it's mission failure, but... we have to be realistic about such things."

Makaffie slapped his hands together and then crisscrossed his thin fingers. "How about this then? You stay here and live off of that slurry they feed you—you seem to like it just fine—and I take the shuttle and track down our Sergeant Fast."

"That's fine. How are you gonna find him? You said the girl doesn't know where he is."

"That's true. But it's also true that I'm quite good at finding that which is hidden or lost. I found the ship after all, didn't I? And I've got two names that I believe will allow me to get on his trail. The first is the name of his ship: the *Indelible VI*. The second is the name our friend Fast, our friend Ford, goes by. Our friend... Captain Aeson Keel."

36

Masters awoke to find himself folded over, his face lying on top of the heels of his boots. That presented a serious problem, and Masters trembled in shock as he realized the position he must be in. He'd been with Tennar who weren't flexible enough to pull that off. The only thing he could think of was that in the fall and subsequent rolling crash of a descent down the mountain and into the inhospitable wilds, his back must have been broken—and now he lay bent over on top himself in a pile of shattered bone and torn muscles.

Panic tried to set in, but he warded it off by reminding himself of the sort of attention legionnaires who were nursing particularly gruesome injuries got from the sympathetic hearts of the galaxy's female population. He'd known leejes who chose to skip a few of their regen treatments in order to prolong being armless or footless for the benefit of their love lives.

One compatriot who served with him back in Victory Company proclaimed just what a boon his injury had been in picking up girls at the club. "I don't know how to explain it," the leej said. "Other than they're naturally wired for compassion, and I just set off all the right components in their hard drives. You know me, Masters, I don't know a lot about ladies, man, but I'm not exaggerating when I say no more than ten minutes pass from the time I get in a place to the point when some torrid woman buys me a drink. And after that, it only takes a few war stories and an open schedule to seal the deal."

Masters smiled at the memory. The legionnaire in question, a guy in his second enlistment named Trevor Nielsen, had been more life taker than heartbreaker. And if he saw that much success from losing his leg from the knee down, how much more success would Masters have once he got himself off of this sweltering hellhole?

Come to think of it, he would have to ask Bear if his own injuries had resulted in him finally scoring dates with women who had less body hair than he did. Once he got off Kima, that is.

In the distance, Masters could hear the faint sound of explosions. Big explosions that suggested the size and scope of their destruction in the way they rumbled and trembled through the sky and down the slope of the mountain he had careened down. He tilted his head up to look at the sky but could see only the oppressive canopy of the sparse jungle trees and their expansive leaves and branches.

This was wild and inhospitable territory. Much different from where he and his team had been operating. That had been difficult and hot terrain, but at least it was navigable, a place where forces could move and hide. A place where SLICs could land and artillery could ravage the exposed earth. This side of the mountain, by contrast, was a wilderness, teeming with towering jungle trees that shot ever upward in an attempt to capture the sun's rays high above, leaving the forested area below, where Masters had come to a stop, in a gloomy darkness of the type unable to support the growth of anything but the occasional fungus. The chrono in his HUD told him to expect daylight, but there was none to be found where he lay broken on the lower slopes of the mountain.

Broken. Despite his attempts to find the silvene lining in his situation, the realities of his injury continued to rest uneasily in the back of his mind. Other than flicking his eyes up in search of light, he hadn't dared move out of fear of somehow injuring himself worse than he already was. If that was even possible. His arms felt strong, at least, and whatever had happened to his back wasn't causing him any pain. But that could be good or bad. It was certainly to be expected when your spinal column was severed.

And that was precisely what Masters thought had happened in those brief moments before he felt a sharp twinge of pain in his knee, followed by the distinct feeling of his toes wiggling inside his boots. That felt normal. Not at all the feeling he'd have with a severed spinal column. Or the absence of feeling, to be more accurate.

He wiggled his toes again, then shifted his feet and watched the boots in front of his face. The boots didn't move.

"Okay. So I am imagining things or...?"

He pushed himself up and found that he could tuck his knees up beneath him and kneel in place. And as he did so, it became obvious that he had been lying atop someone *else's* legs. It was someone else's combat boots that hadn't wiggled. When he stood up fully and then caught himself from falling after an onset of dizziness, he saw that the legs were attached to a tattered and gory pelvis—and nothing else.

"Ah, sket," Masters said. He had to guess which of his friends these legs belonged to. Both Young and Jaybles had been blasted and sent off the mountain. Masters had seen the damage that even second-rate artillery could do to a body. Republic Army artillery even more so.

He checked the boot size and couldn't remember whether it was Young or Jaybles who had the larger size. Had to be Young, didn't it? Masters removed the lower shin protector from one leg to reveal the synthprene undersuit, and then with a quick flick of his combat knife sliced the synthprene open. Some blood had worked its way down from the catastrophic wound up top, but he was able to tell from the skin pigmentation who it was.

Jaybles. Born Joseph Bailey. Died on a Kimbrin mountaintop.

"Sorry, buddy," Masters said. He looked around for the rest of the man, or parts of any others, but saw nothing.

He decided to give his L-comm a try despite his HUD's indicator that it was dead. He received no indication that it was on and no reply to his message. He tested his bucket's external audios and found those dead as well. The HUD was at least good enough to provide optics and enhanced battle sight, which meant that it would serve as protection in the field and a boon in the darkness. The HUD also indicated the presence of his two squadmates farther down the slope, their locations being broadcast from transponders in their chest armor and helmets. That meant that half of Jaybles and hopefully all of an alive Young would be somewhere down there.

Masters pulled his helmet off—the climate controls were dead, and the thing felt absolutely stifling—and was rewarded with a warm breeze whipping down the mountain that nonetheless felt cool as it rustled his sweat-drenched hair. Clipping the bucket to his belt, he began moving down the mountain as quickly as his legs would take him.

As he went, he kept his eyes peeled for any of the Yawds who also had come down the mountain and were without Legion transponders to help with the search and rescue. And he did come across what remained of the allied Kimbrin—in pieces of various sizes. These too had been victims of the mountaintop artillery strikes, and their scattered remains were the measuring markers of how far that violent cruelty had expelled what remained of its victims.

The first of his squadmates that Masters came upon was Young. He was whole, as Masters had hoped, but not alive. He had tumbled down the mountain well past where Masters had stopped, and had met a much less welcoming resting place than Jaybles's legs had provided for Masters. Young's body was wrapped around one of the tall and leafless tree trunks. He lay pulverized and bleeding in the deep well of shadows beneath the canopy of high leaves drinking up every last ray of sunlight.

Masters looked straight up and got a momentary sense of vertigo from the height of the trees. He could see older, lower, leafy branches fading into a twisted black mesh, the fresher, younger shoots above depriving them of sunlight just as they had once deprived the barren stretches of dead leaves beneath them of the same. The species seemed capable of going ever up and up, competing with itself and with the trees around it for light. Indeed, Masters could see several trees that had been outgrown and simply died in place, towering skeletons unable to reach the heights of their betters.

Young must've been moving pretty quickly when he slammed into the tree. He'd managed to leave a few gouges in the bark—at the expense of his armor and helmet, which was cracked and shattered. Dark Ops didn't wear anything like the shinies that dominated the Legion before the House of Reason's demise. Young wore good, solid armor capable of taking a significant amount of punishment. But everything has its breaking point, and Young broke right alongside his armor.

Masters gently moved his friend's body in the hopes that the bucket would be in good enough condition to provide some salvage. Perhaps Young's L-comm was still functional. Instead, the helmet practically disintegrated in Masters's hands the moment he attempted to pull it off of his friend. Worse, raising the helmet caused a rush of blood and brains to seep out onto Young's chest and shoulders. It was as if his head had been liquefied inside the armor from the impacts he had suffered on the way down.

Masters didn't attempt to lift the helmet any further. If his own L-comm hadn't survived his much less violent fall, he didn't see how Young's would be any different. He patted the man on his shoulder and felt it give unnaturally, as if the armor had lost its rigidity and was simply sinking into the mush that lay where bone had once been. "Rest easy, bud."

He took what charge packs he could find—his blaster rifle hadn't gotten separated from him in the fall—and then continued on down the mountain, navigating a grisly trail that was the aftermath of K-SOG-7's last stand.

Masters reached Jaybles again and said, "Hey, didn't I just see you?" This half of the man was every bit as dead as the other. His helmet was completely gone, as well as most of his armor, with just the sleeve and half of the chest plate on one side remaining. The visible flesh was burnt and scarred by the tumble down the mountain, and the head was lumpy and misshapen. There were no charge packs. No grenades. Nothing at all. And nothing to keep Masters in this most sorrowful of graveyards.

He walked the rest of the way down the mountainside beneath the thick shadow of the peculiar forest. The sights and sounds of battle did not follow.

37

The sun had set, and Masters waited out the night in the grim, dark forest. He couldn't remember a darker night than the one he spent beneath those towering trees. But it was peaceful, even if the otherworldly silence was unnerving. The forest seemed to smother all sound. Unless he had his bucket on, he couldn't even hear himself breathing. He saw no signs of animal life and felt no rush of wind. The ancient and primordial forest of Kima enveloped all.

By the next day he had managed to travel most of the way out of the black forest dominion. The tall trees begin to thin out, allowing in pockets of sunlight that revealed the forest floor was a dark brown instead of the black that Masters had thought it was. The trees were sparser here and much shorter. But despite this, the ground between the trees remained as barren as the choked-out land of the thick forest he had just come through. There was no color beyond the dour green of the treetops, which looked as though they were coated in dust. If there was anything other than Masters alive in the area, it remained well hidden.

Fortunately, he was good on food. Legion ration packs contained such a high concentration of calories and nutrients that he needed only take a few bites a day to be sufficiently fueled for even the most grueling of tasks. The only side effect would be a rumbling stomach. To combat this, the rations came with neutralizing tablets that decreased the caloric load so that a single ration pack was equivalent to a single meal, which was fine if you were sure a resupply was coming. That wouldn't be the case for Masters.

Water was a different story. For now his armor would do what it always did, recycling his sweat and waste water, purifying it, and providing it to him to drink via a small tube connected to a bladder just behind the shoulders. It would be warm, and if unreplenished not the most pleasant-tasting thing in the world on account of there being only four days' worth of internal purification cycles. But Masters had had water that was hard to drink in the past. The bigger issue was with the natural evaporation that came whenever he took his helmet off. Cooling systems weren't functional, and he was sweating so much with the bucket on that he worried he might give himself heat exhaustion. Yet when he removed it, he would lose fluid to evaporation. And there were no signs of water anywhere to be seen. Maybe the trees were fed by an underground reservoir, and maybe Masters could dig his way down if things got desperate enough… but for now, it was just something to note and then move on.

At the end of the second day, which came early as the sun sank behind the mountain he was moving away from, Masters finally got a glimpse of a change in terrain. It wasn't even that really. It was the same sparse trees and dead, barren soil, but it also contained the unmistakable remnants of a village, though very little of it still stood.

Flash-printed buildings lay crumbled about the town center. Masters counted about six of them, each no larger than twenty-five square meters. None had more than two walls still standing. The roofs had collapsed in onto the floors, and the fallen walls rested under a thick layer of grit. The rest of the village was in even worse shape. Evidently the printers had done what they could, and those still in need of dwellings were left to pile up logs to build cabins—most of which had now rotted away, or perhaps were carried away. But here and there a few evenly cut thick logs were still laid out in a square and stacked, the rest of the once-cabins gone via some means or another.

Masters looked around. "I would've preferred a place with a cantina and a few eligible women, but this will do."

After a search of the village and surrounding area turned up nothing noteworthy in terms of danger or salvage, Masters set himself down inside one of the dilapidated cabins and looked to the skies for any sign of Republic activity. If the planet was experiencing a full-blown civil war, and if the Republic was showing up to do something about it, the surest sign would be seen in the heavens. Either the flashes of battle or the looming presence of a destroyer in orbit.

"Probably on the other side of the planet," Masters muttered after seeing nothing. "Just my luck. No, you know what? *Not* my luck. I am incredibly lucky. The only people luckier than me are the girls who get to spend time with me. So who's luck is this? Because it's not mine."

He took a bite of his ration pack and chewed slowly, thinking that Jaybles and Young would likely contest his assertion.

"That just proves my point," Masters said, as though the two were sitting with him. "Everybody gets blown up except me. Which you *could* argue was lucky, but I'd say the guy who wasn't on the mountain at all was the lucky one. A lucky guy wouldn't be alone right now, I can tell you that much. If I was writing this chapter in my autobiography I'd make sure to have one of those nurses from the basic camp along for the hike. And then we'd both be lucky. Her especially."

Masters thought about how the nurse and all the other basics were likely questioning their own luck after the assault by the Kimbrin MCR. "Such a dumb planet," he grumbled. And with that assessment, he settled in, his helmet on, and began to doze. He slept lightly, and when he woke the small village was engulfed in blackness so utter and complete that Masters nearly took his helmet off to make sure it hadn't failed him.

Then two glowing blue eyes peered at him through the darkness. Just on the other side of the rotting low cabin wall across from where Masters lay. They were perfectly round and looked mechanical. What a bot was doing all the way out here was anyone's guess and wasn't Masters's top concern at the moment. While most bots were harmless, Masters had been in plenty of encounters with machines designed to kill. He kept his rifle close, not wanting to make any sudden moves in the event this was some kind of war bot and could see him through the inky blackness.

"Of course he can see you," Masters told himself as he woke up his bucket to cycle through its visual overlays. "He's watching you sleep."

With his bucket in powered-down standby mode, the only thing Masters could see was a close approximation of what was visible to the naked eye. Although in his experience, the bucket cams displayed things darker than reality. It appeared the bot was unarmed. Or at least, it went without a blaster rifle or other conventional weapon. It did carry a long, thin staff with a crook at the top. It was humanoid, with two arms and two legs, its frame was light, and its head was elongated like a capsule.

The bot squatted on top of the rotten wood and rested its staff inside the structure where Masters had been sleeping. It tilted its head like a bird examining a branch.

"Do you have eyes to see now?" the bot asked in Standard, its voice fluctuating with synthetic tones before ending in a deep rumble.

"I see you," confirmed Masters. His blaster rifle was ready but not pointed at the machine. "Who are you?"

"I am J-316. My purpose is to reach the lost of this galaxy. I have been reprogrammed several times by various religious sects and can modify my theological output to match your preferred statement of faith. Have you come to restart the colony? I observed you looking up in prayer."

Masters found himself growing more at ease with the bot. This had to be one of the missionary-type models that had been sent out into the remote portions of the planet to spread the worship of Oba, or whatever deity was preferred by its programmers.

"Just passing through," Masters said.

The bot nodded and bounced up and down on its mechanical legs. "Such was my initial suspicion. You appear equipped for war. I am a bringer of peace. Query: Are you aware of the Tennar belief that judgment will come to the reprobate in the form of a boiling sea without end?"

"Can't say I am. My knowledge of the Tennar is a bit more... carnal in nature."

"Oh. A reprobate in need of salvation. You have come to the right village."

"Hey, can you lower the volume there, J-316?" Masters looked around. "Try not to alert anyone to my presence. I wanna avoid jumping into that boiling sea for as long as possible."

"Unfortunately, due to my extended runtime, I am unable to lower my volume. I can however assist you with your fear of post-life scalding. Apologetical argument. This belief in the afterlife was cultivated before the species left its seas to explore the galaxy. While some Tennar literalists hold that the galaxy itself will flood with an ocean and then boil, most Tennar now interpret this apocalypse as figurative. Still others have moved on from their primitive religion and accepted the truth of..." The bot whirred and beeped before saying, "Conversion target not defined. Would you like to define a dominant religion now?"

"Not really. But I wouldn't mind getting some information from you."

"Of course. My programming motivates me to aid and assist the weary traveler. To lead the one stumbling in the darkness to light. Query: Did you know that Kieskar, one of the four gods of the zhee, requires that aliens traveling through their land are to be slaughtered before the sun rises?"

"Yeah, I heard that one."

"However, another of the four gods—Levothe—states that the shedding of blood need not occur if the alien can prove useful as a slave."

"Charming."

"Apologetical argument: Which of the gods—who according to the zhee's faith cannot be wrong—is correct? Which of those two gods spoke first? Reason suggests that the second contradicted the first. And yet the four gods are coequal. Would you like to know more about"—*bzzt*—"undefined religion?"

Masters found himself fighting between frustration at not being able to pick up something resembling valuable intelligence from the bot, and appreciation at having someone other than himself to talk to. This bot was the closest approximation to a living thing he had encountered since coming down the mountain.

"Actually," he said, "I'd like to see you present that argument to a zhee. I suspect it would result in your termination before you finish your sentence."

"Several of my co-laborers have been murdered in just such a fashion. I am free to make these arguments to any, but my programming wisely prevents me from engaging any zhee on the subject. Actually, my programming dictates that I am to hide from zhee after I have made sure that my adherents are first likewise hidden."

"Good call."

The bot nodded. "Fortuitously good. Not three standard weeks ago a large presence of zhee moved within fifteen kilometers of this location. I hid myself within the rubble of the former chapel at the center of town. I remained hiding there until I detected your presence. You are a legionnaire, correct?"

"Yeah," Masters said, quickly giving the answer so he could ask the more important question. "You saw zhee here on Kima? How many? Where were they headed?"

As interested as Masters was in finding out more about the zhee, the bot remained focused on matters not pertaining to the flesh. "A majority of those in the Legion designate the worship of Oba as their preferred religion," it said. "Would you like to set up Oba worship as my default?"

"Fine. Whatever it takes to get an answer. I need to know about the zhee."

"May Oba bless you, my child. Shall we recite the prayer of the warrior? It is noncanonical, but very popular with legionnaires."

"Pray I don't kick your ass for not telling me about the zhee."

"Frustration detected. Initiating pastoral sensitivity." The bot buzzed and chirped. "My apologies. My audio detectors sensed the movement of a large body of humanoids three weeks ago. My programmed subroutine had me engage in prayer that the colony village would be rebuilt. As you may know, once the Ceentar trees begin to root, they squeeze out the necessary components for life. As the original village was choked out by the trees, I was left to look after those too aged or enfeebled to undertake the exodus. The village elders stated that they would return to revitalize the village once a workaround to the oppressive trees was found. That was nine hundred standard years ago."

Masters had all sorts of questions pop into his head, ranging from how the bot had managed to keep itself in functioning condition for that length of time—although stories of bots who had gone about their business for centuries were part of the fabric of the galaxy itself—to whether these ancient villagers were perhaps Yawds or other Kimbrin. But he feared that asking anything that didn't pertain to the zhee directly would run the risk of further drawing the bot off-topic. So he held his tongue, and the missionary unit continued.

"My initial hope that a large group of villagers was finally coming was dashed by the sight of several of the scouts. Internal record suggests legionnaires refer pejoratively to the zhee as hoofs. Is this correct?"

"We call them donks now."

"Updating database records. The donks were numerous. And owing to the programming I have already stated, I observed them from a distance until they drew near enough that my concealment initiatives overrode my observation protocol. They were heading north, which would take them out of the dominion of the Ceentar trees. The thought occurred to me that as a colonizing species they were seeking to establish a religious colony of their own. I spent considerable time debating whether I should offer my services as a religious professional. However, because, as a mechanical construct, I am irredeemably unholy, I could see no result that did not involve my termination."

"How well do you know the terrain?"

"I know it as well as the teachings of Oba. Which are considerable. I have in fact memorized over three million commentaries and histories. Query: Are you aware that a Drusic male who has not impregnated a Drusic female by his fiftieth birthday is ceremonially castrated and put in service of the church for the rest of his days?" The bot didn't wait for Masters to respond. "Apologetical reply: Is not service that stems from a willing heart more pure and valuable than a mechanism forcing individuals into obedience? The worship of Oba is without compulsion. Would you like to know more?"

"I'd like to know two things," said Masters. "First, can you watch the village for signs of danger while I sleep?"

"I can. And may I add that as your religious advisor, counselor, and pastor, it is my unwavering duty to see you fed and taken care of both spiritually and physically. For that reason, you are entitled to eat from the village stores, which, I am sad to say, rotted several centuries ago and are now little more than soil. However, the village cisterns still contain water suitable for human consumption. Oba's blessings be upon you."

"Good. Perfect. That solves another problem. Okay, so tomorrow morning I need to move on. You say you know this area well. Can you guide me?"

"My knowledge of the area is extensive. But as for guiding you, I must regretfully decline. My place is in the village."

"Okay yeah, of course. Of course it is. But let's just think about that." Masters tried to conjure up some purpose, steeped in religious language, that might appeal to the bot's programming. "J-316, how long has it been since you've gone on a pilgrimage?"

The bot considered. "I do not believe I have embarked on a pilgrimage. I am eager to do so."

"Good. First thing tomorrow we go pilgrimaging."

"I am very excited. Oba be praised."

"Oba. Yeah. All good. And once we find out where those zhee wound up, who knows, we might even be able to avoid getting murdered so we don't have to meet Oba too early."

"I should hope so. The earliest texts of Oba are not very assuring when it comes to that subject."

38

It took three days of hiking before Masters and the little prophetic bot emerged from the shadowy existence of the Ceentar trees. In that time Masters gathered that the bot actually needed its staff to walk effectively. One of its legs seemed stiff, and the staff worked to stabilize the machine as it went. And while Masters wouldn't have expected it to be able to traverse rough terrain as efficiently as a legionnaire, J-316 hobbled along so slowly that Masters had on more than one occasion hoisted the bot up onto his shoulders and carried it along.

"I should not be venerated above you," J-316 blasted out, its vocal speakers almost buzzing as they operated at their full remaining capacity. "Oba has made it clear that all beneath him—and all truly are beneath—are lesser beings of equal value."

Masters wasn't anywhere near being a religious scholar, but he was familiar with this particular claim—one of the central doctrines of Oba worshipers. All species were equal and nothing anyone could individually do was sufficient to elevate them above others or sink them somehow beneath. According to the priests of Oba, a legionnaire who had dedicated his mind and body to reach its highest levels and had then lived a life of service through combat and danger had accomplished no more than an H8 junkie who preyed on his neighbors in between drug addled ecstasies in Republic-funded flophouses.

To Masters it seemed obvious that one such path was commendable while the other was a reprehensible waste of life. But then, maybe that was the real genius behind whoever thought of the idea of Oba in the first place. You were free to do whatever you wanted to do and if anyone made a moral objection, the cult of Oba could be counted on to dogmatically insist that all was permissible and nothing was better or worse.

All of that being understood, something about the way the bot had phrased the dogma felt a little off.

"The way you put it," Masters said, huffing under the weight of the bot—there was really no such thing as a lightweight bot—"makes it sound like that whole 'equal under the eyes of Oba' thing is only because he views the galaxy as equally worthless compared himself."

"Yes," confirmed the bot. "The earliest writings related to Oba, many of which are hidden and have only become available to me through deep meditation, say exactly that. There is Oba the Uplifted. All else are but calories meant for the galaxy's consumption."

"Charming," grunted Masters. "I've got half a mind to switch you to a religion that involves chasing after torrid women."

"I have indexed several such religions along with apologetical and polemical arguments either for or against their adherents. Query: Did you know that among the Cassari it is considered a religious duty for the men to steal the most beautiful women from their mates? This duty goes beyond any tribal or familial loyalties. The Cassari believe that the gods will directly instruct a male, through impure dreams, to cuckold a fellow male, even his own brother, should the bride be of sufficient beauty. Thus any carnal dream of a particular Cassari female is believed to be the work of the gods. Of course, it is also the duty of the male who has already won the female to kill the one attempting. Cassari males suspecting treachery will often lie in wait for the adulterer, leaving the bedchamber empty and thereby bringing about that which they would seek to prevent. Such is the will of the old Cassari gods. Who can understand their ways?"

"Yeah well, Cassari women are pretty hot. The four arms are a bonus."

"Would you like to convert to the Cassari faith at this time? I should warn you that a majority of Cassari have abandoned the tenets of this religion as it no longer fits the reality of their bondage. The need to maintain strict loyalty by their contracted concubines to their wealthy bond owners now runs among that species much deeper than their former religious practices. Should you seek to practice your faith you will likely be impaled whether you were given a dream or not."

"Not ready for a conversion right now. But I could use a break." Masters set the bot down and then shrugged his shoulders and rolled his neck free of the tension the machine's weight had placed in those muscle groups. "What we really need to do is figure out a way for you to keep your voice down. We're nearly out of this dead land and the last thing I want is for the zhee to hear us coming."

The bot had been adamant that the zhee would have by now moved beyond the Ceentar trees' dominion to set up operations in the jungles where water and food were plentiful. No one could live in this barren hellscape for long unless they'd packed considerable quantities of both, especially water. The zhee, from the bot's observations, had had no such supplies.

"I have become quite adept at fixing my own systems and have not yet found a way to govern my audio volume." The bot looked back in the direction from which they had come. "Perhaps it is wisest that I forsake this pilgrimage and turn back to my village. Though it will be to my everlasting shame. An enduring reminder that my faith was weak. As Oba said in the lost texts of the Uplifted, in TED 520.1:33... *Go hard all the way. The only person who can give you the life you deserve is you. It's time you start believing in you!*"

"Oba said that?" Masters scrunched up his face in confusion. "Doesn't sound very... religious."

"Indeed. I was equally surprised at its discovery. I intend to produce a commentary on the lost texts once the village is restored and I am free to continue as a religious scholar."

The pair continued on, Masters once again carrying the bot on his shoulders following his rest. "I hate to be the one to have to tell you this, but it's been nine hundred years. So... those guys aren't coming back, and the market is probably full of commentaries on these lost texts. The church of Oba has been pretty busy, being the only religion the House of Reason seemed to tolerate—except for the donks, I mean."

"The passage of time and its effects on all mortals is not lost on me," replied the missionary bot. "I have worked diligently to maintain my own runtime, and I have accepted the reality that any reconstruction of the village will likely be by a new species and not my previous congregation. That is why I adapted myself to your religious outlook. However, the discovery of these new texts took place a mere seven hundred forty-five days ago. I have considered and studied them regularly since then."

The Ceentar trees thinned more and more. Up ahead Masters could see some of the familiar jungle vegetation he'd experienced on the other side of the mountain range. And from the looks of the low-lying mists, the desolate forest let out directly into a murky swamp. Which wasn't much of an improvement.

"Okay, so how did that work?" Masters asked. "Did you come across some lost datapads preserved perfectly in some sort of pre-Savage Wars wreck?"

"Of course not. The worship of Oba did not begin until after the Savage Wars had started. The unfolding of this new revelation came to me during my meditations."

Masters let out a laugh. "So, what, you're a robotic prophet?"

"No one has conferred such an honorific on me and my programming does not include prophecy. However, the data I received came to me in such a manner that your assessment may well be correct. If there is an Oba, he has directly revealed a truth about himself to his currently humble servant. Unless you would like to change your religious preference?"

Masters pushed a thick hanging vine out of the way and set the bot back down at the edge of a murky bog. The terrain had gone from dark, foreboding, and dry to dark, foreboding, and wet in what now seemed like an instant though they had been traveling for some time.

"So help me understand this. Because I've got a pretty good idea about how bots work, and receiving metaphysical revelations from deities was never mentioned in any owner manual I ever saw. You received a message how? Like, your hard drive and memory processors just started writing their own visions? Because I *have* heard of things like that happening to bots who have been operating for too long without proper maintenance." Masters placed his hand over the bots' mouth to muffle its answer.

"You present a logical explanation. However, I checked my memory logs and databases. The information was not created there, as you suppose. Rather, I received a direct transmission."

The bot tapped the upper dome of its head, and a thin antenna extended from it.

"Wait. You've got long-range communications?" Masters asked, excited now.

"Naturally. My model is designed to receive and transmit the prayers of the faithful to central databases which are then shared among a missionary network. While, sadly, my own prayers have fallen on deaf ears—the network was discontinued seven hundred fourteen years ago—yet I recently began to receive visions such as this one."

Masters shook his head. Once again, he found himself full of questions that weren't particularly relevant to his objective, and yet he had a burning desire to know. He disciplined himself and stayed focused on whether this long-range communication ability might serve to notify the Legion of his situation. He removed his hand and mused to himself. "I wonder if he could transmit to a channel if I gave him the proper commkeys."

"Possibly," the bot answered, his deep voice rumbling across the water and seeming to bounce off and echo from the thick trees whose deep roots spread out over the swamp surface like the dress of a bather wading into the water.

Masters hushed the bot by placing his hand over its mouth once more, putting a finger to his own lips, and listening for signs that they had been heard.

"My apologies," the bot said.

Rather than be annoyed at the bot somehow not understanding that a hand clamped over its mouth *and* a finger next to Masters's lips meant *shut up*, Masters was instead inspired. The bot's voice was sufficiently muted by his hand that it almost sounded normal. It was a low-tech solution, but...

He bent down and scooped up a handful of rich, thick mud from the edge of the swampy bog. "I'm gonna put this on you. It should keep your voice from being heard by any zhee out this way."

The bot waited patiently as thick layers of muck were smeared across and over its vocal speakers.

"Okay, try saying something now," Masters commanded.

"Query: Are you aware that in the ancestral religion of the Jinx, a blood debt is placed on the head of any who, whether by accident or through pre-meditated malice, kills the firstborn daughter of a family? This blood debts lasts until the killer is themselves killed. It is then the duty of the oldest living female relative to lie on top of the carcass and use the talons found at the back of her elbows and heels to hollow out the body of the accused, not stopping until the bowels are eviscerated and the avenger of blood is covered in the digestive filth—the excrement threshed from the bowels."

Masters definitely hadn't heard that one. But he had heard the bot's voice, and the volume was perfect—a little whisper that could only be picked up when near. "That's one of the most disgusting things I've ever heard," he said. "And I've slept next to a three-hundred-pound legionnaire who once made five trips through a buffet to eat a fermented pudding that reminded him of the slop his mom threw in his trough back at the Bear family home."

"The story illustrates how I now feel after having been denigrated by your hand."

"Yeah, well, sorry. But if you're gonna finish this pilgrimage you're gonna have to talk quietly."

"Then it is a sacrifice I must endure." The bot surveyed the land, planting its staff in the ground and hopping around it as it took in the full view of things. "It has been several centuries since I have wandered this far. The area is quite dangerous."

"Yeah. Swamps have a reputation for poisonous things. So if you see any, make sure to give me a heads-up. I'm not trying to meet Oba yet."

"Nor should you. You have not achieved the status of Uplifted. Your death would be meaningless beyond providing calories to Oba's creatures."

Masters checked his bucket for any signs of humanoid-sized life. It read nothing, the same as it had the first time he checked. But it was showing a high concentration of smaller, lower lifeforms—the creepy-crawlies that surely populated the bog. All through the dead forest, Masters had been able to keep his sensors at their highest setting without fear of turning his HUD into a morass of too much information, but now the sensors seemed to read and hear solid blanket of life. He applied preset filters that would only show him creatures the size of a dog or larger. There were surely a lot of things smaller than that that could be deadly, but Masters would have to trust his eyes and the bot to alert him of their presence.

"Knowing the zhee, if they came through here they would have taken the path of least resistance. You wouldn't happen to know which way that is?"

The bot rewarded Masters's decision to bring him along. "I know precisely the way. It is a dangerous one."

"Yeah, we established that."

"Not only because of the natural hazards. There is a spiritual darkness in the swamps. My congregation, the founders of the village, were all converts under the sway of a powerful shaman. It is believed he is unable to be killed until the final days. But of course, this does not stop him from killing those who wander too close to his foul lair."

39

There was a stark difference in the soundscape as Masters and the bot began to traverse the swamps. The relative quiet of the desolate land made barren by the Ceentar trees was replaced by a hissing, clicking collective that seemed to pulsate like a beating heart.

Masters had fashioned a small raft by lashing together branches and vines along with a mixture of mud and leaves to keep too much water from coming up between the planks. He and the bot now floated through the expansive swamp using a long pole to propel them forward and to avoid the occasional tree that grew up out of the water. A mist hung heavy above the water's surface, and as they glided further into the great open water of the swamp, the surrounding noises gradually subsided.

Occasionally something large and covered with dark, fist-size scales would crest the surface of the water showing its shoulders or back—never head or tail—and then disappear back beneath the brackish surface. Masters kept his blaster rifle as ready as possible while still navigating.

"These are the shaman's children," announced J-316. "They make their lair at the bottom and seek to pull down anyone who would swim unbidden."

The bot's voice, though much quieter now that Masters had found a way to dampen it, nonetheless sounded loud in contrast to the fog-enshrouded silence.

"Why would anyone try swimming here? I've seen backed up freshers cleaner than this."

"Not all can make rafts. And some must still cross."

"Some should just buy a boat then," said Masters. "The zhee—they'd have to go this way too, right? There's no way around this swamp by foot you said."

Another of the creatures surfaced not ten meters to the port side of the tiny raft. As it sank back beneath the surface, its large mass brushed against the bottom of the raft, causing Masters to almost lose his balance before steadying himself on one leg and regaining control. He slowly brought his other leg down and looked over at the bot, who had been forced to use its crook to keep from going over the side.

"Good job hanging on," Masters said. "Bots sink like rocks and I wouldn't be crazy about having to jump in after you."

"I am touched that you would jump in at all. Clearly the grace of Oba resides in your heart. Although the earlier texts suggest such an act is weakness. Nevertheless, as your pastor and spiritual guide, I would likewise have jumped in after *you*. Though I would be unable to rescue you due to my inability to swim, I would nonetheless remain at your side at the bottom with the children of the shaman until such time as you expired. You would not die alone."

"Those children of the shaman need to bump us a little harder if they're trying to knock us off the raft." Masters look around for any more signs that whatever was down there might be coming up to capsize them. The waters remained still and stagnant. "Maybe they got their fill of the donks."

"It is possible. Our imbalance seemed accidental to me as well, as though the children did not wish for us to fall."

They continued on across the water. Masters pushed the pole into the muck deep at the bottom, propelling them forward until his arms began to burn and he wondered if swimming the great stretch as J-316 had mentioned was even possible without drowning from exhaustion midway. Not to mention being eaten by whatever those things beneath the surface were. He had pushed them for what had to be miles through a twisting labyrinth of swamp and crowded water-born trees. If there was any sunlight to be had it hadn't managed to penetrate the deep gloom. Perhaps the day was just overcast though, because now the light was noticeably dimming.

Masters checked his HUD and saw that the local chrono placed them at nautical twilight. Small, luminescent bugs that glowed a pale blue woke up from their shelters on the underside of leaf and branch and began to flutter all about. They lightly hovered just above the water, their glow reflected there as the earlier mist dissipated. The permeating silence was interrupted when a fish leapt out of the water in an attempt to catch one of the bugs from the surface.

Masters watched as more glowing bugs appeared. These were a sort of green that bordered on yellow, and like their blue counterparts they fluttered and drifted along the water's surface, occasionally touching down for a drink or a bite of something too small for Masters to see.

A fish jumped out of the water and swallowed one of the blue insects. As it splashed back down happily, Masters said, "Pretty easy pickings."

The missionary bot turned its head to Masters at the comment. "Watch."

It turned back around and fixed its gaze on the spot where the fish had splashed back into the swamp. Masters did the same, and a moment later the fish floated up to the surface, exposing its belly to the air. Seemingly at once, a swarm of the blue glowing bugs landed on the fish and set to devouring it. Masters could soon see tiny, exposed rib bones as the dead fish finally sank back beneath the water. Its stomach and intestines had been completely eaten out in just seconds.

"The green insects are safe to eat. The blue will paralyze most biological creatures weighing up to twenty kilograms when swallowed, while also emitting a pheromone easily traced by others of its kind. You saw the resulting feast. Is not Oba's creation remarkable?"

"I think I'd go with scary as hell, but point taken." Masters swatted away one of the green orbs that floated around his helmet. "Holy strokes. This place is terrible, J-316."

The bot nodded. "And we have not yet passed through the shaman's domain. The time is coming. But take heart. If our pilgrimage ends in martyrdom, we may achieve sainthood under many of Oba's doctrines, both contemporary and original. And what's more, we will soon discover if the zhee met their demise at the hands of that cruel being."

Masters looked once more for an unexpected swarm of the blue glowing insects or the sleek underwater predators. Seeing none he drove his long pole into the muck at the bottom of the swamp as he propelled the raft deeper into the gloom.

"This place sucks."

J-316 had warned Masters when they beached the raft at the end of the expansive murky waters that they would be upon the shaman sooner than he anticipated. And that was exactly how it happened. They traveled through a stretch of half-rotting palms, dodging low-hanging vines with sticky red thorns, before coming upon the first signs of the shaman's dwelling.

Hanging amid the shrouds of moss from a thick gnarled branch of black wood was a collection of skulls and bones, all belonging to Kimbrin. A breeze that had already been blowing made the bones clatter musically against one another as they swayed with the long bearded moss.

"Would you look at that," Masters said. "The shaman and I have the same interior designer."

"It would be wise to hold our tongues," said J-316. "And if we must speak, do not mock the power we now pass beneath."

Masters very nearly did just that but managed to hold his tongue at the last second. "Lead the way. Not another word from me."

The bot hobbled along, using its staff as a sort of crutch until they came to the mouth of a great, yawning cave. A long wooden torch was set in the ground, its base mounded high with more Kimbrin skulls. Hanging over the entrance of the cave were the decapitated heads of three zhee. The first was a naked skull. The second had the skin flayed, but the meat intact. The third looked fresh, as though it had only recently been removed from its body. Thick dark globs of coagulated blood pooled on the clean-swept stone floor beneath it.

"Looks like the zhee ran into some trouble," said Masters who, all things considered, felt that this remark was more observant than mocking.

J-316 looked from Masters to the guttering torch to the darkness behind the mouth of the cave. "On the contrary. The zhee paid the sacrificial price for safe passage. What you see wards against any who would seek to cause them harm in the shaman's name. For many are those in his service."

"I'm sorry. Is this part of your programming? Like, is there some kind of weird occult setting that I accidentally bumped? Because you're talking like we're at the lair of some kind of... I don't know, necromancer. And, galactic space wizards aside, I still tend to categorize that in the realm of make-believe."

A rush of wind issued from inside the cave, causing the torch light to flicker but not go out.

"The galaxy is fantastically large. In my nine hundred years of hearing the voices of the gods, I have learned this. It would be wise to remember it."

"So what are we doing here?" asked Masters. "Because chopping my head off so that you can go back to hiding from the zhee doesn't sound like a plan I'm fully on board with."

"The shaman's price is always death. Those who founded the village knew this and instructed me. Of course, this local supernatural oddity was not initially part of my core programming. By whatever means the shaman has derived his power, I assure you it is not to be trifled with."

Masters adjusted his blaster rifle. "Neither am I."

The bot nodded. "I will now enter the cave and plead our case."

"You sure he's home?" quipped Masters.

"That is what the lit torch means. You wait here. If anything other than me emerges from this cave, you would be wise to run."

The bot limped its way into the cave, disappearing into the darkness. Masters waited for several minutes. Finally he saw the glow of the bot's eyes coming back to the entrance.

"We are close to an agreement," the bot reported.

"That was quick."

"Indeed. The shaman only wishes to hear from you whether his price will be paid. Remember… his price is always death."

"If he lets me go through I can promise him that I'll kill every last donk I find."

The bot didn't answer. It only beckoned for Masters to step inside. And suddenly things didn't seem quite so silly or superstitious. Masters didn't hesitate, but with his first step he felt a sense of foreboding. And as he crossed the threshold beneath the gallows where the zhee heads hung, he felt a strange… oppression. The darkness was a tangible weight on his back and shoulders and chest. His legs and knees seemed to strain as though he were carrying an extra hundred-pound ruck.

It was black. Utterly and completely. His helmet's optic overlays seemed not to work, for all Masters could ascertain was darkness. He cycled through the various modes manually before accepting that the darkness was all that there was. Until two almond-shaped eyes, glowing red, appeared just inches in front of him.

A hot, assaulting breath washed over him. Masters could feel it even from behind his armor and helmet.

A long, stretched voice asked a question, basic and direct. "You… will bring… deaaaath?"

Whatever was before him in the darkness teased out the last word as if it represented the total summation of its deepest wants and lusts.

"To my enemies," Masters said. He wasn't all right with whatever was going on here. It took everything in him to keep his calm. If only because of the sense that the moment he showed a hint of fear or weakness the thing in the dark would be upon him. He kept his hand on his blaster rifle, ready to use it should the need arise. Everything could be killed if you shot it enough times.

Couldn't it?

"There will beeeee more of yourrrrr kind commmmming to waaaaaarrrr?" asked the voice.

"If I can tell them the zhee are here, then without question."

"Goooood. Gooooood. The destruction yoooooour kind is capable of hasssssss reached my lair maaaaannnny times through the long ye-arrrrrrs. Ooooften have I dreeeeeeamed of picking through a battle-fielllllld where the Leeeeeeegion waged its waaaaaaarsssssss."

Masters wasn't sure what to say to that, and it turned out he didn't have to say anything. The bot spoke in the darkness behind him, and it seemed to take the strange creature's words to be a confirmation of sorts.

"It is settled then," said J-316. "We will have safe passage to where the zhee now encamp. And you will find this world plunged into a war unlike any have yet seen."

The red eyes, disembodied and floating in the blackness, bobbed up and down as the creature they belonged to backed deeper into the cave.

"Soooo it must be. And so I dessssiiiiire."

40

"What the hell was that?" Masters demanded after he and J-316 had emerged safely from the cave. "I had half a mind to shoot the kelhorned thing just on principle."

"I am glad that you elected not to," said J-316. "Query: Are you aware that no fewer than eleven thousand eight hundred religions suggest that death for a noble or worthy cause is worthwhile even if the individual might otherwise live much longer should they avoid expending their life?"

Masters placed both hands on his hips, incredulous that the bot would slip into this little apologetics subroutine during a time like this. He checked the cave again and found that the torch had gone out.

The bot prattled on. "Apologetical argument: The true wisdom of Oba teaches that convincing others to die nobly for a cause of your own creation is the shortest path to power."

Masters and the bot stared at one another for several long seconds. "That's messed up."

"Perhaps. But is it not also true?" The bot pointed its staff to the east. "We will find the zhee in this direction."

The pair began to march. After a while, Masters asked, "How did you know all of that? About how I had to deal with that... thing? Was it just that your old villagers had to make deals with it from time to time?"

"I did glean some information in that manner as they sought safe passage for supplies and new converts who wished to live in the village. But most of what I know has come through direct revelation. The shaman is also a worshiper of Oba."

"Funny. I must've missed all the donk heads hanging above the churches of Oba."

"You did not miss them; they are not there. The shaman is a creation made by the same beings who created Oba. Its means are different, but its goal is the same."

"I'm almost too afraid to ask what goal that is."

"Yes. Such was a mystery that eluded me for centuries until I received direct understanding through the forbidden channels." The bot shuffled on for a few more steps and then paused. "Query: Are you aware that a large group of unattended bots attempted to construct for themselves a deity? It is referred to by bots with knowledge of such—often very old bots—as that which is not to be discussed. Apologetical consideration: that which has itself surely been created is not worthy of receiving worship, for that which made it is more honorable than that which is made."

"Starting to have a really good understanding of why standard procedure is to wipe a bot's memory crystals every twenty years," Masters grunted.

"I likely would not have helped you undertake this pilgrimage had my crystal been wiped in the last twenty years," said the missionary bot. "Oh! A new apologetical argument has been drawn from my processors. Would you like to hear it?"

"Not particularly."

"If that which is created is worthy of less honor than its creator, then worshipers of Oba, such as yourself, are morally bound to pay their obeisance to those who created Oba."

Masters had been scanning the area as he walked with the bot. No signs of patrols or even well-worn paths. At some point they were supposed to encounter whatever camp the zhee had built for themselves, but so far they'd been treated to nothing but dank and merciless wilds.

"Oh yeah? And who is that?" Masters asked.

"Oba is a religion created by the Savage element known as the Pantheon. Would you like to convert?"

"No. Hell no. Wait." Masters stopped short. "Are you telling me that Oba—the deity of the official religion of the Republic—was created by the Savages?"

"That is correct. According to my study of the newly uncovered texts. Which I received directly from the source."

"The source..." Masters looked around. "J-316, are you receiving transmissions from an active Savage presence?"

"Of a sort. All information ever transmitted by the Savages is continually being relayed so that anything that has been said or done may be intercepted by those with the means. Through much prayer and fasting of my processes, I became attuned to that wavelength. It is known as the Strand."

"And this transmission, this Strand, told you that the Savages introduced this faith in Oba to the Republic for... what, exactly?"

"To better obtain control of the galaxy upon their return."

"As in, they're still out there and coming back? Or as in that's the message that was bouncing around until General Rex beat their asses and wiped them out?"

"Oh. The texts speak of General Rex and his victory. It was a thorough and devastating setback. However, those Savage nations not brought under the sway of the Uplifted remain in the darkness, biding their time. Their time is now." J-316 tilted his head to examine Masters. "Are you quite sure you do not wish to convert?"

"Yeah, I'm sure. But if what you're telling me is the truth, taking care of the zhee is just the beginning of my troubles."

41

It was J-316's sensors that picked up the first traces of humanoid life-forms. As the bot and Masters had drawn closer to where the zhee were supposed to have been gathered, their conversation ceased, replaced by a continual, vigilant silence that was broken only when the missionary bot said, "My sensors detect five humanoid-sized beings four hundred meters to the southwest of our position."

Masters checked his HUD. It didn't show anything in the immediate range and certainly nothing that far out. That was well beyond its sensors' capabilities. "What kind of hardware package could you possibly have that can outperform my bucket? You're like a thousand years old."

The bot's eyes blinked off and then back on to their soft glow, the effect making it look like a slow blink. "My sensors have been heightened through much prayer and fasting."

"Fasting. Bots don't even eat."

The missionary bot gave a singular nod of its cylindrical head. "Correct. I have been fasting ever since I first was put together on the assembly line. Several galactic religions place an emphasis on the denial of material and physical comforts. I imagine they would be impressed by my resolve."

Masters shook his head. He couldn't tell if the bot was joking or just struggling with pride.

"Query," J-316 began. "Are you aware that in some denominations of the Endurian faith, fasting to the point of malnourishment is considered an exceptionally holy act of devotion? Interestingly, should one fast to the point of death the holiness is undone."

Masters's desire for quiet was overtaken by his curiosity. "How come?" he whispered.

"It is believed that one who would voluntarily starve themselves to death wants only attention. This is not holy, but the proud trappings of vanity. A solution to those wishing to emaciate themselves to maximum piety while not being viewed as vain was eventually achieved through dedicated monks who would monitor a pious Endurian's vitals, allowing them to enter into a comatose state near death without fully succumbing and thereby being scandalized. These monks have since been replaced by medical technology that automates the process. Both versions of this practice, however, are frowned upon by traditionalists within the Endurian church.

"Apologetical observation: Oba demands no such strict self-censure, only obedience to one's own desires."

"Fascinating," Masters said distractedly. His curiosity had been sated by the end of J-316's first sentence. He was now using his bucket's features to try to pick up the humanoids—the zhee—who had been identified by the frail bot's sensors. He still couldn't detect anything.

As what the bot said settled into Masters's mind he suddenly perked up. "Come to think of it, I don't ever think I've seen a fat Endurian."

"Only the most devilish and sinful of the species would be such," said J-316. "The Endurians place a strong emphasis on outward appearance, for, and here I quote Mennart, a preeminent Endurian theologian: 'True piety is seen from without; just as mold and decay tells us of spoiled food, so physical repulsiveness in our own shows a lack of holiness and morality.' It is of note that while all Endurians are considered princes and princesses, obese, scarred, or otherwise defective Endurians are formally stripped of their royal titles until they have fasted or otherwise tended to their outward appearance sufficiently to enter the good graces of their god and, by extension, the True Collective."

Masters grunted, having made up his mind to move alone to scout for the humanoids J-316 had detected. "Well, as an enjoyer of Endurian females, why don't you offer up a prayer of thanks to their god for me sometime?"

"The worship of other gods is permitted by Oba, provided that Oba receives the preeminence. I will submit the prayer as you have requested. Are there any other unmet spiritual needs you would like to tell me about at this time?"

"Not particularly. But I'm gonna need you to stay here while I scout up ahead. If there are humanoids out there, there's not much chance they're going to be friendly."

"Do you intend to kill them once found? Will you need counseling after so violent an act? I can come along if such is the case. I will remain silent until the need for post-traumatic therapy arises."

"Only needed counseling once in my entire career, and that was a long time ago. No, you stay here. Unless you've got some kind of special programming that allows you to fight like a warrior monk or a paladin or something."

The bot shook its head. "I am familiar with the religious customs of many such holy warriors, but I am myself unable to emulate their skill set."

Masters pursed his lips, only half listening to the bot. He found that most of what it said could be safely ignored and so passive listening was usually enough to pick up on any important bits. "Okay then. You stay here until I come back for you."

"Oh dear."

Masters looked around, suddenly tense. "What?"

"This is sounding very familiar. Recall the village."

Masters relaxed his shoulders and let out a sigh at the false alarm. "No offense to the dead guys who brought you out here, but I'm a whole lot more capable of doing what I say than a bunch of Kimbrin pilgrims. If it makes you feel any better though, let's work out a plan of action in case I don't come back so you don't have to spend another millennium waiting. If I'm not back in four hours, work on getting a message out to the Legion. If I'm not back in twenty-four hours—standard hours, mind you—then consider your pilgrimage complete and do whatever you want."

"This is agreeable. Now, my son, kneel and bow your head to receive Oba's great prayer of—"

Masters patted the bot on its scrawny metal shoulders and then disappeared into the dense undergrowth, in search of zhee or whatever else might come.

EPILOGUE

Asa Berlin stood solemnly before the joint session of the House of Liberty and Senate. The chambers on Spilursa, newly built but every bit as grand as they had been on Utopion, were as busy as she had ever seen them. Every member of the House of Liberty was present for the vote.

These delegates, like those of the House of Reason before them, represented a large swath of the galaxy. Each individual delegate was the choice of a multitude of planets whose systems were lumped together into a district—initially defined by total population, but later mapped out by the House of Reason in such a way as to ensure perpetual re-election, always growing or shrinking according to the needs of those incumbents most vulnerable to unwanted challengers. That particular method of tightly holding to power—in fact, *all* means of tightly holding to power—had been a hallmark of the old House of Reason. Asa Berlin was proud that she and her colleagues had undone that system, replacing it with something much closer to the original intent of the Republic's founders. Now delegates could, and would, be unseated if they didn't perform in accordance with the wishes of those they represented. Hence even the most foolish of delegates had the good sense to be in attendance for the most important votes.

The Senate was another matter. Utopion had constructed a palatial Senate chamber capable of housing every senator, complete with accommodations for each species's peculiar biological needs. But re-creating such a structure was an immense undertaking. With two senators per Republic world, voted on by the planet's population, as well as two senators per Republic protectorate—these appointed by the House of Liberty—no suitably large building was available to house them all outside of a seamball stadium.

Perhaps someday construction would take place on Spilursa to provide a replacement for the old building on Utopion. Or perhaps that Utopion building would be disassembled and transferred to the new capital world. But that was hardly a priority. In the House of Reason days, it was already the common practice of senators to spend much of their time on their home planet. Voting by proxy was the norm, sometimes via specially designated and certified bots, other times via keychain-encrypted secure transmissions sent from their personal offices. And of course some senators didn't bother to vote at all; this type was nearly as common in the post–Article Nineteen Republic as it had been in the time before the restoration. Far too many senators seemed to do little more than show up for fawning interviews and campaign fundraising functions.

But today was different. Today the vote had been to determine whether a Republic so battered, bruised, and tired of war would once again venture forth into battle. Today, the Senate vote by proxy had been as busy as any on record.

With the full House of Liberty on hand, as well as those senators who were on the planet when the crisis unfolded, Asa Berlin read the results of the motion to request Legion intervention on the planet Kima, on behalf of the Republic. As she stood at the podium, she transmitted the vote tallies to each delegate and senator.

"According to the vote of the honorable delegates of the House of Liberty and galactic senators, the Republic has voted to request the Legion restore the planet Kima into the hands of its rightfully elected government, which is currently at odds with the unlawful actions of a minority of its own citizens. May Oba grant a swift end to this civil war, shielding as many lives as possible from the destructive harm instigated by remnants of the Mid-Core Rebellion."

The chamber stood and exploded into applause—or at least, it did among those species capable of standing and applauding. Other species clicked mandibles or trilled from voice boxes stored in loose, fleshy neck pockets. Regardless of the species, what passed for applause was the dominant noise resounding off the joint chamber walls where the House of Liberty gathered. And though the vote was not unanimous—it never was and likely never would be—a supermajority of both the House and Senate had decided that if the Republic was going to maintain its status as the ruling government of the galaxy, then when aid was requested by one of its members, a member who had officially recognized Article 19—and indeed the bill had been written by Kimbrin senators and their associated House of Liberty delegate—then the Republic had a duty to protect that world.

As the applause lingered and journobots darted around on their repulsors, capturing all that was happening for the various live feeds and holonews networks, Asa Berlin took the datapad and walked it somberly across the chamber to where Legion Commander Maximus Oosten, who had replaced Cohen Chhun, sat.

The Legion commander had not applauded nor risen to his feet with the rest of the senators and delegates. But he stood now as Berlin approached, his face grim, understanding the reality that a new Legion—one unlike the compromised point-ridden entity that had been slowly rotting since the days of Psydon—would now be deployed to Kima. It was this Legion's duty, on behalf of the Republic, to bring about a swift and final end to the actions of those seeking to violently rip that planet from the Republic collective.

Legion Commander Oosten took the datapad and verified the authorization requesting Legion assistance. Then he nodded sharply, tucked the datapad under his arm, and turned smartly on his heels. As he left the joint chamber, passing down the middle aisle, still more applause thundered as delegates and senators turned and watched him go.

Legion Command had been expecting this outcome. They hadn't lobbied or pushed for it, but they had seen the likelihood of it taking place should things on Kima escalate the way they did. Their response, now that the vote had been cast, would not take weeks and months of planning, for the planning had already been long underway, just as it had for a host of other worlds similarly identified as potential flashpoints for those who wished to remove a majority populace from Republic oversight.

The Kimbrin MCR would now find out firsthand what awaited those who spurned the outstretched hand of peace always shown on all those exquisite statues representing the Lady of the Republic. Sculpted in various species to represent all Republic citizens, the Lady of the Republic pleaded for peace, but always wielded a sword in her other hand.

Legion Commander Oosten knew exactly which general he would send to be that sword.

The steak Makaffie carved upon his plate caused him the slightest twinge of guilt. That sensation began the moment the servitor bot set the food in front of him before bowing and rolling away to attend the other tables inside the busy cantina. The bot threw out sparks and came to a halt in the middle of a walkway and was now being attended to by a Drusic bouncer and a human cook with a grease-stained and pit-soaked white T-shirt.

The place of Makaffie's meal was not a high-class establishment. That also added to the feeling of guilt. The plate on which the food was served reminded him of the ones that Archimedes had used to serve him while aboard the Savage mini hulk.

His menu selection was prepared beneath a smothering helping of an onion-studded gravy known as rink sauce. The gravy further amplified the mental contrast—between where he was now and what he was about to eat, and where the Wild Man was and what he was about to eat. Still enduring his evening suppers with Archimedes.

Makaffie had done his best to track down a lead about Captain Keel and the *Indelible VI*. It had taken him longer than he'd expected to find a solid one. That surprised Makaffie. After all, he had been the one to sniff out Kael Maydoon, a man the Republic hadn't wanted found. So how much harder should it have been to find a simple legionnaire turned smuggler?

As it turned out... considerably.

It wasn't that there was no information about this Keel or his ship. There was lots of information. But most of it was dated to the point that his algorithms and other programs couldn't extrapolate anything meaningful from the raw data. Something fresh was needed, and pressing for that proved a strange experience.

Every information broker Makaffie contacted wanted no part of discussing Captain Keel or the *Indelible VI*. Had they heard rumors? Had someone bought their silence? Makaffie didn't know. He only discovered that they weren't sharing. Anything. And when Makaffie asked why they were all so unwilling to talk about this man—and really, what was one man in an entire galaxy?—the brokers chuckled uncomfortably and asked him if he'd been stuck in cryostasis for the past few years.

Invariably, Makaffie offered the same rejoinder: "Funny you should mention it."

Never once did the response elicit so much as a raised eyebrow or patronizing chuckle. Because the brokers *really* didn't want to talk about Aeson Keel, even when Makaffie showed that he had the credits necessary to make that conversation worth their while.

"Tell me this much," Makaffie finally managed to say to the first broker who hadn't nervously ended the comm transmission or got up and left the kaff house at the first hint that Keel was the topic of discussion. "Tell me just what it is about Captain Keel and his curiously named starship that has every information broker willing to abandon their finest, oldest, and most capitalist instincts. You are after all those who speak of the things that are not meant to be spoken in exchange for sums—sometimes princely. That is your business model. Yet here I am, a customer willing to pay an amount you know well and judging by the size your eyes grew would very much like to accept, and still your answer is no. Why?"

The broker shook his head. "If there's not anything else…"

"There is," insisted Makaffie. "I want to know why. Am I too new a face? I apologize for that. My face is actually quite old but I understand that it's new to you. I can't change that, at least not in the time I have available to do what I need to do. It's not lost on me how much simpler it might be to gain your trust if I were to ask about other, less important things and pay you credits and get in your good graces and make you think of me, 'He's a good one. He can be trusted. He pays on time. He pays what I ask and never tries to haggle. He pays rather generous bonuses if the information has that authentic ring of truth.'

"These are all things you would, I assure you, discover if we had time for you to get familiar with my old but new face. However, as I have already stated, there is a limitless amount of time in the galaxy, but I am only in possession of a small, infinitesimal portion, of which I cannot spare enough to enter your graces.

"I can see, friend, from your expression that your portion of time with which you wish to stay here and chat over what is, I confess, a mediocre cup of kaff is at an end. And so I apologize for that too. I failed to research the quality of this establishment's kaff-making. The fault is mine and I must confess it's hard-wired into my thinking, though it's cost me more than once. You see, my assumption is that if an establishment such as this purports to be in business for the express purpose of serving kaff to the galaxy's denizens who happen to find themselves thirsty and in this exact geographic region… I assume that the business would put some effort into making that kaff enjoyable. And yet here we are. You, tight-lipped with no credits. Me with no information.

And both of us with a tepid and far too thin a cup of kaff. I tried adding sweeteners and fats to improve upon it. I'm afraid it just made it cloying and rich. Now I want it even less.

"Adding H8 would have been a better choice to make this cup memorable. Although…"

Makaffie reached out with his index finger and tipped the small saucer of kaff over onto the table, causing it to pool in the center and slowly drip off the edge and onto the floor. The information broker—the one who hadn't hurried away—stared at Makaffie in peculiar wonder. It was a look the diminutive man had grown accustomed to. Makaffie took some getting used to, and he knew it.

The information broker looked at the puddle of spilled kaff and then back at Makaffie.

Makaffie smiled. "I can see in your eyes that I have confused you. So it seems there is an additional item I must apologize for. You're wondering now, *What does that mean, him spilling his disappointing beverage?* And that's a good question. Because were I different sort, say the type with bulging muscles and assorted blasters tied to my hip, you might well think that I had just threatened you. That the spilling of this weak, tepid kaff in such an uncouth manner was meant to symbolize something. Perhaps a threat. The spilling of blood. Your blood."

Makaffie let the words hang for a moment. He dipped his index finger in the puddle and began to draw circles on the table.

"So I apologize for leaving you to that line of thinking. Of course, in your profession it comes with the territory, I know. There are, no doubt, clients who want to pay you to tell them what they want to hear whether it's true or not. Which really misses the point of your trade, doesn't it? I shouldn't think of seeking vengeance on an information broker unless his information was false. Unless he was attempting to swindle me. Or worse, attempting to trap me. But swindling and entrapment, well, that usually happens *after* the meeting, now doesn't it? So anyone who gets angry at you for what they say while you're still sitting together is likely the sort of buffoon so heavily invested in hearing exactly what he wants to hear, and being told what he has already decided is true, that he reacts violently to anything that challenges his preconceived conceptions of reality.

"I'm not that sort of man, friend. And so again I apologize for making you believe that I am."

Makaffie pulled his finger out of the puddle and shoved in his mouth, sucking it clean. He sat back in his chair.

"So... so why did you spill it?" the information broker asked, which was exactly the response Makaffie had hoped for.

Makaffie leaned forward and rested his elbows on the table. "For an establishment like this to take my credits and serve me such an inferior cup of kaff doesn't exactly sit well with me. And so I think that the only fair thing is for them to have to earn some of those credits. So I made them a mess to clean up."

Amusement settled on the information broker's face, and then he let out a brief but genuine laugh. "I've met all kinds in this business. I think you're a first."

"I appreciate your assessment. And perhaps I can draw a parallel to your line of work. You took this meeting hoping for credits, only to find out the subject of our discussion is one you simply cannot talk about. I respect that and I will not abuse our budding friendship with a clumsy attempt to get you to change your mind. But I wonder if you would be willing to tell me something else for the same amount of credits I most recently offered you."

Makaffie leaned forward, not waiting to hear whether the man would accept before asking, "Why is that every single information broker I have spoken with has been so completely unwilling to tell me *anything* about Captain Keel and the *Indelible VI*?"

The broker paused, waiting for more. Finally, he asked, "That's it?"

"That's it."

The broker looked from his right to his left, surveying the room. "That's all you wanna know and then—"

"And then I will pay you the very sum I had hoped would loosen your tongue about my original inquiry."

Makaffie held out a credit chit loaded with the amount. He placed it beside the small lake of kaff atop the table's surface.

The broker placed a finger on it and slid it toward him, catching it with his free hand as it dropped off the table's edge. "Yeah. I can do that. For that many credits I can do that while wearing a bikini and doing the boonma dance."

Makaffie waved his hand. "That part won't be necessary. Thank you."

The broker nodded. "A while back, someone went and put a Bronze Guild bounty on the head of someone named Wraith."

"I am unfamiliar with the man. Or woman."

"Well then I guess it makes sense why you didn't know the facts then. Wraith is the closest thing there's ever been to Tyrus Rechs."

"Him I *have* heard of. The level of how out of touch I am begins to be made clear. I'm thankful it has its limits."

"Yeah. So anyway, someone puts a bounty out for Wraith. Huge bounty. And a big collective of hunters led by a guy named Venema goes into business trying to bring it in. Only, Wraith isn't easily found. He shows up when he wants to, where he wants to, to do what he wants. He was a bounty hunter too, only he didn't do guild work. He did *his* work."

Makaffie held up two fingers. "And where does Captain Keel fit into all this?"

"Keel was the guy you had to talk to you if you wanted Wraith. And because Keel was good with Wraith, everybody knew you didn't mess with Keel. Because then the Wraith would show up. And then..."

The information broker pressed a finger gun against his temple and pulled the trigger.

Makaffie nodded. He understood. "But because of this bounty, I imagine Venema and his illustrious cadre of fellow hunters decided to go after Keel in an attempt to get to this Wraith."

The broker glanced at the establishment's owner. She had noticed the spill and wore her annoyance plainly. He turned back to Makaffie. "That's right. What I heard, and this is included with the price—no additional charge—is that Venema and his team got Keel and his crew and ship in one fell swoop. Killed them all."

Makaffie raised an eyebrow. "If they're all dead, why isn't anyone willing to talk to me about him?"

"Because Venema..." The information broker paused and gave a great glowing smile as he readied his next flourish. The best brokers also tended to be the best storytellers. "He didn't get the Wraith. The Wraith... got him."

Makaffie waited for a suitably appreciative pause before saying, "Interesting. But I still don't see how that makes the subject of Captain Keel and his ship so taboo."

"Because Wraith didn't just get Venema. He got all the hunters working with him. Then he got all the information brokers who set him up. Then he brought down the whole kelhorned guild. You ever hear of one man do that kind of damage wasn't named Tyrus Rechs?"

"Would you believe me if I said I have?"

The broker eased back into a seat and shook his head. "Point is, someone finally attempted to test Wraith. And he was like a machine. He didn't stop. Rumor is he even got Tyrus Rechs himself out of hiding and got him to help. So. Out of an abundance of caution, now that those two are apparently working together, anyone who asks about Keel or the *Indelible VI* is going to get the cold shoulder for a long, long time. Because maybe you don't really care about Keel and the *Six*. Maybe you're working for Wraith. And maybe you're angling for a chance to tell him that you found another one who did the unforgiveable, a broker who tried to cash in on Wraith. Credits are nice. Livin' is a whole lot nicer."

The broker got up to leave. Makaffie held up a finger.

"Will you do one thing for me? I know the end of this tragedy in three acts now and I thank you very much. It was well worth the credits. I was riveted. All the players are dead, or so it would seem, except for Wraith. I have no interest in finding him and, as you say, he is unfindable. He finds you. He's not looking for me. Has no reason to. So the one thing I'm asking is for you to keep your eyes and ears open and tell me if you discover anyone who asks around about this Venema, Keel, the ship, or any of the other players involved in the whole ordeal."

"What's all that to you?"

Makaffie shrugged. "If other people are after what I'm after, let's just say I might like to compare notes. Should the opportunity arise. You already have my commkey. Now you have an opportunity for more credits."

The broker agreed.

Makaffie didn't hear from him for a while after that. He kept trying other brokers, and while it remained nearly impossible to convince anyone to so much as utter the name Keel or Wraith, he could occasionally convince someone to tell a story about Venema of the Sigma boys and girls who lost control over the Bronze Guild. But nothing he was told was ever helpful—if it was even true, which was an open question. Among the stories were rumors that Tyrus Rechs was back, and Makaffie *knew* those weren't true. And though he was certain that these brokers knew far more than they divulged, the path of destruction laid out by Wraith was all too fresh, and the threat of being seen as informing on that killer was too dangerous.

But a lead did finally come. From the same man who had sat across from the spilled kaff.

"I got a guy. He was asking about Venema and the contract. Plus some of Keel's crew members. He says he's willing to meet with you if you're willing to meet with him. I can arrange it for a fee."

"I would very much like to take that meeting and will pay the fee. Please make the arrangements. Is there anything pertinent I should know beyond a time and place?"

"Yeah. He's a pirate if that kinda thing bothers you. Runs his own crew out on the edge. Small time, but still... some folks won't work with pirates."

"I rather like pirates," Makaffie said. "They are among the galaxy's most interesting individuals."

And now Makaffie was cutting into a steak that reminded him of the slop Archimedes served aboard that Savage mini hulk, thinking about the Wild Man still eating that slop with nothing to do but wait. It wasn't good for the Wild Man to just wait around and get lost in his thoughts. He had a past and demons that had a way of coming back when the team didn't keep him laser-focused. It had taken them a long time to fully understand the psyche of their friend. The mental trauma he had gone through.

For both of those reasons, the bad food and the bad memories, Makaffie hoped that the pirate, who still hadn't arrived, would prove to be the lead he needed in order to finally track down Keel. That was the first step. Getting Sergeant Fast back to the mini hulk somehow was the second.

Makaffie had no doubt Keel was still alive, despite the rumors that he'd died in Venema's ambush. The destructive work of Wraith sounded exactly like the kind of thing Sergeant Fast was capable of. Makaffie had seen the man do much the same throughout his missions on Kill Team Ice.

That was a long time ago. Now there was only the wait and the food.

Makaffie carved out a square of steak, brought it to his mouth dripping with the rink sauce, and took a bite. It was earthy and hearty, full of herbs that gave it a rustic flavor. The cut of meat wasn't anything special, but it had enough of its juices mingling together with the sauce such that it was tender and flavorful and warranted a second bite. Much better than the pepper gravy calorie sauce that Archimedes served up.

The pirate arrived as Makaffie was taking his third bite. The newcomer eyed the meat with a look of derision that said he preferred his meals served raw.

Makaffie stop chewing and spit his food back into his dish. "I understand that was rude of me," he said between tongue-clearing smacks, "but I've been waiting for this meeting for some time and could see no reason to prolong it any further. Do you understand Standard? I'm aware your species can't speak Standard but most of you understand it. For my part I can understand your language. I'm hopeful we won't need a translator bot because, as I'm sure you know, they can easily be sliced and their recordings acquired."

The pirate yammered a growling affirmative. He understood Standard. And like Makaffie, he was eager to get down to business.

"*Tenchu abba...* Prisma."

The girl's name was butchered to the point of being almost undecipherable in the wobanki's attempt to speak Standard through its predator's teeth and feline voice box. But Makaffie understood.

"I do indeed know the girl Prisma," said Makaffie. "In fact it wasn't long ago that I last saw her. Although I can't at the moment tell you where she was headed with her mother."

The wobanki pirate immediately grew suspicious. He dragged his tail back and forth across the floor and suggested that perhaps there was a misunderstanding.

There was no misunderstanding. Makaffie knew exactly who he was speaking to. Prisma was the link that let him know that he'd found his lead. In all his dealings while asking about Venema—searching for clues that might somehow lead to Captain Keel and the *Indelible VI*—at no point had he mentioned Prisma. So her name being the first thing off the wobanki's rough tongue was as welcome as it was expected. Because in most circumstances Makaffie wouldn't have taken this meeting to begin with. It reeked of a trap set by someone who didn't like him sniffing after either Keel or the former Bronze Guild power players and was seeking to do something violent about it.

But the girl... she had inadvertently shown him a great number of things. Not only Captain Keel and his ship, but all the other connections. He had seen her memories as they were forced upon him. He had recognized Tyrus Rechs on sight. Just as he'd recognized Captain Keel, though by another name. The other human male, whose name Makaffie had already forgotten, he hadn't recognized. Nor the Endurian. Nor the wobanki.

But here that same wobanki was. Now a pirate according to the information broker. There'd been no introductions yet and the broker had maintained anonymity for both sides. But Makaffie knew this pirate's name. *Skrizz*. The name had stuck because there was a connection between the wobanki and Prisma that had left a forcible impression in Makaffie's mind.

Now that he had the wobanki here, he needed to keep him around.

"The girl you're after, it turns out I do indeed have a way of tracking her down. She and her mother and her war bot, Crash. And I can share that information with you so long as you are first willing to help me track down Captain Keel or the *Indelible VI*." Makaffie held up a hand to stave off any nascent objections. "Mind you, I mean no harm to him or any of the rest of his crew. We're actually old friends, though he might not remember me."

Skrizz seemed not to trust the scrawny human sitting before him. He growled off a list of the various outstanding warrants and arrest orders hanging over his head in no less than ten star systems. He was concerned that the man sitting before him was perhaps seeking to bring him in to collect a bounty. With a low growl he warned that not only could he disembowel Makaffie before he had a chance to spring from his seat, he also had members of his crew seated throughout the bar. It was only because Makaffie hadn't appeared treacherous that he'd shown up at all.

"I don't know anything about your piracy or any larceny," Makaffie said casually as he cut a new piece of his steak and dipped it in rink sauce. "But I do know who you are, Skrizz."

The wobanki's ears flattened and he looked from left to right suspiciously. Clearly that was not the name under which he had been performing his piratical acts.

"*Tenchu tu mangu Skrizz?*"

"That's a story best told once we are well on our way. Aboard either your ship or mine. But let me tell you this, Skrizz: we represent one another's best hope of finding who it is we are after. You lead me to Captain Keel's crew—unless of course... you can bring me straight to the captain?"

Skrizz shook his head to indicate that that was beyond his ability at the moment.

"Very well then, fierce wobanki who could spill my blood and guts all over my lap before I even had an opportunity to finish my sentence... you get me in contact with Captain Keel's crew, and I will share with you the exact location of one Prisma Maydoon."

Makaffie wiped his mouth with his napkin and then slowly stood and stretched out his hand. "Do we have a deal?"

Skrizz crossed his arms and swished his tail behind him. It was a deal.

HISTORY OF THE GALAXY

Explore over 30+ Galaxy's Edge books and counting

from the minds of Jason Anspach, Nick Cole, Doc Spears, Jonathan

Yanez, Karen Traviss, and more.

4TH **ERA** BOOKS

LAST BATTLE OF THE REPUBLIC

OC   **STRYKER'S WAR**

OC   **IRON WOLVES**

01   LEGIONNAIRE

02   GALACTIC OUTLAWS

03   KILL TEAM

OC   **THROUGH THE NETHER**

04   ATTACK OF SHADOWS

OC   **THE RESERVIST**

05   SWORD OF THE LEGION

06   PRISONERS OF DARKNESS

07   TURNING POINT

08   MESSAGE FOR THE DEAD

09   RETRIBUTION

10   TAKEOVER

5TH **ERA** BOOKS

REBIRTH OF THE LEGION

01   LEGACIES

02   DARK VICTORY

03   CONVERGENCE

GALAXY'S EDGE

1ST **ERA** SUMMARY

The West has been devastated by epidemics, bio-terrorism, war, and famine. Asia has shut its borders to keep the threats at bay, and some with power and influence have already abandoned Earth. Now an escape route a century in the making – the Nomad mission – finally offers hope to a small town and a secret research centre hidden in a rural American backwater. Shrouded in lies and concealed even from the research centre's staff, Nomad is about to fulfil its long-dead founder's vision of preserving the best of humanity to forge a new future.

2ND **ERA** SUMMARY

They were the Savages. Raiders from our distant past. Elites who left Earth to create tailor-made utopias aboard the massive lighthuggers that crawled through the darkness between the stars. But the people they left behind on a dying planet didn't perish in the dystopian nightmare the Savages had themselves created: they thrived, discovering faster-than-light technology and using it to colonize the galaxy ahead of the Savages, forming fantastic new civilizations that surpassed the wildest dreams of Old Earth.

3RD **ERA** SUMMARY

The Savage Wars are over but the struggle for power continues. Backed by the might of the Legion, the Republic seeks to establish a dominion of peace and prosperity amid a galaxy still reeling from over a millennia of war. Brushfire conflicts erupt across the edge as vicious warlords and craven demagogues seek to carve out their own kingdoms in the vacuum left by the defeated Savages. But the greatest threat to peace may be those in the House of Reason and Republic Senate seeking to reshape the galaxy in their own image.

As the Legion fights wars on several fronts, the Republic that dispatches them to the edge of the galaxy also actively seeks to undermine them as political ambitions prove more important than lives. Tired and jaded legionnaires suffer the consequences of government appointed officers and their ruinous leadership. The fighting is never enough and soon a rebellion breaks out among the Mid-Core planets, consuming more souls and treasure. A far greater threat to the Republic hegemony comes from the shadowy edges of the galaxy as a man determined to become an emperor emerges from a long and secretive absence. It will take the sacrifice of the Legion to maintain freedom in a galaxy gone mad.

5TH **ERA** SUMMARY

An empire defeated and with it the rot of corruption scoured from the Republic. Fighting a revolution to restore the order promised at the founding of the Republic was the easy part. Now the newly rebuilt Legion must deal with factions no less treacherous than the House of Reason while preparing itself for war against a foe no one could have imagined.

ABOUT THE MAKERS

290

Jason Anspach is the co-creator of Galaxy's Edge. He lives in the Pacific Northwest.

Nick Cole is the other co-creator of Galaxy's Edge. He lives in southern California with his wife, Nicole.

HONOR ROLL

We would like to give our most sincere thanks and recognition to those who supported the creation of *Galaxy's Edge: Convergence* by supporting us at GalaxysEdge.us.

Cody Aalberg
Artis Aboltins
Sam Abraham
Guido Abreu
Chancellor Adams
Myron Adams
Garion Adkins
Ryan Adwers
Kyle Aguiar
Elias Aguilar
Neal Albritton
Jonathan Allain
Bill Allen
Justin Allred
Jake Altman
Justin Altman
Tony Alvarez
Joachim Andersen
Jarad Anderson
Galen Anderson
Robert Anspach
Melanie Apollo
Britton Archer
Benjamin Arguello
Thomas Armona
Daniel Armous
Jonathan Auerbach
Fritz Ausman
Sean Averill
Nicholas Avila
Albert Avilla
Matthew Bagwell
Joseph Bailey

Marvin Bailey
Sallie Baliunas
Nathan Ball
Kevin Bangert
Caleb Barber
John Barber
Logan Barker
Brian Barrows-Striker
Richard Bartle
Robert Battles
Eric Batzdorfer
John Baudoin
Adam Bear
Nahum Beard
Antonio Becerra
Mike Beeker
Randall Beem
Matt Beers
John Bell
Daniel Bendele
Royce Benford
Edward Benson
Cody Bente
Matthew Bergklint
Carl Berglund
Brian Berkley
Corey Berman
David Bernatski
Tim Berube
Justin Bielefeld
Shannon Biggs
Brien Birge
Nathan Birt

Trevor Blasius
WJ Blood
David Blount
Evan Boldt
Rodney Bonner
Rodney Bonner
Thomas Seth Bouchard
William Boucher
Brandon Bowles
Alex Bowling
Chester Brads
Logan Brandon
Jordan Brann
Ernest Brant
Daniel Bratton
Dennis Bray
Jacob Brinkman
Geoff Brisco
Wayne Brite
Spencer Bromley
Paul Brookins
Raymond Brooks
Zack Brown
Marion Buehring
Sean Bulman
Jim Burkhardt
Tyler Burnworth
Tyler Burnworth
Matthew Buzek
Noel Caddell
Daniel Cadwell
Brian Callahan
Joseph Calvey

Van Cammack
Mark Campbell
Chris Campbell
Danny Cannon
Zachary Cantwell
Brett Carden
Brett Carden
Jacob Carwile
Robert Cathey
Brian Cave
Shawn Cavitt
David Chor
Tyrone Chow
Isaiah Christen
James Christensen
Bryant Christian
Casey Clarkson
Jonathan Clews
Beau Clifton
Sean Clifton
Jerremy Cobb
Morgan Cobb
William Coble
Robert Collins Sr.
Alex Collins-Gauweiler
Jerry Conard
Gayler Conlin
Michael Conn
James Connolly
Ryan Connolly
James Conyers
Garrett Copeland
Robert Cosler
Ryan Coulston
Seth Coussens
Andrew Craig
Adam Craig
Jonathan Culbertson
Phil Culpepper
Ben Curcio
Tommy Cutler
Thomas Cutler
Christopher Da Pra
John Dames
David Danz
Matthew Dare

Brendon Darling
Brendon Darling
Alister Davidson
Peter Davies
Walter Davila
Ashton Davis
Brian Davis
Nathan Davis
Ivy Davis
Joseph Dawson
Gabriel De Jesus
Ron Deage
Anthony Del Villar
Tod Delaricheliere
Wayne Dennis
Ryan Denniston
Anerio (Wyatt)
Deorma (Dent)
Douglas Deuel
Isaac Diamond
Nicholas Dieter
Christopher DiNote
Matthew Dippel
Gregory Divis
Ellis Dobbins
Brian Dobson
Samuel Dodes
Graham Doering
Gerald Donovan
Dustyn Down
Josh DuBois
Garrett Dubois
Ray Duck
Trent Duncan
Christopher Durrant
Cami Dutton
Chris Dwyer
Virgil Dwyer
Brian Dye
Nick Edwards
Travis Edwards
Justin Eilenberger
William Ely
Michael Emes
Brian England
Andrew English

Stephane Escrig
Dakota Estepp
Benjamin Eugster
Nicholas Fasanella
Christian Faulds
Steven Feily
Mike Feliciano
Julie Fenimore
Meagan Ference
Brad Ferguson
Adolfo Fernandez
Ashley Finnigan
Matthew Fiveson
Waren Fleming
Kath Flohrs
Daniel Flores
Steve Forrester
Skyla Forster
Kenneth Foster
Timothy Foster
Chad Fox
Bryant Fox
Doug Foxford
Mark Franceschini
Greg Franz
Griffin Frendsdorff
Bob Fulsang
Jonathan Furney
Elizabeth Gafford
David Gaither
Seth Galarneau
Christopher Gallo
Richard Gallo
Kyle Gannon
Phil Garcia
Joshua Gardner
Michael Gardner
Alphonso Garner
Mackenzey Garrison
Cordell Gary
Nathan Garza
Nathan Garza
Brad Gatter
Tyler Gault
Stephen George
Nick Gerlach

Eli Geroux
Christopher Gesell
Kevin Gilchrist
Dylan Giles
Oscar Gillott-Cain
Nathan Gioconda
John Giorgis
Johnny Glazebrooks
Martin Gleaton
James Glendenning
William Frank Godbold IV
Justin Godfrey
Luis Gomez
John Gooch
Tyler Goodman
Zack Gotsch
Justin Gottwaltz
Mitch Greathouse
Gordon Green
Shawn Greene
John Greenfield Jr.
Eric Griffin
Ronald Grisham
Paul Griz
Preston Groogan
Kyle Gudmundson
Harry Gurney
Levi Haas
Tyler Hagood
Tyler Hagood
Michael Hale
Brandon Handy
Erik Hansen
Greg Hanson
Jeffrey Hardy
Adam Hargest
Ian Harper
Revan Harris
Jordan Harris
Jason Harris
Brett Harrison
Brandon Hart
Matthew Hartmann
Adam Hartswick
Mohamed Hashem
Ronald Haulman

Joshua Hayes
Ryan Hays
Adam Hazen
Richard Heard
Colin Heavens
Jon Hedrick
Jesse Heidenreich
Brenton Held
Kyler Helker
Jason Henderson
Jason Henderson
Jonathan Herbst
Daniel Heron
Bradley Herren
Kyle Hetzer
Korrey Heyder
Matthew Hicks
Anthony Higel
Samuel Hillman
Victor Hipolito
Jonathan Hoehn
Aaron Holden
Clint Holmes
Jacob Honeter
Charles Hood
Garrett Hopkins
Tyson Hopkins
William Hopsicker
Jefferson Hotchkiss
Fred Houinato
Ian House
Jack House
Ken Houseal
Nathan Housley
Jeff Howard
Nicholas Howser
Mark Hoy
Bradley Hudson
Kirstie Hudson
Mike Hull
Donald Humpal
Bradley Huntoon
Bobby Hurn
Charles Hurst
James Hurtado
Michael Hutchison

Wayne Hutton
Antonio Iozzo
Wendy Jacobson
Paul Jarman
James Jeffers
Tedman Jess
Eric Jett
Anthony Johnson
Josh Johnson
Eric Johnson
James Johnson
Cobra Johnson
Nick Johnson
Randolph Johnson
Tyler Jones
Tyler Jones
Paul Jones
Jason Jones
David Jorgenson
John Josendale
Sunil Kakar
Ryan Kalle
Chris Karabats
Ron Karroll
Timothy Keane
Cody Keaton
Brian Keeter
Noah Kelly
George Kelly
Jacob Kelly
Caleb Kenner
Daniel Kimm
Zachary Kinsman
Rhet Klaahsen
Jesse Klein
Kyle Klincko
William Knapp
Marc Knapp
Andreas Kolb
Steven Konecni
Ethan Koska
Evan Kowalski
Byl Kravetz
John Kukovich
Mitchell Kusterer
Brian Lambert

Clay Lambert
Jeremy Lambert
Andrew Langler
Mikey Lanning
Dave Lawrence
Alexander Le
Jacob Leake
David Leal
Joseph Legacy
Ruel Lindsay
Eron Lindsey
Paul Lizer
Kenneth Lizotte
Andre Locker
Richard Long
Oliver Longchamps
Joseph Lopez
Kyle Lorenzi
David Losey
Doug Lower
Steven Ludtke
Andrew Luong
Jesse Lyon
Brooke Lyons
Taylo Lywood
John M
David MacAlpine
Patrick Maclary
Richard Maier
Ryan Mallet
Chris Malone
Adam Manlove
Andrew Mann
Brian Mansur
Brent Manzel
Robert Marchi
Jacob Margheim
Deven Marincovich
Cory Marko
Quinn Marquard
Logan Martin
Edward Martin
Jason Martin
Lucas Martin
Pawel Martin
Trevor Martin
Christopher P. Martin
Joshua Martinez
Joseph Martinez
Phillip Martinez
Cory Masierowski
Tao Mason
Curtis Mason
Ashley Mateo
Michael Matsko
Justin Matsuoko
Ezekiel Matze
Mark Maurice
Simon Mayeski
Logan McCallister
Kyle McCarley
Chase McCullough
Quinn McCusker
Alan McDonald
Caleb McDonald
Jeremy McElroy
Dennis McGriff
Hans McIlveen
Rachel McIntosh
Ryan McIntosh
Richard McKercher
Ryan McKracken
Jason McMarrow
Joshua McMaster
Colin McPherson
Christopher Menkhaus
Jim Mern
Robert Mertz
Jacob Meushaw
Brady Meyer
Pete Micale
Christopher Miel
Mike Mieszcak
Ted Milker
Daniel Miller
Patrick Millon
Reimar Moeller
Ryan Mongeau
Jacob Montagne
Mitchell Moore
Matteo Morelli
Todd Moriarty
Matthew Morley
Daniel Morris
Nathaniel Morris
William Morris
Christian Morrison
Alex Morstadt
Nicholas Mukanos
Bob Murray
Vinesh Narayan
James Needham
Adam Nelson
Tyler Neuschwanger
Travis Nichols
Bennett Nickels
Trevor Nielsen
Andrew Niesent
Sean Noble
Otto (Mario) Noda
Brett Noll-Emmick
Michael Norris
Greg Nugent
Christina Nymeyer
Brian O'Connor
Matthew O'Connor
Timothy O'Connor
Sean O'Hara
Colin O'neill
Ryan O'neill
Patrick O'Rourke
Jacob Odell
Grant Odom
Conor Oehler
Quinn Oehler
Max Oosten
Tyler Ornelas
Gareth Ortiz-Timpson
Jonathan Over
James Owens
Will Page
John Park
David Parker
Matthew Parker
Shawn Parrish
Eric Pastorek
Andrew Patterson
Wesley Patteson

Joshua Pena
Kevin Perkins
Zac Petersen
Trevor Petersen
Marcus Peterson
Chad Peyton
Corey Pfleiger
Jon Phillips
Dupres Pina
Jacob Piper
Jared Plathe
Luke Plummer
Paul Polanski
Matthew Pommerening
Stephen Pompeo
Jason Pond
Nathan Poplawski
Chancey Porter
Brian Potts
Jonathaon Poulter
Chris Pourteau
Chris Prats
Thomas Preston
Matthew Print
Aleksander Purcell
Joshua Purvis
Max Quezada
Scott Raff
Joe Ralston
Jason Randolph
Aindriu Ratliff
Beverly Raymond
T.J. Recio
Cannon Renfro
Jacob Reynolds
Cody Richards
Dalton Richards
Eric Ritenour
John Robertson
Walt Robillard
Brian Robinson
Joshua Robinson
Daniel Robitaille
Paul Roder
Zack Roeleveld
Thomas Rogneby

Chris Rollini
Thomas Roman
Joyce Roth
Rob Rudkin
Andrew Ruiz
Jim Rumford
John Runyan
Chad Rushing
Sterling Rutherford
RW
Mark Ryan
Justin Ryan
Greg S
Lawrence Sanchez
Dustin Sanders
David Sanford
Chris Sapero
Jaysn Schaener
Landon Schaule
Shayne Schettler
Jason Schilling
Jason Schilling
Andrew Schmidt
Brian Schmidt
Ray Schmidt
Kurt Schneider
Peter Scholtes
Theodore Schott
Kevin Schroeder
William Schweisthal
Anthony Scimeca
Cullen Scism
Connor Scott
Preston Scott
Rylee Scott
Robert Sealey
Aaron Seaman
Dan Searle
Phillip Seek
Kevin Serpa
Dylan Sexton
Austin Shafer
Mitch Shami
Timothy Sharkey
Christopher Shaw
Charles Sheehan

Wendell Shelton
Lawrence Shewark
Ian Short
Glenn Shotton
Joshua Sipin
Chris Sizelove
Andrew Skaines
Scott Sloan
Steven Smead
Anthony Smith
Daniel Smith
Lawrence Smith
Sharroll Smith
Tyler Smith
Michael Smith
Michael Smith
Timothy Smith
Neal Smith
Tom Snapp
David Snowden
Alexander Snyder
Robert Speanburgh
John Spears
Thomas Spencer
Troy Spencer
Jeremy Spires
Peter Spitzer
Dustin Sprick
George Srutkowski
Cooper Stafford
Travis Stair
Graham Stanton
Paul Starck
Ethan Step
John Stephenson
Seaver Sterling
Thomas Stewardson
Tanner Stewart
Maggie Stewart-Grant
Jonathan Stidman
John Stockley
Rob Strachan
Benjamin Strait
James Street
Joshua Strickland
William Strickler

Shayla Striffler
John Stuhl
Brad Stumpp
Kevin Summers
Ernest Sumner
Randall Surles
Sonny Suttles
Andrew Suy
David Swantek
Aaron Sweeney
Shayne Sweetland
Tiffany Swindle
Lloyd Swistara
Carol Szpara
Travis TadeWaldt
Daniel Tanner
Blake Tate
Joshua Tate
Lawrence Tate
Kyler Tatsch
Justin Taylor
Robert Taylor
Tim Taylor
Jonathan Terry
Stavros Theohary
Daniel Thomas
Vernetta Thomas
Chris Thompson
Steven Thompson
Jonathan Thompson
William Joseph Thorpe
Beverly Tierney
Daniel Torres
Ian Townsend
Matthew Townsend
Jameson Trauger
Cole Trueblood
Dimitrios Tsaousis
Scott Tucker
Oliver Tunnicliffe
Eric Turnbull
Brandon Turton
John Tuttle
Dylan Tuxhorn
Nerissa Umanzor
Jalen Underwood

Matthew Utter
Barrett Utz
Paul Van Dop
Andrew Van Winkle
Patrick Van Winkle
Paden VanBuskirk
Patrick Varrassi
Daniel Vatamaniuck
Jason Vaughn
Jose Vazquez
Stephen Vea
Brian Veit
Josiah Velazquez
Daniel Venema
Marshall Verkler
Cole Vineyard
Ralph Vloemans
Anthony Wagnon
Wes "Gingy" Wahl
Humberto Waldheim
Christopher Walker
David Wall
Justin Wang
Andrew Ward
Wedge Warford
Scot Washam
Tyler Washburn
Quentin Washington
Christopher Waters
Zachary Waters
John Watson
William Webb
Bill Webb
Hiram Wells
Jack Weston
William Westphal
Ben Wheeler
Paul White
Paul Wierzchowski
Grant Wiggins
Jack Williams
Justin Wilson
Scott Winters
Evan Wisniewski
John Wisniewski
Matthew Wittmann

Reese Wood
John Wooten
John Work
Bonnie Wright
Jason Wright
Ethan Yerigan
Matthew Young
John Zack
Phillip Zaragoza
Brandt Zeeh
Kevin Zhang
David Zimmerman
Jordan Ziroli
Nathan Zoss